FLESH EATERS

MARK L'ESTRANGE

Published 2020 by Evenfall – A Next Chapter Imprint

Edited by Terry Hughes

Cover art by Cover Mint

To my gorgeous little princess Beauty, why did you have to break your daddy's heart? Sleep well my little angel, until we meet again.

1

THE DAZZLING BEAMS OF THE APPROACHING VEHICLE PENETRATED the darkened woods, illuminating the massive trees that draped their branches menacingly over the narrow road where the car was travelling.

As he approached a familiar clearing, Dennis Carter pulled over to one side and killed the engine. Without bothering to acknowledge his travelling companion, he climbed out and walked around to the back of the car.

"Oi, Dennis, what you doin' now?"

He could hear Sharon Spate's whining tone coming from the front passenger seat as he opened the boot and removed the old blanket he kept there for such occasions.

Although he found his passenger's voice intensely annoying at the best of times, Dennis understood sacrifices had to be made if you wanted a decent screw, and Sharon had already proved herself to be an incredible lay. So, as far as he was concerned, it was just a matter of how desperate he was to get his end away compared to how much longer he could bear to put up with her whingeing.

Dennis faked his most disarming smile as he opened

Sharon's door. "Can't have that gorgeous little bum of your freezing now, can we?" He held up the blanket and gave her a sly wink.

Sharon cowered back into her seat. "Not out 'ere," she protested, "it's creepy, an' I've 'eard things about this place."

Dennis frowned. "What things?"

Sharon pulled a face. "You remember those stories about those campers going missin' out 'ere last summer? The police never did get to the bottom of it all."

Dennis could feel his patience starting to drain away. He had only called on Sharon in the first place because Rita had the hump with him, and now, having splashed out for drinks and a pizza, the little slut was playing hard to get.

He had to fight the instinct to grab her by the arm and drag her out of the car. Doing that, he realised, would no doubt kill off any last chance he might have to talk her round to his way of thinking.

Instead, he managed to broaden his false smile even more. "Don't be silly, those stories were all proved to be a load of nonsense written by one of the reporters from the local rag to boost their circulation. My old man told me they coughed to it down at the station."

Dennis's father, Ron Carter, was a sergeant at the local police station. He was nearing retirement, and everybody knew that once Sergeant Carter left, the crime rate in the area would decline almost overnight. Ron Carter had long been suspected of taking kickbacks from local villains in return for tipping them off whenever he got wind of any operation against them in the pipeline.

How he had managed to last this long in the force without being sacked was, in itself, a matter of mystery and conjecture among his fellow colleagues.

Dennis could tell from the expression on her face that Sharon was not altogether convinced by his explanation.

The warm night breeze rustled through the branches above their heads, and brought a welcoming coolness with it. It had been a hot Indian summer day, and the humidity had begun to drop only during the last couple of hours.

Even so, the heat had always made Dennis feel horny. Even as a young boy, once he discovered masturbation, he found himself performing it far more during the hot weather.

Sharon bit her bottom lip and shivered involuntarily. She was clearly not comfortable with their surroundings and turned back to Dennis with an almost pleading look on her face.

Dennis pretended not to notice. "Come on, Shar, be a sport, I took you out for the night when I could've been with me mates watching the football, didn't I? Surely you owe me something for that?"

Sharon was being hard work tonight and Dennis was not sure how much longer his temper would hold. She was not what most blokes in town would class as "girlfriend" material, but she had a reputation for putting out if you treated her to a good night. Dennis himself had been on the receiving end of her favours in the past, when he was desperate, and he had shown her more than enough consideration this evening to be rewarded again.

Then he had an idea.

He slipped his hand into his jacket pocket and produced a small plastic envelope containing a couple of ounces of cannabis. He dangled the pouch between his two fingers and Sharon's eyes immediately lit up.

She made a grab for the bag, but Dennis was too quick.

"Nah, ah, first things first," he said tantalisingly.

Sharon stretched out her hand and curled it around the back of his neck, pulling him towards her until their open mouths met. They snogged for a couple of minutes with Dennis crouching down beside the car. Turning in her seat and moving closer towards him, Sharon let her other hand meander down towards Dennis's crotch, and when she could feel the hardness inside his jeans, she gave him a gentle squeeze, which elicited a moan of pleasure from her partner.

Once they parted, Dennis gave Sharon's hand a gentle tug, which was enough to entice her from the relative safety of the car. The walked down a slope towards a clearing a couple of hundred yards from the car.

It was a clear night and the sky was full of stars.

Dennis placed the blanket down on the ground and kneeled to smooth it out, so that it covered as much ground as possible. Sitting on the floor, Dennis produced a roll-up machine and some papers from his other pocket, and proceeded to create a large joint for them to enjoy later.

Sharon smiled in anticipation as she watched Dennis at work. Standing before him, she slowly started to remove her clothing, one piece at a time, swinging her hips and shoulders as if dancing to music that only she could hear.

Dennis glanced up from his task and smiled approvingly as his date stripped down to her bra, panties and shoes.

She stood there for a moment with her legs apart and her hands on her hips.

Dennis put his handiwork to one side, careful to ensure that the spliff was still on the blanket. He rose to his knees and crawled over to where Sharon stood. He began kissing the tops of her thighs and rubbed his hands up and down the backs of her legs.

As he prodded further with his tongue, he could feel Sharon starting to grow moist under the flimsy cotton of her skimpy knickers.

Sharon closed her eyes and lifted her head back as he probed further and further inside her.

Slipping his thumbs inside the waistband of her panties,

Dennis slowly slid them down the girl's legs and held them there while she lifted each foot in turn and slid them out.

With the barrier discarded, Dennis slipped his tongue inside Sharon's eager opening, swirling it around and lapping at her vulva like a parched man desperate to quench his thirst.

Sharon stepped in closer and grabbed the back of Dennis's head with both hands, forcing him deeper inside her, matching his thrusts with her hips until she orgasmed with a loud cry into the darkened night.

After a few more movements with his tongue, Dennis lay back on the blanket, satisfied that he had done more than enough to earn him the shag he so desperately desired.

Taking her cue, Sharon knelt and undid the belt of his jeans before popping the button and slowly releasing his throbbing member from the confines of his zip. She slid his jeans down his legs and threw them over her shoulders, before she teased his boxers down with her teeth.

Easing forward, Sharon clasped her long fingers around Dennis's shaft and stroked it gently with a gliding motion. Dennis propped himself up on his elbows and watched her practised fingers do their work. Feeling his seed starting to rise, Dennis decided he did not want to waste it by cascading all over Sharon's fingers, so he leaned forward and guided her head towards his erection.

Sharon did not resist. She opened her mouth and took him into it, bobbing her head up and down while she sucked him off.

Past the point of no return, Dennis grabbed hold of Sharon's hair to ensure that her lips stayed in place when he erupted inside her mouth.

Just then, they heard a faraway cry pierce through the night.

It sounded more animal than human and, before he had a chance to react, Sharon had lifted her head away from his penis and shuffled up beside him for protection.

Together they listened in the darkness.

The cry had sounded quite a way off, though not far away enough for comfort.

After a moment, Sharon asked: "What the hell was that?" She kept her voice to just above a whisper, but it was still enough to irritate Dennis.

"Shut up, you stupid bitch, I'm trying to listen!" he snapped.

The sharpness of his retort struck Sharon like a slap to the face, but not enough to cause her to move away from the comfort of his body. If anything, she pulled him tighter, which was enough to annoy Dennis further.

"Get off me!" he spat, pushing her away, "I said I was trying to concentrate."

Sharon could feel her eyes welling up.

Without the comfort of Dennis's body, she became acutely aware of her nakedness, and desperately wanted to crawl away from him and find her clothes. But, even with his attitude, the thought of leaving his side right at that moment was not one she found attractive.

Now she wished she had stuck to her guns and insisted that Dennis just take her home, instead of letting him persuade her to come out here. Why was she so weak? All she ever wanted was to be loved and looked after by a good man. Instead, she always ended up with bastards like Dennis-bloody-Carter, who only wanted one thing, which she was foolish enough to give them.

She scanned the surrounding area, looking for anything moving, no matter how insignificant. But other than the occasional flutter from the trees, there was nothing.

When Sharon turned back to look at Dennis, she could tell from his demeanour that he had relaxed considerably, since they first heard the cry.

Sharon gently tugged the sleeve of his shirt. "Can we go please? I don't like it 'ere?" There was a pleading in her voice that she was not ashamed of showing. She really was frightened and she was willing to do or say whatever it took to convince Dennis to drive them home.

Dennis did not respond immediately, but continued to look straight ahead.

Finally, he said: "That sounded miles away, probably came from somewhere near town. Nothing to worry about."

He did not sound at all convincing, and Sharon was not taken in by his attempt at manly toughness one bit.

"No, she argued, "it came from over that way." She gestured to their right. "Towards the village."

Dennis considered her suggestion. He had to admit, now that Sharon had said it, the noise did sound as if it was more off to one side than behind them. But, since they had not heard anything since, he suspected that, whatever it was, it was no immediate threat to them.

"Whatever it was," he offered reassuringly, "it's gone now." He reached out and placed a comforting hand on Sharon's arm. He could feel the goosebumps on her skin, so he gently rubbed his hand up and down to warm her up.

"Can we go now, please?"

He realised she was not going to give up without a fight.

It was all right for her – he had at least made her come. But she had not finished him off before the cry made her stop and move away.

"Come on Shar," he soothed, "it's all right, I'm here with yer. I won't let anything 'appen to yer. Yer know that."

Sharon looked at him. She desperately wanted to believe him. But she was too afraid now and comforting words were not going to do the trick.

But he was giving her that same smile he had used to talk her round earlier when she did not want to leave the car. She loved that smile of his. It always made her feel all soft and gooey inside.

"Tell yer what," Dennis said. He reached behind him and turned back holding the spliff in his palm. "How about we enjoy this and then we see where things go from there?"

Sharon stared at the roll-up. She had to admit that she was very partial to the occasional bit of puff and, after the shock she had just had, it sounded like just what the doctor ordered.

While she thought about it, Dennis took out his lighter and lit the end of the spliff.

He took a deep drag, sucking the drug deep inside his lungs, and held it there for a moment before slowly releasing the smoke.

He handed the roll-up to Sharon, who took it without hesitation.

They both took it in turns to take deep drags on the spliff until there was virtually nothing left of it. By now, they were both feeling completely mellow, and all thoughts of the terrifying cry they had heard earlier were gone.

They cuddled together on the blanket, and Sharon began to rub herself against Dennis until she could feel him growing hard once more.

Dennis pushed her back on to the blanket and Sharon used her fingers to guide him into her willing cleft. Once inside her, Dennis thrust himself back and forth until he felt himself explode. Sharon, for her part, made all the right noises although, in truth, he was not concerned whether she enjoyed herself or not.

They fell asleep, wrapped in each other's embrace.

THE SOUND of another shrieking cry woke them both with a start.

Dennis sat up, shoving Sharon to one side again like so much discarded rubbish. Neither had any idea how long they had been asleep, but the air felt far colder now than it was when they first arrived there, and the pair of them shivered as the cold night wind cut through them.

This time, neither one of them was under any illusion that the cry came from the direction of the village or of the fact that it now sounded much closer than before.

Without saying a word, Dennis crawled forward on the blanket to retrieve his jeans.

Unlike earlier, there was now some low cloud cover that obliterated much of the light they had been afforded earlier by the stars. Dennis fumbled in the darkness around the edge of the blanket, spreading his hands out wide as he swept through the grass looking for his clothes.

After a moment of unsuccessful searching, he turned to Sharon who was sitting on the blanket hugging her knees to her chest. "What the hell did you do with my jeans, you stupid bitch?"

Now she felt the tears starting trickle down her cheeks. "I don't know," she sobbed, "they must be there somewhere." Then, as an afterthought, she added. "Can you throw me my skirt and top too please?"

"Fuck you!" Dennis yelled, returning to his task. "Find them yerself."

"Oh, you fuckin' bastard, yer all the fuckin' same." Spurred on by a combination of her hatred for Dennis and her disgust at herself, Sharon rolled on to her knees and shuffled forward to join in the search for their clothes.

Initially, the pair of them were reluctant to leave the relative safety of the blanket beneath them, but eventually, realising there was no option if they wanted to succeed in their task, they both stood up and walked around, bending down every time one of them saw something that might be an article of clothing.

After a couple of minutes, they looked at each other, bemused.

"What the fuck's goin' on 'ere?" Dennis demanded rhetorically.

"Do you think someone snuck in while we were asleep and stole our stuff?" Sharon asked, timidly, not especially wanting a reply.

"Fuckers!" Dennis spat, as the realisation of what Sharon had suggested took hold as the most likely scenario.

"Dennis?"

"FUCKERS!" This time he screamed the obscenity into the darkness, almost as if to goad the thieves to come forward and face him.

Sharon wrapped her arms around her, both for warmth and for comfort. She would have some explaining to do when she arrived home clad only in her bra and shoes, but right now, that seemed the least of her worries.

"Can we just go, please, I'm frightened whoever took our stuff will come back."

Dennis fought the urge to scream another challenge into the night. The fact was, he too was now feeling vulnerable with nothing on below, and he knew in a fight his exposed genitals would be an easy target.

Turning, he grabbed the blanket. "Come on, then," he barked, as he made his way back through the trees in the direction of his car.

Sharon had thought Dennis might wrap the blanket around her en route, but he seemed either not to notice, or not to care, about how she might be feeling.

Tearfully, Sharon made after him. She was glad that she had kept her shoes on, at least. The thought of tramping through the woods in the dark in her bare feet did not appeal in the slightest.

Sharon hurried after Dennis until they were only a body-width apart. She did not bother trying to grab his hand or link arms with him as she guessed he was not in the mood for such familiarity.

As they left the path and Dennis's car came into sight, he suddenly slapped his hand against his bare thigh, and stopped in his tracks, almost causing Sharon to crash into him.

"What's wrong?" she asked, timidly.

"My fucking keys!" Dennis yelled. "They were in my jeans!"

The significance of his realisation was not lost on Sharon. She felt her heart sink as she looked over at the locked car. So close and yet so far out of reach.

She waited for Dennis to say something else. When he remained silent, Sharon felt compelled to ask the obvious question, under the circumstances.

"What do we do now?"

Dennis spun around. There was a look of hatred etched on his face.

Without warning, he lashed out and caught Sharon across the cheek with the back of his hand.

The force of the blow sent the girl crashing to the ground.

She held a hand against her burning cheek and looked up at Dennis, the tears now gushing down her face in torrents.

Whether Dennis regretted his action or not, he neither said nor did he show any outward signs of remorse. Instead, he walked back in the direction from which they had both just come, throwing the blanket down as if it might be an encumbrance he could do without.

Sharon watched him go without saying a word.

She no longer cared that she was almost naked, cold and shivery from the night, or miles from home. She had taken just about all she was prepared to put with from Mr Dennis Carter, and now she decided that he could look for his damn keys on his own.

She was going to wrap herself in the blanket, and stay by

the car on the off chance a good Samaritan drove passed and offered her a lift.

Dennis could stay out here all night and freeze to death, and serve him right!

As Dennis made his way back into the clearing to search for his jeans, he thought he saw something from the corner of his eye disappear behind a bush to his right.

He stood there for a moment and stared into the semi-darkness, but there was no further movement from that direction.

If he ever managed to get his hands on the wankers who had snuck out here and pinched their clothes while they were asleep, he would make them pay all right. He would see to it that they regretted this for the rest of their lives.

Dennis continued to stare in the direction where he believed he had seen something move seconds earlier for another moment or two, before continuing with his quest.

He wondered if the bastards were hiding somewhere in the undergrowth, watching him in his fruitless search, desperately trying to not laugh and give the game away.

Dennis found a large stick and used it to swipe away at the long grass in front of him. It comforted him that he also now had a weapon he could use if the perpetrators decided to show themselves.

Of course, he blamed Sharon for all this.

If only she had put out as planned in the first place, then they could have gone back to the safety of the car to roll the spliff. But no, she had to pretend to play hard-to-get and act all afraid when they heard the first cry.

Stupid bitch!

He was glad he had hit her. He might even give her another one when he got back to the car, just to teach her a lesson.

A rustling from behind him made Dennis spin round to see what was there.

It was nothing.

But he had heard it, and it was louder than the sound of trees blowing in the wind.

He waited, his weapon held firmly in his right hand, ready to defend himself.

Then he wondered if it was Sharon behind him. Making her way back to help with the search now that she was finished crying and carrying on like a spoilt brat. Perhaps she was holding back just out of view because she was afraid of Dennis's reaction to seeing her again. So she bloody well should be. But right now, two pairs of eyes were better than one.

"Sharon, get out 'ere and 'elp me look!" He waited. There was no further movement from the bushes.

To hell with her. Dennis continued with his search.

Another sound a few seconds later made him jump.

He spun around. This time, the noise sounded closer than before, but what was even worse, it seemed to him as if it came from all around where he was, not just one point.

Were there more than one of them?

Had they split up and decided to really have some fun at his expense?

Dennis had had enough. Half-naked or not, he gripped tightly to the end of his club and strode towards the undergrowth in front of him.

"Right then, you little bastards, now you're gonna get it!" Dennis took a few more strides before the bushes all around him began shaking violently, as something was moving through them.

Dennis stopped in his tracks, squinting through the semi-darkness to try to see what was there.

"Who's there?" he demanded. Then, "Who the fuck is there?"

As the creatures emerged from the undergrowth, Dennis could not believe his eyes.

Before he had a chance to defend himself with his stick, or even to turn and run, they were upon him, ripping into his flesh and tearing great chunks out of him.

Dennis had no conception of how many of them there were, as they just seemed to be everywhere.

As he went down, Dennis managed to see some of them close-up.

They appeared to be shorter than him, but very stocky and their heads appeared almost to be perched directly on their shoulders without having necks in between.

Their bodies and faces were covered in thick, coarse bristles, and their eyes gleamed bright yellow, with tiny points of black in the middle.

The creatures made no sound other than grunts and growls as they tore Dennis asunder.

Mercifully, he passed out before they ripped his life out of him.

SHARON WAITED in the cold with the blanket wrapped around her shoulders. Unfortunately, it was not long enough to cover her exposed legs as well, so every so often she moved it down and wore it like a long skirt.

Not a single vehicle had passed by since Dennis had disappeared back into the woods, and she was starting to think that she would be stuck out here until he returned with the keys.

If he ever did.

At one point, Sharon even considered walking back into town. She figured it would only take an hour or so, and the walking might help to keep her warm. But she had to admit to herself that she was too afraid to venture off down the road alone.

Dennis might be a complete scumbag, but at least he would

act as a deterrent if some maniac drove by and saw her standing there alone. Even in her heels she guessed she could run back to Dennis before a weirdo could jump out of his car and grab her.

From out of the darkness, Sharon could hear a noise.

She strained to listen, then her heart leapt. It was the sound of a car engine approaching.

Sharon stood in the middle of the road. The thought of stepping into a warm car and being ferried home seemed too good to be true. She turned back in the direction Dennis had gone to call to him, but then she changed her mind and decided to let him stew.

As the car engine grew louder, she could just make out the headlights cutting through the trees which criss-crossed the winding road. It was definitely heading her way.

She felt herself shivering, but she could not tell if it was due to the cold or the excitement at the approaching vehicle.

Then she remembered her concerns about some lunatic driving towards her, and her without the protection of Dennis to rely on.

Sharon moved from one foot to the other, she was torn between her fear of being abducted, and her hatred for Dennis and the way he had treated her tonight.

Before she had a chance to decide on her best course of action, the vehicle came around the bend and into sight.

It looked like an old van and, as it drew closer, Sharon recognised it as belonging to the Craven brothers. They worked in their father's butcher's shop in the high street and were both friends of Dennis.

Just her luck.

Even so, they should still be good for a lift home, if nothing else.

As the van approached, Sharon ran forward and began waving her arms frantically in the air. After a couple of steps, she stopped and managed to catch the blanket before it slipped off her hips to reveal her naked undercarriage.

The van pulled over and Colin Craven leaned out of the driver's window.

"Well now, what have we here?" he sneered, licking his lips in an exaggerated manner.

"Oh, looks like a delivery of fresh meat," piped up his brother Don from the passenger seat.

Sharon reluctantly walked over to the open driver's window. "Hi guys, I'm in trouble. Can you help me out, please?"

"Oh yeah, what kind of trouble could an old slapper like you get herself into that we could help with? We're not fuckin' abortion doctors, yer know?"

Don roared at his older brother's joke.

Sharon managed to keep her cool. She had heard worse from some of the other blokes in town, so now it slid off like water off a duck's back.

"Come on guys, please, I'm stuck out 'ere. Give us a lift into town – it's not like it's out of your way."

Colin glanced over at the car, and recognised it at once. "Where's Dennis then?" he asked, raising his eyebrows.

Sharon turned back for a moment to check he was not about to re-emerge from the trees. "Oh, he lost his keys, so he went off looking for them."

"More like he had a better offer and left you 'ere by the roadside waitin' fer 'im," Don commented with a sneer.

Sharon sighed. "Whatever, can I have a lift or not? I'm bloody freezin'."

The two brothers exchanged glances without speaking, then Colin turned back to face Sharon. "Tell yer what – you give me brother 'ere a blow job in the back of the van, then let me shove it up your arse, and we'll take yer anywhere yer want. Deal?"

Sharon did not need a second to consider their offer. "Fuck off!" she yelled indignantly.

Colin shrugged his shoulders. "Suit yerself, find yer own bloody way 'ome." And, with that, he pressed down on the accelerator and sped off along the road.

For a moment, Sharon was convinced that Colin would stop.

Surely, he was not so hard-hearted as to leave her abandoned out here in the middle of the night.

But to her dismay, the van's lights disappeared around the next bend and, while she waited for the brothers to have a change of heart, Sharon soon realised that the noise from the engine was moving further and further away.

Sharon stamped her foot down hard on the road in exasperation.

With no other alternative left, she walked back over to the car, and slumped against the driver's-side door.

She did not see or hear the creatures emerging from the woods until it was too late.

Not that Sharon would have been able to outrun them but, at least if she had seen them early enough, she might have had time to wave the Craven boys down and give in to their disgusting demands in return for a safe passage.

As it was, by the time Sharon was aware of their presence, she was surrounded on all sides.

For a moment the hulking creatures stood staring at their helpless prey, as if considering their next move very carefully.

Sharon screamed for Dennis to come and help her but, unbeknown to Sharon, Dennis was already long gone.

Dropping the blanket in her haste to escape, Sharon ran first one way then, when that avenue was cut off, she turned and tried to escape by another route. But, every time she took a few paces forward, more of the creatures appeared, blocking her escape.

Sharon screamed and yelled hysterically, until her voice was gone.

Once they had her surrounded, the creatures stopped in their tracks as if awaiting a command.

From behind, a larger version of the creatures emerged from the treeline and strode forward until he reached the circle. Unbidden, the smaller creatures moved aside to make an opening for the new arrival to pass through.

Sharon stood, frozen to the spot in terror, as the head-creature lurched up to her. It stood only a few feet away and began sniffing her, like an animal trying to identify a familiar object.

With her mind gone, Sharon slumped to the ground, unconscious.

2

"OUCH... OUCH... YOU'RE HURTING ME!" KAREN TAYLOR CRIED out pitifully as the sweaty middle-aged man on top of her thrust himself in harder.

"Please stop... take it out... I'm still a virgin."

The man appeared completely oblivious to her anguished protest. If anything, her objections seemed to heighten his arousal.

"Ow... please, sir... I didn't mean to do it... I'm only 15... I won't do it again."

Eventually, Karen felt him erupt inside her. The man's body convulsed for a few seconds before he slumped his full weight on to her tiny frame.

Karen felt the air rush out of her body. She gave him a couple of seconds to finish releasing his load, then she tapped him gently on the shoulder. Taking the hint, the man rolled off her and lay exhausted on his back, taking in huge gulps of air.

Karen slid off the bed and took out a couple of wet-wipes from the packet on the bedside table. Carefully, she removed the used condom from the man's flaccid penis, and disposed of the soggy mess in the bin.

She grabbed her dressing gown from the hook and slipped it over her naked body, before making her way to the bathroom to wash her hands. Karen could hear her mattress springs squeal their objection as the man moved his considerable bulk across her bed to retrieve his clothes. By the time she returned, he was fully dressed.

The man looked at her with a beaming smile. "You're very good," he said, pleasantly. "If you tell me your size, I'll bring a school outfit for you to wear next time, if that's all right, of course?"

Karen managed a half-smile. "We'll see," she answered, noncommittedly.

Just then, they both heard the sound of a baby crying from the next room.

"Look, you'll have to excuse me, my daughter needs feeding," Karen explained, almost apologetically.

"Yes, yes, of course." The man left the room and walked down the hallway towards the front door. He waited there until Karen caught up with him. As she reached the door, he held out his hand. Karen took it and shook, while turning the knob with her free hand.

"Lovely to have met you," the man said as he crossed the threshold, "I sincerely hope I can see you again."

Karen managed another half-smile as she closed the door behind him.

Hurrying into the lounge Karen bent over the travel-cot and lifted her baby into her arms. The little girl stopped crying and began to gurgle as she recognised her mother's smiling face. Karen held her daughter to her breast and kissed her tenderly on the top of her head. Moving to the couch, Karen undid her dressing gown and exposed her breast to allow her to feed.

The sensation of her baby daughter gently suckling on her nipple felt a million miles away from the repulsion she had experienced only moments earlier, when the sweaty businessman was performing the same action.

Karen knew that, if she were going to continue with her present regime, she would have to find a way of compartmentalising her feelings so that her everyday activities did not become too loathsome to her, especially when she needed the money to feed her baby.

Karen gazed around her sparsely furnished council flat. There was hardly enough in it to call it a home, but it was all she had. She reflected on the circumstances which had brought her to this state, and immediately felt the urge to cry. It was a feeling she had grown used to having to deal with over the last three and a half months, virtually since her daughter had been born.

She gazed down at the sweet cherubic face of her baby girl as she suckled contentedly. Although the baby had not been planned, Karen knew that she had made the right choice by deciding to keep her. The baby's biological father had been a mistake she made one night after drinking too much at a friend's birthday party. She had contacted him when she told him she was pregnant as she believed he had a right to know. But it was clear from his reaction that he had no interest in being part of his child's life.

The last Karen had heard about him was that he had taken a job abroad, and Karen could not help but wonder if it was because he was afraid that she might try and bring the Child Support Agency down on him.

If he had taken the trouble to ask, she would have informed him that if he did not want to be around for his child, then she was not going to try to force the issue.

To be fair, Karen knew that there was an easy alternative to her present living conditions. Only last month, her mother had made her an offer to move back in with her. And as her mother lived on her own in a huge Victorian house with four large bedrooms, it was not lost on Karen that by refusing to go she was denying her daughter a much better start in life.

But she also knew that moving back home would be the biggest mistake she could ever make.

Her mother would never forgive Karen for the death of her sister, Josie.

Whether she was conscious that she was doing it or not, her mother had affected a tone in her voice and a look in her eyes whenever she was in Karen's company that exuded accusation to the point of hatred.

To tell the truth, Karen had always known that her parents favoured her older sister over her, even from a young age. But Josie, on the other hand, did all she could to make Karen feel loved and wanted, and would often challenge their parents openly when she felt they were being unfair to her younger sibling.

When their father died, their mother turned to Josie alone for comfort. It was almost as if Karen had ceased to exist. But Josie, try as she might, could not handle the way their mother smothered her without allowing her sister to share the burden.

So, eventually, unable to stand the overwhelming sense of suffocation, she moved away. Of course, their mother blamed Karen, and refused to believe that Josie had not been influenced by her.

After she left home, Josie and Karen grew even closer. They would speak on the phone all the time, text and WhatsApp each other daily, and meet up whenever they could, even if only for a quick coffee.

When Josie died, it hit Karen far harder than her mother would accept. As far as she was concerned, Karen was the cause for all her grief and, although she could never forgive her, blood was still thicker than water, which was why she felt compelled to offer her daughter and granddaughter a proper roof over their heads.

Karen looked down at her daughter, and rubbed the back of her finger against her soft cheek. The little girl smiled up while continuing with her feed. Could Karen subject her little girl to life with her grandmother? Only as a very last resort, she assured herself.

Even if it meant resorting to prostitution to make ends meet.

At that moment, Karen's mobile shrieked into life.

It was a withheld number, as she had expected. With a deep sigh, Karen answered.

"Hello."

There was a slight pause from the other end, then a husky male voice said. "I saw your number online, is that the right place?"

"Yes, that's right," replied Karen, trying to sound as cheerful and welcoming as possible. "Would you like some details?"

"Yes," came the gravelly reply.

"Well, as the advert states, I am in the Stockwell area, I am five feet three inches tall, slim with long blonde hair, and my fees start from 30 pounds for a basic massage."

Karen waited. She could hear the caller breathing heavily down the line. Even though she had only been doing this a relatively short time, Karen had learnt not to give out her address until after she was sure the caller was genuine. It was not always easy to decipher what kind of man you were dealing with, especially as she could not see their faces, so she had to rely on instinct for much of the time.

She could still hear the man breathing as if he was deciding on whether or not to proceed.

"Would you like to make an appointment?" she offered.

"Yes... please."

The "please" sounded more of an afterthought to her, but at least it showed a modicum of manners.

Karen was just about to reel off her address when a sudden

feeling of dread came over her. This was not an isolated incident – since advertising her services, she had often felt uncomfortable enough not to tell her caller where she lived, and the abuse she usually received as a result told her that she had made the right decision.

She waited a moment, still deciding how to proceed.

The caller remained silent, but his heavy breathing made Karen feel more uncomfortable by the second.

Finally, she made up her mind. "I'm so sorry," she apologised, "I've just noticed that I am fully booked for the next couple of days. Perhaps you could call back next week?"

The caller made an odd noise as if he were attempting to extract a piece of food that was stuck in his teeth. His breathing remained slow and heavy.

The silence was beginning to unnerve Karen.

She knew that some people, especially men, found it awkward to communicate with a member of the opposite sex. But, when you could not see their facial expression, it added a certain air of menace, which made Karen feel very uneasy.

Without realising she what she was doing, Karen instinctively crossed her ankles over each other. She considered just disconnecting the call, but even in such a circumstance as this, she did not want to appear rude.

"Are you still there?" she asked tentatively. "If you call back next week, I'm sure I will have a free slot by then."

She waited.

The breathing grew louder as if the caller was trying to eat his phone.

"I'm going to fuck you!"

The snarled statement hit Karen like a slap in the face. For a moment, she could not believe what she had just heard. She moved the mobile away from her ear and stared at it, as if by doing so she might find some kind of answer for the sudden outburst of aggression from the caller.

Her immediate instinct was to switch off her phone, but at the same time she had embedded in her a vein of indignation that would not allow such behaviour to go unaddressed.

"Excuse me," she said, trying to keep the natural panic from her voice. "I do not appreciate your language, and there is no excuse for you to be so rude!"

She waited to allow her statement to sink in.

The caller did not respond.

"I am just trying to make a living here by offering a service to kind, appreciative gentlemen, so I think you need to seek your comfort elsewhere."

"I'm going to fuck you!"

Karen switched off her phone.

Now she felt foolish for trying to reason with the man. Evidently, he was used to dealing with a different kind of woman, perhaps one of those whom she had seen plying their trade at the laybys near docks, where truckers often stopped for the night.

Karen so was glad she had not offered him her address.

Even so, with modern technology being what it was, she had heard that people could get hold of devices just like the ones the police used, that could trace a call even when the number was withheld.

She wondered if she should report the man to the police herself.

Maybe they would trace his call and warn him off.

Of course, then she would have to confess to them the circumstances surrounding why he had called her in the first place, and that was not something she was prepared to do.

Karen knew that what she was doing was not technically illegal, but all the same she was not proud of it, and certainly too embarrassed to explain herself to the Old Bill.

Karen dropped her phone on the couch and returned her attention to her baby.

The little girl had finished suckling, so Karen lifted her over her shoulder and gently began to pat her on the back. While she did so, Karen stood up and walked down the hallway to her front door. She peered through the peep-hole along the corridor that led to the bank of lifts at the far end. The concave lenses distorted her view, making it appear as if everything outside her door was trapped in a folding tunnel.

She half-expected to see a knife-wielding maniac emerge from the stairwell and make straight for her door. But the corridor was deserted.

Karen slid the safety bolt home, and continued her vigil for a few moments more, before finally carrying her baby back into the living room.

3

"'ERE, YOU DON'T WANNA BE GOING DOWN THERE, ME OLD MATE – place is full o' weirdos."

Thomas Sheffield rolled his eyes and tried desperately to keep his temper under control. His doctor had warned him about his blood pressure on more than one occasion, and he was not about to let some local yokel land him in hospital with a stroke or a heart attack.

"Yes, thank you, that's most interesting." Thomas smiled, weakly. "Now, if you would be kind enough to point me in the right direction, I'll be on my way."

The old farmer rubbed his unshaven chin, thoughtfully. "What was it you said you wanted to go there fer again, spoons or somink?"

"Cutlery," repeated Thomas for the third time, wishing he had never brought up the subject in the first place. If only his company would supply their salespeople with decent satnavs, he would not have had to stop and ask directions in the first place. Just his luck that the only soul around for miles turned out to be an inquisitive farmer type with too much time on his hands.

"Cutlery?" repeated the old man, removing his flat cap to reveal a bald pate covered in liver spots. "You got any spare samples on yer?" he looked behind Thomas at the two cases on his back seat.

Thomas sighed, deeply. "No, I am afraid not, now could you please direct me to the village?"

The old man shrugged. "All right, but don't say I dinna warn yer."

Thomas noted the man's directions, then thanked him, curtly, before driving off at speed. He didn't want to give the old fool another chance to offer him the benefit of his expertise about the wisdom of venturing into the village.

Why was it, he wondered, that these tiny out-of-the-way places seemed to breed so many interfering busybodies with nothing to do all day but make up stories about anyone who did not fit in to their way of living?

Well, weirdos or not, he had a chance of a very lucrative order from the owner of the local restaurant and hostelry, and for that, he would drive through the gates of hell itself.

At 52, Thomas Sheffield knew that his way of living was far from ideal. Spending half his life on the road, driving from pillar to post with his sample cases on board, earning the majority of his wage on a commission basis, but it was what he had grown accustomed to, and he was too long in the tooth to change now.

The vast majority of his colleagues at the firm opted for comfortable desk jobs where they either cold-called potential clients, or answered enquiries made online for the company's bespoke china, linen and cutlery service ware. But Thomas had always believed that, if you genuinely wanted to make a business contact for life, you had to meet with your clients face to face.

The quality of the product he was offering was exceptional and top of the range, but it came at a price. As he often explained to his clients, if they wanted to create the right impression for their clientele, then mass produced common-or-garden cutlery was not the way to go.

He still prided himself on having the gift of the gab when it came to clinching a deal, and that was an art that many of his younger colleagues did not have a clue how to learn. That was one reason why they passed so many prospective clients over to him. That and the fact that they were too lazy to get off their butts and drive out to meet with clients in person if they were located more than 20 miles out of town.

After passing through the woods, Thomas came to a fork in the road. There were no signposts for either direction, but he remembered the old farmer had told him to take the left-hand road. Thomas followed the route, which more closely resembled a dirt track than a road, as it meandered through overgrown bushes and trees. He slowed down out of fear that he might hit a large, undetected pot-hole. The last thing he needed was to be stranded in the middle of nowhere.

About half a mile down the path, Thomas passed what appeared to be a long-abandoned graveyard, just off the main route. He glanced over as he drove on, and could just make-out the tops of about 12 dilapidated gravestones, most of which were overgrown with moss.

In the distance, he noticed a small two-story cottage, which from this distance appeared to have been abandoned as long ago as the gravestones. A sudden thought inexplicably crossed his mind. He wondered if the cottage was indeed still inhabited by some wizened old crone and her half-mad son, who lay in wait on dark nights to attack and kill wandering motorists, robbing them of their possessions and burying their remains amongst the forgotten graves.

Thomas felt a sudden urge to turn his car around and drive back, but he shrugged it off and continued on his way. He scolded himself for allowing his imagination to run away with him.

About half a mile after the graveyard, the route opened out to what could be described as a proper road again. Thomas immediately began to relax as he saw several residential properties come into view. Upon closer inspection, Sheffield noticed that they all appeared rather crudely built of stone, with thatched roofs, almost as if the builder at the time received a commission for a job lot. As he drove over a stone bridge with a trickling brook below, he finally saw a sign announcing that he had entered the village.

As Thomas drove through the village in search of the inn, he could not help but notice that curtains fluttered in downstairs windows as he drove past. This was not unusual for a small community where strangers probably did not venture very often. But Thomas had been hoping that this would be a more vibrant area, one that welcomed holidaymakers, and boasted a fine warm welcome by the locals. Otherwise, he doubted that the owner of the inn would be able to attract enough customers to make an investment in fine dining service worthwhile.

Further down the road lay a couple of shops on either side. Sheffield noticed a newsagent, a greengrocer, and a hardware shop. As he passed, by he could feel the weight from several pairs of eyes monitoring his progress.

Eventually, he turned a corner and found his destination.

The large wooden sign announced "Beanie's Hotel, Restaurant and Bar".

Thomas heaved a sigh of relief. From the outside, the premises were certainly impressive in both size and structure, even if they did appear a trifle out of place in such a small village.

There was an ample-sized car park at the rear of the property, so Sheffield took the space nearest to the back entrance, and checked his appearance in his rear-view mirror before entering the bar.

As he had expected, all eyes turned in his direction as he walked in.

Thomas smiled and nodded to the scattering of locals as they supped their pints, and received a few acknowledgements in response.

He made his way over to the bar where a stout middle-aged woman stood drying glasses with a dishcloth.

"Good evening madam," Thomas began, politely, "My name is Sheffield, Thomas Sheffield, I believe I have an appointment with the landlord of this fine establishment."

Without warning, the man squatting on a bar stool nearest to where Thomas stood, suddenly rose to his feet to face him. The man towered a good head and shoulders above him, and Thomas felt himself taking an instinctive step backwards.

The man held his gaze for a moment longer, before he turned on his heel and walked out of the bar. Thomas, realising he had been holding his breath, let it out slowly between his teeth so as not to make the motion too obvious.

Just then, he felt a hand grab his wrist.

He turned back to face the barmaid who now had a broad grin stretched across her face. "Oh yes, of course, my dear, 'e's bin expectin' you. Please follow me."

The woman led Thomas through a door at the back of the bar and into a spacious and well-presented dining area. She signalled for Sheffield to take a seat at a table near the window, and he obliged with a smile.

"Now then, my lovely, I expect you'd like a nice drop o' home brew after your drive? Clear away the dust from the road."

Before Thomas had a chance to reply, the woman had turned and started to make her way back out to the bar area.

He sat there for a while, taking in the charming ambiance

of the restaurant. The furniture was all made of sturdy-looking dark wood, and there was a matching blue and white checked tablecloth covering each table, with a cruet set in the middle of each one.

Thomas studied the ceiling of the restaurant. It had been designed to resemble an upturned ship, which married perfectly with the various maps, ships' wheels, telescopes and other forms of naval equipment that were scattered around the walls.

"Hello, my name's Jodie, what's yours?"

Thomas was startled out of his reverie by a young blond-haired girl who had magically appeared by his side.

He swivelled in his chair to face her. She seemed to be about 12 or 13 years old, and she was dressed in a check shirt, which coincidentally – or perhaps not – seemed to match the tablecloths, and blue denim dungarees. Her blond hair was braided in two pigtails that hung down past her shoulders.

"Well, good afternoon young lady," replied Thomas, holding out his hand, "my name is Thomas, and it's a pleasure to meet you."

Satisfied that he was in earnest, the young girl took his hand and they shook.

"Have you come for dinner?" Jodie enquired. "You're a little early, but I can have a word with my dada and ask him for you."

Thomas smiled. "That's very kind of you, but I'm here on business to see the owner of this fine establishment. Would that be your father?"

The girl nodded excitedly.

At that moment, the woman reappeared from the bar carrying a large tankard.

As soon as she saw the girl standing next to Thomas, she called out. "Now Jodie, I hope you've not been bothering this nice gentleman?"

Thomas held up his hand. "No, not in the least, she has been extremely charming company."

Jodie turned back to him and smiled shyly.

The woman placed the tankard on the table in front of him.

"There you go now, you get that down yer and there's another waitin'," the woman assured him. She placed a hand on the girl's shoulder. "Be a darlin' and go an' fetch yer dada fer this gentleman."

The young girl gave Thomas another smile and skipped away through the tables, disappearing through a double swing door behind a large staircase at the back of the restaurant.

Thomas thanked the woman for his drink. In truth, he was very thirsty and a pint would certainly hit the mark. That said, the tankard seemed to Thomas slightly bigger than the usual pint measure, and he wondered if even this one drink might put him over the limit.

He certainly did not intend spending more time than was necessary in this place.

Thomas raised his glass to the woman who stood by expectantly as if waiting to hear what he thought of the drink. He took a couple of large gulps. The beer certainly went down well, and when he had finished drinking, he complimented her on the brew.

"That's our 'ouse special," the woman informed him. "We brew it 'ere on the premises."

With that, she turned away and went back to the bar.

In spite of himself, Thomas took another couple of large gulps. He could feel the effect of the alcohol already starting to take hold, so he decided to slow down because he did not wish to conduct business with his speech slurred.

As he sat alone in the restaurant, Thomas noticed through the windows that the sun was almost setting. He absentmindedly took several more sips from his tankard as he waited in silence for the proprietor.

After a while, Thomas heard the swing doors through which Jodie had disappeared earlier swing open, and he prepared himself to stand up and meet the owner. But instead, he noticed another young girl walking towards him. For a moment, he thought that it was Jodie returning, but as she drew closer to his table, Thomas realised that, although she was dressed in an identical fashion to the young girl, right down to her pigtails, she was definitely older.

Thomas smiled, broadly, as she approached.

"Hello," she said, sweetly, "I 'ear you're waiting for my dada, 'e won't be long, 'e's just overseeing the first batch of pies for the night."

Thomas estimated that the girl must have been 17 or 18. Unlike Jodie, she wore make-up, nothing too heavy, but just enough to enhance her considerable beauty.

In his haste to stand up and introduce himself, Thomas managed to catch the underside of the table with his protruding stomach, causing the legs to scrape across the stone floor as it moved forward.

He looked up at the girl, embarrassed by his own clumsiness, and saw that she was smiling back at him.

"I'm sorry about that," he apologised, readjusting the table back into its original position. "I think I may need to lose a few pounds."

"Aw, don't be silly, we likes our men with a bit o' meat on 'em round 'ere."

Thomas felt his cheeks flush hotter.

The girl laughed. "I'm Polly. I think you've met my little sister, Jodie?"

She moved in closer, offering her hand.

From this distance, Sheffield could tell that she was not wearing a bra. Her checked shirt was unbuttoned just enough to give him a tantalising taste of the top of her perfectly rounded breasts.

Thomas cleared his throat and offered his hand. As they shook, he could not help but watch her perky breasts jiggle up and down without restraint.

He could feel an erection starting to grow.

Self-consciously, Thomas tried to cover his embarrassment by folding his hands over his lap before retaking his seat.

But it was obvious that the girl had noticed his bulge.

When she caught his eye, she winked at him and smiled.

At that moment, Thomas wanted the ground to open up and swallow him. He reminded himself that he was there to conduct business with the girl's father, and if he caught the salesman acting in any way inappropriately with his daughter, Sheffield knew that he could kiss this commission goodbye.

Thomas tried to settle himself and regain some composure. But Polly seemed to have different ideas. She moved in closer and perched herself on the edge of his table.

"Will you be stayin' the night, then?" she enquired seductively.

Thomas shook his head, more severely than he had intended. After all, he did not want to give offence to what was merely an innocent question.

"No... no, I doubt our business will take more than an hour or so."

Polly leaned in closer, as if she were about to tell him something that no one else should hear, regardless of the fact that they were quite alone.

The top of her cleavage was now mere inches from his face.

Thomas tore his gaze away and forced himself to look up at her.

Polly's beautiful sparkling blue eyes shone down on him like sunlight after a storm.

"My dada never does business with anyone what refuses 'is 'ospitality." She gave him a knowing nod of her head. "An' besides, we have the most comfortable beds in the village."

Polly glanced up to the ceiling as if to emphasise how close the beds were to them right at that moment.

Sheffield gulped unconsciously. He found himself all of a sudden, unable to speak in her company.

Smiling at his awkwardness, Polly leaned in a little further and placed a hand on his thigh. Looking into his eyes, she slid it a little further up his thigh, towards his crotch area.

Thomas desperately wanted her to stop, for fear her father or mother might walk in on them. But, at the same time, a part of him did not care.

"It's a beautiful evenin'," Polly informed him. "After we close, we could go for a walk, jus' you an' me. They reckon they'll be a good moon tonight – shame to waste it."

Thomas swallowed hard, again. "But, what about your parents? What would they have to say?"

Polly lifted her hand off his thigh and wrapped her fingers around the back of his neck. She pulled him towards her until her mouth was only centre metres from his ear.

"I won't say a word, if you don't," she assured him provocatively.

Before he had a chance to answer, Polly flicked the tip of her tongue back and forth against the lobe of Sheffield's ear.

Thomas closed his eyes and moaned softly.

Assured of her catch, Polly slipped off the table and walked back towards the swing doors. As she reached the staircase, she stopped and looked back at Thomas over her shoulder.

"Like I said, it would be a shame to waste it."

With one final wink, she left the room.

4

Karen checked on baby Charlotte for the third time in 15 minutes. As before, her baby was sound asleep. Karen knew that she was growing paranoid, but after that obscene phone call she had received earlier she could not help herself.

In her mind, she had visions of the caller climbing in through her daughter's bedroom window, and her walking in to find him standing over her with a carving knife in his hand. The fact that they were eight floors up and it would be physically impossible for anyone to reach them did not help to allay her fears. As far as she was concerned, that obscene caller could be an acrobat, or one of those idiots she had read about in the papers who scaled tall buildings for their own amusement.

The worst part for her was that she could not seem to shake the man's voice from her mind. His language had been bad enough, but it was the sheer vitriol behind his words that still made her skin crawl.

His deep guttural tone had reminded her of a demon she had seen in a film when she was younger. Karen had bluffed her way into a cinema with a couple of her school friends to see an 18-certificate film when they were only 15. The voice of the actor who played the demon had stuck with her all the way home, and that night she had a nightmare that he was coming after her.

Karen shivered at the memory.

She caught herself rising from her chair to go and check on Charlotte again, but this time she managed to stop herself, and went into the kitchen to put the kettle on.

Once her coffee was ready, Karen took it into the living room and sat down in her armchair to drink it. As she blew on the hot liquid, Karen reflected on the circumstances that had brought her to where she was now.

She had always dreamed of travel, to see the world before she reached 25, and at one point she had been on track to do just that. At the time, she was in a great job with terrific prospects. She still lived at home with her mother and sister, so she was able to save for her future without having to restrict her spending too much.

But it all went horribly wrong the night she went to a party with some of the girls from the office. The evening began in a conventional-enough fashion but, after a while, a group of them decided to extend the night by heading into town to visit a night club.

Somewhere in the early hours, after having way too much to drink, Karen became separated from the group and, as she staggered around the club bumping into people in her search for her friends, she was suddenly grabbed by one of the bouncers and thrown out into the street.

With her handbag still somewhere inside, Karen had no money for a cab. Fortunately, she still had her mobile in the pocket of her jeans, so she managed to call home and convince her sister Josie to come and collect her.

On her way to pick her up, Josie was hit head-on by a drunk driver.

She died even before the ambulance arrived at the scene.

Karen's mother blamed her to this day for her sister's death and, if she were honest, Karen blamed herself, too.

From that moment on, Karen's life was never the same.

Her mother refused to allow her younger daughter to offer her any comfort. In fact, she barely spoke to Karen for three months. She did not seem to comprehend that Karen had not only lost her sibling, but her best friend, too, and her grief was every bit as painful as her mother's.

When Karen could not cope with the atmosphere at home any longer, she moved out.

For a while she moved into a house-share with three other girls, and slowly she began to feel human again.

But then when Charlotte arrived, everything changed.

Karen had to move out of the house as the last thing the other girls wanted was a screaming baby on the premises. For a while, the council put her up at various bed-and-breakfast establishments until a flat became available. Although her firm gave her paid maternity leave based on how long she had worked for them, it did not last for long. And, as she was unable to return to her job because she had no one to look after Charlotte, Karen went on benefits.

The benefits staff took a dim view that Karen claimed she could not – or would not – name the father of her child so that they could go after him for money, so her payments were kept to the basic minimum, doubtless in an effort to make her reveal his identity.

So it did not take long for the bills to start piling up, and Karen found herself waiting in line down at the benefits office at least once a week, seeking assistance.

On one occasion, Karen started talking to one of the other mums who confided in her that she earned extra money by being on the game. Even though it was something which Karen would never have previously dreamed of considering, she was at such a low ebb that the prospect of prostitution as a solution to her predicament almost sounded inviting.

The other girl took Karen's mobile number and promised to add it to the website where she herself advertised.

Karen's phone rang with her first client the following day.

The money was good, and it certainly came in handy. But now here she was, home alone and too scared to switch her mobile on for fear that the same creep would call her back.

She knew she could not keep her phone off indefinitely. No phone meant no clients, and no clients meant no more money.

Karen turned her mobile over and over in her hand.

As she drained the last of her coffee, she decided that she was not going to be a prisoner in her own flat. The caller had no idea where she lived and, if he called again, she would just cut him off, and keep doing that until he grew tired of wasting time.

Determined to feel back in control, Karen switched her phone back on.

For a moment she studied the screen, watching as all her apps appeared.

She waited in anticipation for the creep to try his luck again.

She took a deep breath, waiting for the phone to shudder into life.

Just then, there was a knock at the front door.

Karen shot out of her chair and ran to the kitchen to arm herself. She ripped open the cutlery drawer and grabbed the largest knife she owned.

She could feel her heart racing as she turned to walk towards her front door. She had already convinced herself that it was her obscene caller outside, and she knew she had to do everything in her power to protect Charlotte.

Even at the cost of her own life.

Karen gripped the handle of the knife firmly, afraid that she might drop it as her hands were shaking so much. She gazed down at her mobile in her other hand, her thumb poised over the nine button. If she called the police, there was a faint chance that they would arrive before she had to confront whoever was outside her door. Although the police were regular visitors to her estate, it seemed that, when you needed them, they took their own sweet time to respond.

Karen remembered hearing that a woman over on the next block had called them in desperation while her ex-husband was trying to break down her bathroom door to reach her. By the time they responded, the man had knifed her to death and made his escape.

Karen edged her way along the corridor, trying desperately not to make a sound and alert her unwanted visitor. Without realising it, she was holding her breath as she tiptoed close enough to see through the peep-hole.

The man outside had his back to her.

Karen waited, still refusing to breathe, until he turned around to face her.

Karen exhaled a loud breath as she saw the face of Daniel Sorenson looking at peep hole.

"Dan!" she called out, not waiting for a response as she quickly hid the knife in the hall table drawer and fumbled with the chain and latch, before yanking the door open.

Karen threw herself into his arms before Dan even had a chance to speak.

She hugged him hard. Harder than she had done before.

Karen had met Dan at her sister's funeral. Josie and Daniel had been at university together, and, although they dated for a while, they reached a mutual decision that their relationship should remain as that of just friends.

Karen found herself being immediately attracted to Dan, but due to the awkwardness of the situation, Karen made polite conversation with Dan, but her attention was mainly focused on attempting to comfort her mother, who was inconsolable at the loss of her elder daughter.

When Dan came over to pay his respects one last time before leaving the funeral, Karen had wanted to take him to one side and ask for his number. But she knew how inappropriate such an action would appear to others, especially her mother. So instead, she just shook his hand politely and thanked him for attending.

Even though Karen never forgot about him, she tried as best she could to put Dan out of her mind as she had no way of contacting him. She did attempt to trace him via social media, but without success.

After that, she fell pregnant with Charlotte, and her life spiralled out of control.

Then, out of the blue, Dan contacted her. He explained that he had called her mother to enquire after her, and that she had explained Karen's situation and given him Karen's mobile number asking him to intercede in persuading Karen to move back home.

Regardless of the circumstances, Karen was overjoyed to hear his voice, and since then he had called her regularly and visited at least once a week, always bringing a toy or item of clothing for Charlotte.

When Karen finally released her hold on Dan, she could tell from his expression that he was slightly taken aback by her enthusiastic welcome. Karen felt her cheeks flush, but she was still unable to hide her elation at his arrival. She grabbed him again and held him tightly.

"It's so good to see you," she confessed, "but why didn't you call me first to say you were coming over?"

"I tried, but your phone was off."

Karen bit her lip.

She desperately wanted to confess all to Dan right there and then. Although she had known him only a short time,

Karen was confident that he would not judge her, and she felt so safe now that he was there to protect her and her baby.

But she fought the urge, and decided to keep her guilty secret to herself.

She kissed him on his cheek and released her hold.

"Sorry about that," she apologised, "my phone's been playing up so I switched it off for a while."

They both went in to check on Charlotte, and Dan placed his latest present for the baby at the end of her cot. It was a pink bunny rabbit that automatically played a lullaby when the baby cried.

Karen thanked him while chastising him for spoiling her daughter. Dan shrugged it off as if she were wasting her time admonishing him.

They sat in the living room and chatted over coffee.

During this time, Karen's phone rang three times.

Trying desperately to hide her discomfort, Karen disconnected each call within a couple of rings, before switching the phone to mute.

"I see it's working again," Dan observed.

Karen nodded. "Yes, bloody nuisance calls, probably one of those dodgy insurance companies trying to convince me I've had an accident I can still claim for."

They talked late into the night.

Karen made them some pasta for dinner, and when Charlotte woke for her feed, Dan fetched her and carried her in. Even though they were not lovers, and had not even shared a real kiss, Karen felt no discomfort in exposing her breast to feed her daughter in front of him.

After her feed, Dan insisted that Karen let him wind the baby, which he managed quite successfully, after which Charlotte fell back to sleep cradled in his warm embrace.

Karen felt a slight twinge of jealousy.

Right now, she wanted nothing more than to cuddle up

with Dan on the sofa and fall asleep. But even though they had hugged and kissed several times, he had never made a move on her, which Karen believed might stem from Dan feeling awkward because of his earlier relationship with her sister.

She was beginning to think that if anything was ever going to happen, she would have to be the one to instigate it. Not that that was a problem, but what she did not want was to misread the signals and for them to end up in some embarrassing scene with the two of them feeling too awkward to see each other again.

She needed Dan in her life right now.

But Karen's present situation was such a mess that part of her felt too guilty to allow their relationship to advance to the next stage.

For now, she would have to remain content that he was here.

5

THOMAS SHEFFIELD HEAPED ANOTHER CHUNK OF MEAT PIE ON TO his fork and shovelled it into his mouth. When Thaddeus Beanie had told him earlier that he would never have tasted anything like it, he had thought that the man was just blowing smoke. But he had to admit, this was the most delicious pie he had ever tasted.

His meeting with Thad Beanie had been an all-too-brief one but, by the time the man eventually emerged from behind his kitchen door to introduce himself, the restaurant was beginning to fill up with the first flush of the evening's diners.

Just as his daughter had assured him, Thad Beanie insisted that Thomas stayed the night as his guest, and promised that they would conclude their business over breakfast.

Thomas was in no position to refuse such a kind offer. For one thing, since meeting the owner's eldest daughter earlier that evening, he could think of little else but the moonlit stroll she had suggested, and the possible fun and games that might ensue.

Sheffield did not consider himself to be a foolish sort of person. He never deluded himself that he was particularly attractive to the opposite sex and, as such, a part of him did wonder if Polly's offer was merely a ruse lull him into a false sense so that he would drop his guard and end up offering her father a massive discount when he placed his order.

But there was something in the way she purposely sashayed in front of him whenever she passed his table, and winked at him when no one was looking, that made him think he might be on to a winner, after all.

He had heard it said that in some of these out of-the-way places women appreciated a man with a fuller figure, and Polly had certainly expressed such an opinion when they first met.

But even if it were all a ruse, the meal was excellent, and his host's wife made a point of appearing with another full glass of ale whenever he drained his previous one. Added to which, he was having a totally free night's stay in what was bound to be an extremely comfortable bed, and with the promise of a substantial order to follow the next day.

Things could definitely be worse, as far as he was concerned.

Once he had cleaned his plate, Jodie appeared with a large helping of apple crumble and ice cream. She removed his empty pie plate, and placed his dessert down in front of him.

Sheffield dropped his gaze to his new dish. In truth, he was full fit to bust, but when he glanced back up at the young girl to apologise for having to refuse her kindness, she bent down and whispered in his ear.

"This is from our Polly. She says you will need all your energy for what she has planned."

Thomas blushed, and thanked the young girl for her kindness.

Even after he finished his meal, the restaurant was still full of patrons. During the evening, Thomas had noticed that the restaurant also offered a takeaway service and he saw several customers ordering the house pies in various sizes.

Thomas thought it odd that the restaurant seemed to thrive so well when it only offered one dish on its menu. But he presumed that over time the reputation of the fare had spread far and wide, and he was curious just how far some people might travel for such a delicacy.

He intended to ask Thad in the morning.

Having excused himself from his table, Sheffield ventured outside the restaurant to enjoy the night air, and help his food digest. As he walked through the bar area, Thomas noticed that several of the patrons were enjoying pies with their pints. He drew a couple of odd sidelong glances from some of the male customers as he walked past their tables, but he chose to pretend that he had not noticed.

Thad's wife smiled at him over the bar, while she filled another pint glass from the pump. Thomas waved cheerfully.

Outside, he took in a deep lungful of the crisp country air before making his way over to some empty benches in the courtyard. He sat down and lit one of the large corolla cigars he usually saved for when he had signed a deal. But as far as he was concerned, this one was as good as sorted, so he felt he deserved his treat a little early.

Having finished his cigar, Thomas waited a while longer listening to the sound of night creatures scurrying and scuttling through the surrounding foliage before he made his way back into the bar. He waited for the landlady to finish serving her customer before asking if he could be shown to his room.

The woman led him back into the restaurant and signalled to her elder daughter to show Thomas up.

Thomas followed Polly up the winding staircase that led to the upper floors. He could not help himself but focus on her firm tight buttocks as they peeked seductively out from under her apron ribbons.

They walked through a set of swing doors that blocked out the noise from the hustle and bustle below.

Polly opened a door at the far end of the corridor and handed over the key to Thomas. Having checked that no one else was about, she slipped a hand behind his neck and pulled him down to her height for a kiss. Still concerned that they might be witnessed, Thomas attempted to protest, but before he had a chance, Polly's eager tongue slipped through his lips, and Thomas was helpless to resist.

When the young girl finally pulled away, she said, "See you later," before walking away back down the corridor.

Once inside the room, Thomas saw that someone had unpacked his suitcase for him, and placed his clothes in the wardrobe.

He chose a loose-fitting tracksuit and a pair of trainers for his trek into the woods.

Before he changed, he decided to shower. The last thing he wanted was for Polly to be put off him because of his body odour.

Once he had showered and dressed, Thomas lay on his bed, contemplating the night ahead. After a while, he heard stirrings on the landing outside, followed by doors being opened and closed. It was obvious that the hotel did have some other guests tonight after all.

Eventually, Thomas heard a gentle tapping on his door.

He swung his legs off the bed and settled himself before opening it.

He could not believe how nervous he was feeling.

He opened the door to find Jodie, not Polly, standing outside. She had changed out of her serving uniform and was now dressed in a thick brushed-cotton onesie with various animals depicted on it, and slippers in the shape of rabbits.

Sheffield tried not to look too disappointed. "Hello young Jodie," he whispered, "and what can I do for you?"

Jodie signalled with her index finger for Thomas to bend down to her level, so she could whisper in his ear.

"Polly says you are to meet her out the back. I'll show you the way down the back stairs."

Without waiting for a response, the young girl moved down the corridor towards the fire exit at the end.

Thomas shut his door and followed as instructed. Part of him could still not believe that this was really happening, but he decided to play along and not be too disheartened if it turned out to be nothing more than a juvenile prank.

Jodie pushed open the exit door and stood outside on the wrought iron staircase.

Thomas followed her outside, and once there, the young girl pointed towards an area at the back of the car park. As he squinted in the darkness, Thomas could just about make out the shape of a figure standing in the shadows, just out of reach from the light cast by the overhead parking lights.

He looked back at Jodie who beamed up at him with a cheeky grin.

"I'll leave this on the latch so you can both get back in without disturbing the rest of the house," she assured him.

Thomas could not help but wonder what reason her elder sister had given her for their escapade this evening. But whatever it was, little Jodie seemed completely at ease with it.

He thanked her for her kind assistance, and waited for her to go back inside before he started to make his way down the emergency staircase.

Even as he walked through the car park, Thomas could not help but wonder if indeed it was Polly waiting for him in the distance. It was not until he was within a few feet of her that he relaxed.

Polly smiled at him. "You found me then." She pulled him towards her and their mouths met. Thomas could feel his throbbing member pushing relentlessly against the stretchy material of his joggers, like a frustrated commuter desperate to get off a packed train.

Polly allowed him to run his hands over her lithe body while they kissed.

She, too, had changed out of her working clothes but, unlike her little sister, Polly was now dressed in a silky blouse and mini skirt.

When Thomas dropped his hands beneath her skirt to cup the cheeks of her bottom, he realised that she was not wearing any underwear. He pushed himself against her, writhing in ecstasy as she thrust her hips into his groin.

Without saying a word, Polly pulled back. She grabbed his hand and led him in to the woods behind the car park. Thomas could feel shivers of excitement racking his body at the thought of what they were about to do.

The further they ran into the woodland the denser the brush became. Thomas could feel twigs and branches crunching beneath his feet as tried desperately to keep up with Polly, who appeared to be in an even bigger hurry than him to reach their destination.

Thomas could feel his heart pumping wildly in his chest as he tried to keep his laboured breathing under control. He was afraid to call out and ask the girl to slow down in case she suddenly lost interest in him for being too old to keep up. But he was not sure how much longer he could keep up this pace without collapsing to the ground.

To his great relief, they came upon an opening and Polly stopped dead in her tracks.

The two of them stood there a moment, Thomas doing all he could to keep the sound of his breathing to a minimum.

He noticed that Polly was gazing around them, almost as if she were expecting something or someone to appear out of the darkness.

Thomas surmised that she may have heard something which escaped him. After all, she was familiar with these woods and doubtless more attuned to the sounds of the night.

For his part, he was feeling much more composed having rested, and was ready to continue with their liaison.

Taking Polly's hand, Thomas turned her back to face him and moved in for another kiss.

A sudden rustling from the bushes to his left made Thomas stop and look up. With the lights from the car park far behind them, his eyes had still not adjusted to the darkness. He listened intently. There was definitely something there.

Probably just a wild animal scurrying around foraging for food, was his initial thought. Nothing to be concerned about.

Even so, Thomas still strained to see what might be in front of them.

But the dense mass of foliage just a few feet away seemed to blend together with the night sky to form a uniform darkness that his eyes were unable to penetrate.

Another sound, this time coming from behind, made Thomas spin round. He let go of Polly's hand and came close to losing his footing and taking a tumble. He managed to right himself, but still could not see what had made the sound.

He looked back at Polly.

She was smiling her usual sweet, sexy smile, obviously unperturbed by their surroundings.

Taking a few steps back, she held out her arms as if inviting him to come closer.

Thomas was about to move in when something fell from the trees above and landed squarely on his shoulders, sending him sprawling to the woodland floor.

The thing on his back moved away, allowing Thomas to shuffle forward on the ground in an attempt to escape his attacker's clutches. Looking behind into the darkness Thomas felt his hand land on something unfamiliar. He swung his head back and realised it was only Polly's foot. She reached down and grabbed his hand before helping him back up to his feet.

Thomas was grateful, but still concerned by what had hit him moments earlier.

Once he was standing, Thomas wrapped his arms around Polly as if to protect her, as his eyes scanned the darkness surrounding them.

He was just about able to make out something in the shadows, but it was too indistinct for him to ascertain exactly what he was staring at.

Then Polly began stroking him between his legs.

Thomas turned to stare at her, but she just smiled back at him.

The situation was ludicrous. Polly seemed to be completely unaffected by the fact that something had just attacked him and was doubtless lurking just outside their line of sight, waiting for another chance to pounce. Instead, she seemed intent on continuing with their encounter as if nothing had happened.

For a moment, Thomas lost himself in the pleasure he felt from Polly's rhythmic stroking of his nether region. Even though his instincts were warning him of danger, Thomas could feel his erection growing in response to her touch.

He closed his eyes and moaned, loudly.

He wanted her so badly.

Such was his excitement that Thomas did not notice the lurching figures that gathered around them, cutting off any means of escape for the lovers.

Just as he could feel himself reaching climax, Polly moved her hand away.

Thomas groaned and opened his eyes.

He recoiled at the malevolent glares from the uninvited onlookers.

The creatures were within a few feet of the pair of them. Thomas spun around, realising immediately that they were surrounded. The creatures moved nimbly from one foot to the other, as if awaiting the signal to lunge forward and attack their helpless victims.

Thomas had never seen anything like the things surrounding him. He could feel the menace in their stares – they put him in mind of jungle animals stalking their prey.

He looked over at Polly, expecting her to be on the verge of hysterics. But instead, she was standing quite calmly, with her hands on her hips and smiling at him, just like before.

Thomas opened his mouth to speak, although he was not sure what to say at this moment. He hoped that something would come to mind that might allow him a chance to escape this horrific scene before things became ugly.

But before a single word left his lips, he heard a crashing sound coming from the foliage behind him.

Thomas turned to see another of the creatures, this one slightly larger than the others, emerge from the cover afforded it by the treeline.

The creature glared at Thomas with hideous yellow eyes and, as it moved towards him, Thomas could see the huge pointed fangs that emerged from behind the thing's lips as it snarled at him.

"Thomas, I'd like you to meet my cousin, Gobal."

The voice came from behind him, but it took Sheffield a moment to realise that it was Polly speaking. In his panic, he had almost forgotten that she was still there.

Due to the absurdity of the situation, Thomas caught himself almost about to step forward and offer his hand to greet the creature politely.

But as it was, Thomas was frozen to the spot in terror.

Thomas could hear Polly's now familiar laugh as she walked by him and threw her arms around the creature, giving it a loving hug.

The creature did not respond but kept its eyes fixed on Thomas.

As if they had received some telepathic communication, the other creatures slowly began to converge on their helpless victim.

Thomas, realising what was about to happen, felt a hot stream running down the inside of his joggers. His whole body began to tremble uncontrollably. He knew he had no chance of flight, and to try and fight the creatures off would be futile. For one thing, there were too many of them.

Out of desperation he turned to Polly, a look of pleading on his face.

But all she did was laugh back at him as she hugged her creature again.

With a courage born of fear, Sheffield shot forward and tried to drive a path through the creatures. Putting all his weight into the effort, he was successful in knocking a couple of them sideways, but their companions managed to keep them upright as they were so close to each other.

Thomas swung out wildly with his fists, making contact with a couple of haymakers, but it was all to no avail.

Within seconds the creatures had him on the floor, and this time they all converged on his stricken body as one, tearing into his flesh and ripping him apart with their fangs and claws.

Thomas tried to scream through the excruciating pain, but the sound was lost in his throat as one of the creatures tore out his larynx.

He closed his eyes and awaited death.

Thomas did not have long to wait.

6

KAREN CUPPED HER HANDS AROUND THE STEAMING MUG OF coffee. She lifted it to her mouth and blew on the liquid, causing it to ripple, before she took a sip. The bitter black liquid scalded her throat as it slipped down, but she still savoured the taste.

She had had grown accustomed to drinking her coffee black during her pregnancy. The taste of dairy had made her feel sick during the last six months and, by the time Charlotte had been born, she was used to the taste.

It was almost one in the morning, but Karen was still not feeling tired.

Her mind was a jumble of thoughts that she was trying desperately to organise into some form of coherent order.

Dan had stayed until almost midnight and, all the time he was there, Karen had to fight the urge to unburden herself to him and tell him everything. But something held her back. Was it shame? She could not be sure.

Although Dan was sweet and kind, Karen could not help but wonder if he was the kind of man who could cope with the fact that his girlfriend had been on the game.

Most men would not be able to, and those that could were probably the type who were turned on by the idea. That was the last thing she needed.

But if she stopped prostituting herself, how was she going to manage financially?

She could hardly expect Dan to help her out, even if they were together as a couple.

It might be different if they had been together for a while, but how could she expect him to help her pay her bills at the very start of their relationship?

Karen knew that the obvious choice, if she wanted a relationship with Dan, was to move back in with her mother. That way, she would at least be comfortable, with no more money worries. She would have to give up the game, which would be wonderful, and her mother could babysit for her when she and Dan went out.

But no sooner had she convinced herself that that was her best option, she could hear her mother's voice in her head, berating her for all the mistakes she had made with her life, and reminding her that Josie would never have been so foolish.

Karen sighed, and took another sip from her mug.

Outside, rain was beginning to splatter the windows. She took her drink over to watch the surrounding buildings through the tear-stained glass. This was how she liked to see the area where she lived. Damp and sodden. There was something about the surrounding tower blocks that made Karen feel depressed whenever the sun was shining on them.

She followed the trail of a single raindrop as it manoeuvred its way down the outside glass.

Suddenly, she heard a gentle tap on her front door.

For a moment she stayed where she was, holding her breath.

Who the hell could be calling on her at this hour?

Oh Jesus, not a punter, surely!

Karen let out a deep breath and placed her mug on the table. She edged her way towards the door, careful not to make any sudden movement that might cause her to be heard by whoever was outside.

If it was a punter, it had to be someone who had already been to her place, otherwise how would they know where she lived?

Or it was the maniac who had called her earlier that evening? Waiting until Dan had left to make his move?

Karen chided herself. She had already decided that that creep did not know where she lived, and there was no way of tracing her from the website, so it could not be him.

Slipping off her trainers so as not to make a sound, Karen crept along the corridor towards her front door. She was struck by a sudden feeling of déjà vu as she focused on the peep-hole in the door. When her eye was only a couple of inches away from it, the knock came again. It was still gentle and barely audible, almost as if the person standing outside knew she had a sleeping baby.

"Karen."

She recognised the whispered voice. "Dan!"

She looked through the spy-hole and sure enough it was Dan waiting outside.

Karen quickly unlatched the door and swung it open.

For a moment the two of them merely stared at each other without speaking.

Seeing the puzzled expression on her face, Dan finally broke the silence.

"Sorry," he said, apologetically. "I realise this must seem a tad ridiculous, considering I only left less than an hour ago."

Karen stood back and ushered him back in. She could tell from his jacket that he had been caught in the rain, and she wondered how, as his car should have been parked close enough to her block for him to make it before being pelted on.

On top of which, it had not even started raining until long after he had left.

Perhaps his car wouldn't start and he had been outside all this time trying to fix it.

"Did you forget something?" Karen whispered.

Dan stood there, shivering slightly in his wet coat. "Kind of," he shrugged, "I'm sorry this must seem so weird, but I really need to speak to you about something and I didn't want to wait until another time."

Karen helped him out of his wet coat and hung it up to dry in the airing cupboard.

Karen felt an uneasy knot starting to form in her stomach. What could possibly be so urgent that Dan could not wait to call her in the morning.

Her worst fear, she realised, was that he had discovered her guilty secret.

As they entered the living room, Karen switched on the light, and used the dimmer switch to keep it low. She closed the door behind them because she knew that she would still be able to hear Charlotte if she started crying, and somehow, she felt that whatever Dan was about to reveal might end in raised voices.

They sat down together on the settee and turned to face each other.

Dan took a deep breath before starting. "To start with," he began nervously, "I want to say that I realise I have been a complete coward about this but, since we first met, the time has never felt appropriate."

Karen could tell that he was struggling. "OK."

"The truth is, I think I love you... No, God, what a stupid thing to say! I know I do, and even though we have never even been out on a date together, I need to know if I am just fooling myself or if there's any way that you might feel the same."

Karen sat back, not intentionally, as if she were pulling away from Dan, but more from pure shock over his revelation.

But Dan, too, believed the reflex action meant she was rejecting him.

He stood up and began to make his way towards the door, apologising under his breath as he went.

"No, Dan, please come back," Karen implored, realising what her action must have seemed like to him. "I didn't mean to react in that way, it's just that you took me a little by surprise."

Dan turned. Even in the dim light Karen could tell by his complexion that he was feeling embarrassed.

She smiled warmly and patted the seat next to her.

Dan edged his way back to the couch and sat down beside her. "Well, I've made a proper fool of myself, haven't I?" he said resignedly.

Karen reached over and placed her hand on his knee. "No, you haven't, but you certainly know how to take a girl by surprise, I'll give you that."

Dan smiled, in spite of how he felt. "It's hard to believe how long I have wanted to say that to you. I even walked around since I left you earlier on, just trying to think of how best to approach the subject, and then what do I go and do? Just blurt it out all in one go."

Karen felt herself calm down. Now that she knew what Dan had wanted to say, she felt herself back in control of the situation. In truth, Dan's disclosure made her feel happy inside for the first time in ages. She knew full well what a brilliant father he would be for Charlotte, and even though they had only known each other a short time, she felt as if she could trust him to stay true to his word.

But that was still the problem. They had only known each other a short time, and Karen was not the type to charge into something like this without considering all the potential outcomes.

"So what do you think?" asked Dan, still not able to hold her gaze for any length of time. "Please say something, even if it is, 'Get out of my place, you weirdo.'"

Karen leaned over and planted a kiss on his cheek.

Dan turned to face her, and this time he did not look away.

They both moved in together for a full kiss, their first since they met.

It felt good to Karen. It felt real, as if they both meant it, with neither of them expecting too much from the other.

Dan gazed deeply into Karen's eyes. Their kiss had given him the confidence to take this conversation to the next level.

"Just so you know," he began, still somewhat hesitantly, "if you wanted to, you and Charlotte could move in with me whenever you're ready. I don't live in a palace, but I inherited a house from my grandmother when she passed away last year and, although it is a little run-down and needs a ton of work, it's more than big enough for the three of us..."

Dan's voice trailed away. He suddenly felt as if he was rushing things too much. It was one thing to blurt out his feelings, but asking Karen to move in with him so soon after their first kiss might, he feared, be enough to scare her off.

He reminded himself that he had loved her for a long time, whereas the prospect was completely new to her.

Karen's silence told him he should have waited.

He decided not to push the issue, and wait for her to consider it in her own time.

Karen could not get her head around Dan's proposal. Yes, it would solve all her immediate worries, both financial and otherwise. But, could he be in love with her after they had known each other for such a short time? What was more, was she in love with him?

She had to be true to herself if nothing else, and the fact was, as much as she liked Dan, it was too soon for her even to contemplate being in love with him.

It was not that Karen was so unromantic that she did not believe in love at first sight. Nor was it the fact that all the men who had knocked her off her feet during her adolescence had all only been after one thing. It was more the fact that she needed to ensure that she only make good choices for the sake of Charlotte. Not that Karen considered becoming a prostitute as being a particularly good choice, but it was a means to an end, and a sacrifice she was more than willing to make for her baby.

Furthermore, if she and Dan were to have any sort of future together, they could not begin their relationship with a lie.

Although her mind was a jumble of emotions, Karen knew that one issue had to be addressed before they could go any further.

She held out her hand. "Come here, please, Dan. There's something I have to tell you."

Dan looked perplexed. Previous experience had taught him that such an announcement did not bode well for whatever came next.

He walked over and took the proffered hand, holding it firmly in his own, and sat down beside her.

Karen felt a sudden tightness in her throat. There was no easy way to say this.

"Dan, you really do mean a lot to me, and I love the fact that you are willing to open your home and heart to Charlotte and me but the fact of the matter is that..." Karen took another breath and closed her eyes. It had to be all or nothing for this to stand a chance of working.

"What is it, darling? You can tell me anything." Dan's tone was soft and comforting, but Karen knew he was not expecting the answer with which she was about to hit him.

She opened her eyes, and looked deep into his. "Dan, until recently, I have been working as a... prostitute."

For a few moments, Dan did not speak.

Looking at his face, Karen could tell that he was desperately trying to process what she had just said.

He opened his mouth to speak, but no words came out.

Before she could stop him, Dan snatched his hand back and stood up from the couch. He strode over to the window and stood there with his back to Karen, watching the rain splatter down the pane.

Karen felt the air being sucked out of her, as if she were reeling from a punch to the stomach. In an instant, she had gone from being too cautious to consider Dan's offer to wishing she had kept her mouth shut about her how she had been feeding herself and her baby lately.

As she looked at the back of Dan's head, she wished above all else that he would turn around and rejoin her on the sofa. She imagined him throwing his arms around her and telling her not to worry and that everything was going to be all right, and that whatever she had done was in the past.

But instead, he just stayed as he was, gazing outside.

As time passed, and Dan still did not move, Karen resigned herself to the fact that, after tonight, she would probably never see him again. But as much as it hurt, she guessed she could not blame him. Most men would have a hard time accepting the fact that the girl they were in love with had been on the game.

Karen could feel the start of tears brimming, but she fought to keep them back.

Although they had never officially started a relationship, Karen could already feel the loss, and it hurt.

Eventually, Dan turned back to face her.

To her amazement, Karen could see that he, too, had been crying. As if suddenly realising that he was giving himself away, Dan rubbed his hand across his face to clear away the streaks.

Karen fought the urge to run up to him and hold him.

His expression showed a combination of sorrow and pity,

but it soon changed to one of anger. Dan shoved his hand in his trouser pocket and pulled out a couple of 20-pound notes. He crumpled them in his fist before throwing them on to the floor.

"What do I get for that, then?" He almost spat the words out, his face flushed with rage.

Now Karen felt her own anger rising. She did not deserve this!

"A blow job, but you'll have to wear a condom like all the rest!"

They stared at each other for a few seconds, neither speaking, but both breathing heavily, as if desperate to keep control.

Finally, Dan strode purposefully towards Karen, until he was standing directly in front of her.

Karen looked up into a face she barely recognised. His lips were pursed tightly together, his eyes still ablaze with fury.

She cowered inside, but refused to show any outwards signs of fear. She was convinced that Dan was going to strike her before he left.

Instead, he fell to his knees and took Karen's hands in his, and kissed them gently.

Dan looked back up at Karen.

His fierce expression was now replaced with one showing understanding and a longing to comfort.

"If you needed money that badly, why didn't you just ask me?" It was more of a plea than a simple question.

Karen squeezed his hands. "I couldn't... please understand, I just couldn't."

She could feel her tears returning. Karen dropped her head until her chin hit her chest. Part of her was still too ashamed to look Dan in the eyes.

Dan placed both of Karen's hands into one of his, and used his free hand to raise her chin gently so that they could make eye contact once again.

"You don't have to go to bed with me just because you need

money. I'll gladly give you whatever you need, no conditions attached."

Karen could hear the genuine sincerity in his voice. Gazing back at him, she knew he meant every word.

Karen wiped away her tears. "And you don't have to give me money to go to bed with you, you're welcome any time."

Dan raised himself off the floor and the two of them kissed.

Although it was only their second real kiss since meeting, they both poured a great deal of passion into it.

7

INSPECTOR KEITH JACOBS LOOKED UP FROM THE FILES ON HIS desk and strained to hear what the commotion outside his office was all about. Unable to make out the exact content through his office door, he rose from his chair and decided to investigate.

In the foyer he found his desk sergeant trying, unsuccessfully, to calm down an irate man who was leaning on the counter and shaking his fist in the air as he shouted.

Jacobs recognised the man as Charlie Spate, the local odd-job man and town drunk. Judging by the man's condition it was obvious to the inspector that he had already enjoyed a skinful that day, even though it was still not even noon.

As Jacobs approached the desk, the uniformed sergeant turned and gave him a look that conveyed he had all but given up trying to reason with the drunk. Jacobs nodded for the officer to stand aside to allow him to try his luck.

"All right, Charlie, keep it down, there are officers back there trying to get their heads down," Jacobs kept his expression stern, though his words brought a smile to his sergeant's face.

Charlie squinted up at Jacobs as if he were trying to see him through bright sunlight. It took him a moment to realise who it was standing before him. Charlie Spate was a semi-regular visitor to the station, usually as the result of being arrested for causing a disturbance at one of the local hostelries or, on occasion, the bookies.

Jacobs had been the officer left to release Spate on more than one occasion, so the two knew each other, even if only professionally.

"Oh, Inspector Jacobs, thank God." The man attempted to stand up without the support of the counter, almost losing his balance in the process. He managed to grab the side of the glass partition just in time to keep himself upright. "They've taken my little girl, my Sharon," he jabbed a nicotine-stained finger over his shoulder for emphasis. "Those bastards down there in that fuckin' rat 'ole have kidnapped my little girl. You 'ave to 'elp me."

"Who exactly has kidnapped your daughter?" Jacobs asked, perplexed.

Charlie wiped his jacket sleeve across his nose, smearing a trail of mucus along his unshaven skin.

Jacobs winced, plucked a couple of tissues from the box on the desk, and handed them over.

Charlie took the tissues without using them. "You know 'oo I'm talkin' about, those fuckin' weirdos in that shit 'ole near the woods."

"He means Thorndike, guv," the sergeant leaned in and whispered. "He reckons his daughter was up there the other night and now she's being held hostage by the villagers."

Jacobs glanced at the officer, frowning.

The desk sergeant merely shrugged his shoulders in response, and twirled his index finger beside his ear to indicate that Spate was mad.

Charlie caught sight of the gesture and turned to face the

sergeant. "Don't you fuckin' take the piss out of me, you bastard, I can still fuckin' take care of the lot o' yer, and those bastards in that pissin' place. I'll fuckin' show yer all."

With that, the man let go of the partition and attempted to make a boxer's stance with his fists held high in the air. He threw a punch at no one in particular, and the wild swinging motion caused him to lose his balance. Before either officer could reach through the partition to grab him, Charlie hit the counter with the side of his head, before sliding down to the floor.

Both officers made their way around to the front and lifted Charlie off the cold lino floor, before carrying him over to the bench in the waiting area.

By now, Charlie had started whimpering, and tears were rolling down his cheeks. He was still somehow clutching the tissues Jacob's had given him, so the officer pointed to them and told him to wipe his face.

"They've got me little girl, guv, they 'ave, I know they 'ave," Charlie mumbled through the tissue paper while attempting to blow his nose at the same time.

"Shall I chuck him in one of the cells guv?" asked the sergeant. "They're all empty at the moment – he can sober up in there."

Jacobs ignored the offer.

Instead, he squatted down on his haunches in front of Charlie. "When was the last time you saw Sharon, Charlie?" he asked, with genuine concern in his tone.

The man looked at him through tear-stained eyes. "It was a couple of nights ago, she went off to work at the Dog, same as usual, but she never come back that night. I went down there and spoke to Toby behind the bar. 'E reckoned she had gone off with some lad, but 'e didn't know where."

"So, what makes you think she ended up at Thorndike?"

Charlie leaned in closer as if about to reveal a secret.

Jacobs felt guilty for pulling back, but the stench of the man's breath forced his hand.

"I bumped into those Craven brothers in the high street just now, they reckon they saw 'er up in the village on their way back into town. They said she was with someone but they didn't know 'oo. They offered 'er a lift 'ome, but they reckon she said she'd come back with the lad. I 'aven't seen 'er since." Charlie lunged forward and, before he could stop him, Jacobs felt Charlie's grubby hands pulling on the lapels of his jacket. "You've got to 'elp me." He implored pitifully.

Jacobs extricated himself from Charlie's grasp, and stood up.

Turning to the sergeant, he said. "Maybe the cells aren't such a bad idea, just until he sleeps it off. We'll need a coherent statement from him once he's sobered up."

The officer looked confused. "What, you mean you're taking his story seriously, sir?"

Jacobs nodded. "Just until we can verify his daughter is safe and well. Do you know her by any chance?"

The sergeant scratched his head. "Well, I've seen her about town a couple of times, not really to speak to other than to order a drink when I'm in the Dog and Duck."

Jacobs thought for a moment. "Well for a start, let's get someone down to the pub to speak to this Toby person he mentioned, and then let's see if those Craven brothers can verify his story."

The uniformed officer spread his arms out wide. "Are you serious, guv'nor? I've got two in court, another three escorting those burglars up to London, one off sick, and everyone else is already on a call."

Jacobs shot his eyes up to heaven. "Well let's hope no one decides to commit a crime in the near future, otherwise we'll be right up the Swanee without a paddle."

Jacobs helped the sergeant to manoeuvre Charlie into a cell.

The man was obviously distraught and, in Jacobs's opinion, it was not fair to assume that he was talking nonsense just because of his condition.

He knew that the desk sergeant was not simply fobbing him off by saying he had no one available to start the investigation. Since transferring to this quaint, if not somewhat remote, part of Cornwall, Jacobs had grown used to filling in for the lack of uniformed bodies whenever necessary. Cutbacks had slashed the station's staffing levels to the bone but, to be fair, the overall lack of crime in the area was one of the reason's Jacobs loved the pace of life down here.

It was a far cry from the hustle and bustle he had experienced in Liverpool when he was first promoted to inspector. And, although there were many at his old station who voiced the opinion, behind his back, that he was leaving because he couldn't hack it, deep down, he didn't care what others thought.

Now 42, Jacobs had given his life to the force. He had spent enough time on the front line dealing with all manner of thugs and scumbags and he felt that he deserved a change before he burnt out completely.

He had never married, nor had he even been in a relationship that lasted more than a couple of years. His love life, such as it was, was littered with one-night stands and short-term liaisons, again as a direct result of the job. In fact, by the time he reached 30 he had come to the conclusion that the force was in his blood and that, no matter what, he would always put the job first.

No woman was ever going to accept that.

THE LOUNGE BAR at the Dog and Duck was just beginning to fill up with the lunchtime crowd when Jacobs arrived. He ordered himself a beer and a sandwich and took a seat by the window, overlooking the garden.

When the barman brought him over his order, Jacobs flashed his warrant card and asked for Toby.

"I'm Toby," replied the barman, eyeing him suspiciously.

"I believe you spoke to Charlie Spate recently concerning the whereabouts of his daughter, Sharon?"

Toby physically relaxed. "That's right, he came in here looking for her but, as I told him, I haven't laid eyes on her since she left the other night with one of our regulars. The silly cow has dumped me right in it. I'm two staff down as it is and then she decides to do a disappearing act."

"So, you know who it was she left with?" Jacobs raised his eyebrows. "Only Charlie seemed to think you didn't."

The barman looked embarrassed. He took the seat opposite Jacobs. "Look, I told Charlie that because I didn't want him going off all half-cocked. He came in here pissed as usual, and Dennis Carter is a good bloke. You must know him – his dad works at your station."

"He does," Jacobs confirmed, surprised by the revelation.

"Yeah," Toby assured him. "Ron Carter, old bloke, white moustache, been there for ever."

Indeed, Jacobs did know Ron Carter. Word around the station had it that, if he were not about to retire, he would be heading for a disciplinary board.

"Come on Toby, we're dying of thirst here."

Toby turned around to see a large man in work overalls leaning against the bar. In his hand was an empty pint glass.

"In a minute, you impatient sod. Can't you see I'm busy?" Toby's tone had an edge of humour to it, and Jacobs guessed that the customer must be a regular as he seemed to take the insult in good stead.

Toby turned back to him. "Look, sorry, Inspector but I need to get back before I have a riot on my hands." He began to rise.

"Just one last thing," Jacobs held up his hand, and Toby reluctantly sat back down. "Have you seen Dennis in here since he left with Sharon that evening?"

Toby thought for a moment before shaking his head, slowly. "I don't think so, but to be honest, he could have slipped in for a quick pint when I was out the back."

Jacobs thanked him for his time, and Toby returned to his eager customers.

While he ate, Jacobs called the station. The desk sergeant who had helped him with Charlie Spate answered. Jacobs made enquiries about Ron Carter, and was informed that he had been on holiday for the past week and was due to return the following day.

Jacobs asked for his address, deciding that it might be worth his while calling round there on the off-chance he might find Dennis and Sharon shacked up together.

On his way out of the pub, Jacobs gave Toby his card and asked him to give him a call if either Sharon or Dennis put in an appearance.

8

KAREN WATCHED AS HER MOTHER PLAYED WITH CHARLOTTE, cradling the baby in her arms and making gurgling sounds to emulate those of her granddaughter.

It hurt Karen that she felt an actual pang of jealousy that she could never remember her mother showing her such affection when she was little. But then, she reasoned, if she had been the same age as Charlotte, she would hardly remember.

There was certainly no recollection from later years.

Enid Taylor looked extremely fit for her age. But then some might have put that down to the fact that she had never known hardship or physical labour throughout her life.

Her husband's career supplied them with ample finances to allow Enid to spend her days as a homemaker. Even then, she had a small army of staff to complete the more mundane tasks around the house, such as cleaning, cooking and ironing. She even hired au pairs to help with the girls, mainly to afford her the luxury to focus her attention on arranging dinner parties and coffee mornings, for one of the many social groups of which she was a member.

Karen could not remember a single night growing up when

her mother had come upstairs to tuck her in or read her a bedtime story.

Karen had always felt that her parents had children only because it was the expected thing for a young and up-and-coming couple to do. Furthermore, Karen was convinced that her parents would have been quite happy to stop after her elder sister had been born. It was never said to her directly, but deep down, Karen always felt that she had been a mistake.

Enid Taylor had always lived by her own rules of dignity and observance, and she had worked tirelessly to instil those virtues into her offspring. She believed in honouring thy mother and father, saying grace before meals and prayers at bedtime, and adhering to strict formality at all times. As far as she was concerned, there was a place for everything, and everything belonged in its place.

The fact that Karen had had a child out of wedlock was bad enough, but not even being in contact with the father, in Enid's eyes, made everything 10 times worse.

Karen hoped that the idea of her moving in with Dan would appeal to her mother. After all, it would mean that Charlotte would have a father figure and, in time, if things worked out, they would be married and, in her mother's eyes, respectable.

But as with everything where her mother was concerned, Karen had no idea what her reaction would be until she had explained her plans.

"Mum," Karen began, trying to keep the nervousness out of her voice. "I've met someone, and... well, we've decided to move in together."

Enid Taylor immediately stopped paying attention to her granddaughter and looked up, her brow furrowed. "What are you talking about?" she demanded. "Why am I only just hearing about this?"

Karen blushed. She could not help it, but in her mother's presence she was always reduced to an eight-year-old child.

She took a deep breath. "To be honest, we have only just started dating, although I have known him a while..."

"And you're already talking about moving in together?" her mother butted in, not giving Karen a chance to finish her sentence. "Don't be so absurd, you cannot just meet someone one minute and move in with them the next. You were raised far better than that!"

Karen had been dreading this moment ever since she decided to come over.

True, she had not expected her mother to be over the moon about the situation, but even so, she had been hoping for something a little more encouraging than her mother's usual indifferent or even hostile routine.

"I thought you might be happy for me," Karen ventured, hoping to veer on to her mother's sympathetic side.

"Happy!" her mother almost shouted, then, realising she might upset Charlotte, she rocked the baby back and forth until she was confident her anger had not affected her. "Who is this man anyway?" she continued, keeping her voice low and steady. "I take it he's not my granddaughter's real father?"

"No, he's not, but he's happy to take on the role. His name is Dan."

"And where did you meet this night in shining armour?" Although her voice was quiet, there was no attempt to disguise the sarcasm in Enid's tone.

Karen bit her bottom lip. She had toyed with the idea of lying about where they had met as she did not wish to cause her mother undue distress. But part of her thought it would be better to let the truth out from the beginning, just in case it reared its head at some later date and caused another argument.

"To be honest, I met him at Josie's funeral. He works at the library."

The mention of her dead daughter's name in the same

sentence as the man Karen was planning to move in with, was all the ammunition Enid Taylor needed to effect her favourite position of righteous indignation.

"At your poor sister's funeral? Are you serious?"

Karen knew the touch paper had been lit, and all she could do now was sit back and try to defuse the situation whenever the occasion presented itself.

Her mother was going to have her say, no matter what.

Enid stood up and placed Charlotte gently in her carry-cot.

She turned and placed her hands on her hips. "Are you telling me that while your poor sister was being laid to rest, that you were busy flirting with a complete stranger at the graveside?"

"Oh Mother, it was nothing like that, for God's sake." Karen's exasperation was evident, and her plan to try and calm things down had fallen at the first fence.

Enid's face clouded over. "Do not take the Lord's name in vain in this house, young lady!" She shook her index finger at her daughter for emphasis. "Your sister was not even in the ground, and you were prepared to run off with this fellow. Have you no shame?"

Karen had to force herself to stay seated.

If it had not been for the fact that she did not want to upset Charlotte, she would have been more than ready to give her mother a taste of a few simple home truths.

Instead, Karen bit her tongue. "Mother, you're making it sound as if he was with Josie and I stole him. They were only friends, nothing more."

"Because your sister had more dignity than to run off with the first layabout who gave her the eye."

"Dan is not a layabout," Karen retorted, defensively. "How can you say such a thing when you don't even know him?"

"I can guess his type," Enid insisted. "What decent young man asks a girl to move in with him without even being introduced to her mother beforehand, eh? You answer me that?"

Karen could feel her anger rising. "Oh Mother, stop pretending that we live in the last century. Times have moved on, and you need to, too."

Enid moved in closer. "If your poor father were alive today, he'd show this young man the meaning of the word respect. Why isn't he here now, introducing himself? If his intentions are honourable, what's he got to hide? Answer me that, if you can."

"He did want to come over and meet you, as it happens, but I was too ashamed to bring him."

"Ah-ha, so now the truth comes out. You're ready to move in with him but you're too ashamed of him to show him off in public."

"It's not him I'm ashamed of, it's you!" The words had left Karen's lips before she had a chance to check herself.

The second she spoke she regretted it.

Even more so when, within seconds, her mother began to cry.

Throughout her adult life, Karen had been of the opinion that her mother could turn on the waterworks at will. Yet, despite that, it was a line of defence that always served to destroy Karen's resolve, and she was convinced that her mother both knew that fact and exploited it.

Even so, Karen immediately felt guilty. She stood up and walked towards her mother with the intent of giving her a hug and apologising for making her cry.

But as soon as she began moved towards her, Enid turned her back on her daughter and walked over to the sideboard to fetch a tissue to wipe her tears.

Karen checked on Charlotte and saw that the baby was sound asleep. She returned to her chair and sat back down, waiting for her mother to compose herself.

Once Enid was sure that her actions had taken the desired effect, she walked back over and retook her seat, still dabbing her eyes.

They sat in silence for a few minutes until Karen felt it was safe to continue their conversation.

"Mum, you have to face facts, I'm a single mother with no visible means of support, living in a shabby council flat on a crime-ridden estate. What kind of start in life is that for Charlotte?"

Enid's superior countenance returned. "You can always come and live here with me; this house isn't exactly small."

Karen stared up at the ceiling for inspiration. This was an old conversation they had had many times before, and Karen was determined not to give her mother another chance to turn on the tears.

"We both know that wouldn't work, Mum, so please let's not start on that again."

Enid sniffed and wiped her eyes. "Well, all I can say is that it comes to something when a mother and daughter cannot live together under the same roof. I only hope that you do not have to suffer the same hurt from Charlotte one day, then you'll remember this day."

Karen sighed. "Well, if I ever do, then I'll only have myself to blame."

Enid stood up and walked over to a bin in the corner of the room to dispose of her damp tissue. Turning back, she said. "It's Mrs Coyne's day off today, so I'll just go and make us some tea."

With that, she strode purposefully from the room.

Karen slumped back in her chair and let out a deep breath.

She hoped, for now at least, that the worst was over.

9

Jacobs entered the Craven and Sons butcher's shop to find Pete Craven serving alone behind the counter. As there were only two customers waiting, and not wishing to cause Pete any unnecessary embarrassment at his place of business, Jacobs decided to let them finish before he asked to speak to his two sons.

Once the shop was empty, Jacobs explained why he was there, and Pete showed him into the back where his sons were busy chopping meat and sawing bones.

Both boys looked up in surprise when they saw who it was their father was bringing to see them.

"Try not to keep them too long," Pete said, "unless you want to take both of them down to the nick and throw their lazy arses in jail." With that, he turned and walked back into the shop.

The two brothers exchanged furtive glances as Jacobs drew closer.

Colin turned off the bone saw and moved over so that he was standing in front of his brother. Jacobs surmised that the elder brother had taken on the responsibility to answer his questions.

"Hello lads," he began, cheerfully enough, not wishing to raise their level of suspicion any higher than it obviously was already. "I was wondering if you could go over what happened the other night when you met Sharon Spate on the Thorndike road?"

Don Craven immediately blushed red and stared down at the floor.

"Like we told 'er dad," Colin began, keeping his voice steady, "we were on our way home when we saw her standing by Dennis Carter's car at the side of the road. We stopped and asked if everything was OK, and she said that Dennis was in the bushes, takin' a pee. We offered 'er a lift home, but she reckoned she was waitin' for Dennis, so we drove home. That was it."

Jacobs nodded. He noticed that Don was still avoiding his gaze.

"Is that your recollection, too?" He made sure he was looking directly at Don when he spoke. The younger of the two brothers, realising from Jacob's question that he needed to respond, looked up sheepishly and just nodded.

"Did you actually see Dennis Carter with her?"

Both brothers shook their heads. "No," replied Colin, "but it was definitely 'is car, and Sharon told us she was with 'im, anyway."

"So, when Her father asked you earlier, why did you tell him you weren't sure who she was with?"

"Come off it," Don finally pipped up, "Charlie's off 'is 'ead 'alf the time, we didn't want 'im goin' after Dennis for no reason."

Jacobs nodded. "Yeah, that's what Toby down at the Dog and Duck just told me. Have either of you seen Dennis since that night?"

The brothers shook their heads again.

Jacobs waited for a moment. Although their explanation made perfect sense, it still came across to him as somewhat too well rehearsed. Almost as if they were trying to hide something.

The question was: What?

Plus, the fact that Don Craven could not seem to hold his gaze for more than a split second, made Jacobs's copper's nose twitch. But even so, at this point in time, he had no reason to suspect that the brothers had committed a crime. At least, not as far as Dennis and Sharon were concerned.

Jacobs knew that, whatever it was they were hiding; he could easily weasel it out of the younger brother if he spoke to him alone. But he decided there was no reason to raise any suspicion for now.

"OK, lads, thanks for your help. Do me a favour, if you see either Dennis or Sharon, ask them to call the station, just to let us know they are all right."

Jacobs noticed both brothers physically relax their shoulders.

As he turned to leave, another thought struck him.

He spun back around. "Just one thing," he said and noticed Don take a tentative step back behind his elder brother. "What were you two doing in Thorndike in the first place?" Tiny place like that, no clubs or anywhere for young blokes like you to hang out, what was the attraction?"

The brothers looked at each other, as if for inspiration.

As the seconds ticked by, Jacobs could almost feel the tentative tension between the lads growing more palpable.

This time he had really caught them off guard. Whatever they had cooked up between themselves concerning their encounter with Sharon, they obviously had not anticipated his latest question.

He gave them a few more seconds to stew, then he said, "Well?"

Colin turned back to face him, his expression brewing a storm cloud of frustration and panic. His brother Don, once more, had taken up his usual stance of staring at the ground, leaving his brother to act as the mouthpiece for both of them.

"We'd been to the inn in the village," Colin blurted out, lowering his voice so that Jacobs had to strain to hear. "But please don't tell our dad, he'd go mad if 'e found out we were buying pies from anyone else."

Jacobs glanced over his shoulder to make sure their father had not come back in behind him. "Pies?" he echoed, incredulously.

Colin signalled with his hands for Jacobs to keep his voice down.

"Yeah, pies," Colin reiterated. "The ones they serve at the inn are out of this world, so we sometimes go up there for a pint and a pie, but our dad would go spare if 'e found out we prefer their ones to 'is, so please don't let 'im know."

Both brothers looked at Jacobs, and for the first time he saw genuine concern in their eyes. Their explanation made a certain amount of sense to him, and it would explain their reason for being there in the first place, so he decided to let it drop.

Once Jacobs had left the shop, Colin turned to his brother. "That was a stroke of genius, don't yer think?"

Don was visibly shaking. "What if 'e comes back? If 'e goes to the inn and speaks to the owner, an' 'e tells 'im about the real reason we go there, 'e'll know we were lyin'."

Colin grabbed his brother roughly by the shoulders. "'E's 'ardly gonna tell 'im we sell 'im knocked-off meat that past its best, is 'e?"

"But what if 'e does?" Don insisted.

"Then 'e stands to lose a lot more than us, don't 'e? 'E could lose 'is bleedin' licence, so why would 'e chance it?"

Colin could tell his brother was not completely sold, but he also knew him well enough to trust him to keep his mouth shut. They had a tidy little business on the side keeping old man Beanie supplied with dodgy cuts of meat, and it was in all their interests to keep their dealings between themselves.

Colin knew that his brother was more afraid of their father finding out than anything else. Pete Craven was not above knocking ten bells out of his boys if he felt the situation warranted it. But they both knew the risks when they started their little sideline, and this business with Dennis and Sharon was no reason for them to come unglued.

Whatever had happened to their mate and his girlfriend was nothing to do with them.

KAREN STEERED the pushchair through the labyrinthine cement corridors underneath her building, careful not to wake Charlotte as she entered the lift. She hated having to use the lift, but there was no physical way she could carry her baby and the pram up the stairs to her flat.

The acrid stench of stale urine assaulted her nostrils the minute the metal door slid shut, trapping her inside. She managed to hold her breath for most of the journey, but it still made her feel as if she needed a shower when she emerged on her floor.

The reek from the lift was certainly something Karen would be more than happy to leave behind when she moved in with Dan. That, along with the noise whenever one of her neighbours believed that they had the right to blare their music out without consideration for anyone else, regardless of the hour. Or the screams from any of the many couples in her block who frequently decided that their argument was so fascinating that they continued it in the communal corridor for all to appreciate. Yes, Karen was beginning to feel very grateful for Dan's kind offer. She only hoped that in time she would grow to feel the same way about him as he did for her.

Once inside, Karen left Charlotte asleep in her carry-cot, and went into the kitchen to boil the kettle.

As she reached into a cupboard for a mug, her mobile went off. She could see it was an unknown number, and it reminded her that she needed to speak to her friend who had added her number on to her contact website, to have it removed.

"Hello."

"Oh, hello," replied a timid male voice, "I don't know if you remember me, but I called on you the other day. I'm the one who asked if you would wear a school uniform for me."

Karen cut him off. "I'm really sorry but I'm afraid I don't see clients any more. Sorry."

There was a brief pause on the other end, before the man continued. "Oh, I see, that is a pity. Did I mention that I would be happy to pay more for you to wear it, double in fact?"

Karen sighed. "Look, I'm really sorry but as I said, I no longer entertain clients, so please call one of the other numbers on the site."

She did not give the caller a chance to say anything else before she switched off the call.

Karen made her coffee and carried it into the living room. She kicked off her shoes and switched on the television, keeping the sound low so as not to wake her baby.

While she thought about it, she called the girl whom she had met down at the social office to ask her to remove her details from the site. The call went straight to voicemail, so Karen left a message, thanking her, but stressing that she had decided the business was not for her.

As she sipped her coffee, her phone came to life.

She saw it was Dan's number. "Hiya," she said cheerfully.

"Hi darling, how was your day?"

"Oh, we went to visit grandma and filled her in on the situation."

"How did that go?" Karen could sense the tension in Dan's voice.

"Um, let's just say she will get used to the idea," Karen answered tactfully.

Dan laughed. "It went that well? I should have come with you – I feel like such a coward."

"Probably best I went alone. Now that she knows, it won't seem so strange when we go there together."

"Yeah," Dan agreed, "you're probably right. Anyway, reason I called, how do you fancy meeting me for lunch tomorrow?"

"Great, what time?"

"Say one o'clock. Can you meet me at the library?"

"Yeah, no problem, looking forward to it."

"Me too. How's Charlotte?"

"Still asleep, she missed her afternoon nap at my mum's so I thought I'd let her catch up. I'll wake her soon for her dinner."

"OK, I'll see you tomorrow darling, love you."

"Me too."

Karen waited for Dan to end the call.

It still seemed strange hearing him say he loved her, but she had to admit that she was beginning to like the way it sounded.

Now she came to think about it, Karen had not actually used those words herself. She wondered if deep down there was something preventing her from saying it to Dan.

She shook off the thought. As usual, she was overthinking the situation. She would say it when the time was right, and Karen was sure that it would simply roll off her tongue when she did.

Her mobile rang again. Without looking at the screen, Karen answered it, thinking it would either be Dan again or her friend she'd left the voicemail for.

"Hello."

There was no answer.

"Hello," Karen tried again, "is anybody there?"

She could sense someone was listening on the other end.

Then, she heard their breathing as it grew louder.

"I'm going to fuck you!"

Karen almost dropped the phone. She was sure it was the same voice from the other evening. Keeping the phone pressed to her ear, Karen slipped off the sofa and walked back out into the hallway to check she had locked the front door, properly.

The breathing on the other end continued.

Once she had shot the chain bolt home, Karen switched off the call.

She stood there for a moment, catching her breath.

Whoever it was, he already had her number, so even taking it down from the website was not going to make a difference. He could still call her whenever he chose.

Her mobile rang again.

This time Karen looked at the screen. It was a withheld number.

It had to be him again.

"Hello," she said uncertainly.

More heavy breathing.

"Who is this?" she demanded, still trying not to raise her voice and wake Charlotte who was still sleeping soundly only a few feet away.

"I'm going to fuck you!"

Karen had had enough. "Listen to me, you fucking pervert, I've called the police about you, they're probably tracing this call right now so if you know what's good for you, you'd better run!"

Again, Karen terminated the call without giving the caller a chance to reply.

Ten seconds later, it rang again. Another withheld number.

Karen terminated it without answering.

She switched her mobile to silent, and shoved it in her jeans pocket.

Within seconds she could feel it vibrating against her thigh. It continued until her voicemail broke in. She wondered if the creep would leave her a message. Something she could take to the police. They had voice recognition equipment; they could probably trace him through that.

She waited for her phone to stop buzzing, then retrieved it and checked for a message.

There was none.

Karen considered calling the police, then stopped herself.

Would she have to reveal how the creep obtained her number in the first place?

She thought about it for a moment.

There was no need to go into details, just report the calls and leave it to them.

Karen gazed at her phone, almost willing it to come to life again, as she decided that would be the catalyst to persuade her to enlist the police's help.

The phone stayed silent.

Just then, Charlotte woke and started crying.

Karen picked her up and carried her into the living room to feed her.

10

Charlie Spate held the butt of his shotgun tightly under his arm as he threw his head back and poured another generous helping of whisky down his throat. Once he had been released from the police station that afternoon, he had decided that the only way he was going to get his daughter back from those damn villagers was by going in and rescuing her himself.

They had no right to lock him up in the first place, and saying that it was for his own good was just a load of bollocks. When this was over, he planned to sue the county for false imprisonment.

Those stupid coppers should be charging in mob-handed, or even liaising with the army to search that village from top to bottom, not fobbing him off with excuses.

Well, he would show them. Charlie Spate was no fool. He knew there was something queer going on in that place, and no one was going to tell him otherwise.

He remembered years ago when he had driven over there one day to tout for business. He figured there must be at least a few properties that needed their lawns attending to or their brickwork repointed. He could turn his hands to most things and, if he was paid cash in hand, he always kept the price down.

But it still made him shiver when he recalled the eerie sensation that had crept into his bones when he drove over the bridge and entered Thorndike. As he walked through the cobbled streets knocking on doors, he soon realised from the few that were actually answered that his presence was not appreciated.

Eventually, he gave up and went to the pub for a couple of pints to drown his sorrows.

But even in the familiar surroundings of a bar, Charlie had never felt so uncomfortable. It felt to him as if every eye in the place was watching him. He gulped his pint down as quickly as he could and left.

His feeling of unease did not start to dissipate until he drove back over the bridge.

That was the one and only time Charlie had ever set foot in the village, and he had sworn to himself he would not do so again. But this was different. This was his little girl, his only child. She was all that he had since his wife had run off with that lorry driver from London. The old tart, he was better off without her moaning.

But his little girl was another matter. She knew that he could not cope without her. She always looked after her old dad, making sure his dinner was on the table before she went to work, and with her serving at the Dog and Duck, he was always assured of a couple of free pints when Toby had his back turned.

Yes, she was a good girl. But now the stupid bitch had gone and managed to get mixed up in God alone knew what with those freaks in the village. Still, it would serve her right for being so irresponsible and leaving her poor father to fend for himself.

Even so, she had been there long enough now, so Charlie

would have to swoop in and rescue her. Then she would be grateful, and maybe next time she would listen to him about not venturing too far away from home.

Charlie took another long swig from the bottle. He was already down to the label, so decided it might be best to save the rest for later. He placed the bottle in his jacket pocket and checked to make sure he had plenty of spare shells, before leaving his house.

The last of the evening sunlight had slipped away and the sky had been transformed from a rosy red to a dull, leaden grey. Charlie climbed behind the wheel of his old work van, and placed his shotgun on the seat beside him.

Once he drove out of the town, he left the relative comfort of the street lights behind, and the road leading to the village became dark and menacing.

Charlie placed his hand on his shotgun for reassurance, then snatched it back to grab the wheel as something shot out in front of him, making him swerve to avoid it.

More by luck than by skill, he managed to keep his van on the road.

By the time he reached the turning that would take him into Thorndike, the first of the evening's stars had started to poke through the pitch-black blanket of night. Charlie slowed down as the terrain beneath his tyres grew more irregular, and he turned his headlights to full beam to help him negotiate the track.

As he approached the bridge that led into the village, Charlie pulled over to one side and switched off his engine. He decided that another snifter of Dutch courage was in order before he entered the fray.

He wound down his window and rested his elbow on the frame while he drank.

A sudden cry pierced the darkness, almost making Charlie drop his bottle.

He reached out for his gun and held it firmly in both hands, with the barrels poking out of the open window.

That had sounded like a human cry, not just a nocturnal animal, he thought.

Charlie listened intently, but all he could hear for the moment was the wind rustling through the branches of the surrounding trees, and the occasional hoot of a faraway owl.

He cursed the police officers for not taking him seriously.

By rights it should be them out here now, doing the job that his taxes paid for. Instead they were probably safe and warm back at the station, while here he was, out in the elements, exposed.

Charlie watched for any movement in the murky shadows in front of him, but his eyes strained to make out anything specific in the darkness.

What the hell had made that scream?

Fumbling with one hand, Charlie managed to locate the cap from his whisky bottle and replaced it, holding the bottle between his thighs.

Once he was satisfied the cap was secure, he placed it back in his pocket, breathing a sigh of relief that he had not wasted any of the golden nectar.

The force of something crashing into the side of his van almost knocked the vehicle on to its side. It teetered on two wheels for a split second before falling back into place.

The shock of the impact coming out of nowhere made Charlie let go of his shotgun and the weapon slipped out of the open window and landed on the ground outside.

For a moment, Charlie sat there in silence, his mind trying desperately to assess what had just taken place. Whatever had crashed into him must have been large, not to mention strong, as it was no easy feat to almost upend a van.

Charlie had often heard stories about wild cats being scene in the vicinity, but this felt more like a charging bull. It was possible that one had managed to escape from some farmer's enclosure, but if so, what possible reason would it have to attack his van?

He turned around and looked out of the windows. Miraculously, none of them had been shattered by the impact. There was no sign of anything outside. Charlie considered the possibility that whatever had hit him had knocked itself unconscious, or even died as a result. Perhaps it was lying dead next to his vehicle.

Either way, Charlie felt too vulnerable for comfort without his trusty shotgun for protection.

Having satisfied himself that there was nothing lurking outside waiting to pounce, Charlie opened his door and stepped out on to the roadway. He crouched down and managed to locate his gun, thankful that he had kept the safety catch on, otherwise it might have discharged when it hit the ground and splattered one of his tyres with buckshot.

Cautiously, he made his way around the other side of his vehicle.

Even in the darkness he could make out the huge dent in the side of the van. Whatever had hit it must have been quite a size. He surveyed the surrounding area, but there was no sign of his attacker. Obviously, it had not knocked itself out from the impact after all.

Charlie swept his hand along the length of the dent. As deep as it was, he hoped that his old mate Doug down at the garage would be able to knock it out for free. He would buy him a pint next time they met down the pub.

As much as he was relieved that the damage seemed minimal, Charlie reminded himself that if the police had done their job he would not be in this situation. For that matter, if his stupid tart of a daughter had not allowed herself to be carried off by some Jack-the-bloody-lad he could be in the local himself now, enjoying a pint.

His anger at both his daughter and the police spurred him on.

Charlie left the van and decided to make his way over the bridge on foot. The sight of a man carrying a shotgun down the street might raise a fuss in some places, but he was confident that would not be the case in this weird village.

As he stepped away from the van, something leapt out of the shadows and knocked Charlie off his feet, sending him tumbling down the slope. He felt the wind being driven out of his body as he slammed against the cold hard ground.

Before he finished tumbling, he lost his grip on his shotgun once again.

When he came to a halt, Charlie lay there helpless while he tried to pull himself together.

He had no idea what had hit him, but it had to be something strong and incredibly fast.

Once he could take in a complete breath again, Charlie crawled towards the nearest tree, and propped himself up into a seated position. As he squinted into the darkness, he became aware of the shadows around him coming to life.

He felt a stinging pain in his side where he had been hit, and had to lean over to ease the pressure. Charlie could feel bile starting to rise in his throat, the hot sting of whisky mingled with his stomach acid until he could hold back no more. He leaned over and searing hot vomit spewed out of his mouth and nose. Choking and spluttering, Charlie made his way on to all fours, hoping that it might help to open up his windpipe and allow him to breath more easily.

The creatures waited, patiently, as if already aware that their prey had nothing left to fight with. Once Charlie had stopped retching, the first one grabbed him roughly by the head, twisting it to one side before sinking its fangs deep into the soft tissue.

Once it had ripped out a huge chunk of flesh, it dropped

Charlie's limp body back to the ground, as the others gathered to watch him convulse and writhe on the floor, until he was dead.

Once the show was over, the creature hoisted Charlie's lifeless body on to his shoulder and carried him into the village.

This one was destined for the pot.

11

Jacobs mulled over the selection of missing person files scattered across his desk. It struck him as somewhat odd that, when everything was on computer, his predecessor had insisted on keeping paper files. But he presumed it was probably through force of habit as the previous inspector was from a time before computers were the norm.

There were 18 in all, some going back as far as 10 years. Most concerned strangers who might or might not have been visiting his town at the time of their disappearance.

In many instances, those who had reported their loved ones as missing could not be one hundred per cent sure that they were actually in the vicinity, only that they had mentioned earlier that they might be heading that way.

Among those, there were also three files concerning local residents who appeared to have just upped and left without mentioning to anyone where they were going or why.

Jacobs read through the reports on those ones again. It appeared as if his predecessor had made various enquiries and filled in the basic paperwork, but there was no real evidence of a proper investigation.

All three reports concerned local villains, and from what he could glean from the files, no one really missed them, and that included their nearest and dearest. One of the reports from the wife of one of the missing men mentioned in her statement that she was glad to see the back of him.

Under those circumstances, Jacobs understood why so little appeared to have been done to help locate the men.

But, most interesting of all, was that in each case, the village of Thorndike had been mentioned as the last known location the three missing men had been heading to.

Jacobs picked up the most recent file. It was dated a month before he arrived in town to take up his new post. It concerned a young couple who were hiking through Cornwall and ended up staying at a youth hostel run by an elderly couple in Thorndike. According to the file, the couple went to the local inn for dinner before returning to the hostel, and in the morning the man woke up to find his girlfriend missing.

The report stated that when questioned, no one in Thorndike remembered seeing the girl, and the elderly couple, as well as the staff from the inn, insisted that the man had arrived by himself. The landlord stated that having drunk too much home brew, the man became abusive when refused service, and had to be escorted out by some of the locals.

Judging by his final report on the case, Jacobs's predecessor had suspected that the young man in question was making up the story about being with his girlfriend to save face after she had left him, presumably after an argument. Either way, the young man eventually left the village and was not heard from again.

Jacobs stared at the screen in front of him. He checked over the details he had inputted concerning Dennis Carter and Sharon Spate. He still was not completely sure that they were in fact missing, but he felt it would be remiss of him not at least to open a file on them, especially with Sergeant Ron Carter returning from holiday the following day. Whatever else the man was suspected of, he had a right to know that everything was being done to find his son.

There was still a chance the two of them would turn up by tomorrow. It was perfectly reasonable to consider the fact that they had just taken themselves away for a romantic getaway for a couple of nights. After all, Dennis might not consider telling his father as he, too, was away, and Sharon might have told Charlie but he'd been too drunk to remember.

But then there was Toby at the pub. If Sharon was taking off, she would have cleared it with him first. Unless she really did not care about her job. But from what Toby had told him, there had not been any argument or falling out, so why should she just disappear like that? It just did not add up.

Jacobs found himself wondering if there could be any substance in Charlie's ravings about the village. The Craven boys had certainly said that they saw Sharon there on the night she disappeared, and they were adamant that, although they did not actually see him, they recognised Dennis's car.

Jacobs glanced at the time on the screen. It was a little after 9.30.

He needed a drink. It had been a long day, and the village inn in Thorndike would be as good a place as any.

By the time Jacobs reached the turn-off for the village, Charlie's old van was nowhere to be seen. As he crossed the stone bridge on his way into Thorndike, Jacobs was struck by the eerie stillness of the village. Although there were several dim lights visible behind curtains and blinds as he passed the houses along the main road, he sensed that those inside were watching his progress from their darkened upstairs windows so as not to be discovered for being inquisitive.

Jacobs found a space close to the entrance of the inn and went inside.

As he entered the bar, the volume of conversation dropped noticeably.

Every eye in the place seemed to be on him. Even those who had their backs to him, seemed to turn their heads just enough it to be able to stare at him sidelong.

Jacobs nodded a greeting to a couple of the patrons as he made his way towards the bar. The responses were unencouraging, but at least the noise level from those around him began to increase once more.

The woman behind the bar gave him a big welcoming smile. "Good evenin' sir, and what might I get for you on this cold night?"

Jacobs relaxed, even though he could still feel the icy stares in his back from those behind him. "Thank you," he smiled, surveying the pumps before him. "I think I'd like a pint of your home brew, please."

The woman's grin seemed to spread even further across her chubby face. "An excellent choice sir, even if I do say so myself."

Jacobs paid for his drink and, while it was being pulled, he spotted an empty table near the log fire in the corner of the bar. He took his drink over to it and sat down in the worn leather armchair.

From his vantage point, Jacobs was able to survey the entire room. Although most of the patrons had returned to their conversations, every so often Jacobs caught one of them glancing in his direction.

He waited for the head of his ale to form properly before taking his first sip.

The ale tasted good, and Jacobs realised just how much he needed it as his sip became a gulp, and then another.

By the time he had finished half his pint, Jacobs was already feeling the effects of the strong brew. He closed his eyes for a moment and listened to the quiet crackling of the logs as the flames licked them into submission.

Jacobs almost dozed off, when suddenly he felt someone treading on his foot.

He looked up. There was a beautiful young girl standing over him. Jacobs estimated she was probably no more than 16 or 17.

Her cheeks were flushed in embarrassment. "Oh, I'm so sorry, sir. I'm the clumsiest girl you'll ever meet." She quickly removed her foot from his, almost losing her balance in the process.

Jacobs reached out a hand to assist her, grabbing her gently by the elbow.

"Thank you," she said, gratefully. "See what I mean?"

Jacobs smiled up at her. "You're welcome," he replied.

The girl began to wipe clean the table in front of him with a damp cloth. She was dressed in a skimpy cotton vest and a pair of faded jogging pants and Jacobs could not help but notice her bare breasts as she leaned over to complete her task.

He checked himself for staring at such a young girl, and picked up his pint to allow her to wipe where the glass had been.

"I don't think I've ever seen you in 'ere before," the young girl said, making a final sweep of the table with her cloth.

"No, it's my first time, I'm afraid," replied Jacobs, keeping his eyes on her face.

The girl stood up and looked down at him. "My name's Polly, by the way," she offered her free hand.

Jacobs shook. "Keith. Lovely to meet you."

"Are you from around 'ere, or just passing through?"

"I actually live in the town, so you could say I'm local." Jacobs smiled, feeling slightly embarrassed by the fact that he could feel himself stirring. He casually moved his legs closer together to help hide his growing erection, but to his horror Polly appeared to notice what he was up to, and for a moment, she switched her gaze directly at his crotch.

When she looked back at him, Jacobs was unable to hide his embarrassment.

He almost shrank into the chair when Polly leaned down and placed her hand on his thigh before whispering in his ear. "Well, let's hope we see you in 'ere again soon, eh?"

She lingered there for a moment.

Jacobs could smell her scent, a combination of pears and honeysuckle that he found intoxicating. With the strong ale inside him, it took all his self-control not to plant a kiss on her lips.

Finally, she stood up, out of reach.

Polly winked at him as if she knew what he had been thinking, and Jacobs felt his cheeks flush until they burned.

Satisfied she had completed her task. Polly turned and walked away to attend to some of the other tables in the bar.

Jacobs fought the urge to look around to watch Polly as she worked. Instead, he focused on the fire until he could feel his cheeks calming down.

He finished his drink and hoisted himself out of the comfy chair.

The sudden movement caused the room to spin, and for a second, Jacobs had to steady himself on the arm of his chair.

The ale had a mighty kick, there could be no mistake about that.

He too his empty glass over to the bar.

There was no sign of the young girl, and Jacobs presumed she had disappeared behind the swing doors at the far end of the bar.

"Another?" asked the barmaid pleasantly.

Jacobs shook his head. "No thank you, I'm driving."

The woman nodded. "Better safe than sorry, eh?" She smiled, taking his dirty glass and placing it upside down on a tray in front of her. "Take care now."

"Thank you, I will." As he turned to leave, Polly was

standing directly in front of him. He had not noticed her enter the bar again, much less sidle up to him.

They bumped into each other, and Jacobs instinctively shot out his arm and grabbed Polly once more to stop her from falling.

She let out a tiny squeak of shock and surprise before steadying herself.

"Polly!" the barmaid called out. "For the love of God girl, I've never known a creature clumsier 'an you."

"No, please," Jacobs offered, "it was my fault for not looking where I was going."

"Oh, you are sweet," replied Polly, and before he had a chance to react, she pressed herself against him and gave him a lingering kiss on the mouth.

When she pulled away, Jacobs felt the loss, keenly.

"Now don't you go bein' a stranger," she warned him, mockingly.

Before he had a chance to answer, she moved around him and went behind the bar to join her mother.

Once outside, Jacobs took in several deep lungfuls of the night air as he walked to his car. He had to admit that he was somewhat confused by the young girl's attention towards him. But he was not naïve enough to believe that she was coming on to him. More than likely she was putting on a show for the amusement of the regulars.

Making fun of the outsider.

As he approached his car, Jacobs saw something out of the corner of his eye dart into the shadows. He looked up and his senses sharpened as he took in the surrounding area. In the meagre light offered by the nearest streetlamp he was unable to work out what had caught his eye, or where it had gone.

For a moment, he felt a shiver as he imagined whatever it was, staring at him through the darkness.

He waited, holding his breath.

Nothing else seemed to stir, but he could not shake the feeling that he was being watched.

He considered venturing forward to check the area, but he reasoned without adequate light he would more than likely end up falling into a ditch, or at the very least, tripping over something in his path.

After a few minutes, Jacobs slipped in behind the wheel and drove out of the car park.

Visiting Thorndike was not an experience he was likely to forget in a hurry.

As his car left the inn, several figures emerged from the shadows to watch the red tail lights from his vehicle as they disappeared into the distance.

BACK IN THE BAR, once the door had swung shut and Jacobs was out of sight, Mavis Beanie grabbed hold of her eldest daughter's arm and yanked her, hard.

"Ow, Mama, that hurts," Polly squealed, obviously taken by surprise by her mother's sudden action.

The woman held her face directly in front of her daughter's. "What on earth did you think you wus doin' girl? Don't you know better than to mess with a man like that?"

Polly looked genuinely shocked. "Like what, mama? 'E was only a man."

"Yer stupid young fool, can't yer smell a copper after all these years?"

Polly could feel a single tear brim over the edge of her eye and trickle down her cheek.

Her bottom lip began to protrude, just as it always had done since she was a child and was caught doing something she knew she should not have.

"I'm sorry, mama, I was only funnin' with 'im."

Mavis stared deep into her daughter's eyes, clearly not moved by her attempt to gain sympathy. "Now you listen to me, my girl. The trouble with you is you learns too fast – I should never 'ave let your dada allow you to go with your cousin so young. You need to keep control of that power of yours, I told yer before 'ow easy men is to take under yer spell."

Polly nodded her understanding. "I'm sorry, Mama, it won't 'appen again, I promise."

"You just see it don't, my girl, or yer dada will birch you bloody, understand?"

Polly nodded again, more frantically this time.

Mavis released her hold and gave her daughter a peck on the forehead to show that she had been forgiven.

Polly wiped away her tears and smiled before going back to her work.

12

Karen checked the time as she climbed the stone steps that led to the entrance of the library. She was only a few minutes late for their lunch date, which, considering how long the bus took in traffic, was not so bad.

She held open the heavy swing door to allow an elderly man to exit, which he did without acknowledging her assistance.

The minute she entered the building, Karen was struck by the same feeling of wonder and awe she had often experienced as a girl on school trips and excursions to museums and art galleries. She gazed up at the high oak-panelled walls that rose to meet the ornately carved beams that criss-crossed the ceiling, and echoed with the sound of footfalls on the polished parquet floor below.

Karen always attributed her feelings to the fact that she always felt out of place in such surroundings. A direct result – she surmised – of the fact that she never reached the top stream at school as she always put her energy and enthusiasm into sports, rather than her studies.

She saw Dan standing at the far end of the library, speaking to another employee who was pushing a cart loaded with hardbacks. As soon as he saw her, Dan waved and walked over to her.

He pecked her on the cheek.

"Sorry I'm late," she whispered, "the bus took an age."

Dan looked puzzled. "Where's Charlotte?"

"Oh, I left her with a friend – I didn't want to risk her screaming the place down. She hates bus journeys at the best of times," Karen explained.

"That's a shame, you could have shown her off to the others." Dan took her by the arm. "Come on, let me introduce you, I've told them all about you."

Karen felt herself blush as Dan led her across the floor towards the man he had been speaking to when she arrived.

"Karen, this is Jerry, we started here together."

The man held out his hand towards her, while attempting to balance a stack of books in the other. "Lovely to meet you. Dan's told me all about you."

Karen smiled awkwardly. "Nice to meet you, too," she replied.

"Ssshh!" They turned in unison to see a sour-faced elderly woman sitting at the table directly behind them. Her index finger was pressed firmly against her mouth as if to emphasise the fact that they were talking too loudly.

Jerry turned back to Karen and pulled a face that almost caused her to burst into a fit of laughter. She managed to contain it by holding her hand over her mouth and feigning a cough.

Dan led Karen over to the main desk where he introduced her to the two women working behind the counter. The first was a middle-aged woman with grey streaks and a pair of glasses that she wore around her neck at the end of a lanyard. She looked up when Dan introduced them and smiled briefly before returning to her paperwork.

The second, by contrast, was a young girl with stringy blonde hair and a chubby round face that still showed the scars of teenage acne, which she tried to hide under heavy make-up. She smiled warmly at Karen and made a joke about making sure Dan bought her an expensive lunch.

After that, Dan led Karen over to a large oak door at the far end of the library. The brass plaque stated that it was the domain of the Head Librarian.

"I'd better introduce you, otherwise Miss Sharp will take umbrage," Dan explained.

"That young girl behind the counter was really friendly," Karen whispered.

"Lucy, yeah, she's really sweet, smiles all day long."

"Unlike the sourpuss beside her," Karen remarked, keeping her voice down so she couldn't be heard by anyone else.

Dan laughed. "Oh, don't mind Corrine, she's just sore that she wasn't given the head librarian's job when the old one left."

"She certainly looks stern enough for the post," Karen observed. "Don't tell me they found someone even more severe?"

"You tell me," replied Dan, knocking gently on the door before entering.

Miss Sharp was not at all the image Karen had conjured up. For a start, she appeared to be in her early twenties, and was extremely pretty, although she seemed to be trying to hide her looks behind thin-rimmed wire glasses, and with her jet-black hair tied tightly in a bun.

She wore deep-red lipstick which contrasted quite powerfully against her pallid complexion.

To Karen's surprise, the woman rose from her seat and walked around to meet the pair of them, offering Karen her hand. Karen estimated she could not have been much above five feet in height, and that included the four-inch stilettos she wore on her tiny feet.

She reminded Karen of a porcelain doll.

"So you're the famous Karen?" she said, smiling approvingly. "Dan didn't mention how pretty you were, although, he does speak of you in very glowing terms."

"Thank you," answered Karen, trying to disguise her awkwardness at being complimented in such a way by a woman who sounded much older than her tender years.

Although they had finished shaking hands, the librarian kept her slender fingers wrapped around Karen's hand as she casually allowed her gaze to wander over her frame.

She released her hold just before it became too uncomfortable, but even then, Karen felt as if Miss Sharp had done so reluctantly.

Dan, too, must have sensed Karen's uneasiness, as he cleared his throat and announced that they had be going before his lunch break was over.

To his quite obvious astonishment, Miss Sharp placed a comforting hand on his arm and said: "Take as long as you need, Dan – special occasion and all that."

With that, she winked at Karen before turning on her heels and walking back to her desk.

Once outside the building, Dan let out a deep breath. "Well, that was certainly not the prim and proper Miss Sharp I am used to. She's normally so strict on punctuality and lectures us about not overrunning our breaks. She almost had Lucy in tears the other day when the poor girl arrived five minutes late for work."

"Must be the affect I have on people," smiled Karen, "though to be perfectly honest, she did kind of give me the creeps, the way she was looking over me."

"Yes," agreed Dan, "I noticed that too. Again, not her usual behaviour." He grabbed Karen by the hand. "Come on, let me introduce you to the delights of the local carvery."

They walked down the high street, oblivious to the fact that they were being observed from behind a lace curtain in Miss Sharp's office.

Once they were out of sight, the librarian moved back to her desk and lifted the receiver from the phone on her desk. She punched in a string of numbers and waited while the phone rang in her ear.

"Hello," came a voice on the other end.

"It's me," replied Miss Sharp. "How are you fixed for this weekend? I might have a very suitable couple for you."

AFTER THEIR LUNCH, Dan walked Karen to the bus stop and waited until the bus arrived. As they kissed goodbye, they clashed noses, neither of them reading the other's sense of direction. They both laughed before trying again.

Once he arrived back at the library, Corrine on the front desk informed him that Miss Sharp's wanted to see him in her office.

Dan felt a sudden weight in the pit of his stomach. Miss Sharp did not make a habit of calling her team into her office unless they had incurred her displeasure in some way.

He knocked and entered.

"Dan, please come in and shut the door."

He did as he was told and walked over so that he was standing in front of the head librarian's desk.

"Please sit down." Miss Sharp removed her glasses and massaged her nose before continuing. "According to my records, you are overdue some annual leave," she informed him.

Dan thought for a moment before replying. "Really? I was sure I had already taken my entitlement for this year."

Miss Sharp referred to a file on her desk. "Not according to me. You still have three days that you need to take before your new entitlement commences in a couple of weeks."

Dan beamed. "Really, well what a lovely surprise. I must tell Karen. Perhaps we can go away for a short break."

Miss Sharp closed her file and placed it back on the desk in front of her. She replaced her glasses and leaned back in her chair, making a steeple with her fingers. "Well, actually, I might be able to help you out there."

Dan frowned. "Really, how do you mean?"

"Well, I was planning to visit some friends down in Cornwall this weekend, but unfortunately something else has come up. The upshot is that the cottage I was going to stay in is going begging. It belongs to a friend and she spends half the year abroad, so she invites friends like me to stay there free of charge, more to keep an eye on the place than anything else."

Dan nodded. It sounded like a terrific idea, yet something deep down made him feel uneasy about accepting. He suspected it was because Miss Sharp had never seemed like the type to make such an offer, especially not to one of her employees.

"Wouldn't your friend object to a couple of total strangers using her place for a holiday?" he asked, still not entirely sure he wanted to accept.

"No, no not at all," Miss Sharp assured him. "In fact, I only found out this afternoon that I would be unable to go, so I contacted my friend and asked her. She had no qualms whatsoever, once I gave her my personal assurance that the pair of you were totally trustworthy."

Dan smiled. "Well, thank you, Miss Sharp, I don't know what to say. This is extremely kind of you."

"Not at all." The librarian waved the matter aside with a flick of her hand. "Think nothing of it. It'd be a shame to see the place go to waste – it's absolutely beautiful down there. The village itself is only a few miles from the sea, and there's a charming old inn in the village that serves the most delectable cuisine. Mention me to the owner when you go, they'll look after you."

Before Dan had a chance to reconsider, Miss Sharp was on her feet and walking past him towards the door.

Dan stood up and followed her.

She stopped with her fingers wrapped around the handle. "Now you go and inform that lovely girlfriend of yours and we'll hear no more of it. I'll let you have the details this Friday. If you drive down on Saturday, you don't need to be back at work until Thursday." She looked him straight in the eyes. "In fact, if you decide you want to stay on until the end of the week, I'm sure that I can let you have a small advance on your next entitlement."

Without giving Dan a chance to respond, Miss Sharp opened the door and waved him out.

As Dan exited her office, he could see his colleague Jerry across the floor, slotting some returns back into place. The minute he saw Dan emerge from their boss's office, he walked over to him.

"What was all that about?" Jerry whispered. "Was she having a go at you for being late back from lunch?"

Dan shook his head. "No, in fact, she told me to take as long as we wanted."

Jerry gave him a suspicious stare. "Are you mad, Razor would never offer one of us something like that." Jerry had given the head librarian the nickname of "Razor-sharp" just after she first arrived at the library. He only used it in front of Dan and Lucy, as he did not trust Corrine not to grass him up to their boss.

Dan nodded. "I know, but not only that, she has offered us a chance to stay at a cottage in Cornwall that belongs to a friend of hers for free this weekend."

"What!" Jerry's voice rose above an acceptable level, and Corrine shot him a stern "Shhush!" from her desk.

"I know," Dan replied, "I was as shocked as you are. I'm just going to call Karen now and tell her the good news." Dan was just about to turn to leave when he had another thought. "Here, do you fancy a pint after work?"

Jerry nodded. "You bet," he replied, "I need something to get over the shock of what you've just told me."

13

KAREN WAS JUST GETTING OFF THE BUS WHEN SHE RECEIVED Dan's call. The noise from the high street made it hard for her to hear what he was saying, so she shuffled into a shop doorway and pressed a finger in her other ear to drown out the sound.

Just like him, she too was taken aback by the offer, but a break from London sounded too good to pass up, so she agreed excitedly.

Karen stopped off on the way home to pick up a bottle of wine from the supermarket.

When she reached her block, she took the lift to the floor above hers and made her way along the corridor to her friend's flat.

Janice Brown answered the door in her usual short leather skirt and tight blouse. At 55 she had managed to retain the figure that had attracted three ex-husbands, not to mention a host of male admirers.

Karen could never remember a time when she had not seen her friend dressed up to the nines. No matter what time of day, she had never seen her wear jogging pants or jeans, or even flat shoes, and she had never once caught her without full make-up. Even when she had to drop Charlotte off early in the morning so that she could make a hospital appointment, Janice opened the door in full make-up, with her hair looking as if she had just stepped out of a salon.

Janice prided herself on her appearance and, to her, the idea of comfort was kicking off her shoes before lifting her feet on to her couch at the end of the day.

Karen had met Janice in the lift lobby when she first moved to the block.

She had been trying to juggle the pram and too much shopping when Janice came to her rescue, and the two of them just hit it off.

Janice loved children, even though, or perhaps because, she could not have any herself, and she volunteered to look after Charlotte whenever her work allowed.

"Come on in me darlin', little one's fast a-kip," Janice informed Karen with a smile as she welcomed her inside.

Karen handed Janice the bottle of wine.

"Now what's this for?" asked Janice, scanning the label.

"Karen shrugged. Just a little thank you for all your help, I don't know how I would cope without you."

Janice used her free arm to hug her. "Oh, you are a silly, I told yer before, I'm more 'an 'appy to look after me little treasure whenever yer want."

Karen walked into the living room and went straight over to Charlotte's carry-cot, which was wedged into a large armchair adjacent to the radiator. As Janice had mentioned, the baby was fast asleep on her back, with her head turned slightly to one side.

Karen watched her for a moment and was tempted to bend down and kiss her daughter. But rather than risk waking her she merely smiled down at the little girl with pride, and walked over to the settee.

closer on the sofa as if she were about to unfold a secret, and she was afraid that someone might overhear. "I remember once, me and me first 'usband were watchin' one of them old porno films, you know, the ones where the women all have huge tits and no cellulite, and the men all 'ave dongs like bleedin' German sausages."

Now it was Karen's turn to stifle a laugh.

Janice was not distracted by her friend's reaction. "Anyway," she continued, "my first 'usband was a big bruiser, six-foot odd an' built like a brick shit 'ouse. So, we're both pissed watchin' this porno, an' then during the film, this woman ties this collar around this bloke's neck an' starts to lead 'im around the floor like a bloomin' dog. Suddenly, me 'usband turns to me and asks me if I'd do that to 'im."

Karen looked shocked. "And did you?" she asked incredulously.

Janice looked at her. "Of course I did, no 'arm in it. But the thing was, it really turned 'im on. Made no difference to me, but from that day on, anytime I wanted anything from 'im, all I 'ad to do was whisper in 'is ear that I would be puttin' his collar on 'im that night an' takin' 'im fer a walk. 'E gave in every time." She nudged Karen's arm, almost spilling her drink. "An' let me tell yer, girl, the screwin' 'e gave me after one of them sessions lasted fer 'ours."

Karen emptied her glass and swallowed the contents in one gulp. "So your husband enjoyed being led around the house on a dog's lead?" she asked, not wishing to allow the doubt in her voice make Janice think that she did not believe her.

"Yep." Her friend nodded. "An' let me tell yer somethin', there's millions of wives out there who'd love to 'ave their 'usbands under that much control, an' all I 'ad to do was dangle the lead, an' 'e would come running, do anything I asked."

Karen had a sudden thought. "Just a minute, is there something about Dan that you know that you're not telling me?"

Janice shook her head before draining her own glass. "Not at all, me duck, I'm jus' sayin' that with some blokes, if yer wants to keep them loyal an' faithful, yer 'ave to be prepared to play their little games, that's all."

Karen nodded her understanding. Although, the sudden image of her leading Dan around the floor on a dog's lead made her stomach churn. She sincerely hoped that after all she had had to put up with from her clients, that he at least would have a more vanilla-style attitude towards sex.

On her way back to her own flat, Karen could not help but ponder what Janice had told her. She wondered what her response would be if Dan suddenly came up with some kind of sexual fetish which she found abhorrent, or disturbing.

She had to consider the possibility. After all, if he did harbour such thoughts, chances were that he would not divulge them to her straight away. Rather he would wait until he was sure that she was open to such an idea.

But what if she never was? What would he do then? Go looking for his thrills elsewhere, as Janice had suggested?

Karen shook her head. These were questions which deep down she hoped she would never have to deal with. Janice was a lovely woman, and a good friend, but some of the weirdness she came out with made Karen wish that she could just block out the thought and pretend as if she had never heard her in the first place.

This was definitely one of those occasions.

The lift stopped and the iron doors slid open, creaking from overuse and a lack of maintenance. Karen wheeled Charlotte's pram along the landing towards her door.

The baby was still sound asleep, and had not stirred a muscle when Karen lifted her carry-cot to attach it to the frame.

As she slotted her key into the lock, Karen had a sudden urge to turn around. As she did, she thought she saw a dark shadow disappear behind the frosted glass of the stairwell at the far end of the landing.

She waited.

The corridor before her was deserted. The only movement she could detect was from the stairwell door as it swung back and forth of its rusty hinges.

So, there had been someone there.

The question was, had whoever it was simply been on their way out, or had they actually been watching her?

Karen quickly opened the door and manoeuvred the pram inside.

Once she was safe behind the closed door, she slid the safety bolt home and peered through the peep-hole to see if anyone had re-emerged from the stairwell.

The corridor was still deserted.

Karen stayed there for a couple of minutes before she let the cover of the peep-hole drop back into place.

Karen unhitched the carry-cot and took Charlotte into her bedroom. She placed the apparatus inside her daughter's wooden cot without lifting her out first, as she did not wish to risk waking the sleeping baby until it was time for her next feed.

She looked at the time on her phone. Dan would be leaving work any minute. Karen wondered if she should call him and ask him to come over, but she stopped herself before pressing the call button. She took a deep breath and waited.

The last thing she wanted was to make Dan think that he was being saddled with someone suffering from paranoia. After all, she had no proof that she was being watched and, if it had not been for those nasty phone calls, Karen doubted that she would be this concerned about a swinging door in her hallway.

Karen walked into her living room and switched on the television.

As she slumped down on the sofa, her mobile burst into life.

She lifted it up and stared at the screen. It was a withheld number.

Karen felt her blood run cold.

She switched it off without answering.

DAN LOCKED the library door behind the last borrower and walked back into the main reading area.

Miss Sharp and Corinne had both left for the day, which always made the others feel a little less tense and somewhat more playful.

Jerry Grayson was busy stacking the newspapers before placing them in their recycling bin.

"Come on then, old son," Ben called, "those beers won't drink themselves."

Jerry looked up from his task and grinned. "Music to my weary ears."

"Oh yes, and what's all this about, then?" asked Lucy, walking up behind him with a trolleyload of books for reshelving.

"It's our bi-monthly boys' night out," replied Ben, "no girls allowed."

"Well that's not very diverse," Lucy grumbled, sidling up next to Jerry, "no one ever asks me out for a drink, or anything else, for that matter."

"Serves you right for being so ugly," Jerry teased, winking at Dan.

"I beg your pardon!" Lucy exclaimed indignantly, while casually placing the heel of her boot in the middle of Jerry's instep and pressing down with all her weight.

Jerry's face contorted, sharply. "Ow, that's me bleedin' foot," he yelped.

"Oh, I am so sorry," said Lucy apologetically, "I didn't see you there."

She twisted her heel back and forth for emphasis before removing it from Jerry's foot, and casually pushing her trolley towards the nearest set of shelves.

While Lucy proceeded to put away the books on her trolley, Jerry perched himself on the edge of the nearest desk and began to massage his injured foot.

Dan could not stifle his laughter.

After a moment, Lucy sauntered back over to the men and plonked herself down next to Jerry, her bottom nudging against his. "You know," she began, "we should all go out together one evening. Dan could bring Karen and we could make up a four-some. What do you think, Dan?"

Dan shrugged. "Sounds good to me."

Jerry looked from one to the other, and then back again. "Hang on a minute," he protested. "Don't I get some say in all this?"

"No," replied Lucy sternly. "You just get to do as you're told." With that, she planted a kiss on his cheek before he had a chance to pull away, and slipped off the table to make her way back to her task.

Jerry finished rubbing his foot and stood up. "I've had enough of this," he announced, "come on, mate, take me away from this evil harridan."

Dan wished Lucy goodnight before turning to follow his friend who appeared to be limping in a far more exaggerated manner than Dan thought strictly necessary.

"Goodnight, Dan... Goodnight, misery!" Lucy called.

Jerry did not turn around, but waved her off with his hand as he hobbled out of the door.

Once outside in the street, Dan turned to his friend. "My

God, man, didn't mother nature bless you with a penis?" he asked wryly.

"What's that supposed to mean?" Jerry asked, standing on one leg and rotating his ankle as if attempting to get his circulation restarted.

Dan gasped. "Come on, you know Lucy fancies you. Why do you always give her such a hard time?"

Jerry pulled a face. "She's too young for me, for one thing," he replied.

"Shouldn't you let her be the judge of that? The age gap isn't that wide, and besides, she's lovely. You could do a lot worse."

Jerry looked over his shoulder as if to ensure that Lucy had not followed them outside. "Yeah, but, it's never a good thing to date someone you work with, especially in such a small team."

"What, are you afraid Corinne would grow jealous?" Dan asked with a smirk.

"Very funny," Jerry said, frowning as he checked his ponytail was outside his collar. "You know what I mean, if things went south it would become awkward working so close together, that's all I mean."

"So, if it wasn't for that, you'd ask her out?" Dan seemed determined to elicit a definitive answer from his colleague.

Jerry thought for a moment, then said: "I suppose I might. Who knows?"

They crossed the road and made their way towards the pub.

Jerry strode up to the bar to order their first round, while Dan found them a table by the window. He stared out at the passers-by on the street while he waited. Dan had never been a huge fan of the high street. As far as he was concerned, there were too many people crammed into too tight a space, most of whom could not even bother to look where they were going. Usually, they were more interested in what was happening on their mobile phones.

Strange though it was, since he and Karen had officially

been together, such mundane thoughts no longer seemed to bother him.

He knew that he was completely smitten with her, and the warm feeling that pervaded his body whenever he thought about her convinced him that she was the one.

Dan consider giving her a quick call just to say hello but, before he had a chance, Jerry returned with their drinks.

They clinked glasses and each took a long swig.

"Boy, I needed that," confessed Jerry. "Been one of those days I thought would never end." He placed his glass back on the table. "So, tell me about this wonderful offer Razor made you."

Dan wiped froth from his mouth. "It's the weirdest thing. Right after I came back from lunch, she called me into her office and sprang it on me. She was apparently planning to go and stay in a cottage owned by some friends in Cornwall, but something came up so she can't make it. Anyway, she offered the place to me for the weekend in her place. She was quite insistent, too. It was almost as if she was making me an offer that I couldn't refuse."

Jerry grinned. "Careful there – next thing you know you'll wake up with a decapitated first edition Hemingway in your bed."

Dan nodded. "It did feel a bit like that," he admitted. "I don't know why but I always feel nervous when she calls me into her office."

"We all do," agreed Jerry. "It's like that episode of the X-Files where the boss of this marketing office is really an alien beetle, or giant wasp or something, and whenever he calls a member of staff into his office, he infects them with a poison, and turns them into creatures just like him." Jerry shivered at the thought.

Dan laughed. "I must have missed that one," he said. "At least this time she wanted me for something nice."

Jerry took another sip of his drink. "Don't you think it's a little odd though?" he asked, seriously. "I mean, to make you an offer like that out of the blue?"

Dan thought for a moment. "I know, but I can't think what kind of ulterior motive she might have for doing it, so maybe she's not so bad after all."

Jerry shrugged. "I'll reserve my judgement on that one for now," he offered, making no attempt to keep the sarcasm from his tone.

"Yeah, maybe you're right," Dan said thoughtfully. "But I've told Karen now and she's looking forward to it, so I can't back out."

Just then, Dan noticed Lucy emerging from the library across the road.

He watched as she locked the main door, and pulled the gated screen across the entrance. "And speaking of good deeds," he said, signalling to Jerry with a nod of his head. "Why don't you ask her to join us, I'll bet you'll make her day."

Jerry pulled a face. "You're not going to let this drop, are you?" he asked, exasperated.

Dan grinned as he lifted his glass to his mouth. "It's only a drink after work, for goodness' sake –you're not asking her to move in with you."

Jerry sighed and plonked his glass down on the table. "Your round, I think," he stated, pushing his chair back as he stood up.

Dan drained his pint as he watched his friend leave the pub and cross the road to catch Lucy before she left. He smiled to himself when Lucy linked arms with Jerry and marched him back across the road towards the pub.

14

Richard Drake turned in his seat and glanced down at the girl he had tied up on the floor of his van. In the shadowy light, he could just about make out her shape. The cable ties he had used to bind her hands and feet still held her fast.

She had come around from the chloroform he had used to knock her out about half an hour ago. At first, she had struggled and lashed about wildly, but now she had calmed down, probably spent from the exertion.

Through the gag he had placed in her mouth, he could hear her muffled whimpering.

He smiled to himself and continued driving.

This latest victim was going to be his third kill. From tonight, Richard Drake would officially be known as a serial killer.

Drake could feel his erection pushing against the stretchy fabric of his jogging pants as he conjured up images of what he intended to do to his helpless victim.

As far as he was concerned, the reason so many wannabe serial killers were caught so early on in their careers was as a direct result of their lack or organisational skills. Now he, on the other hand, made a point of carefully planning each attack, and not leaving anything to chance.

His first two victims still had not been found.

In fact no one, not even those numbskull coppers on the television, even knew for sure that they were dead.

Drake made sure that, when he buried his victims, he buried them deep. Far away from each other, and in the remotest places he could find.

Of course, there was always a chance that some wild animal might dig one of them up. But even then, he had spent his life ensuring that he never came to the notice of the police. In fact, he did not have so much as a parking ticket to his name. So there was no record of him on any DNA database and he intended to keep things that way.

Even so, Drake was pragmatic about his situation. One day he would be discovered, but he intended that day to be far away in the future, by which time he would have a story to tell that would keep the news media and their readers agog for ages.

In his mind, once he reached a total of 50 victims, he would allow himself to be caught after sending the police a series of clues as to his identity. After all, there was no point being the most prolific serial killer in England without anyone ever knowing his name.

Yes sir, one day the name of Drake would be up there next to all the greats. But first, he needed a name. Bundy had "The Deliberate Stranger", Gacy "The Killer Clown", Ridgeway, "The Green River Killer". Even Kemper, who murdered only a handful of women had "The Co-ed Killer" for his nickname, so Richard Drake needed a name on a level with his peers.

Problem was, he couldn't think of one himself, so he would have to leave it to the papers, once his trail of destruction was discovered.

Still, that was OK – most of the others had been given their nicknames by the press.

He had been driving for just over two hours since trapping his victim and, as was his usual habit, he had kept mainly to B roads to avoid cameras. He could smell the sea, so he knew he must be somewhere near the coast by now, so Richard decided that he would stop at the next deserted piece of land he came across.

After another 10 minutes or so, he saw a turn-off that led across a field towards a dark clump of trees at the far end. Richard had not seen anyone in his rear-view mirror for at least the last mile, so this might be the perfect location for him to have his fun.

He followed the road through the trees until his vehicle was completely hidden from the road.

Drake turned off the engine, and climbed over the front seat in to the back of the van.

The girl, doubtless sensing that her ordeal was about to become even more horrendous, began to shuffle and fight against her restraints.

Drake laughed at the futility of her endeavour.

Straddling her flailing body, Drake slowly removed the pillow case he had placed over her head. In the dim light, the pair of them looked at each other. The girl's eyes were wide with panic as she tried desperately to plead and reason with her captor through her gag.

Drake leaned in and began to trace a line across the girl's soft white cheek with his tongue. The girl turned her head as far away from his as possible, and groaned her disgust.

Without speaking, Drake slipped off his victim and grabbed a long hunting knife with a serrated edge from underneath the passenger seat. With one movement, he severed the tie that bound her legs together.

Before she had a chance to react to her sudden freedom, Drake grabbed her by the ankles and stretched her legs wide apart. Holding one in place with his foot, he tied the other to a bracket on the side panel. Once he was satisfied it was secure, he repeated the task with her other ankle, and sat back on his haunches to admire his handiwork.

Using his knife, Drake proceeded to slice through the girl's clothing until her entire torso was laid bare before him.

Unable to wait any longer, he lifted himself up and removed his joggers and shorts, discarding them to one side. He moved forward on to the naked girl and began to rub his throbbing member against her soft white skin.

After a while, Drake placed his calloused hands on the girl's exposed breasts, and squeezed and kneaded them roughly, pinching her nipples tightly between his fingers until he heard her scream in agony behind her gag.

He moved forward and placed his erect penis between her breasts, and continued to massage and fondle them so that they enveloped his erection, encasing it in warm pink flesh.

As his excitement reached its apex, Drake could hold back no longer.

He slid down the girl's tethered body and forced himself inside her.

The girl screamed in agony as Drake shoved himself in deeper. He thrust forward and back with ever-increasing momentum until, in a final rush of excitement, he ejaculated inside her.

Drake reluctantly withdrew his member before he was finished, but it was all part of his ritual. He held his penis firmly in one hand, and rubbed it back and forth until every last drop of his ejaculate had spouted out, on to the girl's bare flesh.

He sat back for a moment to catch his breath.

After that, Drake took hold of his knife and, using the tip of the blade, began to trace a pattern through his hot semen on the girl's body. Every now and then, he would push the point, ever so slightly, into her soft flesh. Just enough to make her jerk and squeal, but not hard enough to break the skin.

He toyed with her like this for almost half an hour. He spread his white goo over her breasts and along her neckline like soft butter on toast, until eventually it dried and became impossible to work with.

All the time he was playing with her, Drake could feel his manhood starting to recharge until eventually he was ready for the next assault.

Drake pulled a length of thick rope from under one of the benches that ran along the sides of the van. Holding it between his hands, he made a point of snapping it back and forth in front of the girl, as a way of building up the anticipation of her fear.

Placing the rope across her neck, Drake pushed it tight against her skin, pressing down on her windpipe until he could feel it restricting her air flow.

The girl's eyes bulged in their sockets as she fought against her gag to breathe.

Drake smiled down at her. He traced a path across his lips with his tongue.

Keeping the pressure on the girl's trachea with the rope, Drake entered her once more.

With each thrust inside her, Drake shoved the rope harder against his victim's throat.

The girl's face began to turn blue as her eyes continued to bulge, and her expression showed she was still unable to comprehend why this was happening to her.

By the time he came again, the girl had mercifully passed out due to lack of oxygen.

Drake released his grip on the rope, and continued to jerk back and forth inside her until he was completely spent.

Exhausted, he rolled off his bound victim, and lay beside her on the floor of the van, breathing rapidly. Drake knew from past experience that he was good for another go. But first he would need a while to recharge his batteries. A little nap usually did the trick, and he could feel himself dropping off when, suddenly, there was a knock on the van door.

Drake sat up, shaking his head to clear his lethargy.

Was that really a knock, or had he already drifted off and dreamt it?

The back doors were solid metal, so there were no windows for him to look out of to check if anyone was there.

He waited for a moment.

What if it was the police?

Surely not out here, in the middle of nowhere!

How the hell did they find him?

Drake felt a heavy sickness in the pit of his stomach. It had to be them. No one else in their right mind was going to approach a deserted van in the middle of a wood, especially at this hour, and knock on the door to see if anyone was inside.

It had to be the law.

Drake's mind raced. He could picture the scene. Him being led away from the court, a burly copper on each side, his hands cuffed behind his back. His mother in the gallery, crying her eyes out. His stupid half-wit of a brother and that snotty bitch of a sister-in-law, peering down their noses at him as he was led away to serve a life sentence.

Drake shivered. He was not ready for prison. He had not done enough yet to earn the respect of his fellow inmates.

There was another knock on the van door. This time it was harder and more persistent.

Drake swallowed hard. There was no escape. Even if he tried to drive away the coppers would give chase and catch him before he even made it back to the main road. His clapped-out old van would be no match for their vehicle.

The girl on the floor beside him stirred and moaned.

Instinctively, Drake raised the knife, thinking he would have to keep her quiet.

As he was about to bring the knife down in an arc, he stopped himself and thought for a moment. Right now, all they had on him was kidnap and rape. They had no idea about his previous victims. He could make up some yarn about the girl being into it. She asked him to help her live out her fantasy.

It might all sound implausible and, of course, she would deny it, but a decent brief could at least plant the seed of doubt in the mind of a half-baked jury. Of course, the girl would claim she was held against her will and raped, but again his lawyer could argue that she was ashamed of being discovered by the police during the escapade, and having to face up to her parents and boyfriend, if she had one.

It might just work.

Feeling a little calmer now, Drake leaned forward and released the catch on the back door, before pushing it open.

"Hiya," said Jodie, smiling cheerfully. "I don't suppose you could give me a lift; I've been walking for ages and I'm shattered?"

The shock of seeing the young girl standing there instead of the police, stunned Drake into momentary silence. She was dressed in a tee-shirt and a pair of dark satin shorts, which were grossly inadequate for the cold night air.

Jodie crossed her arms and began rubbing herself as she hopped from one foot to the other. "Please mister," she said, pathetically, "I'm already late home, and my dada is going to give me hell."

Drake wiped the back of his hand across his mouth, and licked his lips. The girl could obviously see that he was naked, but his appearance did not seem to bother her in the least.

He looked past the shivering girl and gazed furtively into the night behind her. There did not appear to be anyone else about, so perhaps she was in earnest after all.

Not taking the time to consider why such a young girl would be out on her own in a place like this, Drake moved to one side to allow Jodie to enter.

He was poised for the moment when she noticed his bound and gagged victim on the floor. His plan was to grab Jodie from behind before she began screaming.

But to his amazement, the second Jodie saw the girl she squealed with delight, clapping her hands together.

"Oh wow!" she said initially, as Drake closed the van door behind them. When he turned back, Jodie was kneeling beside the helpless girl, and appeared to be stroking her face.

Drake frowned. This was not the reaction he had been expecting.

When Jodie turned back to face him, even in the dim light, Drake could see that her cherubic cheeks was flushed with excitement and wonder.

But even so, he was not expecting to hear what came out of Jodie's mouth next.

"Oh, please say that I can join in?" she pleaded, "I won't tell anyone, promise."

Drake was taken aback. He could not believe what he was hearing.

"Join in what?" he replied, anxiously.

Jodie sighed loudly. "You know what I mean," she said, not attempting to hide the indignation in her voice. "You've both been fucking in here – I can smell it. Is she your girlfriend?"

Drake cleared his throat. "Well, sort of," he spluttered nervously, still unable to comprehend what was happening. Alarm bells were ringing in his head – there was something not quite right about this girl. For one thing, she only looked about 13, if that. But the way she was talking it was obvious to Drake that she was not like any 13-year-old he had ever met.

Without another word, Jodie pulled off her tee-shirt, revealing her naked breasts.

Drake could not help himself. His eyes fixed on her pert, firm nipples as Jodie massaged them with her hands in front of him.

Drake could feel his erection returning.

Noticing the effect she was having on him, Jodie giggled.

She reached forward and took hold of his penis and started to stroke it gently. Drake closed his eyes and moaned. This was something he was not used to, a willing companion.

He could feel himself growing at her touch.

"That's better," Jodie chirped. "Come on then, you can take me from behind with that, if you like."

She let go of him and slipped her shorts down over her trainers.

Straddling Drake's victim, Jodie began to massage the woman's naked body, bending down to take her nipples in her mouth as she sucked and nibbled on them like a voracious baby hungry for its mother's milk.

Drake could no longer control his ardour. Yes, Jodie was younger than his other victims, but he was beyond the point of no return, and willing or not, he would have to bury two victims tonight, so he was determined to make it worth his while.

Drake shuffled up behind Jodie and felt between her legs for her opening.

To his surprise and delight, it was moist and, when he slipped his fingers inside her, Jodie leaned back her head and sighed loudly.

Unable to resist any longer, Drake removed his hand and used it to guide himself inside the girl. Jodie gasped at the sensation, and lowered her head once more to continue licking the dried semen from the naked girl's body.

Drake gripped Jodie by the hips and thrust himself deeper inside her. He relished the feeling of being with someone who did not struggle or fight back.

He jerked himself faster and faster, until he could feel his seed starting to rise once more.

It felt to him as if the whole van was moving along with his thrusts, such was the intensity of his momentum.

Then he realised that the van really was moving.

He stopped himself in mid-thrust and gasped as the entire van continued to shake from side to side as if it was being buffeted by a freak hurricane.

Drake removed himself and sat back on his haunches.

He realised that in his excitement he had dropped his knife, so he frantically tried to locate it in the semi-darkness.

Jodie too stopped what she was doing, and turned back to face him.

"What's the matter?" she enquired nonchalantly, as if oblivious to the violent shuddering of the vehicle. "Why have you stopped? I was enjoying that."

Unable to trace his weapon, Drake looked up at the girl in amazement.

"Can't you feel the fuckin' van shaking?" he spat out. "It feels like the whole fuckin' thing is about to go over!"

"Oh that," Jodie replied, shrugging, "it's just my cousins playing about. Don't let them put you off."

"Who?" Drake screamed, scrabbling in the darkness, trying to locate his clothes. His nakedness suddenly made him feel extremely vulnerable.

Before Drake had a chance to retrieve his underwear, both the van's back doors were simultaneously ripped off their hinges.

Drake turned, just in time to see two massive fur-covered arms reach in and drag him outside by his legs.

He tumbled from the vehicle and hit the ground hard, rolling over several times before he knew what had hit him. The landing knocked the wind out of him, and as he tried desperately to take in a breath, Drake was grabbed by several more pairs of huge, rough hands, before being viciously torn apart, limb from limb.

Jodie watched the onslaught from the van with childlike wonder.

Once the excitement was over and the creatures were tucking into their victory feast, the largest of them lurched forward and stood in front of the open van.

Jodie hopped down, and stepped back into her shorts, holding her tee-shirt under her arm as she did so. Once she was fully dressed, she turned and pointed back to the naked woman lying in the van.

Gobal crawled inside the vehicle, making it shake from side to side as his enormous bulk squeezed itself inside. The creature ripped the ropes that bound the helpless woman from the brackets to which Drake had tied them, and carried the woman out into the night in its huge arms.

Once back outside, Gobal crouched down so that Jodie could hop on its shoulders.

The creature stood back up and steadied itself, before turning to grunt an order at its minions.

Then it gently carried the two women away into the night.

15

KEITH JACOBS LOOKED UP FROM HIS PAPERWORK AS THE commotion outside his office grew in volume. Whatever was taking place, he felt confident that the desk sergeant could handle it. They were a breed all their own, and each of them took great pride in their ability to deal with whatever was thrown at them.

Jacobs tried to ignore the din and returned to his work.

Just then there was a frantic knocking on his door, which made the frosted glass rattle in its frame.

Before Jacobs had a chance to react, the door shot open and Sergeant Sid Carter strode into his office, and right up to his desk.

"What's all this I'm hearing about my Dennis?" he demanded, not giving Jacobs a chance to respond. "I've been trying to reach him all day, now Bill outside tells me he's been missing for a couple of days. Why wasn't I contacted? What action has been taken to find him?"

Jacobs rose from his chair and walked around his desk.

He placed a comforting arm on the sergeant's shoulder, and tried to reassure him.

"Sit down a minute, Sid," he suggested calmly. "Let me shut the door for a bit of privacy and I'll explain everything."

Sid Carter stayed standing for a few seconds, his breathing coming in short bursts, his face flushed with rage. He waited until Jacobs had closed the door before finally taking the offered seat.

Jacobs walked back around and sat opposite him.

Sid Carter looked at least 10 years older than his real age. A combination of smoking 40 Marlboros a day, plus his love for the bottle, had definitely left its mark on his overall wellbeing. Although Sid was the same ten-and-a-half stone he had been for most of his adult life, he walked with a pronounced stoop, and even climbing the 10 stairs from the ground to the first floor left him gasping for breath.

His weathered skin, which stretched tightly across his cheeks, had the same dark pallor as that of the drunks he would often have to lock up for the night for their own safety. It was a sure sign that, like them, his liver was starting to lose the battle against his daily alcohol consumption.

These days, his hands shook so violently that even typing in the simplest details on the main computer could take him up to three attempts. He always cursed the keyboard for being too small, but everyone at the station knew the truth, and they all suspected that he did too.

Carter instinctively reached into his coat pocket and pulled out a half-open packet of Marlboros. He had already slipped one between his lips when it dawned on him that he could not smoke inside, so he took it out and replaced it in the pack.

With nothing constructive to so with his hands, Carter sat there fidgeting while his superior explained the situation.

"Now Sid, I don't want you to worry, we don't have any concrete evidence that Dennis is actually missing."

"Then what was Bill talking about?" Carter jumped in, not giving Jacobs a chance to finish.

Jacobs held up his hands to calm the man down. “If you'll let me finish, I'll tell you everything we know, all right?”

Carter slumped back in his chair with an audible, “Humph!” and folded his arms over his chest.

Jacobs continued: “Charlie Spate came in the other day, drunk as usual, carrying on that his daughter hadn't come home from work the previous night. Now, from what we can ascertain, she was last seen with your Dennis on the woodland road, but the witnesses stated there was nothing untoward taking place, and everything seemed fine.”

“So where is he now? Who said they saw him with that Sharon? He wouldn't look twice at that little tart – he's told me so before.”

Jacobs took a deep breath. Well, according to the Craven brothers...”

Before he had a chance to finish, Carter jumped out of his chair, knocking it over in his haste. “Those two little bastards, you can't believe anything they say. They were probably up to no good and my Dennis caught them. They've probably done something to him, and that Spate girl, you need to drag them in here for questioning!”

As he spoke, Carter's eyes began to bulge in their sockets to the extent that Jacobs almost believed they were about to pop out on stalks.

Jacobs sat back in his seat and rubbed the bridge of his nose between his thumb and forefinger. He could tell this conversation was going nowhere, and that Sid Carter was in no mood to listen to sense.

Carter's breath started coming in rasping heaves, as if something was stuck in his windpipe, forcing the air through a tighter gap than it was accustomed to.

For a moment, Jacobs was genuinely concerned the man was going to have a heart attack right in front of him.

He stood up and walked over to his colleague.

Looking him straight in the eye, he said. "Listen Sid, I understand you are upset, you've just come back off holiday and your boy isn't answering his phone, I get that. But just think for a moment, has he ever gone off without telling you before?"

The question took Carter aback. He stared into space for a couple of seconds, before answering. "Well… Yes, he has, but he always came back."

"Right," replied Jacobs, "and for how long has he gone absent before, can you remember?"

"Eh, a couple of days, maybe." Carter thought hard. "There was that one time he disappeared for almost a week, little shit went to some music festival or something, too bloody stoned to call his old man."

Realising what he was saying, Carter calmed down. He bent down and picked up his chair and placed it back in front of the desk.

"Sit down," said Jacobs, soothingly, "and let's see if we can figure something out. How's that?"

Carter lowered himself back into his chair, and sat there with his shoulders slumped forward, while Jacobs walked back to his seat.

"Now then," continued Jacobs, "the Craven brothers were adamant that they saw Sharon Spate on the woodland road, and that she was standing next to your lad's car. When they asked if everything was all right, she assured them that it was, and that Dennis had gone back into the woods to have a pee."

Carter's eyes shot up. "So they never actually saw my boy?"

Jacobs shook his head. "No, but as I said, they recognised his car and Sharon told them he was there with her." He could tell from his expression that Carter was not convinced by his explanation, so he added. "What plausible reason would the boys have to lie? I spoke to them myself."

Carter shook his head. "Those Craven lads have been up to

no good for as long as I can remember. My Dennis was always telling me about their plans and big ideas." He leaned forward in his chair and pointed with his index finger. "What if they've kidnapped my Dennis and Sharon, because they threatened to expose them for whatever it was they were doing?"

"Oh, come on, Sid. I appreciate you're a little on edge, but kidnapping seems a little far-fetched for the Craven brothers, don't you think?"

Carter opened his mouth to speak, then thought better of it. He sat there for a moment, breathing through his nose, his nostrils flaring with the effort.

Jacobs rested his arms on his desk and linked his fingers together. "If it helps," he began, "I took a drive up to Thorndike last night to see if there was any sign of either Dennis or Sharon, or his car, but there was nothing untoward going on."

Sid Carter looked up. "Thorndike! You didn't say he'd gone up there. Place is full of nutters – you must know that."

"Oh, come now, Sid, just because the place is secluded and they keep to themselves doesn't make them 'nutters', as you charmingly put it."

Carter bounced on his chair as if he was not sure whether to stand or stay seated.

His hands began to shake more frantically. "Why didn't you tell me he'd been seen up there, he knows better than to be going up there, especially at night!"

"Look, Sid." Jacobs scratched his head. It was obvious to him now that nothing he said to his colleague was going to keep him happy, short of launching a full-scale attack on the village to find his son. "I can understand your frustration, but you yourself just admitted that Dennis is not averse to going off on his own from time to time."

Sid Carter kept his mouth shut. Jacobs could tell that he did not relish being reminded of his earlier confession, but at least it seemed to do the trick.

"Why don't you just go home and try calling him again, leave him a message telling him to call you back asap." Jacobs purposely kept his tone calm in an effort to placate Carter. The last thing he wanted was the man rushing out and doing something stupid.

"I can't, I'm back on duty tonight," Carter replied, dejectedly.

"No problem," Jacobs said, reassuringly, "I'll get one of the other lads to cover for you. You take another day off, or a couple if you think you need it. Dennis will be back home before you know it."

Carter considered the suggestion. He had had a long drive back that afternoon and his throat was decidedly dry from the road. A skinful in the Dog might be the very thing to take his mind off Dennis. Stupid little bugger was probably shacked up somewhere with Charlie's daughter, anyway.

"All right," he sighed. "If you reckon it's for the best."

"That's the spirit." Jacobs smiled. "Now you go and phone that son of yours and give him an earful. He'll be back with his tail between his legs in no time."

Carter stood up to leave.

Opening the door, he turned back to Jacobs. "But you will keep looking for him, won't you?"

"Of course," Jacobs assured him. "I'll make sure the night patrols are instructed to call in if they see him."

Reluctantly, Sid Carter shuffled out of the door.

"WELL, THAT WAS..."

"Gruesome? Horrendous? Painful? Shall I go on?" Karen offered as she settled Charlotte into her car seat.

Dan smiled, "Well, I was going to say awkward but then, I was trying to be polite."

"You needn't bother on my account," Karen assured him, climbing into the passenger seat beside him. "I've known my mother a long time, so I already knew this was going to be a mistake."

Dan shuffled uncomfortably in his seat. "I just thought it was the right thing to do, meeting your mother before we go away for the weekend. I actually thought she might appreciate the gesture."

"The only thing my mother appreciated was the chance to pass some snide comments while she looked down her nose at you."

Dan started the engine and checked his rear mirror before pulling out.

After a moment, he said. "Well, it's done now. Hopefully, the next time won't be so uncomfortable."

"I wouldn't put money on it, knowing my mother." Karen turned back to check on Charlotte. Her baby seat was reversed to protect her neck in case Dan had to brake suddenly, so Karen could not see her face. But she could hear the baby gurgling happily while she watched the multi-coloured toys on the elastic string attached to the chair's frame.

Dan had insisted that he meet Karen's mother before their trip.

Karen understood his reasons, but she also knew her mother extremely well, and although she had tried to warn him of what he was in for, Dan insisted that they go ahead.

All evening, Karen's mum ignored him by pretending to play with her grandchild, and on those occasions when she did deign to ask him a question, she invariably sniffed the air in self-righteous disgust when she heard his answer.

Karen did her best to keep the conversation going but, even for her, the strain became too great, and eventually she made their excuses and they left.

She felt sorry for Dan having to sit through such an ordeal, but she had warned him what to expect, so he only had himself to blame for his persistence.

The worst part of it all was that Karen's mother did have some valid observations scattered among her back-handed sneering. When she said that the two of them had known each other for only five minutes, and it was far too soon to contemplate moving in together, she was not altogether wrong.

Deep down, Karen still had doubts about whether she was doing the right thing. She had to admit to herself – if no one else – that were it not for her financial situation, she would have insisted on waiting a while before making her decision. She did not doubt Dan's sincerity, and she felt as if she should be more grateful that he was willing to take her and her child on, especially as it meant her being able to get off the game.

But she could not help the nagging doubts that plagued her mind.

Still, only time would tell.

They made good time back to Karen's block. Dan carried the sleeping Charlotte up to the flat in her car seat, and Karen managed to settle her into her cot without waking her.

Dan declined Karen's offer of coffee as he was opening the library the following morning.

When they kissed goodnight at the front door, Karen allowed it to last as long as Dan wanted. His hands slipped down her back and clasped her buttocks firmly, squeezing and kneading them through the fabric of her trousers.

When he held her close, Karen could feel the first stirrings of an erection pressing against her pubic area. She really was not interested in anything but a good night's sleep after the ordeal with her mother. But she felt she should at least make the offer.

"Are you sure you don't want to stay?" she asked half-heartedly.

Dan pulled back and shook his head. "Don't tempt me, please, I've got an early start."

Karen smiled and tried to look disappointed.

They kissed again, this time just on the lips, and Dan left.

Karen watched him until he disappeared into the stairwell at the far end of the corridor. She waited another moment before she closed the door.

She hated the fact that she was relieved that he had decided to go home.

Karen really wanted to want him more, but it just was not happening.

On the couple of occasions that they had made love, the act was what Karen would best describe as "clunky". It was as if their bodies were not yet in tune. Dan was not what she would call a skilled master at the art of seduction, and his foreplay, such as it was, left a little to be desired. But she hoped that as time went on, they would become more accustomed to each other's needs and wants.

He had not managed to enter her on his own, and seemed a little frustrated that she had to guide him with her hand, but that was a skill which she believed would come in time.

Karen had not orgasmed on either occasion, but she pretended she had, not wanting to make Dan feel as if he had not satisfied her. She had read articles from women who claimed that they had done the same thing for their entire married lives, and that they only truly experienced fulfilment when they relieved themselves. Or, in some cases, when they experimented with other women.

Karen's mobile suddenly sprang into life.

She gazed at the screen. It was a withheld number.

Tentatively, she held the object to her ear and answered the call.

Immediately, she heard the familiar sound of heavy breathing on the other end.

Instinctively, Karen turned and shot the chain across her door.

Before the caller had a chance to start speaking, Karen cancelled the call.

She waited for a moment, staring at her screen.

After a few seconds, the phone burst back into life, the same "withheld" message on the screen.

Karen took a deep breath and disconnected the call without answering it.

She turned her phone off.

An idea struck her which sent an immediate shiver down her spine.

How was it that this obscene caller seemed to know exactly when she was alone?

Was he watching her?

Switching off her hall light, Karen made her way into the living room. She stood at the window and stared out at the numerous windows of the other tower blocks that stretched before her, as far as the eye could see.

Was he behind one of those blank glass rectangles? Watching her with his binoculars or telescope from the safety of his flat?

The thought made her feel physically sick.

Karen drew every curtain shut. As tired as she was, she now needed the company of light and other human voices.

She slumped down on her sofa and switched on the television.

Sleep would have to wait.

16

Colin Craven swung the old delivery van from side to side as he tried to negotiate the rough track that led up to Thorndike village. He always preferred taking the woodland path, despite the rocky, pot-holed, branch-strewn condition of the road. There was far less chance of their being seen on this particular stretch, and that, in itself, had its advantage.

Beside him in the passenger seat, his brother Don fiddled with the knob on the van's antiquated radio. Finally, he reached the station he had been looking for, and raucous R&B blared from both speakers.

"Whoo, now that's what I'm talkin' about," he cried, taking another drag on the spliff held between his lips, before passing it to his brother.

Colin placed the can of lager he was drinking between his knees, and took the spliff. He sucked in a deep lungful of skank, and held it for as long as he could before releasing the smoke out in a winding tunnel.

Although Colin had the headlights on full beam, he did not notice the huge pothole in front of them, until the van's front wheel hit it with full force, causing the van to buck. The plastic crates in the back lurched to one side as the van righted itself, just before Colin managed to hit another, equally large crater, which caused the crates to topple over on to their sides, spilling their contents across the van's dirty floor.

Realising what had happened, Colin slammed on the brakes and skidded the van to one side of the road.

"What's up?" asked Don, obviously shocked by his elder brother's sudden action.

Colin turned to face his sibling. "Are you fuckin' kiddin' me?"

Don merely shrugged and took another swig from his can.

"The fuckin' meat is all over the floor, you idiot!" Colin yelled, raising his hand as if to strike his brother.

Don instinctively cowered back in his seat, until Colin lowered his hand.

Realising what his brother had said, Don turned in his seat and glanced into the back of the van. Sure enough, he could see the crates of meat they had stolen from their father's shop lying on their sides, with some turned completely upside down.

From a combination of the beer he had been drinking and the joint his brother had rolled for them; Don could not help but see the funny side of their predicament.

He lifted his head and laughed out uncontrollably, into the night.

After a moment, Colin grabbed his brother by his shirt collar and pulled him about, roughly. "Will you get your fuckin' 'ead back on straight?" he shouted., "We 'ave to get this shit sorted before we get to the inn. Old Thaddeus ain't gonna pay us the full amount if 'e sees the stuff 'as been covered in dirt from the floor, is 'e?"

This scolding seemed to have the desired effect, and Don straightened himself up in his seat and placed his half-full can in one of the plastic holders between the seats.

"Sorry, bruv," he muttered apologetically.

The brothers climbed out of the van and went around the back. When Colin opened one of the doors, unbeknown to him, one of the crates had been wedged up against it, and it fell out in front of them, spilling the meat on to the woodland floor.

"Shit!" Colin shouted. "'Elp me get this lot up, for Christ's sake."

The two of them worked together, righting the fallen crates and replacing the spilled meat back inside. Those pieces which appeared particularly muddy, they wiped with their shirttails until the worst of the dirt was gone. Working in the butchers all day, they already smelt of raw meat, so the latest addition could hardly make their situation any worse.

Once they had completed their task, Colin surveyed the crates once more, to ensure they were neatly stacked and unlikely to topple again.

Suddenly, he frowned. Pointing inside, he asked, "Why are there two red crates in here?"

Don, who had already been making his way back to his side of the van, came back and followed his brother's finger.

He scratched his head before answering. "Don't know, does it matter?"

He could see immediately by the scowl on his brother's face that it did matter, although for now he was at a loss to know why.

"What?" he asked, feeling uneasy that his elder brother was not explaining himself.

"I told you to only load the black crates, because they were the ones with the cheap cuts and bones." Colin slammed his hand against the side of the van in frustration. "The red crates had the good stuff for the shop. Dad's goin' to notice it's missin' when he opens up in the morning, and he's going to realise what we've been up to."

Don thought for a moment.

It was true, now that he mentioned it, he did remember his

brother's instructions, but he must have just been carried away and loaded the red ones without realising it.

Even though he would never admit it, Don Craven looked up to his brother and would do anything he could to try to impress him.

Dejectedly, he looked at the ground and kicked a stone away into the darkness.

Colin took several deep breaths before slamming the van doors shut.

He often despaired at his younger brother's antics, but part of him blamed himself for not checking before they set off.

"Come on," said Colin, "it's too late to do anythin' about it now."

"Can't we just take the red ones back to the shop once we're finished at the inn?" Don asked, hopefully.

"Not now they're covered in mud and shit," replied Colin. "It's one thing to sell 'em cheap to old Thad, but quite another to try and get them past Dad."

They climbed back into the van and drove the rest of the way to the inn in silence.

Once they arrived, Colin parked up at the back of the building, reversing the van so that the back doors were in front of the loading area.

Colin knocked on the door while Don started to unload the crates.

Thad Beanie opened the door after a moment, and smiled at the brothers.

"Come on in lads," he beamed, "bring those crates through to the back room, as usual.

While they unloaded the meat from the van, Thad disappeared into the back of the loading dock, and re-emerged a few minutes later with a tray with two medium-sized pies on them. He placed them down in front of the boys, and took a brown envelope from his back pocket and handed it to Colin.

Colin opened the envelope and counted the cash, while Don eagerly set about eating his pie.

"Enjoy," said Thad, "you've earned it."

Colin finished counting the money, then looked up at Thad. "It's not enough," he said awkwardly.

Colin Craven was a big lad for his age, and years of humping around sides of beef and crates of meat had put a fair bit of muscle on his bones. But even so, Thad towered over him and was at least twice as broad into the bargain, so Colin was in no doubt that the man could probably kill him with one almighty blow.

Don stopped eating and stared at his brother. He too knew just how easy it would be for Thad to take care of the pair of them. Even two against one, they would not stand a chance against this meat-mountain of a man.

Thad's brows furrowed.

It was obvious that Colin's announcement had taken him by surprise, and he could not hide the fact.

He took a couple of deep breaths while he kept his gaze focused on Colin.

Colin felt himself shrink inside, and did all he could not to let it show on the outside, but he was already regretting his statement.

Eventually, Thad spoke up. "So why the sudden change in our arrangement?" he asked, keeping his voice steady.

Colin gulped, inadvertently. "Sorry," he muttered, "it's just that our dad's getting suspicious and we brought along a couple of crates of the really good stuff to fill out the order. We might have to pay him for those out of our wages if he finds out."

Thad considered Colin's explanation, while he rubbed his unshaven chin.

After a moment, he leaned forward. Colin felt sure that he was going to grab him and throw him out on his ear. But instead, Thad clapped him on the shoulder and smiled.

"Get that pie down yer, boy," he said with a grin. "I'll be back in a minute with the rest of yer money."

Colin and Don both heaved a sigh of relief after the big man had left.

"Fuck me," Don whispered, "I thought we was both for it, then. What made you suddenly ask for more dosh?"

Colin shrugged. "Like I said, we might 'ave to pay dad back." He took a large bite of his pie. The gravy streamed down his chin, but he ignored it while savouring the flavour. Once he had swallowed, he continued. "An if we don't, we're quids in."

Don laughed and took another bite.

From behind them, they heard a door opening.

Don quickly gulped down his latest mouthful, and wiped his sleeve across his mouth.

Colin, noticing his brother's reaction, spun around, fearing Thad had returned with a large axe or knife in his hand.

Instead, he was relieved to see Polly walking towards them with a tray, upon which there were two tankards.

She sashayed over to where the brothers stood frozen to the spot, and placed the tray down in front of them.

"There you go, boys – thought you might need a little something to wash down your pies."

Neither brother could respond right away.

Both could feel their tongues growing too big for their mouths as they ogled the young girl.

Polly, as usual, was dressed in her serving uniform, which served only to emphasise her gorgeous figure underneath.

She watched with great amusement as the two brothers stood there like statues.

"Well, eat up," she said encouragingly. "I like to see a man enjoy his food."

As if on command, both brothers immediately took a huge bite from their pies.

Neither brother noticed Thad reappearing, until he was

directly behind his elder daughter. “What you doin’ out here?” he asked Polly, smacking her playfully on the rump.

Polly tuned and smiled up at him. “I thought the lads could do with a drink after their long drive,” she replied.

“She’ll make someone a handsome wife someday, eh, lads?” Thad winked at the brothers.

Polly blushed. “Dada!” she rebuked him coyly.

“Now go on back inside,” Thad told her. “Your sister can’t cope on her own for too long.”

Polly turned back and smiled at the lads. “Hope to see you again soon,” she said, before turning and leaving the room.

Once she had disappeared through the door, Thad took out two 20-pound notes and handed them to Colin.

“I’ve checked that extra meat you brought,” he informed them. “Top quality stuff. Will that cover it?”

Colin folded the bills and put them in his top shirt pocket. “That’ll do nicely,” he agreed, still focusing on the door through which Polly had left.

Matilda Fox opened her eyes and blinked at the gloom. As her vision began to focus, she tried to sit up, but her entire body ached, and fought her all the way.

When she finally managed to move to an upright position, she realised that she must be in some sort of cave. The floor beneath her was strewn with leaves, thick grass and dead flowers and, in the distance, she could see the faint glow of a fire, sending flickering shadows across the walls.

Her mind could not envisage how she came to be here.

The last thing she remembered was leaving the beach and heading for the car park to grab a coat from her car. She and some friends had met up with some surfers they had started talking to the previous evening in a club, and they had invited them down to the beach to watch them surf and have a party on the sand.

She had a vague recollection of two of her friends stripping off and diving into the sea, and the rest of them cheering them on while they huddled around the camp fire and barbecued sausages on the portable kits one of them had brought for the occasion.

But after that, the rest was a complete blank.

Matilda looked around her at the solid rock walls. There was no discernible entrance to be seen, and she wondered if perhaps she had passed out and been carried inside by one of the surfers.

Either way, she seemed fine in herself, except for the fact that her body ached as if she had been on a 10-mile hike.

She threw back the blanket that covered her body.

It was then that she realised she was naked.

Instinctively, Matilda wrapped her arms across her breasts as she looked around for her clothes. But they were nowhere to be seen.

She forced herself to stand, wrapping the old blanket around her for protection.

To her left, the cave was mostly black, the shadow from the firelight ebbing out before it reached that side. She considered venturing into the darkness to explore her surroundings, and possibly locate a way out. It was obvious from the fact that there was a fire just around the corner to her right, that someone must have made it, and right now she could not be sure whether that person was friend or foe.

Just then, she heard somebody moving about just beyond the next turning where the fire was. Matilda froze – whoever it was they must know she was there. The question was, did she want them to know that she was conscious?

She listened intently. It sounded as if there were several sets of feet scurrying around just out of sight. What seemed particularly odd to her was that, whoever was there, they were not speaking to each other.

Carefully, Matilda edged her way towards the bend in the cave, praying that her approach would remain undetected, at least until she could ascertain who her captors were.

Try as she might, she could not fathom a single innocent reason why someone would keep her stripped naked inside a cave. If it turned out to be some sort of joke involving those surfers, they would soon discover the sharp edge of her temper.

The rough stone floor beneath her bare feet was difficult to walk on, rather like pebbles on the beach, but sharper and more jagged. Matilda placed each foot gently in front of her to test the ground before allowing her weight to press down.

A sudden scream as a result of standing on a pointy rock would give her away in an instant.

As she reached the bend, Matilda stayed back for a moment and continued to listen.

From around the corner she could still hear the sound of shuffling, as well as the fire crackling, but still no one spoke.

Then she heard a cry.

It sounded like a baby, only there was something guttural, and more sinister about the noise that came out of its mouth.

Matilda listened for a moment, still too afraid to peek around the corner.

Someone was moving, presumably to comfort the crying baby. If indeed it was a baby. There was definitely something not quite right about the infant's weeping.

Matilda steeled herself. She could not stay where she was, and she did not have the courage to venture further into the cave in the darkness. Whatever was on the other side of the bend, she would have to venture out and see for herself.

Just as she was about to step forward, Matilda noticed that the baby had stopped crying.

She could hear other sounds now, slurping, sucking noises

had replaced the weeping. It sounded to her like a baby suckling from its mother's breast.

Perhaps that was all it was. One of the surfers had a wife or girlfriend, and she was using the cave for some privacy so she could feed her baby.

As to why they had brought Matilda inside was anyone's guess. Perhaps she had slipped on the rocks and been knocked unconscious when she went to fetch her coat from the car? It had to be some perfectly innocent explanation.

Matilda lifted back her shoulders and stepped forward, taking the bend in the cave to present herself to the party on the other side.

The scene that faced her was not one her brain could comprehend, before the shock of it caused her to pass out.

17

Don Craven's head smashed against the side window as his brother skidded into the turning.

"Ow! Watch where you're goin' – that fuckin' hurt." Don sat upright and rubbed the side of his head where it had just made contact with the glass.

"D'yer wanna drive?" his brother asked, sneeringly.

"Well I can't do a worse job than you. Slow down, fer fuck's sake."

"Stop whining – we'll be 'ome soon," Colin reminded him. "Then you can go to bed and wank yerself off thinkin' about that Polly down at the pub."

Don blushed red, in spite of himself. It was true that Polly was stunning, and as they were a similar age, he had fantasised about taking her out since the moment he first laid eyes on her.

But the truth was that he did not have the courage to ask her.

For one thing, there was that huge brute of a father of hers. Don very much doubted that he was Thad's idea of a suitable boyfriend for his elder daughter.

Secondly, although Polly often flirted with him whenever

the boys were making a delivery, the fact was she did the same thing with his brother, and he had seen her do likewise with some of the men in the pub.

Perhaps she was no more than a prick-teaser?

Even if that were the case, Don would not refuse the chance to find out for himself.

"OK," he replied. "I'll fantasise about Polly, while you jack off thinking about 'er little sister."

"Shut up, yer pervert, she's only about 12 or 13." Colin took his hand off the steering wheel and slapped his younger brother on the side of the head.

"Aren't you always tellin' me if they're old enough to bleed, they're old enough to butcher?" said Don, rubbing where the slap had landed.

Colin looked over at his brother, then burst out laughing.

Don joined in and playfully slapped his brother back.

They were now entering the main road back in to town. There were still no street lights for a mile or so, but the familiarity of the district caused both brothers to relax, now that they were far enough away from Thorndike.

Although they made several excursions into the village to sell off cheap cuts of meat to Thad, neither brother looked forward to the trips, even if there was a pint of home-brew and a tasty pie in it for them.

The fact was that both of them had always felt an uncanny sense of foreboding whenever they entered the village.

When they were youngsters, their father had always told them to keep away from the place. But once they were old enough to explore, they disobeyed their father's instructions and dared each other to go.

Even though it was early afternoon on a bright sunny day for their first venture, once they crossed the boundary into Thorndike, it was almost as if the village was trapped in a different season.

The very air seemed dense and much colder than it had been in town that day.

The clouds hung low above the village, and completely masked the clear blue sky and fluffy white clouds they had seen earlier.

There was also an eerie mist that appeared from nowhere and seemed to cover the entire area, as if it were being wrapped inside a cold, dank blanket.

The worst part of all was that, as both boys had egged each other on to make the trip, neither of them wanted to be the one to suggest turning back, even though they both desperately wanted to do so.

Colin, being the eldest, felt it was his duty to show his younger brother that he had no fear. But he could feel his legs shaking violently inside his jeans as they walked further and further into the village.

The pair walked down the deserted high street, feeling as if they were being watched by a thousand eyes, from behind the curtains of the windows they passed.

The mist grew so thick, that whenever one of the boys turned back to check if anyone was following them, they could not see more than a few feet ahead.

Suddenly, Don stopped dead in his tracks and reached out to grab his elder brother.

When Colin followed his gaze, he could see the outline of a large man, standing just on the edge of the mist so that his outline was distorted.

From this distance, both boys could see that the man was holding something down by his side, but it was impossible for the moment foe them to ascertain what it might be.

The boys stayed put. Neither of them felt safe enough to venture forward. Colin would later use the excuse that he felt he should stay back so as not to leave his younger brother behind.

But the truth was that he was just as frightened as Don.

As they both stared at the figure lurking in the gloom, it began to walk towards them, swinging the object he held in his hand from side to side, like a pendulum, preparing to strike.

After a few strides, he swung the item above his head, and held it aloft.

It was only then that the boys realised the man was carrying an axe.

The pair of them turned on the spot and began to run back the way they had come.

Neither of them stopped running until they had left the village and were back on the road into town.

It was a long time before either of them ventured back into Thorndike.

As Colin sped into town, feeling the combination of his earlier spliff and his pint at Thad's, a figure darted out into the road.

Don yelled to his brother to look where he was going, grabbing on to the side panel above his window to brace himself for the inevitable impact.

With a reflex action that was born more of luck than skill, Colin swung the wheel at the last minute and managed to veer the van off to one side, just missing the careless wanderer.

Once they were safely past the person in the road, Colin braked hard and brought the van to a stop.

Both brothers jumped out, intent on confronting whoever it was that had almost caused them to crash.

"Oi, dickhead," yelled Colin, striding towards the man, "what the fuck do you think yer doin'?"

Don quickly checked over his shoulder that there were no witnesses. He knew what his brother's temper was like, and he almost felt sorry for the bloke who was about to get the crap kicked out of him.

"Oi, I'm talkin' to you." Colin walked up behind the staggering man and grabbed him by the shoulder. As he swung him around, ready to land his first punch, he stopped himself.

It was Sergeant Sid Carter standing before him.

Colin immediately dropped his hand to his side, but his face still displayed the pent-up rage he was feeling.

Sid Carter was obviously the worse for wear. He stood on the spot, trying to regain his balance after Colin had yanked him around.

Once he was steady, he focused his vision on the two men before him.

"Ah, the two Craven lads, I was lookin' for you two!" He wagged his index finger at them, still barely able to stand upright.

"Fuck!" Don exclaimed. Ever since the night they had seen Sharon Spate on the Thorndike road, and not bothered to help her and Dennis, they had feared that sooner or later either Charlie or Sid would catch up with them, demanding an explanation.

Colin managed to shake off his initial shock at seeing the policeman in the road.

"Never mind that," he shouted, "what the fuck are you doin' wanderin' around the middle of the road, at this time of night? I could've killed yer."

Sid was not perturbed by the younger man's anger. He reached out and grabbed Colin by the lapels of his denim jacket, and dragged him closer until Colin could smell the acrid stench of whisky on his breath.

"Now you listen to me, yer little squirt," he said, his voice low and menacing. "You're goin' to take me to where you last saw my boy, right now, d'yer understand?"

Colin tried to pull away from the officer, the smell of his breath from such close proximity made him want to gag.

But Sid held tight, and Colin soon realised if he were to try to wrench himself free, the chances were that he would pull Sid over on top of him.

The last thing either of the brothers needed was trouble with the police. So Colin decided, that if they did not do as Sid demanded, with his position, he could make life very difficult for them once he was sober.

"All right, all right, we'll take yer," he replied reluctantly. "I don't know what good yer think it will do, but if that's what yer want, fine."

Sid stared deeply into Colin's eyes, as if attempting to ascertain if the man was in earnest, or would just run off the minute he let go of him.

Don strode over to stand next to his brother. "Col," he stammered, looking at him nervously.

"Just shut it, all right," his elder brother had obviously made up his mind, and Don knew better than to try arguing with him.

They helped Sid into the van. Don sat in the middle so that Sid could lean out of the open window. Cold as the night air was, neither of them relished the prospect of the officer spewing his guts up all over them.

Colin drove back towards the village. The more he thought about it, the more he realised that they had nothing to hide. No one need ever know that they refused to give Sharon a lift, and if she did ever turn up and accused them, they could always continue to deny it.

As it was, they had not even seen Dennis that night, so they had nothing to lie about there. If Sid wanted them to show him the spot, then fine. If it kept him happy and meant he would leave them alone, it was a small price to pay.

Colin made a conscious effort to drive more slowly back up to the village than he had on the way back down. The ground beneath his tyres was too uncertain for him to risk a puncture by driving too fast. On top of which, with Sid in the van in his condition, Colin did not want to risk any sudden jolts.

Once they reached the spot where they had last seen Sharon, Colin pulled over and switched the engine off, but left the headlights on.

Somehow, being parked up here late at night made him revert to being that young boy in the mist all those years ago.

By now, Sid had slumped forward in his seat.

“Silly bugger doesn’t even know we’ve stopped,” Don remarked. “Why don’t we just drive back to town an’ tell ’im we stopped an’ ’e ’ad a look around? ’E’ll never remember, anyway.”

Just then, Sid raised his head. “We ’ere?” he called out.

Colin sighed. “Yeah, this is the place but, like I said, I don’t know what you expect to find up ’ere.”

Without replying, Sid opened his door and almost collapsed on to the road, just managing to retain his balance in time to keep himself upright.

The brothers stayed in the van as Sid made his way around the front and sidled up to Colin’s window.

With a speed that surprised both brothers, Sid reached in and grabbed the key from the ignition, pulling it out before Colin could react.

“Hey, what the fuck you doin’?” Colin yelled.

Sid smiled, and tapped his nose. “Just in case you boys decide to drive off and leave me stranded out ’ere.”

Sid pushed himself away from the old van and staggered across the road towards the grass verge.

“What the fuck are we supposed to do now?” Don asked, unable to keep the panic from his voice.

Colin thought for a moment, then said. “Come on, we’d better keep an eye on the stupid prick before ’e slips and falls down the hill, takin’ our keys with ’im.”

The brother alighted from their van and made their way over to where Sid stood, surveying the area around him.

In the faint light afforded by the van's headlights off to their side, it was almost impossible to see more than a couple of feet into the darkness. Even so, Sid appeared to be scanning the ground as if he were staring through a microscope.

After a moment, he asked. "Yer sure this is the exact spot?"

"Yeah," Colin replied. "This is where we saw 'is car parked, an' Sharon reckoned 'e 'ad gone down there towards the lake to have a pee."

Sid nodded. "Come on, then," he said as he began to take a few tentative steps down the slope.

The brothers looked at each other in disbelief.

"I ain't goin' down there in the dark," Don squeaked.

"Suit yerself," Sid called back. "you boys can just wait there fer me to return."

Colin sighed, and swore under his breath. "Come on, we need to make sure 'e gets back in one piece, otherwise we'll 'ave more explainin' t'do."

Reluctantly, the two men followed behind.

On their way to the lake, the brothers ended up having to half-carry their unwanted guest, as Sid was incapable of keeping upright as he negotiated the uneven terrain.

There was no moon to guide them, and low clouds scudded across the sky, blocking any light from the stars that might have helped them.

Finally, they reached level ground once more and they could see the lake ahead of them as it stretched out into the distance.

Sid managed to grab hold of a large stick, and used it to sweep the ground in front of him as he searched for any sign that his son had been there.

The brothers stood back and watched. Neither felt inclined to help, deciding that, with or without their assistance, the officer would take just as long as he wanted until he was satisfied.

Eventually, they grew bored with waiting, and both slumped down on some nearby logs.

Don removed another joint from his top pocket and placed it firmly between his lips.

"What the fuck yer doin'?" demanded Colin, indicating with his head towards Sid, out in front of them.

"Oh, like 'e's goin' to notice – or care," Don replied defiantly, lighting the end with a match.

Colin shrugged, and waited for his brother to take a long drag before holding out his hand for his turn.

The brothers took it in turns until the spliff was finished.

Sid was still foraging around by the water's edge and, just as Don had speculated, he was oblivious to the scene taking place behind him.

The night air was growing colder, and Don shivered as he zipped up his jacket.

"How much longer are we goin' to give this?" he asked, the joint starting to make him feel drowsy.

"Not much longer," Colin replied, cupping his hands together and blowing into them. "I'm getting' sorely pissed off with all this!"

From behind, they heard a rustling in the bushes.

Don spun round, almost toppling off his log. "What was that?" he asked, his eyes trying to focus in the darkness.

"Probably just the wind," replied Colin. "Stop pissin' yerself."

Unconvinced, Colin continued to stare back up the slope towards the road.

He waited, holding his breath. From the corner of his eye, he saw something move off to his right.

Colin swung round again, but once more there was nothing to see.

From out of the night, there came a malevolent cry that sounded as if it were emanating from every direction at the same time.

It sounded more animal than human but, even so, like no animal either of the men had ever heard before.

The two of them jumped from their perches in unison, and began to scour the area.

"See, I told you there was something there!" Don announced triumphantly. "What the fuck is it?"

Colin shook his head. "How the fuck should I know." He turned back around to see what Sid's reaction was. The officer was obviously too engrossed in his search to have heard the cry.

"What the fuck do we do now?" Don asked, his voice almost pleading for his brother to act.

Colin stared back into the shrubbery which covered the slope, clearly unnerved by what they had just heard.

"Right," he announced, decidedly "fuck 'im, I'm getting' my keys back an' we're leaving, right now!"

Don followed close behind his elder brother as he strode towards the lake and the oblivious Sid.

When they were close enough to him, Colin called out. "Sid, give me back me keys, we're leavin'. You can fuckin' stay out 'ere all night if yer want, but we're off!"

Sid turned, suddenly aware of the advancing men.

He held up his stick. "What're you talkin' about? I'm not leavin' until I find something that proves my boy was 'ere."

"Good," Don chimed in, "but you're stayin' alone. Now give us the keys."

Sid took a tentative step backwards, waving his stick in front of him as if to keep the brothers at bay. "You ain't goin' nowhere until I'm finished," he insisted.

"Stop being a prat," said Colin, stopping in his tracks. He and Don were no more than a couple of feet away from Sid, and his menacing stick was close enough to make contact if they moved any further forward.

Sid turned his attention on the elder brother.

He shook his stick at the man's face, his expression contorted into a scowl of pure malice. "What are yer afraid I might find, eh? Evidence that you two 'ad something to do with my lad's disappearance?"

Sid lunged forward.

Colin just managed to take a step back in time before the point of the stick made contact with his face.

"Stop it, yer fuckin' lunatic," he shouted, ready to dodge another blow should it come. "We never 'ad anythin' to do with Dennis, or that stupid tart 'e was with. Now give me the fuckin' keys!"

As Colin tied to grab the stick from Sid, the officer moved it away and aimed a swing at his head. But before he had a chance to let fly, Don moved in from his other side and landed two hard punches in his gut.

Sid shouted out in agony and slumped to the floor, the stick falling from his grasp.

Colin immediately moved in and placed a well-aimed boot in the man's side.

Sid rolled over on to his back, the wind knocked from his body.

Instinctively, he lifted his knees towards his chest and wrapped his arms around them.

Don moved in from behind and kicked Sid in the back, twice.

For the next minute, the brothers took it in turns to lay into the fallen officer with kicks and punches aimed at any uncovered part of his body.

Neither seemed concerned that they might do the man permanent damage, their fury egged on by their attempt to impress each other and fuelled by the strength of their latest skunk wrap.

The fact that he was an officer of the law no longer held any sway with either of them.

Eventually, they grew tired of the assault.

By now, Sid was lying on his front, his arms and legs splayed out.

He wasn't moving any longer, but the brothers could still hear a faint groan escaping from his lips.

Colin bent down and rifled through Sid's pockets until he located his van keys.

Once he had retrieved them, he turned to his brother who was still staring down at the prone body, transfixed.

"Come on, let's get out of 'ere," he ordered.

They left Sid behind as they made their way back towards the hillside.

As they started to climb their way out, they heard the something moving around ahead of them.

Both men stopped dead in their tracks, and scanned the area for any sign of movement.

There followed another rustling off to their left, then one to their right.

Don turned to his brother, his knees trembling. "What the fuck is that?" he asked, his voice starting to quiver. His one hope was that his elder brother would respond with some comforting words.

Instead, Colin ignored him, and continued to squint in the darkness for any evidence of what might be stalking them.

Before they had a chance to move again, another high-pitched cry pierced the darkness. Only this time, it sounded much closer than before.

Their father had insisted on taking them both to an abattoir when he felt they were old enough to understand. In his mind, it was only natural for a future butcher to see what preparing the animals for the butcher's slab, entailed. So, both men knew the sound animals made when they called out.

But this was completely different from anything either of them had heard before.

In fact, right now neither of them was altogether sure that it was an animal, after all.

Colin took a step back.

Unnerved by his brother's display of weakness, Don gulped hard, and followed suit.

They both knew that they were stuck. There was no point in turning back to the lake. Although they were both good swimmers, neither of them was in any state to make it across to the other side.

If they decided to run along the shore, either way would just lead them to more dense woodland and whatever was lurking in the shadows could doubtless just follow them until they grew too tired to fight.

Their best chance was still to make a run for it, and try to reach their old van before they were caught.

Without speaking, Colin put his head down and began to run forward.

Don, taken by surprise at his brother's sudden movement, slipped as he tried to follow him. He came down hard on the ground and smashed his knee against a loose rock.

"Oww!" he cried out, feeling deserted by Colin's flight. He looked up, and saw that his brother was gaining ground up the slope.

Rubbing his knee, Don stood up and ran after him, his knee throbbing every time he put weight on that side.

Colin was almost out of sight, cloaked by the overhanging trees and bushes ahead.

Don bit his bottom lip against the pain, and leaned forward to try and pick up some momentum.

Ahead of him, he heard a sound that reminded him of a carcass being ripped apart.

From out of the darkness, something bounced down the slope in his direction.

Don stopped where he was, and waited while trying to focus on the object falling towards him.

When it was within a couple of feet, he recognised it.

It was his brother's decapitated head.

Half out of his mind with shock, Don stooped to pick it up once it was within reach.

As he stared into his brother's dead eyes, he did not see the creatures descending towards him until it was too late.

18

In her dreams, Matilda Fox was being chased through a labyrinth of tunnels, and although she could not see her pursuer, she knew exactly what it was.

The tunnels were dark, almost pitch, and Matilda had to trust wherever she placed each foot that there would be some solid ground beneath to support her.

The creature roared its frustration at not being able to locate her. The sound echoed throughout the tunnels, and made her redouble her efforts.

She knew there was no escape.

She had been here before.

At each turn and bend Matilda could feel herself heading deeper underground, minimising any chance she might have of escape.

The only entrance was far behind her now.

That was where the creature had dragged her in from the beach.

She could still smell the awful stench of his body odour, which he had tried to mask by spraying himself in too much deodorant. His breath too smelled strongly of alcohol and nicotine. The combination of the aromas mingled in the air to give off a pungent musty smell, which made her want to retch.

Matilda tried to remember how she had managed to break free of his grasp, but her memory was hazy. All she knew for sure was that he had threatened to kill her when he caught her, but first, he intended to do unspeakable things to her.

In the distance, Matilda could hear a voice. It spoke to her in soft, lulling tones that tried to reassure her that she would soon be safe and out of danger.

She wanted to believe it. To know that somewhere up ahead lay her salvation. But a part of her wanted to distance herself from the voice, almost as if it were trying to lead her down the wrong path and lull her into a false sense of security.

But the voice was so sweet and innocent, Matilda could not help but believe the words it spoke.

The fetid stench of her attacker, which had assailed her nostrils until now, was suddenly replaced with something pleasant and inviting.

Unable to resist, Matilda stopped in her tracks and took in a deep breath, infusing her lungs with aromatic smell, and eradicating the foul odour emanating from her pursuer.

As she inhaled, the sweet voice encouraged her to open her eyes.

When she did, she saw a gentle, smiling face, staring down at her.

"Hello," said the same sweet, melodic voice. "My name is Jodie. How are you feeling?"

Matilda tried to sit up, but her body still ached from before, and it took her a couple of attempts before she could prop herself up against the stone wall behind her.

She looked around frantically.

There was no one else to be seen except the young girl in front of her.

Although the cave was dark, with no daylight seeping in,

there was a large fire burning a few feet away from them, and the light from it cast a warming glow, which radiated around the walls and ceiling, making it seem almost inviting.

"I hope you don't mind, but I washed you down while you were asleep. You were quite mucky from before?"

Matilda looked down at her body, it was then that she realised she was naked, with her breasts on display. The blanket that covered the rest of her body had obviously slid down when she sat up.

Embarrassed, she cupped her hands over her boobs.

Jodie laughed. "You needn't worry about that – we're both women, after all."

Matilda looked at the girl. She estimated that she could not be older than 13 at most, but there was something almost worldly about her that made her speak and act like someone much older.

"Did that nasty man hurt you?" Jodie enquired, looking solemn and concerned. "You don't need to worry any more. He can't hurt anyone now – my cousin took care of him."

Matilda's mind was swimming. Her recollection had not fully returned, but Jodie's words made her think of the creature from her nightmare. His pungent odour returned to invade her nostrils for a second, but was thankfully replaced when Jodie removed the cover from the pot she had in front of her.

Matilda suddenly realised she was ravenous. She breathed in deeply, savouring the gorgeous aroma.

Jodie stirred the contents several times before lifting a spoonful towards Matilda's mouth.

"Now try some of this," Jodie suggested. "It'll make you feel better straight away."

"What is it?" asked Matilda, her voice shaky.

"It's one of my mama's special recipes, just try some and see if you like it."

As if in response, Matilda's stomach rumbled loudly.

The smell was too inviting to dismiss.

Matilda leaned forward and accepted the offered spoonful.

The moment the stew entered her mouth, the succulent meat melted on her tongue, stimulating her taste buds and exploding in an eruption of flavour.

Matilda swallowed and instinctively opened her mouth, ready for some more.

Jodie continued to spoon in mouthful after mouthful, like a mother feeding her child soup while they are ill in bed.

The delicious stew warmed Matilda from the inside, making her feel human once more.

When she had eaten all she could, she held up her hand, and apologised to Jodie that she could not take another mouthful.

"How was it?" asked Jodie, grinning. "Bet you've never tasted anything like it before," she added confidently.

Matilda shook her head. "You're not wrong there," she agreed.

Feeling less self-conscious, Matilda uncovered her breasts, and looked around her again for any signs of familiarity.

Jodie's words about a "nasty man", brought back a partial memory of her being grabbed from behind while she was walking to her car.

"What am I doing here?" she asked.

Jodie placed the spoon back in the pot, and leaned back on her haunches.

"You still don't remember, do you?" she asked sympathetically. "Well, I was out walking in the woods with my cousins, and we came across this van parked near the wood. I felt that something was wrong, so I knocked on the door, and this horrible man opened it, that's when we saw you inside, naked, and all tied up and gagged."

The shock of Jodie's retelling of the circumstances surrounding her discovery sent a shiver down Matilda's spine.

In the back of her memory, there was an evil man leering over her while she struggled to free herself.

Slowly, the full horror of her experience returned.

As she relived the ordeal, Matilda felt hot tears starting to streak down her cheeks. She wiped them away with the back of her hand.

Jodie leaned forward and placed a comforting arm around her shoulders.

"You don't have to worry any more – he's gone now. I told you, my cousin took care of him."

Matilda wiped her nose with the back of her hand. "Was it your cousin who brought me here?" she asked tentatively.

Jodie nodded. "Yes, you're safe here."

"And where is 'here', exactly?"

Jodie moved back. For a moment she appeared to be lost in thought, almost as if she were trying to answer a difficult question.

Finally, she replied. "This is where my cousins live. It's quite safe, no one will hurt you while they are protecting you."

Matilda looked puzzled. "But this is a cave, isn't it?"

"Yep," replied Jodie, "I love it down here. My sister and I used to come here all the time when we were little."

Matilda decided it was best to choose her words carefully. She was not entirely sure what was going on, but she decided she needed Jodie's help, regardless.

"Jodie, I am very grateful for everything you and your cousins have done for me, but I would really like to go home now, if that's all right?"

Jodie looked perplexed. The furrow lines which appeared across her forehead seemed out of place on someone so young.

"What's your name?" she asked, moving off track "I've told you mine."

Matilda took a deep breath. Although she was feeling stronger after her stew, she was not in any state to make a run for it, so she thought it best to play along for the moment.

"I'm Matilda," she replied, holding out her hand.

Jodie shook it. "Nice to meet you, Matilda."

Matilda smiled back. "So now we're proper friends, can you show me the way out so I can go back home?"

The furrowed brow returned. "I'm sorry, but it's not that easy. You see, my cousins want to meet you properly."

Matilda nodded. "I see, and I would like to meet them so I can thank them for rescuing me. But, couldn't we do that outside, in the open?"

Jodie shook her head. "Oh no, it's daylight now, they don't go out in daylight."

"How come?"

"They're cave dwellers," Jodie announced proudly, as if it were the most natural thing in the world to say by way of explanation.

"Cave dwellers," Matilda repeated, an uneasy feeling starting to form in her stomach.

"That's right, we were all cave dwellers initially. I come from generations of cave dwellers, going back centuries. My dada can tell you all about our family's history."

The urge to make a break for it was building momentum inside Matilda.

She began to wonder if Jodie had somehow escaped from a mental hospital, the way she was talking. But that made even less sense. How could someone so young have brought her to this cave? Let alone saved her from her attacker?

Plus, judging by the girl's complexion, she certainly did not appear as if she had spent any great length of time below ground.

What's more, if, as she said, her cousins were down here somewhere, they were hardly likely to allow her just to leave.

They were obviously keeping her down here for a reason.

Matilda looked Jodie straight in the eyes. “Jodie, I'm really very frightened. I don't like it down here, so please show me how to get out.”

Jodie placed a comforting hand on Matilda's shoulder, rubbing the bare flesh, sympathetically.

“Look,” she began, “I know it can be a little scary – you're not the first one we've brought down here – but you'll soon see that there's nothing to be afraid of.”

Matilda's appeal to the girl's better nature had fallen on deaf ears. If anything, Jodie's words sent a further shiver down Matilda's spine.

What did she mean: “You're not the first one”?

Matilda instinctively pulled back.

Jodie sighed. “I can see I'm going to have to introduce you to my cousins so that you can understand what I'm saying.”

With that, Jodie turned around and called out into the darkness beyond the roaring fire.

The sound she made was like nothing Matilda had ever heard before, and she could not believe that it was coming from the girl.

Within seconds, Matilda could hear the sound of shuffling and grunting echoing from around the next bend.

When the creatures finally came into view, Matilda believed that she had indeed gone mad herself.

She opened her mouth to scream but the sound refused to come out.

As the creatures barged each other for a better look at her, Matilda pushed herself as far back against the stone wall as possible.

Jodie turned to her and smiled, reassuringly. “These are my cousins,” she announced proudly, standing up and walking towards the largest one and wrapping her arms as far as she could around its enormous girth.

Looking back down at Matilda, she continued. "And this is my cousin Gobal, who saved you from that nasty man I was telling you about."

Matilda smiled back, but it was no longer the smile of a sane woman.

19

KAREN AND DAN FINALLY ARRIVED AT THORNDIKE AT SIX O'CLOCK in the evening. The drive down from London had taken over seven hours because Dan decided to take mainly A and B roads instead of the motorway after it was announced on the news that morning that the police had closed it off in both directions due to a major accident.

Furthermore, whenever Karen needed to feed or change Charlotte, it made more sense to stop rather than keep moving.

Dan used Google to direct him the last 10 miles as he was too tired to negotiate the country lanes with their hit-and-miss signage.

When they pulled up in front of Moorside cottage, Dan switched off the engine and stretched his arms out to relieve the stiffness from the journey.

"Boy," he said, glancing over at Karen. "That was a drive and a half."

"It didn't help that the motorway was closed," she agreed. "Perhaps we should have tried to cut back in on it further on?"

"Maybe," Dan surmised, "but the problem with incidents like that is that they end up having a knock-on effect all the way down the line. Then you end up stuck in a jam because everyone has had the same idea."

Karen unhitched her seat belt and leaned over so that she could see Charlottes face. The baby was sound asleep in her rear-facing car seat.

"Do you want to slide her out while I go and open the door?" asked Dan, smiling.

"Sounds good to me," Karen responded. "But could you take her carry-cot out first? I don't like leaving her hunched up in her car seat for too long?"

"Will do, ma'am," Dan said in his best American accent. He leaned over and gave Karen a kiss before sliding out of his seat.

The gateway to the cottage was enveloped by two over-grown hedges on either side, which crossed over at the top to form an arch.

Once they were through the opening, the sight of the cottage made them both stop in their tracks.

The building looked very much like somewhere that had not been occupied for several years. The whitewash on the walls was chipped and uneven, and there were entire areas no longer covered where the paint had been worn away.

There were large quantities of moss and weeds growing both in the small front garden and under the window ledges. In some cases, it seemed as if the greenery was the only thing that was keeping the windows in place.

The glass in the window frames looked as if they had never seen water, and even from this distance with the failing light, they could both see that several roof tiles were missing.

The two of them looked at each other with wry smiles.

"Miss Sharp did say that this was someone's home, didn't she?"

Dan nodded. "Yep, according to her, she was only going to stay here because they were away."

"Where, in prison?" Karen joked. "It looks as if no one has lived here in decades."

She did not wish to sound ungrateful. After all, this was a free holiday. But by the same token Karen felt she herself would have been too embarrassed to offer such a dilapidated property as a potential holiday home.

"Do you think there's any chance that the inside might be in better shape?" Dan asked, trying to keep a positive mood. "Perhaps the owners are too old or infirm to maintain the outside."

"Mmnn." Karen did not sound convinced. "Well, there's only one way to find out."

Dan moved forward with Charlotte's carry-cot swinging at his side, and retrieved the key his boss had given him from his jacket pocket.

The key, like the escutcheon of the lock, was old and a little rusty. For a moment, Dan was afraid that it might even break when he tried to turn it.

It took a little effort, but the key finally worked, and they both heard the heavy bolt slot back into the holder.

"Here goes nothing," Dan said, pushing the door open.

The door creaked open on rusty hinges that had obviously not seen oil in a good while.

The inside of the cottage was dark and foreboding.

Dan slipped his hand and felt along the wall until he located the light switch.

When he flicked it on, they were both pleasantly surprised to see that the inside was far pleasanter than the outer façade had led them to believe it would be.

Dan heaved a huge sigh of relief. Although he had nothing to do with the state of the place, he did feel responsible for bringing Karen out here. He was glad now that he had not built up too unrealistic a picture of their venture down here.

Since first seeing the property, Dan had resigned himself to the fact that he would have to find them a local hotel for their break, a prospect he did not relish after the long drive.

Dan walked inside and held open the door for Karen to manoeuvre Charlotte's car seat through.

The downstairs was open-plan. There were two armchairs by the fireplace with matching footrests in front of them, and the ceiling was criss-crossed by dark wooden beams. A small couch tucked was away next to a door that Dan suspected must lead to the kitchen, and two matching sideboards stood on opposite sides of the room.

To the right there was a flight of stairs leading to the second level, with a very ornate bannister on the near side.

Dan closed the door behind them to keep out the night chill.

"Well, I've seen worse," he ventured. "What do you think?"

Karen turned to him and smiled. "Not bad at all," she replied. "Well done you."

In reality, Karen found the cottage a little eerie. It was nothing specific that she could point to, but just a feeling deep within her. But she brushed the thought aside and decided she needed to be more sympathetic to Dan's feelings.

"Come on," he said, cheerily. "Let's explore."

They transferred Charlotte into her carry cot without waking her.

For a moment, Karen was afraid that Dan might suggest that they leave the baby in the living room while they explored the rest of the property. But her uneasy feeling about the place would not permit such an action, so she was prepared to carry her baby if necessary.

As it was, Dan lifted the carry-cot up by the handles once Charlotte was settled, without being asked, so Karen need not have concerned herself.

They went through into the kitchen, which was larger than

either of them had expected, given the size of the rest of the cottage.

On one side sat a range cooker which looked big enough to cook a feast for a family of 12. The sink was one of those rectangular porcelain ones such as Karen remembered seeing in stately homes on school trips, and it looked large enough to bathe a baby elephant in.

There was a large fridge, and separate freezer towards the back door and, in the middle of the room stood a sturdy wooden table with six chairs arranged comfortably around it.

Next to the range, Dan spotted a pad with written instructions on how to work the cooker, as well as details of where everything was stored, and the instructions for lighting the pilot to ensure they had hot water.

Upstairs, they found two bedrooms, one far larger than the other. The bigger of the two had twin beds with a side table in between them, one large wardrobe, and a dressing table with a vanity mirror in an oval frame.

The smaller one had a single bed at one end, and two full-size wardrobes.

The single bed was unmade but there were several sheets, pillows and blankets folded on it, ready for use.

As with the fireplace downstairs, the two upstairs had been prepared with paper, kindling and wood, ready to be lit.

The bathroom did not have a shower option. It contained a fairly large bath, a sink with a small cabinet on the wall above it, and a toilet with an old-fashioned tank and chain above.

Dan walked in and tested the chain. To his relief, it still worked, although the sound of the tank refilling seemed to reverberate throughout the cottage.

He looked at Karen. "I'll have to try and hold it in if I need to go during the night," he said with a smile. "That noise could wake the dead."

"Or at the very least, little one here," she replied, nodding towards the sleeping Charlotte.

They went back downstairs and checked over the instructions they had been left.

There was milk, butter, cheese, and eggs in the fridge, tea, coffee, and sugar in one of the cupboards and fresh loaf of uncut bread, together with a selection of biscuits in the bread-bin.

There were also instructions on how to reach Beanie's Inn.

The welcoming gifts made Karen feel a little more relaxed about staying there.

Walking back into the lounge, Karen shivered as a cold draught hit her.

"Shall we light the fire?" Dan suggested. "We can leave it blazing while we go out for dinner. It'll be lovely and warm by the time we get back."

Karen considered his suggestion. Even though the grate had a metal grille in front to contain the fire and stop logs rolling on to the carpet and there was a mesh firescreen, she was still concerned that ashes might spit out and land on it. She had seen too many public-service broadcasts about how easy it was to start a fire, and the last thing she wanted was for them to be responsible for burning down someone else's cottage.

"No, let's leave it. There's no point heating the place when we're not here to enjoy it."

Dan looked surprised. "I wasn't sure if you still wanted to go out this evening. Isn't it getting past Charlotte's bedtime?"

Karen peered over at her daughter. "No, she's sweet, so long as the place isn't too noisy, she should be fine."

"Well, according to the instructions, it's only about a five-minute walk, so if it's unsuitable we can always try to find somewhere else or get a takeaway."

When they arrived at the inn, the bar area was crowded with Friday-night regulars. Everyone stopped their conversations and turned to look at them when they entered. It reminded Dan of one of those old western films when the gunslinger enters the saloon.

The uncomfortable silence lasted mere seconds before patrons went on with their conversations. To Dan and Karen, though, it felt like hours.

Karen looked back at Dan and gave him a nervous smile.

He pulled a face in response which at least made her smile.

Then, from out of nowhere, a large woman emerged from the crowd, and strode over to them with a beaming smile on her face.

"Hello," she said, offering her hand, "my name is Mavis Beanie. Welcome to our little establishment. Now let me see, you must be Dan and Karen, is that right?"

Karen accepted the woman's hand and shook it. "Yes, that's right," she replied, curiously.

Dan did the same. "I take it my boss told you that we were coming?"

"That's right, my dear." The woman peered into the carry-cot. "What a beautiful angel. We hadn't been told about her – how simply gorgeous."

"Thank you," said Karen. "This is my daughter Charlotte, I hope it's OK to bring her in here, if she starts crying or causing a scene I will take her outside."

Mavis stared at both adults. "I'll have none of that 'ere," she insisted. "This little one can scream the place down if she likes, I'll send this lot packin' before I turf her out."

Karen smiled. "Thank you, that's very nice of you."

"Not at all," Mavis insisted. "Now you both follow me and we'll get you settled an' fed. I hope you're both hungry."

"Famished," Dan assured her.

The locals scraped their chairs back as the trio approached

to allow them access to the restaurant. Karen caught a few eyes on the way through that made her feel slightly uncomfortable. The men, especially, did not try to disguise the fact that they were taking delight in looking her up and down.

She heard Dan behind her saying a few hellos as they walked, but she heard no one respond.

Once they were through to the restaurant, Mavis led them at a table in the corner that had a reserved sign on it and sat them down.

"Now, you make yourselves comfortable while I fetch you a pint of home brew," she said, patting Dan on his shoulder. "And would you like the same?" she asked Karen. "Or would you prefer something a bit lighter?"

"A dry white wine would be lovely," Karen replied.

Mavis did not wait to see if Dan had any objection to his order.

They placed Charlotte's cot on a chair to one side, where no one would bump into her if they were passing.

The restaurant was fairly busy, with only a handful of vacant tables.

Unlike in the bar, here no one took any special interest in them, although a couple of heads turned briefly in their direction as they sat down.

"At least it's warm in here," Karen whispered.

"Mmnn," agreed Dan, taking her hand. "And can you smell those pies? I think I could eat a dozen myself right now."

Karen nodded. She had to admit the aroma certainly brought on her appetite.

There were no menus on the table, which was not particularly odd – in any decent restaurant, the waiting staff brought the menus with them when they approached the table. But when she gazed around the room, it seemed to Karen as if everyone was eating the same meal.

Perhaps, she thought, Friday night was pie night.

There appeared to be only two waitresses serving. Both were dressed identically in plaid shirts and dungarees. The younger of the two did not look old enough to be working, in Karen's opinion. But, seeing them together, they looked so much alike, Karen concluded that they were probably members of the owner's family.

The younger of the two walked over to their table after setting another couple's food down for them.

"Hello," she said, brightly, "my name is Jodie, and I will be serving you tonight. Would you like something to drink?"

"The lady who showed us to our table has already gone to fetch our drinks," Dan informed her. "Is there a menu we could see?"

Jodie gave him a puzzled look. "Menu?" she responded. "We don't use those here – everyone comes from far and wide to sample my dada's meat pies. They're the best in the world."

"I'm sure they are lovely," Karen piped in. "What type of meat are they, or is there a selection?"

Jodie laughed. "They're a family secret, been handed down over generations, they're very nice."

Just at that moment, Mavis returned with their drinks.

"Now Jodie, I hope you are looking after our guests?" she asked, placing their drinks in front of them.

"Oh, yes mama, I was just telling them about... Oh, my goodness, she's adorable, what's her name?"

Moving around the table to allow her mother to put down the glasses, Jodie had noticed the carry-cot on the chair between them.

A broad beaming smile crossed her face as she peered over at Charlotte.

"Her name's Charlotte," Karen replied, smiling.

"How old is she?" Jodie asked eagerly.

"Just over three months."

"Oh, look at her, Mama," Jodie cooed. "Isn't she the most precious thing you ever saw?"

Mavis Beanie placed her plump fists on her hips and frowned at her younger daughter. "Now Jodie, you know better than to be bothering customers."

Karen turned back. "Oh, really, she's not being any bother," she assured Mavis.

"Well, thank you for your kindness, young miss, but she has a job to do 'ere an' it won't 'appen all by itself, will it, Jodie?"

Jodie looked up at her mother, suitably admonished. "Sorry Mama, but she's so adorable."

"And these people are so hungry, so get about your work!"

Jodie blushed red and turned to go back to the kitchen.

"I'm sorry about that," Mavis apologised. "She's still very young and apt to forget herself."

"Really, it's no problem at all," Karen assured her. "She seems a lovely girl, very polite. I take it she's your daughter?"

"That's right, my lovely, and there's 'er big sister over there." She nodded towards Polly on the other side of the room, where she was carrying a bottle of wine over to a table of four.

"You must be very proud to have them working for you?" Dan chipped in. "Most girls their age would want to be out on a Friday night, with their friends."

Mavis smiled, but the expression did not quite reach her eyes. "Oh, they know their place, my girls, I'll give 'em that."

At that moment Jodie reappeared from the kitchen, carrying a tray. As she approached their table, the aroma that escaped from under the pie crusts assailed their nostrils, causing both Karen and Dan to release an unconscious murmur of appreciation.

"Well, I'll leave you both to it. Enjoy your meals." With that. Mavis left to return to the busy bar.

Jodie placed a plate in front of each of them.

Each plate contained a large slice of meat pie, a dollop of buttery mashed potato, and a side dish of carrots and peas.

After she had laid down the plates, Jodie lifted a gravy boat on to the table and set it down in the middle.

"I'll be back in a moment," she assured them.

Dan and Karen inhaled deeply to savour the delicious aroma.

"Wow, this smells wonderful," Dan said. "I didn't realise how hungry I was until just now."

"Me neither," agreed Karen. She looked over to see that Charlotte had woken. The baby smiled up at her mother with beaming bright eyes.

Karen leaned over and gently stroked her daughter's cheek with her finger.

She felt a twinge of guilt for not picking her up. But she had changed and fed her before they came out, and as Charlotte appeared content just to lie there for the moment, Karen decided to wait and see how much of her dinner she could consume before she was interrupted by her baby's grizzling.

Jodie arrived back at their table. She placed a wicker basket with an assortment of bread rolls, and a silver dish containing individual pats of butter, each wrapped in silver paper, down in front of them.

"There now," she said, proudly, "is there anything else I can get for you?"

Karen and Dan both shook their heads.

"No thank you," Dan assured her, "everything looks delicious."

He reached over to grab the salt shaker.

Jodie's hand suddenly shot forward and grabbed his hand before he had a chance to lift the condiment out of its holder.

"You should really try my dada's pie before you add anything to it," she advised earnestly. "His gravy is especially meaty."

Taken aback, Dan nodded his assent.

Jodie's hand lingered a moment longer before she released him.

"Bon appetit," she said with a smile.

She peeked over at Charlotte. "Now you let me know if there's anything I can get for you, little one," she cooed, grinning when the baby appeared to smile back up at her.

With that, she turned and left them to their meal.

20

INSPECTOR KEITH JACOBS HAD NOT HAD THE MOST FRUITFUL OF days. For a start, he slept through his alarm, which naturally meant he was late for work. In his haste to try to save time, he managed to slip over in the bath and bang his forehead on the side. Then, to add to his misery, he also managed to cut himself shaving, and his chin was still bleeding when he arrived at the station.

As he was assigned to such a small county station, it was not as if he had a senior officer breathing down his neck. But all the same, he felt it was important that he project the correct image to his subordinates, and being on time for work was a basic example of probity, which he was keen to exhibit.

The desk sergeant casually glanced over at the wall clock when he wished Jacobs good morning. It was a subtle gesture, but did not go unnoticed.

He had overslept because he had spent a restless night, worrying about the business with Dennis Carter and Sharon Spate.

Neither Charlie Spate nor Sid Carter had reported that

their offspring had returned home, so Jacobs knew that it was only a matter of time before he would have to launch a full investigation.

In anticipation, he decided to delve into the archives and fish out any old cases involving disappearances connected with Thorndike.

The officer in charge of their archive was a portly man, with a very pale complexion. A consequence of spending most of his working day underground, Jacobs suspected.

The archive contained rolling shelves, crammed with paper files, most bursting at the seams and held together with criss-crossed elastic bands.

The officer in charge evidently loved his job, and was happy to talk ninety to the dozen about his system of stacking and maintaining files.

There was a computer on his desk, which Jacobs suspected was specifically placed there so the officer could register and check the location of his files without leaving his desk.

But it was obvious to Jacobs by the fact that the screen was blank, and the hard drive was not even switched on, that this officer was of the old school who preferred to do things the traditional way, before computers were introduced to help make their lives easier.

Sure enough, when Jacobs asked about Thorndike, the officer's eyes lit up.

"Why are you interested in that place?" he asked curiously. "Don't go tellin' me there's been another disappearance down there?"

"Another one?" Jacobs enquired, his curiosity piqued. "Why, do you know of others recently?"

The man shook his head. "No, not recently. Last one was over a year ago, if I remember correctly. I've got the file down 'ere, 'ang on a minute." And with that, he disappeared around a corner and returned several minutes later with a thin blue file under his arm.

He handed it to Jacobs. "Not much in there," he explained. "Bloke who made the complaint only came into the station once. Claimed we weren't taking the disappearance of his girlfriend seriously enough, an' 'e was going to solve it 'imself. Never saw 'im again."

Jacobs flicked through the scant file. The officer was correct, all it contained was the original complaint form, dated and stamped over a year before.

"And this is all you've got?" asked Jacobs, curiously. "The way you were talking, I thought there had been a raft of unexplained disappearances involving the place."

"There 'ave," the officer replied excitedly. "They go back 'undreds of years. In fact, the first inquiry this station ever 'ad was concernin' someone going missin' after telling people they were going down there."

"When you say hundreds of years, are you being serious?" asked Jacobs, shocked by the officer's revelation.

"Absolutely," the archivist assured him. "When this station first opened, they transferred all the records about incidents from this area over here. Some of the accounts are so old, I'm surprised they're not written on parchment." The officer laughed at his own joke.

"And those reports are just gathering dust down here?" Jacobs asked incredulously.

The officer nodded. "Yep, the idea is that when we finally get our scanner, I can transfer them so that we have a digital copy. Some of the older cases are virtually crumbling to dust, so there's no guarantee I can save all of them."

Jacobs thought for a moment. "And are you saying that all these files concern disappearances reported from Thorndike?"

"Well, no, I didn't say all of them," the officer answered defensively. "But there are still a fair few that are technically open. You know what it's like, Inspector – someone reports someone missing then they turn up, and no bugger bothers to tell us, so the file remains open. No one looks into the case again, unless there's a review commissioned." Jacobs knew all too well how true the archivist's words were. He knew of thousands of missing person files left open from his time in London, so it did not surprise him that even in a relatively small town and no bugger bothers to tell us, so the file remains open. No one looks into the case again, unless there's a review commissioned."

Jacobs knew all too well how true the archivist's words were. He knew of thousands of missing-person files left open from his time in Liverpool, so it did not surprise him that even in a relatively small town like this, such instances were still occurring.

"Tell me," he enquired, "other than this one, when was the last official missing person complaint lodged from Thorndike?"

The officer scratched his chin, thoughtfully. "Well, I'll have to check, but off the top of my head, there have been a couple per year going back at least 10 years."

"All still officially open?" Jacobs asked, not attempting to disguise the astonishment on his face or in his voice.

"Well, yeah, I suppose. It's like I said, when these people turn up, no one bothers to tell us." The officer turned and glanced down the nearest aisle. "I keep them mostly together, especially the ones where someone has run off after a fight with their other 'alf. You can bet yer life they'll be back once they've cooled down."

Before this conversation, Jacobs had no idea how potentially serious the situation in Thorndike might be.

It was such a small village, he could not fathom how so many people could go missing from there without one of his predecessors looking into the cases in more detail.

He decided he needed to read some of those reports before

deciding as to whether or not to bring the situation to the attention of his superiors.

He hoped that Dennis Carter and Sharon Spate were not the most recent victims in a long list of similar incidents.

He turned back to the archivist. "Could you fetch me all the reports concerning these disappearances going back over the last two years?" he asked, holding up the file in his hand. "Only the ones that have remained open."

"Right you are, chief," the officer replied cheerfully. He seemed happy enough to oblige, and Jacobs wondered if being stuck down here underground meant that he did not have many visitors, or requests of this nature.

It was usually the case that those who worked in the archives had been taken off regular duties due to ill health or age.

Jacobs wondered what the man's story was. But before he had a chance to ask, he had disappeared around the corner, whistling tunelessly to himself.

Jacobs worked through lunch, trying to make head or tail of the poorly kept files the archivist had found for him.

It was obvious from some of the written reports that the officers investigating the incidents did not take them too seriously. In fact, most coppers knew from experience that the vast majority of missing-person cases ended up with the supposed victim being found safe and well within a relatively short time.

Those cases where the victim was not found eventually led either to a murder investigation or a cold case.

All the cases Jacobs had read about involving Thorndike did not appear at first glance to follow any specific pattern. The victims were both male and female and of varying ages. Most were visitors to the area, which would make Dennis and Sharon, if they turned out to be missing, the first local victims on record.

Several of the files stated that when the victims were reported as missing, their nearest and dearest could not say for sure that their loved ones had gone missing in the area. Only that they had mentioned visiting it in previous e-mails or texts, without confirming they had arrived.

Jacobs concluded that such a circumstance would doubtless account for the lack of time and effort put into such an investigation.

Even so, none of the cases had been closed, which presumably meant that none of the victims had reappeared. At least, not as far as the police were concerned.

Jacobs was relieved that, at least for the moment, Charlie Spate and Sid Carter were not hammering on his door demanding action. But even so, the longer their kids were unaccounted for, the more likely it was that he would end up having to ask for outside help.

The only lead he had thus far was the statement given by the Craven brothers. They were the last people to see Sharon and Dennis before they vanished into thin air.

It occurred to Jacobs that perhaps he had better reinterview them, this time more formally.

He did not suspect that the brothers were in any way involved, but there might be something that one or both of them saw on the evening in question that might be pertinent to an upcoming investigation.

Jacobs knew that if he did end up having to ask for help, he needed to ensure that he had all his facts properly collated and ready to pass on to his superiors.

It was starting to get late, and Jacobs could see through his window that the sun was on its way down.

Grabbing his jacket from the back of his chair, Jacobs informed the desk sergeant on his way out that he was going back to speak to the brothers again, at their father's shop.

By the time he reached the butcher's, the door was closed and the shutters had been pulled down.

Jacobs went in to the newsagent next door to make enquiries, and discovered that the two lads lived with their father above the shop, so he walked around the side of the building until he found the right front door.

Pete Craven answered the door after several knocks. From his appearance, Jacobs deduced that the man had been in the middle of washing after a long day handling raw meat.

The butcher eyed Jacobs suspiciously.

Before Jacob's had a chance to say anything, Pete cut him off.

"Oh, fer God's sake, what 'ave the two little bleeders been up to now?" The butcher asked, rubbing remnants of shaving cream off his face with the end of the towel he had wrapped around his neck.

Jacobs frowned. "Sorry, I don't understand," he replied.

"My two lads, tweedle-dumbass an' tweedle-dumber. I take it yer 'ere because they've got themselves into some sort of bother?"

"Not exactly," Jacobs responded, suddenly concerned that the man obviously did not know where his sons were. "In fact, I was hoping to speak to them again about the night they saw Sharon."

Jacobs could see the cloud of confusion starting to drift over Pete's eyes.

"I take it they're not here?" Jacobs continued.

Pete Craven took in a deep breath before replying. "No, they're not, but I'll tell yer why, should I?"

Jacobs nodded.

"I noticed this mornin' that the little buggers 'ave nicked a tray of me best steak. How they thought I wouldn't notice is anyone's guess, but I'm sure that's why they've been too afraid to show their faces 'ere today!"

"So you haven't seen them all day?" asked Jacobs, considering Pete's explanation.

The butcher shook his head.

"Why on earth would they steal meat from you?" Jacobs asked, curiosity getting the better of him.

Pete leaned against the door jamb, exposing his overgrown armpits to the detective.

"Because the pair of them don't 'ave the brains they were born with," Pete scoffed. "I turn a blind eye to them now an' again when they nick some of the cheap stuff. I know they're probably sellin' it on to someone who isn't too worried about where it comes from. But this time they've cost me some real money, an' when they get back, they know what's waiting fer 'em both!"

Jacobs thought it prudent not to ask what that was, but he could hazard a good guess.

"Have you any idea where they might be hiding out?"

Pete shook his head. "Could be anywhere, knowin' them. Probably sleeping off the booze they bought after selling my good steak. Well, I hope they think it was worth it when I catch 'old of 'em."

It was obvious from his manner that Pete was not at all concerned with the fact that his sons had not returned home the previous night.

Furthermore, as he appeared to have no idea where they might be, Jacobs concluded that any further questioning would be a waste of time.

He gave Pete a card with his mobile number on it. "Just ask one of them to give me a call when they come back."

"Yeah, OK," replied Pete, backing away. "If they are still able to once I've finished wiv 'em."

After Pete closed the door, Jacobs returned to his car and sat in it, thinking.

There was a nagging thought at the back of his mind that

he should take the brothers' disappearance more seriously than their father was doing. At this stage, it was not worth launching a full-blown investigation, but there was nothing stopping him from making a few discreet enquiries.

He remembered one of the brothers telling him that they sometimes went to the pub in Thorndike for a pie and a pint. Jacobs considered the possibility that a place such as that might be just the sort of establishment two young entrepreneurs could offload some knocked-off meat.

It was a start, at least, so Jacobs decided to take a drive down there, just on the off-chance he might spot their van in the car park.

When he arrived at the inn, the car park was almost full. Even though it was Friday night, Jacobs still thought it odd that so many people were there so early. It made him wonder if the brothers were not exaggerating about the pies, after all.

He found a spot towards the far end, close to the entrance to the woods, and searched among the other vehicles to see if he could spot the butcher's van.

Having come full circle, without success, Jacobs decided to have a look around the back of the inn, just in case there was an overspill area where the lads had parked to stay out of sight.

As Jacobs walked past the outside patio area, where several tables and chairs were set out for anyone brave enough to endure the cold, he could see through the side window that the bar area was heaving, which was no surprise considering the number of vehicles in the main car park. He walked past the large refuse area, and peered around the corner. The parking area was only large enough to house a couple of vehicles, and neither of the ones there resembled a butcher's van.

As he came back around the corner, the back door leading into the inn swung open.

Jacobs stopped and looked over to see Polly exiting with a large plastic bucket.

She made her way over to the bins. Without noticing Jacobs standing there in the shadows, Polly lifted the large plastic lid on one of the refuse bins.

Jacobs wondered if he should cough, or clear his throat to announce his presence. The last thing he wanted was for the young woman to catch sight of him and think he was spying on her.

Before he had a chance to signal, Polly turned and shrieked, dropping the bin at her feet.

Jacobs held out his hands. "I am so sorry – I didn't mean to startle you," he said apologetically.

"What are you doing there?" Polly demanded. "You scared me half to death."

Jacobs walked over towards her. "I really am sorry," he reiterated. "I was looking for a vehicle which I thought might be parked behind the inn."

Jacobs stopped in front of Polly and bent down to retrieve the bucket. Fortunately, it had landed upright, so none of the waste material inside had spilled out on the ground.

"Permit me," he said, smiling. In his haste as he lifted the bucket, Jacobs caught his tie between his hand and the plastic rim. Unable to grab it, he concentrated on tipping the contents into the receptacle Polly had just opened.

Jacobs could feel his face flush.

Polly had not moved back when he recovered the bucket, so now she was no more than a few feet away from him. He could smell a light fragrance which he suspected was her perfume. It wafted towards him on the night air, and filled his nostrils with the pleasant scent of fresh-cut flowers.

Once the bucket was empty, Jacobs closed the lid, and turned back to face Polly.

She was still looking at him, her eyes full of suspicion and intrigue.

"Why were you looking for a vehicle behind my dada's restaurant?" she asked him forthrightly.

Jacobs opened his mouth to answer, but nothing came out.

He felt foolish at his embarrassment. After all, he was there in his official capacity, so he had no reason to prevaricate, or try to avoid the question.

Yet something about Polly made him feel like a teenager trying to ask the most beautiful girl in school out on a date.

He chided himself for his ridiculous sentiment, and reached into his jacket for his warrant card.

He held it up, close enough so that Polly could see it in the dim light cast down on them from the back entrance.

"I'm a police officer," he explained, trying desperately to keep his voice level. "I am investigating a suspected disappearance, and making a search of the area in case the victim's vehicle is in the vicinity."

Polly's eyes opened wide. "Wow," she exclaimed. "You're a police officer, I had no idea. How exciting."

Jacobs smiled and placed his ID back in his pocket.

Although he felt himself relax, now that he had explained his presence, he still felt a shiver of excitement run down his spine at Polly's response.

She was obviously impressed by his badge and that made him feel slightly giddy.

Polly was, after all, a stunningly beautiful girl, but he was old enough to be her father and was well aware that he should know better than to flirt with her.

"So, can you tell me about this missing person you're looking for? Perhaps I've seen them." Polly took another step closer, so that the two of them were barely a foot apart.

"Well, "Jacobs stammered, "to be honest, I can't really discuss it at the moment. It's still very much in its early stages."

Polly looked disappointed, and did not try to hide it.

"What makes you think they might have been here?" she

asked, focusing on Jacob's crumpled tie, and stroking it with the back of her hand in an effort to straighten it.

Jacobs could feel his reserve starting to slip.

The mere touch of Polly's hand against the fabric, was starting to give him an erection.

Reluctantly, Jacobs took a step back, just far enough to make a point.

Polly looked up into his eyes, a bemused expression on her face.

The two of them stood in silence for a moment.

Finally, Polly asked. "While you're here, would you like a pint and one of my dada's meat pies? He's just made a fresh batch."

The thought of food made Jacob's stomach start to growl.

Not having eaten since breakfast, he could certainly do with some sustenance.

He looked over at the inn, then turned back to Polly.

"It looks a little crowded in there tonight," he said.

"Friday night is one of our busiest," Polly replied, "but I can still find you a table if you're hungry."

Jacobs chewed his bottom lip inadvertently. "To be honest," he explained, "I'm not really comfortable in large crowds. Perhaps another time."

Polly moved forward. "Are you hungry?" she asked purposely.

On cue, Jacob's stomach rumbled again.

"Come with me." Without waiting for an answer, Polly led him towards the patio, and dusted down a chair with a towel from her apron. "There you go," she announced, proudly. "You sit there, and I'll bring it out to you."

Jacobs felt compelled to comply.

He took his seat and watched Polly disappear back inside the bar.

As he sat there, listening to the racket from within the pub,

Jacobs shivered and wished that he had agreed to go inside after all.

The prospect of eating his dinner out here on such a cold evening, was not exactly appealing, but he felt that now Polly had made the arrangement it would be churlish to refuse the offer.

From above, he suddenly heard the sound of one of the outdoor heaters come to life.

He looked up and watched as the dome-shaped object began to glow red.

Within minutes he could feel the comforting warmth from the glow-lamp reach his tired shoulders.

It really made all the difference and, even with the breeze, Jacobs was more than comfortable, and now looking forward to his meal.

After a few minutes, Polly re-emerged from the inn with her sister in tow.

They were both carrying trays, and placed them on the table in front of the detective.

There was a full meal of pie, mashed potato, and vegetables, and a pint of home brew, which Jodie proudly placed before him.

Jacobs was about to introduce himself to Jodie, but before he had a chance, Polly turned to her and said: "Thanks, Jodie." With that, the young girl lifted her apron tails and made a slight curtsey, before spinning around and walking back into the inn.

"Now then," said Polly, her voice almost stern, as if she were speaking to a minor. "You get that inside you, and I'll be out to check on you when I've finished serving inside.

"Thank you," replied Jacobs, "it all looks magnificent."

Before she turned to leave, Polly leaned over and cupped his chin in her hand, giving him a quick squeeze between her thumb and forefinger.

Jacobs could not help but smile warmly in response.

He watched Polly sashay back to the inn. As she opened the door, she stopped and looked back over to him.

Jacobs raised his glass to her in salute before she went back inside.

21

DAN STUMBLED, TRIPPING OVER HIS OWN FEET, AND LURCHED forward. He managed to stop himself from falling by grabbing hold of the handrail that ran the length of the patio and down the few steps which led to the car park.

In his effort to stay upright, he let the door swing back.

Karen, realising what was about to happen, stuck her hand out and just managed to stop the door before it crashed into Charlotte's cot.

This was why she had insisted on carrying her daughter home, instead of allowing Dan to undertake the task, even though he insisted on doing it, and even became quite vocal inside the restaurant.

Karen had never seen him drunk before, and she had to admit to herself that it brought out a side of him she did not like, or appreciate.

As it was, he had only had three pints of home brew with his dinner, which did not seem particularly overindulgent to Karen. After all, it was Friday night. But the ale must have been far stronger than Dan anticipated. Even after only two pints, he almost fell over when he stood up to use the bathroom.

In fairness to him, he did not order a third pint. But the landlady brought one out regardless.

Karen did not want to seem like a nag, but she did ask him if he could handle another, and Dan seemed confident enough at the time.

Karen was glad she had stuck to water after her first glass of wine.

But then, she knew she had to put Charlotte's wellbeing first.

When Dan reached the bottom step, he slumped down on to it and leaned to one side against the balustrade. He sat there for a moment, seemingly oblivious to Karen's presence, and sucked in a deep lungful of the night air, letting it out slowly through his mouth.

"Feeling a little worse for wear?" Karen asked, not bothering to conceal the edge of sarcasm in her tone.

Dan turned to look up at her.

The stare from his eyes told her all she needed to know.

Dan smiled, but it was not his usual cheerful beam, more like that of a man unaware of his circumstances.

Karen considered leaving him there to sober up while she took Charlotte home. But he had the keys, and besides, she knew she would feel guilty if she did so.

The question was what to do now.

At that moment, Charlotte stirred in her cot, and started grizzling.

Karen knew she needed another feed, and possibly a change of nappy.

She needed to get back to the cottage, but with Dan out of it he was going to be more of a hindrance, than a help.

"Come on Dan," she urged, "I need to take Charlotte back, it's freezing out here."

"Yep," Dan slurred, holding on tightly to the bannister rail as he tried to lift himself up.

It took him three attempts, but finally he made it to a standing position.

"Boy, that stuff was stronger than I thought," he murmured, more to himself than Karen. "OK, Danny boy, steady does it."

Dan managed to push himself away from his makeshift crutch without falling over.

Karen switched Charlotte to her other hand, so that she could link arms with Dan to help guide him home. She was a little concerned that, if he fell, he might inadvertently take her with him, but she decided the risk was small enough to risk it.

Besides which, if she felt that Dan was losing his balance, she could always slip her arm out of his and move to one side before he went over.

It was slow going, but they made it back to the cottage in one piece.

Karen had to remind Dan that he had the front door key in his pocket.

Then she had to wait for what seemed like an age for him to locate it.

The inside of the cottage seemed even colder than outside. Dan immediately announced that he was going to light a fire, but Karen convinced him to wait until she had sorted out Charlotte.

Once the baby was fed and changed, Karen lit the fire in the large bedroom.

The warmth from the crackling wood spread out through the room, making them feel more human again.

Karen set up Charlotte's crib in the corner of the room, and placed her sleeping baby inside.

Once she was sure everything was ready, Karen went back downstairs to find Dan fast asleep in one of the armchairs. She considered waking him and attempting to help him up the stairs, but decided instead to let him sleep it off.

She brought down a couple of blankets from the small bedroom and draped them over him as he slept.

Karen fed a few more logs to the fire before she slipped in between the crisp, soft sheets.

She was asleep in seconds.

JACOBS DRIED himself off after his shower, and stood in front of his bedroom mirror with a towel wrapped around his waist, checking himself out.

His body was reasonably trim, considering his age, which was more down to luck than planning. He had never really taken much notice of what he ate or drank and, as for exercise, he preferred to watch sports on the telly rather than actively take part.

He sighed to himself resignedly.

Was he making a huge mistake by going back to the inn tonight?

After he had finished his delicious pie and pint of ale, Polly had come back out to see him, with another pint of home brew on a tray.

Jacobs knew he should refuse as he was driving, but as Polly had already pulled it and brought it out for him, he could not refuse.

She stayed with him while he drank.

The ale was slipping down wonderfully, and Jacobs could feel it warming his insides, and relaxing him to the point of sleepiness.

Somewhere during their conversation, Polly convinced him that he should come back later, after the restaurant was closed, and join her for a late-night stroll in the woods.

There was something in the way she spoke which made

him feel as if the invitation was not merely for a walk, but something rather more personal.

Although she was young and beautiful, Jacobs felt as if she were making a play for him, which made him feel extremely flattered. But, the sensible copper in him was sending warning flashes to his brain, telling him to back off and make his excuses.

Whether it was the ale, or just his hormones being spurred into action by such a lovely young girl, either way, before he could stop himself, Jacobs had accepted her offer and the two of them finalised their plans.

Polly had explained that, for obvious reasons, she needed to sneak out after her parents had gone to bed, so they arranged to meet at the edge of the car park, near the woods.

Jacobs drove home with his insides in turmoil.

Did the girl really want to sleep with him, or was he simply deluding himself, having mis-read the signs, due probably to the drink.

Once home, Jacobs showered, brushed his teeth, and smothered himself with his most expensive cologne.

Thinking about the night ahead, he dressed himself in a tracksuit and picked his sheepskin coat from his wardrobe to keep out the cold.

He checked the time and found he still had over an hour to wait before driving back there.

Jacobs decided to watch television in the meantime, even though he found he was unable to concentrate on anything with his mind racing about the night ahead.

When it was finally time to leave, Jacobs wrapped himself in the comforting warmth of his coat, and set off, taking care on the road as could still feel the after-affects from the ale.

On Polly's instructions, Jacobs parked as close to the wood as he could, making sure that his car was in shadow so that it could not be seen from the inn.

He waited inside.

With the engine off, it soon became too chilly to be comfortable, and Jacobs wondered if he would be better off going outside and walking around, to help keep out the cold.

Before he decided, he noticed a door at the top of the fire escape opening, and Polly exiting on to the fire escape.

His stomach churned with excitement.

These were not the actions of a professional police officer, and he knew it. But he put aside all concerns when he saw Polly approaching his car.

She was dressed in a mini skirt, with a puffa jacket zipped up to her neck. She was wearing white pumps, and her long blonde hair was tied back in a ponytail.

She reminded Jacobs of a cheerleader.

He opened his door and slid out from his seat.

When Polly reached him, she threw her arms around his neck and pulled him in for a full kiss.

Jacobs did not resist. He could not, even if he wanted to.

When they pulled apart, Polly took him by the hand and led him into the woods.

"Come on," she coaxed. "There's a lovely spot a few hundred yards in. No one will disturb us there."

Jacobs followed along like a puppy being led by its owner.

Sure enough, after a few hundred yards, they reached a clearing surrounded by undergrowth on all sides.

Jacobs could hear the soft lapping of the water from the lake, just over the next ridge.

There was a half-moon sitting above them, which cast a peculiar range of shadows across the clearing. For a moment, Jacobs was convinced that he could see figures moving behind the bushes in the shadowy moonlight, but before he had a chance to voice his concern, Polly had pulled him down to the ground, and was sitting astride him, kissing and caressing his face and neck with her well-manicured fingers.

Jacobs was lost in the moment.

He responded hungrily to the girl's affections, reciprocating as best he could within the confines of his thick coat.

Jacobs could feel the goose bumps on Polly's thighs as he stroked them, tenderly, slipping his fingers beneath the thin material of her panties, and cupping her small, well-rounded buttocks in his palms.

Polly moaned loudly, responding to his touch.

She helped ease him out of his sheepskin so that it lay beneath them like a soft mattress, and unzipped the top of his tracksuit so that she could gain access to his neck.

After a while, Polly sat up and undid her own jacket, letting it fall behind her on the ground. She was wearing only a flimsy T-shirt underneath and even in this light, Jacobs could tell she had no bra on.

Smiling down at Jacobs, Polly grabbed hold of his hands and slid them underneath the soft fabric so that he could fondle her breasts. She could feel his growing erection beneath her.

Polly started to grind her hips against his rising bulge, sliding back and forth until his eyes told her that he would not be able to hold back for much longer.

Polly moved down Jacob's legs and eagerly pulled down his joggers and released his engorged organ from his shorts. She bent down and took him in her mouth, sliding her tongue along the shaft of his penis, and flicking her tongue along its head.

Jacobs could feel his seed starting to rise.

It was all happening so fast, he was unable to control himself.

For a brief second, it occurred to Jacobs that he did not have any condoms on him.

He wondered if perhaps Polly had thought of it.

He wanted to ask her, but before the words could form in

his mouth, Polly slipped off her knickers and guided Jacobs inside her.

It was too late now. All caution was well and truly cast to the wind. Jacobs held back as long as he could, while Polly gyrated on top of him.

He ran his hands up and down her spine, feeling the tender, smooth flesh beneath his fingers.

Polly grabbed him by the hair with one hand, and leaned forward as she too began to reach orgasm.

Jacobs thrust upwards to meet each one of her movements. Their bodies moved together in perfect synchronisation to create the legendary beast with two backs. So engrossed in the moment was he, that Jacobs was completely unaware that just behind him there was gathered a small army of creatures, each watching the scene with only one thought between them. To feast on him once the union was complete.

Jacobs managed to hold back just long enough for Polly to reach orgasm. When he finally released his torrent, he let out a small cry of fulfilment.

Polly leaned forward and covered his face with her naked breasts, mashing them against him as his eager tongue sought out one of her nipples.

She lifted her head and stared at the creatures, who were readying themselves for the attack that was to follow.

Polly gave a subtle shake of her head and Gobal immediately understood the message.

He turned on the spot and melted back into the darkness, followed by the rest of his pack.

WHEN POLLY RE-ENTERED the inn via the fire escape, her mother was waiting for her in the shadows.

She grabbed the startled girl roughly by the wrist, and swung her around until her back was against the nearest wall.

"Where the 'ell 'ave you been, young lady?"

Polly knew instantly that her mother already knew the answer to her own question. Even so, she thought there might just be a possibility that she had only noticed her missing after she had left, had therefore had not seen her meet with Jacobs in the car park.

"I was just going out for a walk, mama," she lied, trying to hold her mother's suspicious gaze. "You know I like to get some fresh air before bed."

Mavis Beanie leaned in closer until they were almost touching noses. She closed her eyes and began to inhale deeply.

When she opened her eyes again, Polly could tell that her game was up.

"Yer think I'm stupid, girl," her mother spat. "I can smell 'im all over yer."

Polly gulped. "It was only a bit of fun, mama. No harm came of it."

Mavis squeezed her daughter's wrist until the girl began to yelp.

"Ow, mama, you're hurting me," she pleaded, already suspecting that it would fall on deaf ears.

Without responding, Mavis marched off down the corridor towards the first room. Once there, she flung open the door and dragged Polly in after her.

The woman plonked herself down on the corner of the bed and yanked her daughter across her lap.

"Now then, my girl," she said, "I warned you what would 'appen if yer went with that copper, didn't I?"

"But mama," Polly protested, "he's really nice, he's not like the others, I promise."

"Shut up," Mavis snapped. "You was warned, and now yer goin' to get it."

With that, she lifted Polly's mini skirt up, and pulled her panties down past her thighs, revealing the girls naked bum cheeks.

"Now hold still," Mavis commanded, "or I'll fetch me slipper."

The threat was enough to make Polly bury her face in the bed covers to stop herself from crying out. As hard as her mother's spankings were, she knew from experience that her slipper hurt even more.

As Mavis slapped her right palm down on her daughter's bare bottom, over and over, she grunted with the effort. After 10 spanks, her hand was starting to sting, but she refused to give up until she was sure her daughter had learned her lesson.

Once the spanking was over, Mavis allowed Polly to stand up.

"Now then my girl, 'ave you learned your lesson proper?" she enquired, using the emphasis in her voice to ensure that her daughter knew there was only one acceptable answer.

Polly stood rubbing her sore bottom with both hands, and nodded.

"Yes Mama," she replied softly.

Mavis could see two trails of tears leading down her daughter's face. She pulled her down gently, and Polly fell to her knees, resting her head to one side on her mother's lap.

The woman began to stroke her daughter's hair gently.

"There, there, come on now, it's all over," Mavis coaxed. "You know you done wrong, an' you've bin punished, so let's 'ave no more to say about it."

"Yes Mama," Polly responded, her voice muffled by her mother's dressing gown.

"Yer know 'ow careful we 'ave t'be, yer've always known.

We're not like other folk, we can't just pick an' choose 'oo we see an' 'oo we don't."

Polly nodded her understanding once more.

Once Polly's tears were dry and she had stopped snuffling, her mother gave her a hug and a kiss and sent her off to bed.

Mavis hoped that this would be the last of the matter.

But something deep down told her that was not going to be the case.

22

Sometime during the night, Karen felt the covers being pulled back as Dan joined her.

The fire had burnt out, so she figured it must be several hours since she had left him downstairs.

His body felt like ice as he snuggled up to her, wrapping his arms around her for warmth.

Karen suddenly caught a whiff of his breath. The smell was pungent enough to make her gag. She surmised that he had probably thrown up during the night, but had not bothered to brush his teeth afterwards.

She turned her head and buried her face in the pillow to tray and block out the stink.

They were woken early the next morning by Charlotte crying.

Reluctantly, Karen threw back the covers and shivered as she went to the crib to see to her daughter.

Dan stirred, then turned over and went back to sleep.

Karen pulled on some joggers and wrapped her dressing gown around her shoulders for warmth, then sat with Charlotte to feed her.

She watched Dan as he slept.

So far, this had not turned out to be the romantic weekend she was promised, but she hoped that Dan would at least have learned his lesson, and stop after his second pint next time.

It took a while for Charlotte to settle after her feed so, by the time Karen managed to slip back into bed, the sun was starting to appear outside the window.

The sound of Dan coughing and spluttering brought Karen out of her dream.

She looked at her phone on the table next to her and saw that it was already 11 o'clock. She turned to see Dan on his knees beside the bed, his head buried in the mattress as he tried to stifle another fit of coughing.

Karen felt a twinge of guilt that she did not feel a tad more sympathetic towards her boyfriend. But then, she comforted herself that it was his fault, after all, thinking that he could handle more drink than was good for him, like some adolescent teenager trying to impress his mates.

The noise that Dan was making, finally woke Charlotte, and the baby began screaming to announce the fact.

Karen slid her legs from under the covers. She noticed that she had kept her track pants on after waking up earlier to feed her daughter, and she was glad of it now as the cottage was as cold as ice.

As Dan sloped off to the bathroom to empty his stomach again, Karen pulled on a jumper and slipped her feet into her fleece-lined ankle boots. She grabbed her dressing gown from the chair she had draped it over earlier and put it on, wrapping the cord around her waist and tying it in a bow.

She picked Charlotte up and held her over her shoulder, cradling her neck with her hand.

Karen carried her daughter downstairs and sat in the armchair where Dan had fallen asleep the previous night.

She pulled her dressing gown apart and lifted her jumper

to see if Charlotte wanted feeding. The baby immediately began to suckle hungrily, so Karen leaned back in the chair and let her daughter drink her fill.

After a while, Dan struggled down the stairs, looking very much the worse for wear. He had pulled on the same clothes he had been wearing the day before and, from his wet hair, Karen surmised he had been splashing water on his face after throwing up.

Although his condition was of his own making, Karen could not help but feel sorry for him when she saw the hangdog expression on his face.

"What in name of all that's holy was I drinking last night?" he asked pitifully.

"Something called home brew, I think the landlady said it was called. I take it you're not a fan?"

Dan slumped down in the armchair opposite Karen, and held his head in his hands.

"I'd offer to make you some strong black coffee," Karen said, "but I'm afraid someone else needs my attention even more."

Dan looked up and realised what she was alluding to. He attempted a smile, but he only made it half way.

Once Charlotte had finished her feed, Karen carried her over to Dan. "Can I trust you to look after her while I make us both a coffee?" she asked, trying to keep the sarcasm from her voice. She really did feel sorry for him, but she was still concerned that he might not be capable enough to take care of Charlotte right now.

Dan nodded, and held out his arms.

Karen carefully placed Charlotte against his shoulder, and waited for him to wrap his arms around her before she let go.

She made them both some strong black coffee and brought it back in to Dan.

Karen placed their mugs on the small table next to each of

their chairs and, before she retrieved her daughter, she lit the fire and replaced the metal guard.

By now, Charlotte had managed to doze off in Dan's arms, so Karen took her and placed her in her carry-cot to sleep.

She took her seat, and watched Dan trying desperately to sip his scolding coffee before it had started to cool.

The air in the cottage began to warm up almost immediately as the heat radiated out

from the crackling logs.

They stayed there watching the fire until they had finished their coffee.

"Better?" asked Karen.

"A little," Dan agreed, "I don't suppose you have any painkillers on you, by any chance?

Karen shook her head. "Sorry, I usually keep a supply at home, but didn't think to bring them with me."

"Not to worry," Dan sat forward in his chair, rubbing his temples. "I might have to go and find a chemist."

"Is it that bad?" Karen enquired, wondering if she should volunteer for the trip, as she was by far the steadier of the two of them, at this moment.

Dan nodded his head in response. "I think I may be in the grip of the mother of all hangovers," he admitted.

Karen glanced over at the carry-cot. It was not that she did not trust Dan to be responsible with Charlotte but, given his present condition, she was still concerned that he might trip over, or stumble, carrying her back to his chair if she woke up while Karen was out.

The other option was to put her in her pram, but that was still in the boot of Dan's car, and she would need Dan's assistance to take it out.

Added to that, and she hated to admit it, even to herself, but she found the village a little creepy. On their way back from the inn last night, she felt sure that people were watching them from the shadows.

A couple of times, while she was attempting to keep Dan upright, she had looked up and could have sworn that she saw people dart behind hedges up ahead.

It was almost as if the entire village was curious to see who the strangers were.

Karen concluded that such behaviour might not be that out of the ordinary in such a small community, where everyone knew everyone, and newcomers were always to be treated with suspicion.

But, all the same, it still unnerved her enough that she did not fancy venturing out alone, even in broad daylight.

Then, she had another idea. "How about if I fix us some breakfast?" she offered. "Some egg, bacon and fried bread might just help to soak up all that alcohol."

Dan held up his hand for her to stop talking, and slapped his other one against his mouth.

Karen took the hint. "Not a great idea then?"

Dan shook his head.

After a few moments longer, Karen stood up. "Another coffee?" she asked, "I could do with one."

Dan shook his head once more. "No thank you," he groaned, "I think once you get back, I'll go and look for that chemist before this hangover ruins our entire day."

DAN SPENT the best part of an hour searching in vain for a chemist. He managed to find a newsagent at the far end of the village, and the owner informed him that the nearest chemist would mean a drive into town.

Dan knew he was in no fit state for that right now.

He managed to buy some paracetamol from the newsagent and a bottle of water, so at least there was something inside him fighting his hangover. It was not much, but it would have to do for now.

It was a clear day, with low cloud, but at least it was dry and not too cold. So, instead of walking back along the main road to the cottage, he decided to take a longer route through the woodland, and down by the lake. As he was unfamiliar with the area, he followed the signs, and it was not long before he could see the water through the trees.

The sight of open water had always had a calming effect on him, ever since he was a child, so Dan hoped that perhaps a couple of minutes by the lake might help the tablets do their job.

There was no one on the lake, which Dan found a little odd.

It was almost afternoon and he would have thought that those who owned boats in the vicinity would have looked forward to the weekend to take them out.

There were bound to be fish in the lake, and as there were no signs forbidding fishing, Dan also found it strange that no one seemed to be taking advantage of the mild weather.

Dan found a suitable tree stump and sat down to listen to the sound of the water lapping against the shoreline.

This was certainly not how he imagined Karen and he would be spending their romantic weekend away. What's more, he knew that it was all his fault. He would have some making-up to do, once he was feeling more human again.

After about 10 minutes, the paracetamol started to kick in.

Dan leaned forward with his elbows resting on his knees, and watched the ripples on the water as a flock of ducks waddled by in the distance.

He could feel himself starting to drift off.

"Hello again," said a cheerful voice beside him.

Startled, Dan sat up, and saw Jodie standing next to him.

"Oh, hello," he said, only vaguely remembering the young girl from the restaurant.

"What are you doing out here, all alone?" she asked, placing the wicker basket she was carrying down on the ground. "Please tell me you haven't had a fight with your girlfriend?"

Dan laughed. "No," he assured her, "nothing like that. I just needed a walk to clear my head. Your mother serves a mean pint of beer, and no mistake."

Jodie laughed. "That she does," she agreed. "You're not the first person I've known to suffer the after-effects of too much home brew."

Dan glanced down at the girl's basket. It was covered with a chequered cloth, so he could not see what the contents were.

"What's in there?" he asked, nodding towards it. "Are you going on a picnic?"

Jodie seemed to have to think for a moment before she answered.

"No, not as such," she answered. "I am going to see a friend of mine who's not feeling well. I'm taking her some supplies from my mama."

Jodie began to rub the crook of her arm where the handle of the basket had lain.

Dan could see the red mark it had left.

"That looks sore," he observed. "Is it heavy?"

Jodie nodded. "It is a little, my mama always makes too much, but my friend can't get out at the moment and I don't have time to make two trips. I still have my chores back at the inn to do."

Dan felt sorry for the girl.

Now he remembered, she had been very attentive to them the previous evening, and she appeared to dote on little Charlotte.

"I don't want to intrude," he said, "but would you like me to help you carry your basket to your friend's place? It looks like your poor arm could do with a rest."

Jodie's eyes lit up. "Would you?" That would be so kind. It's not far," she assured him.

Dan hoisted himself off his stump.

As he bent down to pick up the basket, Jodie leaned in and gave him a kiss on his cheek.

Dan smiled at the girl and felt himself blush a little.

He held out his arm. "Lead the way young lady," he said.

They walked together for about 15 minutes, with Jodie chatting animatedly for most of the time. She seemed extremely curious to know what he and Karen were doing in the village, and how they came to be there.

Eventually, they left the lake and Jodie took Dan along a path which was so well hidden that, if she had not known it was there, Dan would have never seen it.

They walked up the hill, through the bushes, some of which were taller than Dan.

His original plan had been to just drop Jodie off at the door of her friend's house, but now he was afraid he might need her to find his way back.

As they entered the woods, the trees that towered over them blocked out most of the daylight, making it almost appear as if it were dusk, rather than early afternoon.

"Almost there," Jodie announced brightly.

Dan stopped and looked around them.

They seemed to be in the middle of nowhere.

Before he had a chance to enquire as to what she meant by "there", Jodie grabbed him by the hand and pulled him towards what looked like a large mound of earth, off to one side.

On closer inspection, Dan saw that it was actually a rock formation that appeared to be covered in thick moss, almost as if it had been camouflaged to conceal it.

Dan looked on quizzically as Jodie produced a torch from her pocket and switched it on.

Satisfied that the beam was strong enough, she tugged on Dan's hand, but this time, he refused to budge.

"Hold on a second," he objected. "Where exactly are we going now?"

Jodie turned back, and smiled. "This is the entrance to a tunnel," she informed him. "It leads to the other side of the hill, saves us going up and over. My friend is only a few minutes away now."

Jodie could tell by Dan's hesitation that he was not altogether convinced by her explanation.

He looked around them apprehensively.

There was no one else in sight.

In fact, now that he came to think of it, they had not passed anyone since they set off from the lake.

Jodie's brows knitted. "What's wrong?" she asked.

Dan felt a little foolish that he was so uneasy about entering the structure when young Jodie showed no such apprehension.

"Maybe it would be better if we took the long way over the hill?" he suggested.

"That's silly," Jodie chided. "It's only a couple of minutes through the tunnel, but it takes ages over the hill and back, and I need to be back soon, for my chores."

Dan could not hide his reluctance to venture forward.

Jodie sighed, and held out her hand towards the basket. "It's OK," she assured him. "If you're afraid of going through, I can take it the rest of the way. But I am very grateful for all your help, I always struggle to carry it this far when I'm alone. It's not too bad when Polly comes with me, then we take it in turns, but she was too busy this morning."

Dan squeezed her hand. "Don't be silly," he said, reassuringly. "I can't let you lug this thing the rest of the way. That's what you've got me for." He winked.

Jodie smiled, and turned to lead the way through the entrance of the cave.

Once inside, Jodie's torch was soon the only illumination they had to see where they were going.

Dan's trepidation about this part of the venture was as strong as ever, and he found himself holding on to Jodie's hand for dear life.

He felt ridiculous that he, a grown man, should be scared of using this route, when it was obvious that little Jodie had used it countless times before and she was not in the least bit frightened.

Dan knew he would never have forgiven himself if he had sent the girl in here alone, regardless of how confident she was, or how many times she might have been this way in the past.

They meandered around the various twists and turns chiselled out of the rock, and Dan had the distinct impression that the farther in they went, the deeper underground they were going.

Jodie chattered on regardless, her sweet voice echoing back at him from the solid walls and ceiling.

From up ahead, Dan could see a light emanating from around the next bend.

He heaved a huge sigh of relief that they were finally heading towards daylight, and a way out.

As they neared the turning, Dan could see shadows dancing on the walls, cast no doubt by the light ahead. It seemed odd to him that daylight alone could cause such an effect, but Jodie seemed unconcerned and continued to lead the way, pulling him along behind her.

When they finally made the turn, the sight that met Dan's eyes was enough to make him reel back in shock. The light he had seen came from a fire, rather than daylight.

Sitting around the fire were a dozen or so creatures, the like of which Dan had never set eyes on before. As they came into view, the creatures all turned in his direction and, one by one, they began to rise to their feet.

Jodie let go of Dan's hand and walked towards the largest of the creatures.

Dan was in a quandary.

His instinct was to flee but at the same time, he was afraid for Jodie who clearly did not seem to appreciate the danger they were in.

Dan looked on in astonishment, as Jodie reached the mammoth creature and proceeded to try and hug him, even though her slight arms could nowhere near reach around the thing's massive chest.

Dan opened his mouth to call out to her, but he could not find his voice. His vocals cords were as frozen as his legs appeared to be.

He saw Jodie mouth something to the monster before her, but he was too much in shock to hear her words.

As if on some silent signal, the creatures all converged on Dan.

At the last second, he found his legs again, but it was too late. Dan turned to run, but before he could take a single step forward, the mob was upon him.

He heard his bones crack, and felt the searing pain as his limbs were ripped from his body.

Then, mercifully, death claimed him.

23

JACOBS DRAINED HIS THIRD CUP OF COFFEE FOR THE MORNING. Usually, he tried to space his caffeine consumption throughout the day, but he had slept badly, hardly at all, if he was honest, and he needed the boost to bring him back to life.

One of the many disadvantages of his profession was a distinct propensity to overconsume hot beverages, at least until it was deemed appropriate to switch to alcohol.

That decision, he knew from past experience, was one that varied greatly, depending on how much pressure he was under during any particular investigation.

He knew of colleagues back in Liverpool who, over time, had slipped into the habit of adding a shot of scotch to their first tea or coffee of the morning and, for some, that crutch was the only thing that made it possible for them to cope.

Jacobs, however, was not so much stressed as he was confused.

His tryst with Polly the previous night had left him with a jumble of emotions he could not understand.

Jacobs was an attractive man for his age, and although he had often been on the receiving end of welcome glances from members of the opposite sex, he knew that his pulling power did not extend to beautiful young women such as Polly.

If he was honest, the only time in recent years when women as young as Polly had made any such advances towards him, was when he was seconded to the vice squad, and then it was only from young toms looking to make a deal to avoid arrest.

Jacobs was in no doubt that Polly had made a play for him, and not the other way round. For a start, he would not have had the courage, or the confidence, to ask her out in the first place, let alone suggest that they take a midnight stroll down to the lake.

He had often heard tell of young girls who had what was known as "daddy issues", that was to say they always seemed to go for men several years older than them, and not out of desperation, more out of choice.

If that were the case with Polly, so be it. If her feelings lasted a month, a year, or for ever, so be it. In any case, Jacobs was already smitten by the young girl. But what he needed to be careful of, he warned himself, was falling desperately in love with her, only to end up with a broken heart.

Their age difference was not that unusual in this day and age. He had read hundreds of stories about young girls falling in love and marrying men much older than themselves. But then, the objects of their affections tended to be very rich older men, and their union often did not last much past a year before they were fighting over the spoils in a divorce court.

Well, he was certain that Polly was not after his money. He had none, and she probably realised that from his job, and the fact that he was working from such a modest station in a rural district such as this.

Then what was it that she found so attractive about him?

Jacobs checked himself for wasting so much thought and effort on the subject.

It was probably only a one-time thing, anyway. Maybe Polly

was the kind of girl who tried it on with all newcomers to the area, just for her own sport and entertainment.

Nothing wrong with that, as far as he was concerned. Nonetheless, he could not deny that he hoped there was more to it than that.

His mobile sprang into life on the table next to him.

"Jacobs," he answered.

"Good morning, sir," came the professional response. Jacobs immediately recognised the voice of one of his desk sergeants. "I'm sorry to bother you on the weekend, but we've had a call from Pete Craven, the butcher."

"Oh yes?"

"He said he spoke to you yesterday concerning the disappearance of his sons."

"Well, to be accurate, I spoke to him about it. He didn't seem that concerned either way. Why, what's he saying now?"

"Apparently, they still haven't surfaced, and he finds that odd as Saturday is his busiest day, and the boys have never let him down like this before."

Jacobs rubbed his eyes to clear away the sleep.

"Is he ready to make a formal missing-persons report?" Jacobs asked, already suspecting what the answer would be.

To his surprise, the sergeant answered, "Not exactly. I asked him that same question, naturally, but he just kept saying he wanted to speak to you again, in person."

Jacobs groaned. "Was he at least prepared to come into the station?"

"Well, he said he wanted you to go back to his shop. There was something he wanted to show you."

"Right."

"I didn't want to insist he came down here, just in case whatever he had to show you had some pertinent bearing on the case. But I can call him back if you want?"

"No, that's all right, Sergeant, I need some fresh air."

"Right you are, sir. Shall I call ahead and let him know you're on your way?"

Jacobs thought for a moment as he struggled out of his chair.

"No, don't worry, I won't be long. Besides, he had ample opportunity yesterday to take the matter seriously, so another hour shouldn't make any difference."

Within the hour, Jacobs had showered and dressed, and was on his way to the butcher's. He did not bother to shave, as he liked to give his skin a rest at weekends, when he could.

By the time he was parked up outside, it was almost one o'clock, and there was only one customer in the shop.

Jacobs walked in and waited patiently while Pete served her.

The woman was talking nineteen to the dozen about her husband and his lumbago, and how difficult it was for him to struggle out of the door each morning to go to work, and how she thought he was milking it as an excuse not to help her around the house.

Once he had wrapped her meat, and given back her change, Pete cut her off in mid-sentence and told her he needed to speak to Jacobs, urgently.

The woman turned around and looked at Jacobs, clearly put out by the fact that he was the cause of her not being able to finish her conversation.

Once Pete had ushered her out of the door, he locked it and turned the sign around to show he was closed.

The butcher looked somewhat sheepish to Jacobs as he asked the officer to follow him into the flat above the shop.

Once they reached the top of the stairs, Pete led the way along the landing to the boys' bedroom.

It was obvious from the state of the room that Pete allowed his lads to live in their own mess if they so desired. The two beds at either end of the room were unmade, with the duvets slung back, half hanging on the floor.

There were piles of dirty clothes littered throughout the room, mingled with shoes and muddy boots and trainers, none of which appeared to Jacobs ever to have been cleaned.

The fact that Pete made no excuse for the state of the room told Jacobs all he needed to know about their domestic arrangements.

Pete walked over to a chest of drawers that stood to one side of the room.

He opened the top drawer, and produced a small Ziploc plastic sandwich bag and held it up for Jacobs to see.

Jacobs walked over to where the butcher stood, and surveyed the bag and its contents.

It appeared to be half full of marijuana.

Jacobs looked back at Pete. The butcher could not hold his gaze, and looked at the floor. His overall body language showed how uncomfortable he felt about the situation.

Jacobs took the bag from him, opened the zip, and sniffed at the contents.

"It's pot, all right," he confirmed, before resealing the bag and passing it back to Pete.

Pete looked back at him, his face turning crimson.

"Do... Do you think they might be involved in some kind of drugs gang?" he asked, sheepishly. "You hear about these things goin' on all the time."

Jacobs fought hard with himself not to laugh.

It was obvious from his demeanour that Pete had thought long and hard about this, before calling him over.

"Based on the evidence I've seen here," he answered, "I'd say it was more likely that your lads enjoyed an occasional bit of puff behind your back." He pointed at the plastic bag. "But there isn't even enough there to arrest them for intention to supply, so I very much doubt that they are involved in anything quite so shady as a drugs cartel."

Jacobs could see the big man's shoulders relax.

Pete released a huge sigh. "When I found this," he explained, "I thought the silly buggers 'ad got themselves caught up in somethin' dodgy, and perhaps that's why they 'aven't come 'ome."

"So I take it you haven't heard anything from either of them yet?"

Pete shook his head. "Nah, nothin'. That's why I started to panic when I found this gear," he held up the bag for emphasis. "Well this little lot's goin' straight down the toilet, that'll teach 'em."

"In light of the fact that they still haven't contacted you, would you like me to open an official missing-persons report on them?" Jacobs asked, feeling that Pete was likely to be more responsive than yesterday.

The butcher thought for a moment, rubbing his unshaven chin with his hand.

"Nah, don't bother – they'll turn up."

Jacobs was surprised by his answer, but Pete knew his sons better than he did, so all he could do for now was offer advice, and make himself available if he was needed.

Even so, he felt it was his duty to express his concerns to their dad.

"Are you quite sure you don't want to make it official just yet?" he asked, giving Pete another opportunity to change his mind. "If you have any inkling where they might be, I'd be happy to check it out."

Pete looked at him. "Little sods left me short on my busiest mornin'. One of me Saturday workers called in sick as well, I was right rushed off me feet."

He seemed still to be pondering Jacobs's offer of assistance.

After a moment, Jacobs offered. "You said to me yesterday

that they nicked some of your best meat to sell on to someone. Have you any idea who that might be?"

Pete thought for a moment. "Well, I don't like to sound racist, I'm really not like that, but there are some very dodgy takeaway places down along the coast, and God alone knows what they're sellin'. I bet they'd jump at the chance to get their 'ands on some decent meat."

Jacobs nodded. "I see, nowhere near here you can think of, though?"

Pete's brows furrowed.

He stared into space for a moment before answering. "Well, now you mention it... Nah, they wouldn't, don't worry," he said, thinking better of it.

But Jacobs was not willing to let the subject go just yet. Even if it did not lead to anything now, it might be useful information as a starting point.

"No, go on Pete, where were you thinking of?" He urged.

Pete sighed. "Well there's a place in Thorndike, just outside of town, I've 'eard they sell the most wonderful pies there, but some of me customers 'ave been there fer dinner, and say they've seen some odd goin's-on taking place round the back."

"Did any of them elaborate?"

"'Ow d'yer mean?" Pete looked at the detective curiously.

"Did any of them say exactly what they saw that made them suspicious?"

Pete shook his head. "Nah, just that the owner seemed to be collectin' meat from a large container out back, an' when they looked closely, they said it was not properly wrapped, or sealed, or anythin'. Made them wonder 'ow safe it was to eat."

Jacobs nodded.

It was not much of a lead, but it was something.

If he was honest, it was also an excuse to visit the inn and maybe see Polly again.

At least then he would know by her reaction if last night was a one-off, or the start of something more permanent.

———

WHEN JACOBS ENTERED THE BEANIES' inn the smattering of regulars in the bar turned their heads in his direction once more.

This time, however, their gaze did not linger, and they soon returned to their drinks.

Mavis Beanie gave Jacobs a wide smile as he approached the bar.

"Hello my lovely, nice to see you back 'ere again," she grinned. "Pint of the usual, is it?"

Jacobs shook his head while he removed his badge from his inside pocket, to show her.

"No thank you," he replied. "I wonder if I might speak to the proprietor for a moment?"

Mavis did not bother to study the ID card. She merely glanced at it, her smile fading slightly.

"What seems to be the trouble?" she asked, frowning slightly.

Jacobs kept his best professional face on, although, he allowed the corners of his lips to lift just a tad. The last thing he wanted to do was alienate anyone working at the inn unnecessarily. After all, they were bound to be friends and family of Polly's and, for now at least, he hoped that he might become a regular fixture there.

"It's nothing to concern yourself with," he assured Mavis. "I'm just making some general enquiries concerning local food outlets, and this place just happens to be within the remit of my investigation."

"Oh, I see," she replied, clearly not convinced everything

was as innocent as he was making out. “Well, my ’usband is the proprietor. If you wait ’ere I’ll go an’ get ’im for yer.”

Jacobs nodded his appreciation, and Mavis disappeared through the doors which led into the restaurant area.

Jacobs stayed at the bar, moving to one side to allow drinkers to gain access. There were a couple of young girls serving, who Jacobs surmised must be extra weekend staff.

Mavis Beanie strode through the restaurant, forcing a smile as she acknowledged some of the lunchtime diners.

Jodie was busy serving, along with a couple of part-time waiters whom they hired from an agency to help cover busy periods.

When Mavis entered the kitchen, Polly was setting out a tray with vegetables and gravy. She smiled when she saw her mother enter. But her smile faded the minute she saw the cross expression on her face.

Without saying a word, Mavis grabbed her eldest daughter by the arm and dragged her over to the ovens, where Thad Beanie was in the process of taking out a batch of freshly baked pies.

His initial smile faded, too, the instant he saw his wife’s countenance.

“What’s up, luv?” he asked, setting the hot pies down on the counter.

Mavis spun her daughter around by her arm, propelling the girl towards her husband.

Polly squealed in pain and almost lost her footing, but her father managed to catch her and keep her upright.

Thad Beanie stared at his wife. “What the ’ell is goin’ on?” he demanded. “You nearly ’ad the girl over.”

Mavis planted her chubby fists firmly on her hips. Her breathing was laboured. “Why don’t you ask that slut of a daughter o’ yours, what she was up to last night, eh?”

Thad looked down at the terrified girl.

Polly looked back at her mother, hurt that she had betrayed her after already punishing her the previous night for her escapade.

"Well, girl?" Thad turned his daughter to face him. Now his expression matched his wife's, but on him, it looked even scarier.

Polly's bottom lip began to tremble and she could feel a couple of tears trickle down her flushed cheeks.

"Out with it!" Thad demanded, grabbing Polly by her shoulders with his huge, calloused hands and shaking her so that her head flipped back and forth.

"Dada, I'm sorry," Polly sobbed, "I didn't mean nothin' by it."

"By what?" Polly could tell her father was on the verge of exploding, and she needed to start explaining before he passed the point of no return.

"She was out last night with a copper, if yer please," Mavis chimed in, unable to watch the scenario unfolding before her, even though she was its instigator.

Thad stared deeply into his daughter's eyes. He could tell immediately that his wife was not joking.

"A copper!" he growled, his grip tightening on Polly's shoulders.

"An' now," continued Mavis, "'e's outside in the bar, wantin' to speak to you about summat to do wiv our food."

Thad's nostrils flared, and he looked as if he were about to breath fire.

When he was this angry, his eyeballs always seemed to turn black and an inhuman stare radiated from them, something that Polly had witnessed only once before.

"I'm sorry, Dada," she repeated, the words barely making it passed her tears.

Thad bared his teeth and grunted before shoving his daughter to one side.

Polly's shoulder slammed into the oven door, but she was too distressed even to notice the pain.

Thad took several deep breaths to try to calm himself before he marched past his wife and headed for the restaurant.

Once he was gone, Polly looked at her mother, the figure a blur before her eyes.

Mavis shook her head. "What 'ave you done now, girl?" she asked, sighing.

Polly threw herself into her mother's arms and sobbed into her apron.

Mavis folded her fleshy arms around her weeping daughter. She was already starting to feel sorry for telling her husband about Polly's nocturnal pursuits. Neither she nor her husband had ever frowned upon their daughter's sexual appetite. In fact, they had positively encouraged it.

From the time their daughters had reached puberty, they had allowed them to mate with their cousin Gobal and the rest of the tribe. Such was the way with their kind – procreation meant everything. And whether they produced a human-like offspring or another bestial one did not matter – the important thing was keeping their kinfolk flourishing.

The outside world would never understand their ways, and the Beanie clan did not care one way or the other.

Those who were born to the tribe stayed with the tribe and lived life underground, away from prying eyes. On the other hand, those who turned out human lived among the rest of society in various guises. But they all helped one another and never forgot their roots.

Above all, they stayed well away from those in authority, and never gave them a reason to interfere with their way of life.

That was their first rule of survival, and Polly should have known better than to lie with one of them, without making sure they were taken care of by the tribe afterwards.

Mavis let Polly sob out her tears before holding her out at arm's length and wiping away what was left with her thumbs.

"Now," she began, sympathetically, "you go an' wash yer face, and get back out there to see to our customers, understand?"

Polly nodded dejectedly.

"I'm going back to the bar to see what this copper wants wiv yer dada. I only hope it doesn't lead to anything, that's all."

"I'm sorry, Mama," Polly whispered, her tiny voice barely audible from all the crying.

"What possessed yer to leave 'im alive once yer'd 'ad yer fun, girl? That's what I can't understand."

Polly shrugged her tiny shoulders. "I think I may love 'im, Mama. I'm sorry."

Mavis stood back, clearly startled by her daughter's revelation.

"Love 'im!" she cried. "By all the stars, yer only met 'im five minutes ago. What the 'ell 'as got into you, girl?"

Polly had no answer to offer. Instead, she just gazed into her mother's eyes and gave her a half-smile.

Mavis shook her head in disbelief. Her suspicions from the previous night were bearing fruit, and it did not bode well for the clan.

24

When Thad entered the bar, cheers erupted from the drinkers assembled there.

There were shouts of, "Come an' 'ave a pint with us," and, "Thad, over 'ere, mate," from the regulars. But Thad simply waved and smiled, while he scanned the area for Jacobs.

Finally, he noticed a stranger standing by himself at the far end of the bar, without a drink in his hand. He assumed that had to be the copper his wife was referring to.

Thad walked over and offered his hand.

"Thad Beanie, Officer. My wife says you want to 'ave a word with me concernin' our food. I 'ope there 'asn't been any complaints."

Jacobs shook the offered hand. "No, let me assure you, it's nothing like that," he replied, holding Thad's gaze. The innkeeper's hands were like shovels and completely encased Jacobs's one. "Do you think we could go outside a moment?" he asked, retrieving his hand. "It would be a little more private."

Thad nodded. "Lead the way, officer," he said, nodding towards the main door.

Once outside, Jacobs led Thad around to the back of the inn.

He remembered standing there, what seemed like a lifetime ago, when Polly had come out of the back door and caught him loitering around the bin area.

The thought of the young girl caused a stir in his loins, and although there was no way Thad could have noticed it, Jacobs could still feel himself starting to flush a little.

Once they reached the bins, Jacobs turned to Thad.

"I hope you don't mind me dragging you away from your work, but we're investigating a complaint from the food industry watchdog," he lied, trying to keep a straight face. "It appears that some restaurants and takeaways in the vicinity have been buying their meat from, shall we say, some illicit sources."

Thad thought for a second, then shook his head. "Well, it's news to me, Officer – all my meat comes from local farms and legitimate meat outlets. I've got all the paperwork and certificates to prove it, if you'd like to see 'em?"

Jacobs glanced around. There was nothing he could see which matched the description that Pete had given him of an old outhouse.

In fact, the only thing out here at the back, other than the bins and recycling containers, was an old wooden shed. Hardly the place to store meat, Jacobs thought.

All the same, he had to start somewhere.

"Do you mind me asking what you keep in there?" he asked, pointing to it.

"Oh, nothing much really," replied Thad. "A few tools, and a couple of old meat saws."

Jacobs nodded. "Is it all right if I take a look?"

"Not at all," said Thad, glancing around them to see if anyone else was watching. "It's a bit musty in there, so I warn you now, yer nice clean clothes might not smell the same when we come out."

As they approached the shed, Jacobs realised that it was in fact, made of plastic, not wood. The plastic was coloured to make it appear like wood and was very realistic.

There was no padlock on the shed, and Thad slid back the bolt and stood back for Jacobs to inspect the interior.

Jacobs did not notice the crafty sweep of the carpark Thad made, before they entered.

When Jacobs opened the door, he was immediately struck by a strong, rancid odour, which came from within.

So taken by the vile stench was he, that Jacobs did not notice Thad bend down and grab hold of a large club from just inside the door.

Jacobs held his nose between his thumb and forefinger.

"Christ almighty," he said. "You weren't kidding about the smell, were you?"

Thad held the club behind his back, relieved that there were no severed body parts within the shed. This was the dumping ground for Gobal and the rest of the tribe to leave the remains of their victims.

Thad usually checked the shed each morning but, typically, today he had forgotten.

Jacobs looked back at Thad. "What is that smell?" he asked, still holding his nose.

"Well, that comes from the scraps of meat left behind on the old saws," replied Thad, pointing towards the jumble of saws and blades stacked against the far wall of the shed. "I must admit, I didn't bother to clean 'em off when I bought my new electric meat saws last year. Over time, the meat rots and then you get this stink."

It certainly sounded feasible to Jacobs.

"Have you considered getting rid of them?"

Thad nodded. "One of them things on me list – I've just been so busy lately. I'll see to it, though, Officer, rest assured."

Jacobs stepped back and went to close the shed door, hoping that it would at least shut off part of the vile smell.

From behind, Thad raised the wooden club into the air, aiming for the back of Jacobs's head. Before he had a chance to swing it down, a scream from behind caught them both off-guard.

"Dada!" It was Polly.

Thad immediately dropped his arm down to his side.

Jacobs, still unaware of Thad's intentions, watched Polly as she walked towards them from the back door of the inn.

She looked every bit as beautiful and angelic as she had the previous night.

To Jacobs, it still felt somewhat surreal that this gorgeous young girl before him was the same one he had made love to in the woods.

As she drew closer, Jacobs noticed that her face was puffy and tear-stained. His initial instinct was to reach out and hold her but, remembering who was standing beside him, he held himself in check.

Polly smiled at her father, but it seemed a tad strained to Jacobs.

"Mama says she needs you in the kitchen, Dada," she said, keeping her voice steady.

"Oh, right," Thad replied, clearly flustered. He turned back to Jacobs. "I'd better go, the boss is callin'. Why don't you stay for a pint an' a pie, on the 'ouse?" He held up his hand. "That's not meant as a bribe, yer understand, Officer."

Jacobs laughed good humouredly. "Well that's extremely kind of you, I don't mind if I do, thank you."

Under normal circumstances, Jacobs would have refused the offer. He had known of colleagues in similar circumstances who had come unstuck when, further down the line, defence barristers had tried to allege that they had intended to accept a bribe.

But Jacobs was too excited at the prospect of seeing more of Polly, even if it was just to watch her walk back and forth across the restaurant floor, while she served him.

Jacobs smiled at Polly, but to his surprise, she looked down at the ground awkwardly.

He wondered then if perhaps she was not as worldly as he had first thought, and maybe last night's little adventure had left her feeling ashamed.

He sincerely hoped that she was not regretting her actions after all.

"Polly 'ere will show yer the way to yer table. I'd better get meself in," Thad said, before walking back towards the door Polly had just left.

Even now, as Jacobs watched the innkeeper leave, the club in the man's hand did not register in his mind. He was still too focused on Polly.

Once Thad was out of earshot, Jacobs turned to Polly.

"Hello, again," he said, quietly. "Did you have a good night's sleep?"

He knew it was a stupid thing to say, but Jacobs was not sure how to start the conversation. He was still feeling a little awkward that, moments before, her father had been standing next to them.

He presumed from what Polly had told him the previous night, that her parents were none the wiser about their tryst.

Polly nodded her response, but kept her gaze down towards her shoes.

Checking that the coast was clear, Jacobs stretched out and gently touched her under her chin, lifting her face up.

To his surprise, Polly pulled away. "Don't, please," she muttered under her breath.

"I'm sorry," Jacobs replied. "I didn't mean to upset you."

Polly looked up at him, embarrassed.

She looked over she shoulder to check the coast was clear.

Once she was satisfied, she turned back to Jacobs. "My mama and dada know about last night," she confessed, clearly nervous about admitting it.

"Oh, really?" Jacobs was shocked. Officer of the law or not, he was still surprised that neither of Polly's parents had mentioned anything to him this afternoon.

He had merely assumed they were unaware of the matter.

Jacob's sighed. "I take it they weren't all that enamoured when you told them?"

"I didn't tell 'em. Mama was waitin' for me when I got back. She saw me slippin' out to meet you."

"Ah, I see." That was all Jacobs could think of to say. He was feeling particularly foolish, as, due to his age, he felt that he should be man enough to go and speak to Polly's parents and explain himself.

But there was something at the back of his mind that alerted him to the fact that there must be a reason why neither of them had said anything to him already.

Especially Thad.

He had had an ideal opportunity while the two of them were out here alone.

"Is that why you've been crying?" Jacobs enquired. "They didn't... They didn't hurt you, did they?"

Under normal circumstances, Jacobs would not have felt the need to ask such a question.

Polly was, after all, an adult in the eyes of the law, and old enough to make her own choices. But there was something odd about the family dynamic that made him feel uneasy. He could not quite put his finger on what it was, but even the way Polly still called her parents "Mama" and "Dada", at her age, did not seem conventional.

"Polly?" he pressed. "Have they hurt you in some way?"

Polly shook her head. "No," she lied. Her bottom cheeks were still stinging from the spanking she had received last night, and she was dreading the beating she was likely to receive from her father, now that he knew the truth, too.

What's more, he was going to be even madder with her for stopping him from killing Jacobs that afternoon. But as soon as she saw what he was about to do, she had been compelled to shout out, to save her man.

Without another word. Polly rushed forward and fell into Jacob's arms.

Taken aback by her unexpected action, Jacobs hugged her close, and gently kissed the top of her head.

She smelt of a combination of freshly baked bread and those delicious pies her father made.

They stayed together for several minutes, before Polly reluctantly let go.

"Come on," she said, cheerfully. "Let's get you that pie and pint."

With that, she gave him a peck on the end of his nose and led him by the hand back into the inn.

KAREN PUT Charlotte down in her cot. The baby gurgled happily as she stared up into her mother's eyes. Karen stroked her daughter's cheek with the back of her forefinger until the child eventually turned her face and fell asleep.

Karen sat back down in the armchair. She had kept the log fire burning throughout the afternoon, although she had added more wood to it only when it appeared as if it were about to go out.

She did not relish the prospect of using their entire supply on their first day there. Especially as she had no idea where they could find more. She suspected that there might be a shed or some form of shelter out at the back, which might contain extra stock. But as it was already starting to get dark, Karen did not fancy the idea of venturing out there, and stumbling around in the dusky light, having seen how unkempt the back garden was when she peered out earlier.

Dan had been gone now for almost four hours.

By the second hour, Karen was beginning to grow concerned, so she tried to call him, only to find that he had left his mobile behind on the bedroom table.

She waited patiently, watching television or reading some old magazines she found in a cupboard, drinking more coffee than was good for her – anything to help pass the time.

She even managed to doze off for a while in front of the fire.

But now, however, she was convinced that something might have happened to Dan.

Karen knew that he had set off to find a chemist, and if he hadn't been able to do so, he might well have ventured into the town to locate one.

As he had left his mobile behind, it was not inconceivable that the journey might have taken longer than he anticipated, but once there, surely he could have found a taxi or mini-cab to bring him back sooner than this.

With the sky growing darker, Karen decided to draw the curtains and turn on some lights. If nothing else, it gave her some comfort.

She had made herself some bacon and cheese sandwiches earlier in the afternoon, when hunger convinced her that she could no longer wait for Dan's return. Besides which, she was confident that his hangover, even with the intervention of a medical remedy, would not be sufficiently eradicated to allow him to face food.

Although Karen was growing more concerned for Dan's welfare as the afternoon turned to evening, there was a part of her which was still angry at him for overindulging the night before.

Were it not for that, they might have spent the day driving down to one of the towns on the coast, and exploring the myriad quaint lanes, packed with any number of boutiques and independent shops, some of which had doubtless been in the same family for generations.

It would have made a nice change from the hustle and bustle of London, where you had to push and shove your way wherever you went, with no one giving any consideration for the fact that you were carrying a young baby.

This weekend had not, so far at least, turned out to be the romantic getaway Karen had been promised.

Where on earth could Dan be?

As much as she feared that something untoward might have befallen him, a part of her wondered if perhaps he had decided to slope off somewhere for a "hair of the dog", as some people were known to swear by them as an ideal cure for hangovers.

If that were the case, she was not going to be best pleased on his return, and Karen had vowed to make sure he was aware of it.

On the other hand, Karen could not believe that Dan could be so irresponsible.

There was no way he would just leave her and Charlotte alone all day while he was supping beer in some pub.

Which only left one other alternative. Something must have happened to him. The question was, what?

It could be that he had had an accident, perhaps a fall. Maybe he was lying in a ditch somewhere between here and the town, and his cries for help had gone unheard because the road was so remote that nobody had passed him.

Or, he might have been hit by a car, taken to hospital, but no one knew who he was, or how to contact Karen.

But that made no sense. He had his wallet on him, and he

would have credit cards and his driving licence inside, so the authorities would know who he was.

However, that still did not give them a link back to her.

At least if he had had his mobile on him, they could have gone through his call list until they came upon her number.

Karen checked her phone for the umpteenth time that day, but there were no missed calls.

She decided to leave it for another hour, then she would decide what to do.

Karen threw another small log on the fire, and curled up on the armchair, tucking her legs underneath her.

Eventually, she dozed off.

25

MATILDA OPENED HER EYES. THE NOW FAMILIAR SIGHT OF THE cave roof, with the shadows of the open fire dancing across it, came into focus.

She had no idea how long she had been there, and only the vaguest notion of how she came to be in the cave to begin with.

For the most part, Matilda had drifted in and out of consciousness, while the male versions of the hairy cave-dwellers, took it in turns to rape her.

Matilda did not resist any more as resistance was futile. The creatures were far too strong, and there were more of them than she could possibly hope to struggle free from. So instead, she would just lie back and allow them their sport, not bothering to acknowledge their presence, even when there was a change of partner, which occurred several times during each session.

At times, she could hear the creatures mating with each other. Although it always took place out of sight, occasionally Matilda could make out their shadows on the stone walls in front of her. The screeches and cries they made during their mating rituals would, under normal circumstances, have made her block her ears in an attempt to drown out the sound.

But now that, too, had become something her mind refused to register.

The young girl who came to feed her, Jodie, had informed Matilda that she would be looked after and kept safe inside the cave, and that the tribe would ensure that no harm came to her while she was in their care.

In fact, she was, according to Jodie, a vital part of the survival of their clan and, as such, she would be treated with dignity and respect, at all times.

The words never prompted Matilda to respond.

She would sit there, mutely, opening and closing her mouth when Jodie asked her to, so that she could spoon in the hot casserole that she always brought.

In between the times when Matilda was either being fed or molested, her mind preferred to close down completely, thus allowing her body to rest, and recuperate, before the next onslaught.

Within minutes of waking, Matilda could hear the familiar grunts and growls from her hosts, as they somehow seemed to know that she was awake, even though they were all out of sight.

Matilda waited, placidly as, one by one, heads began to peer around the corner of the cave, followed by shuffling and jostling, as the male creatures approached her, eager to continue mating with their compliant partner.

Without thinking, or even acknowledging the action, Matilda spread her legs as wide as she could, ready for the first assailant to take up position.

Once again, her mind carried her away to a distant place, where she would not be able to see of feel the atrocity that was about to befall her.

KAREN STIRRED FROM HER SLUMBER, and picked up her mobile to check the time.

It was a quarter past seven, and she noticed that she had received no messages or calls while she slept, which was hardly surprising as Dan had forgotten to take his phone, and even if he found a call-box, she doubted he could remember her mobile off by heart.

Karen struggled into an upright position, and stretched the cramp out of her limbs.

Beside her, Charlotte lay awake in her crib, looking straight up at her mother, and gurgling happily.

"Hello you," Karen cooed, "and how long have you been awake, eh?"

She reached down and placed her hand on her daughter's tummy, gently rocking the baby from side to side.

Charlotte smiled and chuckled as she played with her.

The fire had nearly died, and Karen could feel the chill of the evening air starting to penetrate the cottage. She considered placing another log on the fire, but then decided there was no point, as she had already made her mind up to go back to the inn, to see if, by chance, they had seen Dan.

The thought of going out was not exactly welcoming, but the inn was only a five-minute walk away, and Karen felt in need of some fresh air, having been cooped up inside all day.

She checked Charlotte's nappy, which appeared to be dry, but decided to change it anyway, just to be on the safe side.

Once she had bundled Charlotte up against the cold, and placed her snugly in her carry-cot, Karen pulled on her coat and gloves, and made sure she had both her mobile and Dan's in her pocket.

Before leaving, she checked to make sure the fire guard was securely in place.

As she opened the front door, an icy draught of air rushed at her, sending a shiver through Karen's body. She steeled herself against the cold, and locked the front door behind her, before setting off down the road.

Although the walk was short, by the time she had reached the inn, Karen was starting to feel in need of something warm and nourishing inside her.

As soon as she opened the main door to enter, the delicious smell of freshly baked pies wafted in from the restaurant, and Karen could feel her stomach grumble in anticipation.

The bar appeared to be even more crowded than the previous evening, which came as no great surprise to her, it being a Saturday night.

Karen caught the eye of the lady behind the bar who had welcomed her and Dan in the previous evening, and as Karen manoeuvred Charlotte's cot through the crowd, the woman came around the bar to meet her.

"Hello again," Mavis Beanie greeted her, "and where's your young man this evening?"

Although the bar was quite noisy, and not the best place to hold a conversation while holding her sleeping daughter, Karen decided to take advantage of having the woman's full attention to make her enquiries.

"Actually," she began, trying to keep her voice low enough so that the men sitting at the nearest table could not overhear. "I was hoping you could tell me."

Mavis stared at her quizzically. "'Ow's that, then?" she asked.

Karen tried to think of the best way to phrase her next sentence, without making it sound as if she and Dan had had a fight, and he had stormed off.

"Well," she began, "he woke up this morning a little worse for wear, and slipped out to find a chemist."

Mavis laughed. "Ah, that'll be my special home brew – it can have that effect."

The woman's raucous laughter made a few drinkers nearby turn in their seats to see what the fuss was about.

Karen was not pleased about the extra attention, but she felt it unwise to ask Mavis to keep her voice down, in her own pub.

"The thing is," Karen continued, "he still hasn't come back, and now I'm starting to get worried."

Mavis's smile was replaced by a deep frown. "Oh, I see, well 'ave you tried callin' 'im?"

Karen nodded. "Yes, I did, but he forgot to take his phone with him. I wondered if perhaps he had dropped in here to ask directions."

Mavis thought for a moment, rubbing her chin, then she shook her head.

"I'm sorry my dear, I certainly 'aven't seen 'im today." Then her face lit up as another idea took hold. "I'll tell yer what, why don't you bring that little sweet'eart o' yours through to the dining room, an' I'll ask me daughters if either of 'em 'ave seen 'im. Yer never know. An' as yer 'ere now, yer can stay fer a bite, on the 'ouse o' course. 'Ow's that?"

Karen's original idea had not been to stay for dinner.

But she had to admit the thought of going back to the cottage for a cheese sandwich did not compare to the succulent dinner on offer.

She nodded her agreement, and Mavis led her through the bar crowd to the restaurant.

Once through the double doors, the atmosphere in the restaurant was much serener than in the pub, with diners focusing on their meals and speaking in quiet voices.

Mavis found them a table, with plenty of room for Charlotte's cot, and rushed off into the kitchen to speak to her daughters.

Minutes later, Jodie came through into the restaurant, carrying a tray of food for another table. She smiled at Karen on route to her destination, and once she had served the couple sitting there, she made a beeline for Karen.

"Hello again," she said, smiling broadly. "Mama says you're looking for your boyfriend, can't believe he'd run off and leave a beautiful woman like you behind."

Karen smiled back. "Thank you," she replied, trying to sound as cheerful as she could.

"Do you mind if I take a peek?" Jodie asked, already leaning over Charlotte's cot.

"Please do, I'm afraid she's just fallen to sleep."

"Oh, what a little angel," said Jodie, holding her hand against her heart. "It makes me feel broody just looking at her, she's so gorgeous."

"Thank you," said Karen, unsure as to why she felt embarrassed by Jodie's comment. But it did sound an strange thing for someone so young to say.

Karen had often heard that country folk spoke and acted differently to townies, so she decided it must just be a figure of speech, and not worth fussing over.

"Now then," Jodie continued, looking up from the cot. "Dada does a special pie for Saturdays, so you're in for a treat. Would you like me to fetch you something to drink?"

"Oh, er, a dry white wine would be lovely, thank you."

"A large one?"

Karen thought for a second, then replied, "Oh go on then." She was having dinner there after all, and this way she wouldn't have to order a second glass.

"Won't be a tick." And with that, Jodie went through into the bar.

Karen took the time to survey the rest of her fellow diners.

She was sure that several of them had been in the previous evening, although she could not swear to it.

If that were the case, then at least it spoke volumes for the quality of the food.

She had to admit, last night's pie was the best she had ever tasted, and, according to Jodie, she was in for another treat tonight.

As Jodie reappeared with Karen's wine, Polly came through the kitchen door and brought Karen her dinner.

"Mama told us you're looking for your young man," Polly said, placing the various dishes of pie and assorted vegetables around Karen's table. "I doubt 'e'll go too far, knowin' 'e 'as you to come back to."

"That's just what I said," Jodie chimed in, handing Karen an extremely large glass of wine.

Once the girls had left her table, Karen stared at the delicious-looking meal that had been laid before her.

It looked as if it was far more than she could manage, but another rumble from her stomach reminded her of just how hungry she was.

As she ate, Karen could not help but look over every time someone came through from the bar. Each time she hoped it would be Dan, having finally returned to the cottage and realising she was out, deciding that the inn was the most logical place to find her.

But on each occasion, she was left disappointed.

As delicious as the food was, Karen was too worried about Dan really to enjoy it.

She accepted a second glass of wine from Polly, almost without realising she was doing it. Karen glanced down at her baby, feeling a slight twinge of guilt as she took a sip from her second glass. Even the wine here was good, and for a house white, it tasted better than some of the expensive stuff she had bought, back when she had a career and a decent wage.

Eventually, Charlotte woke up and started crying.

Karen tried to soothe her, but she was having none of it.

She picked her daughter up out of her cot, and straight away felt that she needed changing.

The other diners smiled whenever they caught her eye. She presumed that many of them could sympathise, having been in the same situation themselves, from time to time.

Mavis appeared beside her, while Karen was checking the baby's changing bag for supplies.

"Oh, dear me, what a noise from such a tiny baba," the woman remarked, leaning over and stroking Charlotte's ear with her finger. "Now then, what's all the fuss about, little one?" she asked, in her most sympathetic tone.

"I think someone needs a change of nappy," Karen informed her. "Do you have any baby-changing facilities down here?"

Mavis laughed, her sizeable girth wobbling with the effort.

"No such luxury, I'm afraid." She stared around the room until she caught Jodie's eye, then signalled for her to come over.

"Oh bless 'er little heart," Jodie said, sidling up to Karen and placing her hand gently on Charlotte's head. "You tell yer aunty Jodie all about it."

To Karen's surprise, Charlotte did seem to respond to the girl's touch. For a moment, she stopped crying and looked up at Jodie, as if in wonder at the appearance of a new face looking down at her.

But, after a moment, she started again. The discomfort of her wet nappy obviously superseded the young girl's affection.

"Now then Jodie, you take the young lady upstairs to one of the rooms, so she can change her baby."

Karen turned back to look at Mavis. "No, really," she replied. "I'm only staying five minutes away. I can just take her home and see to her there."

Mavis shook her head, sternly. "I won't hear anything of the sort, young lady. We've plenty of free rooms upstairs, now take that little treasure upstairs an' sort 'er out, an' let's not 'ear any more of it."

The idea certainly did appeal to Karen.

The thought of carrying Charlotte back along the street, screaming her little lungs out, and then having to change her in what was probably, by now, a freezing cold cottage, did not really appeal.

There was a slim chance that Dan had made his way home, and, for whatever reason, decided to stay put and wait for her, instead of coming out to find her. But right now, Karen preferred Mavis's suggestion overall, and once Charlotte was dry, she could also feed her, and maybe she would drift back to sleep; so, the walk home would be less eventful.

Karen thanked Mavis, and stood up from her chair with Charlotte in her arms.

Before she had a chance to ask, Jodie bent down and picked up the changing bag, slinging the strap over her shoulder.

Karen was too focused on Charlotte to notice the look Mavis gave her daughter, or indeed, the subtle nod the young girl gave in reply.

Once upstairs, Jodie showed Karen into a spacious room, with a double bed and an en-suite bathroom.

The room felt warm and cosy, and Karen could not help but compare it in her mind to the cold, uninviting one she had to look forward to, back at the cottage.

Jodie helped Karen by laying the changing mat down on the bed, and keeping Charlotte amused, while Karen prepared to change her.

Jodie stayed with her while she sorted Charlotte out, keeping her focus mainly on the baby, playing peek-a-boo to take her mind off the ordeal of having her bottom wiped and her nappy changed.

Once Charlotte was clean and dry, Karen sat on the edge of the bed and unbuttoned her blouse, so she could feed her.

Jodie sat beside her, and looked on in admiration. "You're so lucky," she observed. "One day, I hope to have a beautiful baby like yours."

Karen laughed. "There's plenty of time for that," she said, "you should enjoy your freedom while you can. Once you have one of these, your life will never be the same."

Jodie looked surprised. "You don't regret having her, do you?"

Karen shook her head. "I wouldn't say regret, but to be honest with you, she wasn't exactly planned."

"Oh, I see," replied Jodie, thoughtfully. "Did you and your boyfriend get careless?"

"Well, he wasn't really my boyfriend, as such. More like a passing ship, if you take my meaning."

Jodie nodded. "But he seems really happy now," she said, encouragingly. "So at least you know you can count on him."

"Ah, I see what you mean," Karen smiled. "Dan's not Charlotte's father. He and I met later."

"But he is still your boyfriend, so he must love you both, all the same?"

Karen loved the simplicity of the young girl's logic.

She was certainly very mature in her thinking, for one so young, even if she was a trifle simplistic.

"Well," replied Karen, "it's still early days. But you're right, he does seem very fond of us both."

"I think you both look very happy together," Jodie announced, "and he'd be a fool to let you go."

Karen smiled. "That's very sweet of you."

Karen could feel Charlotte had stopped suckling.

She held her over her shoulder and patted her on the back until she burped.

"That's a good girl," Karen said, continuing to stroke her baby's back.

"I think you should both stay here tonight." Jodie suddenly announced, standing up.

The suggestion took Karen a little by surprise.

"Oh, I couldn't do that," she responded. "Besides, I'm only down the road, it's not as if I have to drive anywhere. Not that I could, after all the wine I've had."

"I'm going to talk to mama," Jodie seemed adamant. "We've got plenty of room this time of year, an' you don't want to be walking home alone to a cold, empty house."

Karen had to admit the offer was tempting.

The room was so inviting, she felt as if she could put Charlotte down and fall asleep straight away.

But what if Dan was waiting for her back at the cottage?

Well, it would serve him right for disappearing all day.

No, that was not fair. She had no idea why he had taken so long, but he might have a perfectly reasonable explanation for it.

At the very least, she had to give him the benefit of the doubt.

"I won't hear of it," Jodie announced, walking towards the door. "An' my mama won't either. You're our guest, an' we have a duty to look after you."

Karen could feel herself giving in.

But she knew it was not up to Jodie.

But the longer she stayed in the room, the more enticing the offer sounded.

"OK," she relented, "let me come down and speak with your mum and see if we can sort something out."

"No need," insisted Jodie. "I'll send her up here, you just stay and keep your baby warm, I'll bring up her cot, an' everything will be lovely."

Before Karen could object, Jodie was out of the room, with the door shut behind her.

Karen lay back on the bed with Charlotte on her chest.

The baby was already fighting sleep and, from the look of things, losing the battle.

Five minutes later, there was a knock at the door.

"Come in." Karen sat up to meet her guests, cradling her baby against herself so as to keep her from waking up.

Mavis and Jodie entered the room, both smiling warmly.

The older woman had a small plastic carrier bag in her hand, and a thick cotton nightdress over her other arm. Jodie was holding Charlotte's carry-cot firmly, by the straps, as if it were something valuable that she was afraid of dropping. She made her way over to the bed and peeped over at Charlotte.

"Ah, she's fast asleep. How gorgeous does she look?" she whispered.

Mavis too came over so that she would not have to speak too loudly.

"Now then," she began, keeping her voice down, "Jodie tells me yer thinkin' of leavin' us an' goin' back to that draughty old cottage tonight? Well, me an' Thad won't 'ear of it." With that, she placed the plastic bag on the bed beside Karen.

Keeping a firm hold of Charlotte with one hand, Karen peered into the bag. Inside, she saw a toothbrush, and paste, mouthwash, some cotton wool balls, a bottle of make-up remover, and individual bottles of shower gel, shampoo and conditioner.

"Thank you, that's very kind of you," she said, looking up at Mavis.

"Nonsense," the woman replied. "Now this 'ere is one o' my Polly's nightdresses, it's clean out the wash, an' yer about the same size, so yer welcome to use it."

Karen took the garment, gratefully. "That's lovely, thank her for me."

Mavis grinned, broadly. "Now you settle that beautiful baby o' yours, and I'll be right back with a nightcap. What would be yer poison?"

Karen instinctively went to resist but then, on reflection, after the kind of day she had had, and with Charlotte already fast asleep, a little something to help her sleep might be just what she needed.

"A little brandy might be nice," she smiled.

Jodie busied herself pushing together two large armchairs beside the bed, securing one against the adjacent wall, and then placed Charlotte's carry-cot in the middle.

Karen placed her sleeping daughter inside, and covered her with a blanket.

Just then, Mavis returned with her brandy.

It looked more like a double to Karen, but she did not want to sound ungracious, so she thanked the woman, and both of them left her to sleep.

After finishing her night-time ablutions, Karen came back into the bedroom, and slipped on the borrowed nightdress. It was a perfect fit.

She checked on the sleeping Charlotte once more, before turning on the bedside lamp, and switching off the overhead light.

Karen selected a book from the small bookcase that sat in the corner of the room, and climbed between the sheets.

She read as far as chapter two before knocking back her night-cap.

Karen finally dozed off halfway through the next chapter, with the book lying upon her chest.

26

Once the last of the staff had been seen out of the door, Thad Beanie sat down with his nightly pint of home brew in front of him, and called his elder daughter over to him.

Polly, who had been replenishing the salt and pepper shakers for the following day, obediently walked over to her father's table, and sat down opposite him.

Thad stared into his daughter's eyes, but she was unable to hold his gaze.

He took another long swig from his glass, almost emptying it, and placed it back down in front of him.

"Now then my girl," he began, "s'pose you tell me about this nonsense yer mama's been tellin' me about you and that copper, eh?"

Polly turned her head and glanced at Mavis, who was in the middle of folding napkins. The look she gave her mother was not one of reproach for telling on her to her father. But, more one of pleading desperation.

Both Mavis and Polly knew from past experience that there could be no disagreement with Thaddeus Beanie. He was the head of the household, and whatever he said was law.

It was not another spanking that Polly feared so much as her father's final word on the subject, which once spoken, was never to be rescinded.

Jodie had already been sent up to bed, so there were only the three of them left in the restaurant.

Mavis stopped working and came over to join them at the table.

Polly looked guiltily from one parent to the other.

"Well?" her father insisted. "I'm waitin', girl. What 'ave yer to say fer yerself?"

Before she had a chance to answer, Polly could feel the now familiar hot sting of tears, as they trailed their way down her flushed cheeks.

Her head slumped down onto her folded arms.

"Yer tears'll do yer no good, girl," her father shouted. "Now tell me what's goin' on between you an' that copper, or so help me..."

"Sshhh," Mavis cut in, slapping her husband's hand with her palm. "Yer tryin' to wake up our guest?" she whispered, chastising him.

Thad sat back in his chair, suddenly feeling foolish for forgetting they had Karen staying upstairs. With all the doors shut, the sound of his voice, loud as it was, should not have carried. But even so, he could understand his wife's caution.

Thad drained his glass.

Polly lifted her head. She stared back at her father through her tear-stained eyes, her vision blurred. "I'm sorry, Dada," she blurted, "I think I might love 'im."

"WHAT!" Thad stood up so suddenly, he knocked back his chair, sending it crashing to the floor.

Mavis jumped up and came around to her husband's side.

Before he had a chance to object, she slapped her hand across the front of his mouth to silence him, reminding him, again, why he needed to keep his voice down.

Thad nodded his understanding before Mavis removed her hand.

She bent down to pick up Thad's chair, and grabbed his empty glass from the table.

This was no occasion for sobriety.

While Mavis went out to the bar to replenish her husband's drink, Thad slowly retook his seat, staring in disbelief at his elder daughter.

Neither of them spoke until Mavis came back. She returned with a tray, with a pint for her husband and two halves for her and Polly.

"Now that you've calmed down," she said, placing Thad's pint in front of him, "perhaps we can 'ave a civilised conversation, an' decide what we're goin' t'do about this situation."

Thad looked at his wife, his eyes wide in disbelief. "What d'yer mean, 'do' about it? We 'ave no choice, we can't 'ave the law stickin' their noses in our business. We'll 'ave to deal with 'im like the others."

"No, Dada, please." Polly turned to look at her mother, "Mama?" she sobbed, her eyes imploring her to say something to quell her father's anger.

Mavis placed a hand on her daughter's, and took a drink from her glass.

"This ain't no ordinary situation, Thad, an' you know it, same as I do."

"What d'yer mean," the big man growled, determined to keep control of the situation.

"Polly's not a child any more, no use sayin' otherwise," Mavis continued, keeping her voice steady. "We knew this day would come, sooner or later."

Thad pointed at his daughter. "She's too bleedin' young to know day from night, an' we can't afford to 'ave 'er fallin in bleedin' love with every Tom, Dick an' 'Arry that comes along, yer know that as well as she does."

"I... I didn't mean ter fall in love with 'im, Dada." Polly sniffed. "It jus' 'appened, like that." She slid her hand across the table towards her father's, but at the last moment, he moved his away.

Thad knew how easily his wife and daughter could twist him around their little fingers when they wanted to. Even little Jodie had picked up a few tricks by observing her mother and sister.

Well, there were times when a man had to put his foot down for the good of the family, and this was definitely one of those times.

"Am I the only one 'ere with the sense 'e was born with?" he asked rhetorically. "'Ow exactly are we supposed to entertain the idea of havin' this copper as our Polly's fella, eh? Now, you tell me that."

Mavis thought for a moment.

Having caught her daughter sneaking in the previous night, she knew deep down that there might be more to this than Polly's seemingly insatiable desires. Their conversation in the kitchen earlier had settled it.

But she had been hoping that, in time, Polly would tire of the officer and despatch him with the help of the tribe, before Thad got wind of what was going on.

Unfortunately, that window had passed.

"We can't just kill a copper without it raising all sorts o' questions." Mavis pointed out. "An' if we did, then what would we do? Sit around an' wait fer the army t'be called in to search fer 'is body?"

Thad thought for a moment. "We could always make it look like an accident?" he suggested. "'e could fall an' break 'is neck while climbing one o' the cliffs and crags round 'ere."

"Mama!" Polly sounded desperate as she clutched her mother's hand in both of hers.

"It ain't gonna be that easy, Thad Beanie, an' you know it." Mavis replied, staring directly into her husband's eyes.

Thad harrumphed, and buried his face in his glass as he knocked back half the contents in one go.

"Dada, please let me talk to him?" Polly asked, softly. "If he won't listen, or 'e doesn't understand, then... then we can tell Gobal an' the others, if you like."

"No!" Thad, managed to keep his voice down, but his temper still flared through his expression. "You tell 'im nothin', d'yer understand, nothing?"

He slammed his palm down on the table for emphasis.

Polly knew she had lost her chance.

Once her father had lost his temper, only her mother could calm him down. Polly felt as if all she was doing was fanning the flames. Pleading and begging were obviously not going to work on this occasion, that was for sure, and Polly knew better than to attempt arguing back with her father. Even her mother would not put up with such an action.

Polly ran from the table, leaving her drink untouched.

As she made her way up the stairs, they could hear her trying to muffle her sobs.

Once she was gone, Thad turned back to face his wife. He could see she was not best pleased with him.

"What would you 'ave me do?" he asked, opening both hands in front of him as if to demonstrate his desperation. "We can't jus' let 'er go around with any bloke she fancies, you know that. She's only known 'im fer five minutes – 'ow can she be in love?"

Mavis slid her hand over and clasped Thad's.

"'Ow long after meetin' me did you know, Thad Beanie?"

Thad blushed. "That were different, we wus older," he stammered.

"Not by much, an' you knows it to be true."

Thad looked flustered. He rubbed his hand across his forehead, as if searching for divine inspiration.

Finally, he announced. "We 'ad our parents' permission, an' we were jus' right fer each other. We wus both part o' the clan."

Mavis could not deny her husband's logic. This was one situation where she could not claim to have all the answers.

JACOBS SAT in his car at the edge of the car park, waiting anxiously for Polly to arrive.

She had made the arrangements with him earlier that day, while he was having his lunch. As much as he had hoped that their tryst the previous night would prove to be more than a one-night stand, by the time he sat down to eat, Jacobs had lost his nerve to ask her out again.

He convinced himself that it was merely the fact that he was in a crowded restaurant, with everyone close enough to overhear their conversation. But he knew that in fact, it was just him chickening out.

As he watched Polly sashay back and forth between the tables, delivering steaming plates of pie and vegetables, Jacobs could not believe that they had made love together only a few hours previously.

She was so beautiful, and the way she spoke to the clientele demonstrated how charming and sincere her personality was, too.

Jacobs could still not believe his good luck. After so many years working in Liverpool, which was crammed full of beautiful women, he had landed up in this backwater and managed to catch the eye of the most beautiful girl in town.

When Polly presented Jacobs with his bill, she had written on the back: "Tonight, same time, same place xx"

Jacobs could barely contain his excitement at the prospect of another encounter, especially one so close after last night's.

He spent the rest of the afternoon making the rounds of the many shady-looking takeaways that littered the beachfronts in some of the main towns nearest to Thorndike, but all to no avail. Most denied outright that they would source their ingredients from anywhere other than a legitimate supplier, and those that could not merely shrugged and told him to contact the owner.

By the end of the day, Jacobs felt as if he had been on a wild-goose chase. If anyone knew anything, they were not about to reveal it to the authorities and risk being closed down,

If nothing else, Jacobs hoped that his impromptu visit might have the desired effect of making some of the less salubrious outlets clean up their act, out of fear that a full inspection from the Food Standards Agency might follow.

By seven o'clock that evening, he was shattered and headed back into the station.

The desk sergeant was one Jacobs had only spoken to a couple of times before. He appeared a little young to be in the role, but Jacobs had to surmise he had earned his stripes, so was entitled to the position.

"Anything new come in?" Jacobs asked, standing on the public side of the desk.

The sergeant shook his head slowly. "Nothing to get excited about, chief, there was a report earlier about an abandoned van just outside town but, by the time we had someone to check it out, there was no sign of it."

Jacobs thought for a moment. "What colour was the van in question?"

The sergeant scanned through the report on his computer, before locating the correct section. "Er, it would appear to have been a dark brown, possibly black, not noticed in the area before."

"Definitely not white?" Jacobs enquired. "With the name 'Craven Meats' emblazed across the side?"

The sergeant looked back at the screen, rechecking the information.

"No, Inspector, it was definitely a dark colour, no writing noticed by either witness. Why, are you on the lookout for a van?"

Jacobs nodded. "You could say that – Pete Craven appears to have misplaced his delivery van."

The desk sergeant tapped a few more keys on his keyboard, but drew a blank.

"I can't find a report being filed," he informed Jacobs, "are you sure he said it's been taken?"

Jacobs held up his hand. "It's not that simple, to be honest – the old man suspects his teenage sons have done a bunk with it, along with some of his best cuts of meat, as well as their ill-gotten gains from illegal meat distribution, as well as the possible selling of illegal substances."

"No wonder he doesn't want to make a formal complaint," the desk sergeant concurred. "Should I just ask all patrols top keep an eye out for them?"

"That would be my guess. Well done, sergeant."

With that, Jacobs went back into his office to make a list of those food outlets he had already visited, so he could concentrate on some of the others tomorrow.

With luck, by now word of mouth was spreading and the proprietors were already in the process of cleaning up their act.

Jacobs worked diligently until 10pm, then turned off his office light and made his way out of the door, saying goodnight to the officer left in charge.

Within 20 minutes of arriving home, Jacobs had showered, shaved, applied a liberal amount of his finest cologne, brushed his teeth, taking special care to gargle with mouthwash for the recommended two minutes, instead of just sloshing it around his mouth once and spitting the disgusting cocktail back into the bowl.

He chose another pair of track-pants for the liaison, and a black polo-neck jumper to help keep out the cold. His sheepskin jacket would no doubt act as their makeshift mattress again.

As he drove to the inn, Jacobs could not help wondering where this relationship was heading, if indeed it had a final destination. Perhaps, he thought, Polly had a thing for older men, and was happy to have some innocent fun with them until she grew bored.

Jacobs hoped that was not the case, but he was long enough in the tooth to keep an open mind. After all, if he made a fool of himself, he would have only himself to blame.

As he approached the inn, Jacobs noticed that the place was in darkness and he hoped that meant Polly's parents were both in bed and fast asleep. Although his intentions were honourable, the thought of having to explain his actions to Thad Beanie was not an experience Jacobs relished.

He parked in the same spot as last time, and waited patiently.

Jacobs stared into the woodland, watching the trees swaying in the midnight breeze. The lack of moonlight made it impossible for him to tell where the undergrowth ended and the trees began. Everything blended to a uniform black but, as Jacobs stared ahead, he could have sworn he saw movement from something other than foliage.

As he strained to see better, Jacobs almost jumped out of his skin when Polly began knocking on his side window.

Feeling stupid for allowing himself to be spooked by nothing more than nocturnal shadows, Jacobs opened his door and climbed out of the car.

He smiled at Polly. "Hello," he said cheerfully.

"Can we get inside a minute? We need to talk."

Polly sounded anxious, not her usual breezy easy-going self.

Jacobs clicked the lock button on his ignition key and released the other door locks on the car. Polly opened her side and jumped in, closing the door behind her slowly, so as not to make too much noise.

Once Jacobs slid back behind the wheel and shut his door, Polly leaned over and grabbed his head, pulling him towards her.

They kissed passionately.

Jacob's mind was full of questions as to why Polly suddenly seemed afraid to be seen with him.

He feared the worst. This was to be their last encounter.

When they finally drew apart, Polly looked Jacobs straight in the eye, her face etched with pain and fear.

"What's the matter?" Jacobs asked, not really wanting to hear the answer.

"Do you love me?"

Jacobs moved back instinctively. The shock of Polly's question had him reeling.

It took a moment for her question to sink in.

"Do I, well, I mean..." Jacobs stumbled to find the right words.

Yes, he was very attracted to Polly, what man would not be, and certainly he was extremely flattered by her attention. What's more, if he allowed his feelings and his fantasies to take over, then he could easily fall in love with her, no question about it.

But, on the other hand, he was too long in the tooth to believe in fairy tales, and though, in theory, he had no doubt that the phenomenon of love at first sight existed, he just could not believe it was something that could happen to him.

But, as he stared back into Polly's beautiful green eyes, he was in no doubt that she at least was in earnest.

"It's a simple question, man – do you love me or not?" Polly appeared irritated at Jacob's hesitation. To her it was obviously a simple matter and thus it deserved a straightforward answer.

"Of course I love you." Jacobs blurted out.

Polly flung her arms back around him and kissed him all over his face, barely giving him time to respond.

She finished by planting another lingering kiss on his mouth.

"Right then," she began, decidedly. "We need to get away from 'ere, not just the inn, but the village, even the town, we must get as far away as possible before we can settle down."

Jacobs held up his hand.

"Hang on a minute, what's the rush?"

"My Dada knows about us. We 'ave to get away before 'e finds us."

Jacobs could not hide his confusion. He always suspected that, if her parents discovered what they had been up to, they would not be happy about it, but Jacobs was confident that once he explained his intentions to them, they would understand.

After all, other than his age, what could they possibly have against him?

He could understand Polly's initial panic – she was still young and clearly respected her parents enough not to want to see them unhappy. But he was sure that once they all sat down together and discussed the situation; she would calm down once her parents were on board.

"Polly," Jacobs began, keeping his voice calm. "We can't start our relationship by running away. Your parents will come around to the idea once they see us together."

"No, you don't understand," Polly insisted, grabbing his hand. "My Dada has already made up his mind, 'e doesn't look kindly on anyone from outside our clan, an' as 'is elder daughter, I 'ave a duty to follow 'is wishes."

"Listen," Jacobs, said, reassuringly, "your father will be fine, trust me, he cares for you, naturally, you're his daughter after all..."

"It's not jus' that!" Polly stated, clearly growing impatient with Jacob's failure to appreciate the position they were in. "Look, do you love me or don't yer? Because, if you do, then we need to get away from 'ere tonight! There's no time fer arguing, let's jus' go, please."

Jacobs could see there was no calming Polly down, she had made up her mind that they needed to leave immediately, and no matter what he said she remained adamant.

He was sure that she was overreacting, but trying to explain that to her was proving to be more difficult than he could ever have imagined.

Jacobs was in no doubt that Polly believed her parents would go spare if they discovered their relationship. But that was to be expected, initially. Once they had a chance to grow used to the idea, he was sure that they would come around.

He just needed to convey that to Polly.

Jacobs looked into Polly's eyes and smiled reassuringly.

Suddenly, Polly's eyes widened in terror.

She was not looking at Jacobs, but over his shoulder at something behind him, outside the car.

Before he had a chance to turn around to see what was causing her such alarm, the driver's window behind him shattered, and something grabbed hold of Jacob's collar, pulling him backwards through the now vacant windowframe.

Unable to turn around, Jacobs watched as Polly tried desperately to hold on to him, grabbing at his coat, then his legs, but she was nowhere near as strong as whatever had hold of his upper body.

Once his whole body had been wrenched through the window, Jacobs was released, and unable to make it to his feet in time, he fell to the floor, his back taking the brunt of the fall as he slammed into the tarmac.

Jacobs lay prostrate on the ground, trying desperately to take a breath. The fall had knocked the wind out of him, and as he struggled to regain his composure, something grabbed him and hoisted him off the asphalt.

Whatever had hold of him, it was stronger than any man he had ever come across.

Two powerful hands held him in place, making it impossible for him to turn to see his attacker.

Jacobs fought for breath as he watched Polly climb back out of the car, tears streaming down her face. She was shouting something, but Jacob's head was still ringing from his fall.

Without warning, something wrapped itself around his neck, crushing his windpipe, making breathing impossible.

Jacobs gasped for air, but the grip grew tighter, like an anaconda slowly tightening its grip on its helpless prey.

Through his dimming vision, he watched as Polly ran towards him, waving her arms in the air and shouting.

Then he passed out.

27

KAREN AWOKE REFRESHED FROM HER NIGHT'S SLEEP AT THE INN. The bed was very comfortable, especially compared to the one in the cottage, and with no Dan coughing and spluttering beside her, she had slept right through the night.

Even baby Charlotte had managed to stay the course.

That nightcap had definitely done Karen a power of good.

Stretching, she threw back the covers and swung her legs out of bed.

The morning sun was already pouring in through the gap in the curtains, so Karen walked over and spread them wide open.

Her room looked out on to the front of the inn, and she realised that, had it not been for a few of the homes nearest to the inn, she might have been able to see their cottage from her window.

She wondered if Dan had finally managed to find his way back.

If not, then Karen was going to have to think seriously about involving the police.

Regardless of the fact that he had no way of calling her at present, she could not think of any reason why he should have stayed away so long. So she had to conclude that either he had been involved in an accident or something untoward had befallen him.

Either way, it was Karen's duty to make the appropriate enquiries as no one else even knew he was missing.

Karen interlocked her fingers and, looking towards the ceiling, stretched her arms above her head.

After a moment, she tiptoed over towards the two inverted armchairs that housed Charlotte's cot. Her wonderful daughter must have sensed that mummy needed a decent night's sleep, so did not cry if she stirred during the night.

Karen peeked inside Charlotte's cot and her blood ran cold. The baby was missing.

Karen pulled back the blankets just to make sure her daughter had not somehow slipped below them during the night, but the cot was empty.

In a panic, Karen spun around and frantically began searching the room, unable to fathom how her daughter could have got out of the cot, but equally unable to imagine any other possible explanation.

She checked in the bathroom and even under the bed without success.

Without a care for her state of undress, Karen flung open the bedroom door and stepped out into the corridor.

For a moment she stood in place, turning left and right, desperate for any indication as to where Charlotte might be.

Eventually, she turned right and made her way down the corridor towards the fire exit. In her mind she was already conjuring up all manner of scenarios where someone had sneaked in through the exit and, finding her door unlocked, crept in and kidnapped her daughter.

When Karen reached the fire door, it was locked. A push

bar prevented it from being opened, so Karen grabbed hold of it and pushed, slamming it against the metal frame.

The door flew open, and Karen stepped out on to the cold metal landing in her bare feet. Naturally, there was no sign of any intruders, as the rational part of her mind told her that if someone like that had taken Charlotte, they were probably long gone by now.

Karen stood outside, holding on to the railings for fear of collapsing.

The car park in front of her was empty and fallen leaves skipped across the asphalt, blown hither and thither by the morning breeze.

Her initial thought was to run down the iron staircase and scour the surrounding area for clues. Any sign that the kidnappers had left would be vital to the police – a discarded blanket, one of her little booties, a scratch mitten, anything.

"Karen."

She heard her name being called, but it sounded as if it were from very far away.

Was she imagining it?

"Karen."

Closer this time.

Karen turned, almost in a daze, and saw Jodie walking towards her down the corridor, carrying Charlotte in her arms.

After standing frozen to the spot for a second, Karen leapt into action and ran towards the startled young girl.

"Give her to me!" she demanded, holding out both arms.

Jodie complied, clearly shaken by Karen's tone.

Karen took Charlotte in her arms and cuddled her, kissing the sleeping baby's forehead over and over.

"I'm... I'm really sorry," Jodie mumbled, "I didn't mean to upset you, but I heard Charlotte crying for ages, so I came in to see if there was anything I could do."

Karen stared at the girl, breathing heavily.

"I did knock, a couple of times, but you were dead to the world," Jodie explained, trying to keep her voice steady. But in truth, she was more than a little unnerved by Karen's venomous stare.

Finally, Karen found her voice. "So you thought you'd just come in and steal her, is that what you decided?"

Jodie shook her head. "No, of course not, I did try to wake you up but, like I said, you were sparko. I only took Charlotte to the next room so that she didn't wake you up. She only wanted a cuddle. She was back asleep in no time."

"So why didn't you bring her back into me, then? What were you waiting for?"

Jodie's eyes brimmed over. "I'm sorry, I only wanted to hold her for a bit in case she woke up again. I was about to bring her back when I heard you open your door, but by the time I got up and came into the corridor, you were already at the exit... I'm really sorry."

Karen stood rigid for a moment, her gaze fixed on Jodie, while she tried to calm down. The girl was obviously distressed by her reaction, but Karen felt totally justified for losing her temper.

Who the hell thinks nothing of walking off with someone else's baby? Especially someone you barely know?

Once she began to calm down a little, Karen surmised that, perhaps down here, in this out-of-the-way place, things were different from in London and other large cities. It was possible that Jodie's actions, which were obviously innocent, did not seem so out of the ordinary in such a quaint village setting.

Karen imagined that parents probably still allowed their children to play unsupervised in the vicinity, because they were lucky enough not to have been affected by the rising crime rates that she was used to reading about every day back home.

Either way, Jodie's tears of remorse seemed genuine

enough, and now that Charlotte was safely back in her arms, Karen began to feel sorry for snapping at her.

"It's all right, Jodie," Karen assured her. "I'm sorry I was so angry, you just scared the living hell out of me, that's all."

"I'm really so sorry," Jodie blubbered, rubbing her tears away with the back of her hand. "I should have woken you up. It won't happen again, I promise."

Karen laid a comforting hand on Jodie's small shoulder.

"Come on now," she said, soothingly. "Dry away those tears – no harm done."

Jodie smiled, her eyes glistening brightly.

"Tell you what," Karen continued, "how about, to show me there's no hard feelings, you watch little one for me while I take a shower?"

Jodie's eyes widened. "You mean it?" she shrieked.

"Yep," Karen assured her. "If you're really keen, you can also keep her amused while I change her, how about that?"

JACOBS COULD FEEL his head lolling about from side to side as he finally came to.

His head felt heavier than normal and he found it a strain to lift it off his chest. As he tried to focus his eyes on the scene around him, Jacobs realised that he was bound to the chair he was sitting on by thick rope, which had been tightly looped around his body several times before being secured to a large chimney flue pipe behind him.

On the bench opposite him sat Thad Beanie.

The man was dressed in what had doubtless once been white coveralls, but which were now so stained by blood that they appeared to be more red than white.

Jacobs opened his mouth to speak, but his voice could only rasp out a sound which was barely above a whisper.

When he swallowed, his throat stung with a burning pain inside, as if he had swallowed razor blades.

He gazed around him in the fluorescent light. Hanging from meat hooks scattered around the room, were huge slabs of meat, most of which were still dripping blood on to the concrete floor.

The bench where Thad was sitting also had several smaller cuts, piled on top of each other haphazardly, while others were merely strewn across the bench.

The overpowering stench from the raw meat was overwhelming, and Jacobs could feel the bile rising in his oesophagus. He looked up at the ceiling and swallowed, hard. It was still painful, but at least it had the desired effect.

"So, yer still alive?" Thad Beanie stated gruffly.

Jacobs looked over at the big man. "I guess so," he whispered, wincing with the pain.

"I s'pose you think that because yer the law, you can just chuck your weight aroun' the place an' everyone else 'as to stand in line?"

Jacobs shook his head.

He tried to clear his throat once more, but the pain stopped him midway.

"Yer 'ave no idea 'oo yer dealin' with, do yer?"

Jacobs decided it was safer to just nod and shake his head and let Thad do all the talking.

It would certainly be less painful than trying to reply, right now.

"Our family goes back generations, 'undreds of years. The Beanie clan tradition is one we can all be proud of, an' I intend to keep it goin' fer another 'undred years, d'yer understand?"

Jacobs nodded his understanding, trying his best to appear interested but, in reality, he had no idea what Polly's father was talking about.

Fortunately for him, Thad seemed intent on giving him their complete family history.

"You lawmen are all the same, thinkin' yer so smart an' clever. It's jus' like when the king's men discovered our ancestors' hideout, back in the 16th century, an' dragged 'em out for execution, without so much as a fair trial."

Jacobs could tell that Thad was growing angrier with every word, and his ferment was aimed directly at him, as a representative of the law.

"But, yer see," he continued, tapping his index finger against his temple. "They weren't as clever as they thought they wus, even when they searched the hideout with dogs, they didn't find all the clan, an' several o' them escaped execution by hidin' themselves deep within the cave, an' stayin' there till the king's men 'ad gone away. An' once they were safe, they 'ad nothin' left to do but feed an' breed."

Thad's face darkened, and his brows knitted together.

"But as fer those what were caught, men, women, even children, some younger than our Jodie, dragged out before the screamin' mob an' burnt alive, or strung up from trees, an' fer what?"

Thad slipped his enormous frame off the bench, and moved in closer towards Jacobs, until their noses were mere centimetres apart.

"I'll tell yer what fer, shall I?" the big man said. "Fer discoverin' the pleasure t'be gained by eatin' 'uman flesh."

Thad's words took a moment for Jacobs to take in.

Was he seriously talking about cannibalism?

"What the..." was all that came out of Jacobs's mouth.

His mind raced with the possibilities of Thad's revelation.

He stared back at the big man.

Thad nodded, and moved back to his bench. "That's right, Lawman," he confirmed with a grin. "I'm proud t'be carryin' on the family tradition. Only now, we don't jus' keep the goods fer ourselves, we share it out with anyone 'oo wants a piece."

Thad pointed directly at Jacobs.

"An' that includes you, Mr Lawman."

Jacobs blinked his eyes several times, as if trying to clear away an awful thought which was fighting to force its way into his imagination.

He looked back at Thad, in disbelief.

The big man nodded his head slowly, as if in response to his unspoken question.

Staring back at the hunks of meat dangling from hooks in the ceiling, Jacobs suddenly noticed the resemblance between some of them and human body parts.

He could now make out legs, arms, even whole torsos, leaking out what was left of their owner's blood on to the floor.

Jacobs could fight the nausea no longer.

He just had time to turn his head to one side as the first hot gush of vomit spewed out of him. Jacobs retched and heaved, until he had no more to give.

The fire within his throat was now worse than ever, as if what had initially been a spark had now become an inferno.

From somewhere in the distance, he heard a door opening.

Then a familiar voice. "Oh, Dada please, what 'ave you done to 'im? You said you wouldn't 'urt 'im."

"I said nothin' o' the sort, girl. 'E knows too much."

Jacobs felt a soft hand against his cheek.

He stayed looking away, and coughed himself hoarse.

When he finally turned, Polly's face was in front of him. Her beautiful eyes locked on to his and, for a moment, he forgot why he was there and the danger he was in as a result of what he had just been told by her father.

He wished now that he had just driven away when she begged him to, without wasting time demanding an explanation.

But it was too late for that now.

Polly removed a tea towel from her apron and used it to wipe the remnants of bile from Jacob's mouth.

"Never mind all that, girl," Thad growled. "Go an' fetch a bucket an' mop, an' clean this mess yer boyfriend 'as made, before it stinks the place out."

Polly stayed on her haunches and turned towards her father.

"Promise me yer'll not 'urt 'im while I'm gone," she demanded.

Thad's face grew red with rage.

He jumped back off the bench, and grabbed Polly by her ponytail, pulling her up towards him.

"Ow," she squealed, "yer 'urtin' me."

"I'll do more 'an hurt yer, if yer talk back ter me again," he snarled. "I warned yer to stay away from 'im, but yer disobeyed me. Now, go an' fetch that bucket an' mop, an' no more sauce out o' you, understand?"

When Thad let go of his daughter's hair, she nodded her understanding, before turning away and heading back in the direction she had come.

Jacobs watched her leave, feeling as if his last hope had just gone with her.

28

Karen switched off her mobile, and threw it on to the sofa in frustration. She had just spent the best part of an hour on the phone to the local police station, and the officer on duty who took her call, reminded her of the Keystone Cops silent films they used to show on television during the holidays.

In her mind she had an image of uniformed men running around the station like headless chickens, tripping over each other, and crashing into walls and furniture.

Karen fully understood his rationalisation that Dan was a grown man, and had only been missing for 24 hours, but what she could not forgive was his overall condescending tone. He even managed to make the word "madam" sound as if he were humouring a child.

Karen's account of why they were in the village, and the fact that she was not his next of kin, nor appeared to know who that might be, only added to the officer's assertion that Dan had taken a wrong turn somewhere, and spent the night at a hotel, or guest house.

He assured Karen that the fact Dan had forgotten his mobile back at the cottage was a reasonable explanation as to why he had not been able to contact her, and that he was probably on his way back by now.

He further explained that as it was a Sunday, the station was not fully operational, so he could not spare anyone to come out and see her, but he recommended that, if Dan had not appeared by the same time tomorrow, Karen should come into the station to make out an official missing-person report.

Karen stood there for a moment, staring down at her phone, fuming at it, as if the obstinate man was still on the line.

She considered calling back and demanding to speak to someone in authority, but, she felt sure that under the circumstances, if there were such a person present, they would simply fob her off with the same flannel.

The question was, what to do next?

It was another cold, but crisp and sunny day, and Karen did not want to spend it inside the cottage waiting for Dan to turn up.

She realised, for the first time since yesterday, that she was growing more annoyed at his disappearance than concerned for his safety.

The words from the officer on the phone, echoed through her mind. He was somewhere safe. He had been lost, caught without his phone, and was on his way back.

Karen needed some fresh air. After her shower that morning at the inn, Jodie's mum had made her a delicious bacon and egg sandwich, with thick crusty bread, just the way she liked it, washed down with two large mugs of strong coffee. Now, she needed to walk it off.

After a feed and a change, Charlotte had settled back in her cot, and by the time they had reached the cottage, she was fast asleep, once more.

Karen bundled herself up against the wind, and checked again to ensure there were no messages on either Dan's mobile or hers.

There was a niggling doubt at the back of her mind that, even though he probably did not know her number off by heart, there was still a possibility he would know his own.

In which case, why had he not called? Unless he didn't realise he had left it behind, and thought he had dropped it while he was out. But surely, even then he would try, just in case.

Karen calmed herself. In truth, she could not recite her number off by heart, so, in one respect, it made perfect sense that he was the same.

Karen lifted the carry-cot up by the straps, and carefully placed it on the chassis without waking baby Charlotte. She snapped the locking device into place, and double-checked it, as always, just to be sure.

Once outside, Karen turned left, away from the direction of the inn, so that she could explore the other side of the village.

Those whom she passed along the way, seemed surprisingly reserved for a small English village. From previous experience, Karen had always found villagers to be friendlier than people living in London, and certainly more willing to pass the time of day, and smile.

But the few pedestrians she encountered on her walk, either looked away or crossed the road as she approached, which surprised her, especially as she had Charlotte with her.

Even the occasional Londoner was willing to take a peek in the pram and congratulate her.

Shrugging it off, Karen continued down the high street until she reached the hump-back bridge, which led over a small stream.

The road surface on the other side looked far more rough than the pavement she was on, and the thought of having to negotiate her way with the pram through the fallen branches and rock-strewn landscape convinced her to turn back and retrace her steps.

The sun was at its apex, and heading back towards the cottage, Karen was able to enjoy its full warmth on her face.

On the return journey, she passed even fewer villagers, but still made the effort of smiling when she caught their eye. The most she received in return was an occasional half-smile before they turned their faces away.

Once she reached the cottage, Karen still felt too restless to go back inside, so she decided to carry on with her walk, in the direction of the inn.

As she passed it on the opposite side of the street, Karen could see through the windows that the bar area was busy, as usual. It being lunchtime, she was hardly surprised. She considered stopping in for drink, but decided to keep going instead. Charlotte was starting to grizzle, and there was less chance of her nodding back off inside the bar with all its noise.

Karen walked along the street, until she reached the turning that led down to the lake. The sign said it was only a few hundred yards away and, staring ahead, she saw that the going was relatively well maintained, and should not prove too onerous for the wheels on Charlotte's pram.

Once she reached the lake, Karen sat down on a suitable rock and gazed out at the calm water. She turned the pram to one side so that the sun was not directly on the baby's face, and adjusted the visor so she could see Charlotte from where she sat.

There were a couple of rowing boats on the water, each containing a couple enjoying the afternoon sun.

To her surprise, when they saw her, both couples waved in her direction. Karen waved back, presuming that they were visitors to the area just like her, and not locals, judging by the negative responses she had received in the village earlier.

Karen watched the boats disappear around the bend in the lake. She wondered if there was a boat-hire station nearby, and thought how lovely it would have been to spend the afternoon idly drifting along with Charlotte asleep in her arms and Dan doing all the hard work.

She could feel her irritation grow inside at the thought of all they could have accomplished this weekend, if only Dan had not decided to drink himself into a blind stupor on their first night.

Karen took a deep breath, and waited for her annoyance to pass.

If Dan had not resurfaced by the morning, she resolved to make the trek into town to make a formal statement.

His keys were still back at the cottage, so at least she would not have to rely on anyone else for transport. In fact, now that she thought about it, Karen decided if the circumstances did not change, she would lodge the missing-persons complaint, and then drive home in Dan's car.

There was no reason for her to stay here any longer, especially if, for whatever reason, he was not coming back.

With her mind made up, Karen stretched out the tension that had been building in her shoulders.

"Hi there."

Karen jumped, almost sliding off her rock. She turned and squinted into the sunlight. It was Jodie.

"Oh, my God, you scared the life out of me," Karen said, holding her hand over her chest, as it rose and fell in rapidly.

"I'm sorry, I didn't mean to," replied Jodie sweetly. "I thought you might have heard me coming down the path."

Karen shook her head. "Sorry, no, I was off with the fairies." Her breathing grew steady once more, and she managed a smile.

Jodie looked over into the pram. "How's our little gorgeous angel doin'?" she asked, peering in at the sleeping baby.

"Oh, she's fine, just enjoying the afternoon sun."

Karen noticed the basket Jodie was carrying, covered in a checked cloth.

"Are you off for a picnic?" Karen enquired, nodding towards it.

"Oh this?" She laughed. "No, nothin' so exciting, I'm afraid. I'm just goin' to visit a friend of my mama's who's not very well."

"That's kind of you," Karen observed. "I hope it's nothing serious?"

Jodie shook her head. "No, she jus' fell on the rocks near 'ere and fractured something in 'er foot, so she can't get out at the moment. Would you like to come with me and meet her? She'll be glad of the company."

Karen thought for a moment, then said, "I doubt she'll want a complete stranger turning up on her doorstep, unannounced. You carry on, I should be taking madam back to the cottage for her bath and feed."

Jodie looked shocked. "Oh, you're not planning on spending the night in that musty old cottage, are you? Mama assumed you would stay with us until your boyfriend came back."

Karen was slightly taken aback. "Well, that's very kind of your mother, but I'd really hate to impose."

Jodie shook her head. "It's no trouble. Mama told me to come an' find you once I'd seen 'er friend, to invite you back fer dinner an' offer you a bed for the night. She can't bear the thought of you bein' all alone in that cottage."

Karen thought for a moment. It was certainly a tempting offer. The good food and warm beds back at the inn were far more inviting than being stuck in the dank, depressing cottage, with nothing for company except the television.

Karen bit her bottom lip. "Well, if you're sure it's not too much trouble, I'd love to stay. But your mum must let me pay this time. I can't keep taking advantage of her good nature."

Jodie laughed. "She'd never 'ear of it. Neither would me dada. Mama says you're our guest, an' that's all there is to it."

"She's very kind, and so is your father," Karen responded. "I must admit, I wasn't exactly relishing the thought of another night in that cottage, especially on my own."

"Come on then," Jodie held out her basket for Karen. "Let's go and visit mama's friend, and then we can go home for tea."

Karen took hold of the basket, and placed her arm through the handle so it could rest in the crook of her elbow.

"I'll drive," Jodie announced, releasing the brake pedal on Charlotte's pram, and turning it back towards the path.

Along the way, Jodie explained to Karen that they would need to venture through the tunnel built through the rock, and that for practical purposes, due to the uneven ground, it would make sense for them to take Charlotte's cot off the chassis and carry her.

Jodie allayed Karen's concerns that someone might come along and steal it, reminding her that she was no longer in London, and so had nothing to fear on that count.

As sceptical as she still was, Karen reluctantly did as Jodie suggested.

They hid the chassis behind some bushes so that it was out of sight, at least.

Jodie used her torch to guide the way once they were inside the cave. She had insisted on still being allowed to carry the cot with Charlotte inside, while Karen kept hold of the basket.

As they meandered left and right through the stone structure, Karen was impressed at how adept Jodie was at finding her way through.

"I take it you've been this way more than a couple of times?" Karen asked.

"Oh yes, I've been using this tunnel since I was a child, it's so much quicker than having to walk over the hills around here, and then attempting to cross the busy intersection into town. Not far to go now." Jodie assured her.

Up ahead, Karen saw a light, and breathed a sigh of relief. She was not claustrophobic, but being inside the cave without being able to see daylight at the other end still left her feeling a trifle nauseated.

As they drew closer to the light, Karen realised that it was coming from a fire, not an entrance. She could not understand – who would light a fire down here? Potholers, maybe?

As they rounded the last turning, Karen saw huge fire burning brightly in the middle of the dirt floor. The shadows of the flames licked the walls hungrily, casting shadows far away into the darkness.

Before she had a chance to ask one of the dozen or so questions which had sprung to mind, Karen saw the tribe of creatures emerging from all sides, surrounding them in seconds.

Karen's initial instinct was to grab Charlotte's cot and run from them. She slowly placed the basket on the floor, but when it came time to move, her legs would not budge. She turned to warn Jodie, who seemed oblivious to their impending danger, but she was already walking away towards the fire, with baby Charlotte by her side.

As Jodie approached the next turning, Karen found her feet and ran after her, screaming for her to give her back her daughter.

Jodie stopped when she reached the sleeping body of a young woman, and knelt beside her, placing the carry-cot on the floor beside her.

Charlotte appeared to have woken up, and now she started screaming, her tiny voice piercing the shadowy darkness, and echoing around the walls of the cave.

When Karen caught up to her, she bent down to retrieve her daughter. But even as she reached out to grab the cot's handles, one of the creatures was upon her, dragging her backwards along the floor.

Karen kicked and screamed as she was yanked backwards. Her only concern was for the safety of her precious daughter.

The creature that had grabbed her bore down on her shoulders, keeping her pinned to the floor, as she watched Jodie come back and grab the basket, and take it to the sleeping woman.

As Karen watched, her mind overwhelmed by the scene before her, Jodie shook the sleeping woman gently on the shoulder until she woke up and sat upright against the stone wall, revealing her nakedness.

Next, Jodie undid the cloth covering the basket and produced a large plastic food container from within. Releasing the lid, she took out a spoon and began to feed the woman, as if she were an infant incapable of performing the task herself.

The hands that kept Karen in place, were large and covered in thick, knotted fur.

Karen watched as the woman ate, spellbound by the what she was seeing.

In between mouthfuls, Jodie would reach down and try to lull Charlotte by rocking her cot and speaking to her softly.

Once the container was empty, Jodie snapped the lid back on and popped it back into the basket. She then stood up with the basket in one hand, and Charlotte's cot in the other.

Karen attempted to lunge forward, but the huge hands kept her firmly in place. She had never felt so helpless in her life.

Karen watched as Jodie walked back towards her. She placed the cot on the ground a few feet in front of Karen, and removed her torch from her jean pocket, holding it in the hand with the basket over her arm.

"Would you like to say goodbye?" Jodie asked with a smile.

For a split second, Karen thought the young girl was talking about the woman behind her. But then the awful truth of the matter hit her like a sledgehammer to the face.

Jodie was about to take her baby away and leave her behind!

Karen stared up at Jodie, her head began to shake slowly

from side to side, as if denying the girl permission to take her child. But in reality, it was merely a reflex action.

Karen screamed: "You can't take my baby away from me, please give her back to me."

The mother's plea inspired her daughter to add her voice to the argument.

Jodie shushed the baby, as if it were the most natural thing in the world.

Jodie picked up the cot in her free hand, and stood before Karen.

"Please," Karen pleaded, tears rolling down her cheeks. "I'm begging you, don't hurt my baby. Do what you want with me, but please leave her alone."

Jodie looked shocked. "Hurt this little one?" she said, taken aback. "I'd rather cut out me own eyes first. This little darlin' is goin' to come an' live with me. She's goin' t'be mine now, an' I'm goin' to look after 'er as if she were born to me."

Karen felt an odd sense of comfort at Jodie's statement. At least, her daughter would be safe, so long as the girl kept her word.

Before she had time to consider her own plight at the hands of the monsters that surrounded her, Karen watched as Jodie had moved off, lulling Charlotte as she went.

29

LUCY OPENED HER EYES, YAWNED, AND BLINKED AWAY THE remnants of sleep.

In the bed beside her, Jerry was lying on his side and texting.

As it was their weekend off, they had both decided to make a night of it. Having met in a pub for a drink and a bite to eat, they set off to go clubbing, which was not Jerry's favourite pastime but, as it was officially their first date, Lucy reminded him that it was the lady's prerogative to decide where they went.

Jerry had never heard of that regulation before, but he could tell from her eyes how excited Lucy was at the prospect, so he gave in heroically.

As it turned out, once they had had a few more drinks at the club, and the thumping music enticed them on to the dance floor, the evening went by in a flash. Before Jerry knew it, it was almost three o'clock in the morning and they were announcing final orders.

They had shared their first real kiss on the dance floor, and while they waited outside in the cold for their cab to arrive, they enjoyed their first fumble as well.

Once they reached Jerry's flat, although sweaty and exhausted from the night's exertions, they were too enthusiastic to wait until the next day, and by the time their last piece of clothing hit the floor, Lucy had already taken Jerry inside her.

Their love-making was eager and frantic, and Jerry only just managed to hold off until Lucy orgasmed, before he shot his load.

They slept in until 11 in the morning.

When they woke, Jerry offered Lucy coffee, but she shook her head and silently reached for him once more, pulling him on top of her and massaging his bottom as he slid inside her.

Afterwards, they slept some more, entwined in each other's embrace as the rest of the world outside carried on with its Sunday ritual.

By now, it was almost one in the afternoon, and Lucy turned on her side to face Jerry's back, while his fingers were still tapping away at his phone.

She gently trailed a path from his neck down to the split in his bottom with her fingernails. Jerry squirmed at her touch, but managed to continue until he finished his text.

Once done, he placed his phone back on the night table and turned back to face Lucy.

"Morning," he said.

"Morning," she replied, before cupping her hand behind his neck and pulling him in for a kiss.

Even with the dried perspiration from the previous night's exertions still on her skin, Lucy still smelled intoxicating. It was not from any perfume or body spray, but her natural body scent, which somehow seemed to assail his nostrils, making him want her more.

"Who you texting?" Lucy asked, curiously, peering over his shoulder.

"Oh, no one special, it's just my girlfriend, I was telling her not to come over until I'd got rid of you."

Lucy stared at him, hurt and furious in equal measure.

Then she saw the crafty smile he was unable to conceal, and she knew he was joking.

Lucy tossed him over on to his back and straddled him, trapping his arms by his side.

She was far from fat, but she was heavy enough to keep him pinned down. Her body was hard and firm, like a female weightlifter. Without warning, she dug her fingers into his torso, tickling him furiously.

Jerry laughed so hard that for a moment he could not catch his breath.

Finally, he yelled. "I surrender, I surrender, you win."

Lucy did not let up. "Are you sorry?" she demanded, smiling down at his helplessness.

"Yes, yes, I'm very sorry, please stop."

Eventually, she did. Lucy sat back with her hands on her hips, looking down at Jerry while he continued laughing, still unable to control himself.

"Now," said Lucy, suspiciously, "who were you texting?"

Jerry looked into her eyes. "It was Dan, that's all, I just wanted to know how their break was going."

He sounded genuinely terrified that Lucy might start another onslaught.

Finally, she said. "OK, I believe you, millions wouldn't."

She climbed off him, releasing his arms.

Jerry propped himself up on one arm. He traced her mischievous grin with his index finger, then bent down and kissed her on the lips.

"You're a harsh woman," he grinned.

"Better believe it, chum," she agreed, "and now I know your weakness, I intend to always get my own way, or else." Lucy spread her fingers out, moving her hand towards Jerry's naked body as if she were about to begin tickling him again.

"I said I submit," Jerry yelped, shifting backwards, but not far enough so she could not reach him.

Instead, Lucy let her fingers walk down his torso, until she reached his groin.

She used her index fingernail to stroke the underside of Jerry's penis, tenderly, back and forth, before she slid her hand between his thighs and cupped his ball sac in a soft embrace.

Jerry moaned and closed his eyes, as Lucy's fingers went to work on him. He could feel himself growing hard as she deployed her fingers between his testicles and his organ, sliding them up and down his shaft in a firm but gentle grasp.

"Uh-oh," Lucy announced.

Reluctantly, Jerry opened his eyes. "What's the matter?" he asked, concern in his voice.

"I think the bald-headed avenger has returned for another attack."

JACOBS CALLED OUT ONCE MORE, his voice rasping from the repeated effort.

Thad had warned him before he left, that no one would be able to hear him from down here, but Jacobs felt compelled to give it go, as he decided he had nothing to lose.

Even Polly had explained to him that shouting and screaming would not help, but at least when she said it, unlike her father, she had a tinge of sorrow in her voice.

Jacobs was not sure how long he had been tied up now. When Thad left him to go back upstairs to prepare lunch for their patrons, he assumed the big man would come back down to finish him off once the crowds had departed, so he imagined it had been no more than a couple of hours thus far.

His back ached from being stuck in the same position for so long, and his wrists were raw as a result of him struggling to release the rope that kept him bound.

He knew his efforts were futile. But he was not prepared to give in just yet.

As long as he was still alive, there was a chance he would make it out in the same condition.

His mind reeled from the stories Thad had told him about his ancestors, and how they had been living off human meat right up to the present day. His stomach turned at the thought that he too, albeit unwittingly, had partaken of the same fare, baked into Thad's famous pies.

If that was not bad enough, Thad had also regaled him with tales about how they bred among each other to keep their line pure, and how some of their kind took after their first breed, living in caves and hunting out fresh meat at night.

Those were the ones, Thad explained, who were not able to mix socially with the rest of the clan, so they continued to live out of sight, only venturing out when it was deemed safe to do so.

But the others, the ones like him and his wife and daughters, they lived all over the world, taking on facades that were more acceptable in society, but still breeding among themselves, and still eating human flesh whenever the occasion permitted.

As Thad repeated his ghoulish tale, Jacobs looked over at Polly as if for confirmation that her father was not just spinning a yarn to frighten him off his daughter. But the minute he caught her eye, Jacobs knew that the story was true.

As hard as it was to believe in this day and age, the family were cannibals.

What's more, by the sound of it, there were potentially hundreds of them spread throughout the world.

Thad had even suggested that Jacobs was a hypocrite for

squirming and retching at the thought, while he himself had enjoyed several meals at the inn, and would have continued to do so had he not succumbed to Polly's erotic charms.

Jacobs had to admit, if only to himself, that there was a kernel of truth in what Thad had said. But right now, the thought of those delicious pies made his stomach turn.

He knew that his only hope was that Polly might somehow be able to free him before her father carried out his threat to turn Jacobs into next week's lunch and dinner.

Polly had certainly reacted to the threat with genuine distress, and even threatened to leave home if Thad hurt Jacobs. But her father was having none of it, and warned his daughter that if she continued to protest, he would make her watch while he sliced up Jacobs on the slab.

Polly then threw herself on her father's mercy, pleading with him to spare Jacobs and let them leave together. She swore her allegiance to the family, and promised him that they would never speak a word of what went on in the village, if only her father would let them leave together.

When Polly fell to her knees and pledged her love for Jacobs, he thought for a moment that Thad would relent. The big man's eyes appeared to mist over, and he scratched his beard, thoughtfully.

When he looked down at Jacobs, the officer nodded his head, hoping that Thad would believe that he too was in earnest, and let him go.

But the moment passed, and Thad shook his head as if to clear away the thought. He grabbed his daughter by the arm and yanked her to her feet, ordering her back upstairs to start organising lunch.

As Polly left the abattoir with her father, she looked back over her shoulder, and gave Jacobs a sorrowful smile.

The vision of that smile haunted him now. If only he had listened to her when she was in his car, begging him to drive away with her. Perhaps now they could be miles away, far from her father's murderous reach, and the unspeakable goings-on at the inn.

In truth though, Jacobs had been far too taken aback to respond at the time.

Did she really love him? Or was he simply the best option of escape from the life she was forced to live?

Either way, did he care? The fact remained that they would have been safe right now, and if he were honest with himself, there was no one else he would rather have been with.

Jacobs glanced around the blood-stained room once more. It reminded him of a scene from the Texas Chainsaw Massacre, with the dangling body parts and severed limbs scattered around the place.

There was only one tiny window at the top of the wall to his right and, when Thad turned off the overhead lights behind them as they left, that left Jacobs with the only trace of light between him and the darkness.

Even now, he could tell that the sun was on the wane. The bright sunlight from when he had first opened his eyes and found himself bound to the chair, had turned to an orange hue, signalling the onset of dusk.

Jacobs feared the time he had left was short.

He had never been a particularly religious man, but even so, he caught himself in silent prayer, asking God at least to make his end swift, and as painless as possible.

Under the circumstances, he was not so sure the second part of his prayer was possible.

Suddenly, he heard the sound of a bolt being shot back.

Jacobs strained to turn towards the noise, and saw a tiny sliver of light appear at the top of the stairs, as the door opened for a split second, then was pulled shut.

He waited for the overhead lights to come to life, but the room stayed in shadowy darkness. Jacob's heart sank as he heard footsteps descending the wooden stairs down to his level. This has to be Thad returning to carry out his threat.

He fought against his restraints, putting every last ounce of his energy into the task. But it was all to no avail. The ropes held fast, and Jacobs wished he had attempted one last scream when the door opened. It may have been his last chance of being heard by someone in the restaurant.

As the footsteps drew closer, Jacobs strained in the darkness to make out the silhouette of his approaching executioner. His stomach churned as a cold shiver of fear spread throughout his body.

His end would not be pleasant.

Judging by the dismembered corpses dangling from the ceiling, Jacobs surmised that Thad's system must include severing his victim's throat, then hanging their lifeless form until the blood had drained out of them.

Jacobs closed in his eyes in anticipation.

Then he felt a gentle kiss on his dry lips.

He looked up to see Polly squatting before him, her face mere inches from his own.

Jacobs opened his mouth to speak, but before he had a chance, Polly covered it with her hand. Her eyes conveyed the message that he needed to keep his voice down, so he nodded, dumbly.

"Dada's been watching me like a hawk all afternoon," Polly whispered. "I didn't think I was goin' to get a chance to slip away, but 'e's gone out back to fetch somethin' so I 'aven't got long."

"Can you untie me?" Jacobs pleaded, his voice a husky a croak, which was barely audible.

Polly shook her head. "It wouldn't be safe, Dada will be down to check on you eventually, an' if 'e sees I've meddled with you, it'll be worse fer both of us."

"But he's planning on killing me!" Jacobs urged, his eyes wide in alarm. "If you don't help me, I'm a dead man."

Polly held his face in her hands and kissed him again.

"You need to trust me," she implored. "I've 'eard Dada speakin' to Mama about you, an' she knows 'ow I feel about you. Even though she doesn't agree with it, I think I can talk 'er round to 'elping you, fer me."

Jacobs frowned. From what he had seen of Mavis Beanie, he was far more willing to believe that she would be happier sharpening the knife for her husband than trying to persuade him to allow Jacobs to live.

But what choice did he have? Without Polly on his side, he was a dead man.

"I've got to get back upstairs before they miss me," Polly informed him. "Stay strong fer me."

With that, she kissed him once more before turning on her heels and heading back upstairs.

Jacobs followed her shadow until she exited the door.

Her words left him with some hope, though not enough to relax completely.

30

KAREN FLINCHED WHEN SHE HEARD THE SOUND.

At first, she could not place it. Underground in the cave, every noise echoed and became distorted, and was usually drowned out by the heaving and grunting noises made by the creatures who held her captive.

Since Jodie had left them, Karen had been approached by the pack more than once. She seemed to fascinate them, although she assumed their interest was more carnal than anything else.

She had looked on in horror as a couple of them took turns with the naked woman Jodie had fed. The woman did not scream or cry out, or even flinch at their touch. Instead she remained motionless, a slave to their wants.

Instinctively, Karen kept her knees tight together, although she realised if the pack did turn on her, she would not be able to fight them off. But. Fortunately for her, once they were finished with the other girl, they moved away.

It almost seemed as if they were waiting for permission to attack her.

Karen wondered if it was Jodie who granted them such approval.

Once the pack had settled down on the other side of the fire, Karen approached the young woman cautiously, and whispered to her to try and ascertain if she were still able to communicate or if her mind had gone completely.

After the ordeal she must have suffered during her time down here, Karen believed that she had every right to have relinquished her hold on sanity.

Sure enough, the woman just kept staring straight ahead, her eyes focused on the flickering shadows on the wall opposite.

When Karen touched the woman's shoulder, she did not even flinch, which was no great surprise considering her lack of reaction to being assaulted by the creatures.

Even so, Karen removed her coat and manoeuvred it around the woman's shoulders to help cover her modesty. Once her coat was in place, Karen put her arms around the woman, and held her closely. She had to admit to herself that her actions were note entirely for the benefit of the woman.

Karen, too, was feeling vulnerable, and petrified in case one of the creatures decided to take a turn with her.

Although, if such a horrendous ambush were to take place, Karen did not intend to lie back meekly and accept the consequences as her companion did. Yet she knew that, in reality, she would have little or no hope of fighting them off.

There were far too many of them, and they looked incredibly strong.

Karen had no doubt that if they wanted to, any one of them could probably rip an arm or a leg clean out of its socket.

But the thought of merely lying back and allowing them to have their filthy way with her turned her stomach.

It was then that the irony of her present predicament occurred to her.

During her relatively short time on the game, how many of her clients who lay sweating and grunting on top of her made her want to throw up?

The fact that she had accepted their payment made no difference to her physical feeling of repugnance at their touch.

But she had survived the ordeal because she was strong and she had put her baby's needs first, ahead of her own. And that, she decided, was the mentality she would adopt to make it through this ordeal, should the situation arise.

Fortified by the thought, Karen leaned back against her companion and closed her eyes.

She was beginning to doze when a noise jolted her out of her reverie.

Karen sat up, and looked around her, wondering where the sound had come from.

Had she imagined it?

It had been a short sharp buzz, like the sound a bee made when it flew past your ear on a summer's day. One second there, then gone.

Karen strained to hear above the miscellaneous grunts and snorts made by her captors, as well as the cracks and spits which emanated from the fire, but the sound did not repeat itself.

Dejected, Karen sat back against the stone wall.

Just as she closed her eyes once more, a thought struck her.

How could she have been so stupid?

She lifted herself away from the wall, and glanced sideways to make sure the creatures were not approaching from around the bend.

Fortunately, they seemed oblivious to her movements.

Once she was convinced, Karen leaned over her fellow captive and fumbled inside the pockets of her coat until she located her mobile.

She took it out and looked at the screen.

There was no signal.

Karen held it out at arm's length and moved it around in an arc, but there was still no sign of life. She slumped back against the wall, dejected. If she were honest, she was not entirely surprised at the lack of signal, her package was not the most advanced by any stretch, but that buzzing sound had given her hope.

Karen slipped her phone inside her jeans pocket; on the off chance she might be able to receive a signal later. She had no idea what plans these creatures had for her, although she had a fair idea, after witnessing what they did to her companion.

But there might be a chance they would move her somewhere else at some point, somewhere with a better reception. So it made sense to keep her phone handy.

Karen glanced over at her fellow prisoner. In her rush to locate her phone she had managed to dislodge her coat from the woman's shoulders, even though the girl appeared oblivious to the disruption.

Nonetheless, Karen turned and moved to a kneeling position to allow her to cover the woman's modesty once more.

As she replaced the coat over the girl's body, Karen felt something tap against her thigh.

It felt heavier than the jacket's material alone, so she slid her hand into the nearest pocket and felt something solid.

When she pulled it out, she realised it was Dan's mobile. With everything else that had happened to her this afternoon, she could be forgiven for forgetting she even had it with her to begin with.

Glancing over her shoulder, Karen held the phone up. The signal was weak, but at least there was something there.

Her first instinct was to call the police. But the sound of the creatures shuffling about nearby changed her mind. If they heard her speaking to someone, they were bound to investigate, and that would be that as far as the phone was concerned.

Karen turned the phone towards her and away from the direction of the creatures.

Sure enough, there was a text message waiting. Karen could see it was from Jerry, whom she had met that day at the library. Dan had told her that they were good friends and that he was the sort of person you could rely upon if you were in trouble. It appeared he was about to be put to the test.

Karen cupped her hand around the phone to dim out the light, and gently replied to Jerry's text, pressing each button slowly and carefully, so as not to make too much noise.

JERRY, this is Karen. Dan is missing and I am being held captive in a cave near the inn. Please help me, my life is in danger. DO NOT CALL!! Just text. They can't hear I have a phone. PLEASE HELP!!!

KAREN SENT THE MESSAGE, and waited. Above all else, she hoped that Jerry would not think it was a prank from Dan. She did not know the extent of their friendship, but if this was the kind of thing they did as a joke, then she knew her cavalry might be a long time in coming.

She wondered how long she should give him to respond before sending further texts. Karen checked the time on the phone. It was a quarter to three. Whatever Jerry was doing right now, she hoped he had his phone to hand.

THE DING from his phone next to him, on the nightstand, was enough to rouse Jerry from his afternoon doze. Lucy's head was resting on his chest, her hair covering her face.

Jerry reached over without dislodging her and grabbed his phone.

He had to read the message twice to make sure what he was reading was not just a trick of the light, or due to his blurry vision, having just opened his eyes.

In all the time he had known Dan, this was not the kind of joke he dealt in.

Jerry's first reaction was to call him. But, before he hit the button, he remembered the message told him not to do so.

He lifted Lucy off him, gently sliding her on to her own side of the bed.

Sitting up, Jerry scanned the message for the third time. There was no mistaking the urgency in the words, nor the sheer desperation Karen expressed.

And what did she mean that Dan was missing?

Missing how?

None of it made any sense to him, but the longer Jerry stared at the message on his screen, the more convinced he was that the situation required attention.

He sat up in bed and replied to the text, as instructed:

<u>Do you want me to call the police?</u>
<u>Are you still in the village?</u>
<u>What should I do?</u>

As he sent it, Lucy began to stir beside him. She yawned and stretched, and leaned over to kiss him once on the mouth. He responded, but kept his focus on the phone.

Without speaking, Lucy slid out of bed and walked out of the room, naked.

Jerry only half noticed her leave. His main attention still

riveted to the phone, in case Karen replied. The sceptic in him still held the view that this was a prank, and that, after a few more such texts, Dan would reveal the game.

But the longer it took, the more Jerry came over to the idea that something was seriously wrong.

While he waited, Jerry heard the toilet flush, followed by the sound of the tap running. After that, he could hear Lucy's bare feet slapping on the wooden floor as she made her way into the kitchen.

"How do you take your coffee?" she called, "black or white?"

"Black please, one sugar." It was an automatic response as the question barely registered in his subconscious.

By the time Lucy returned with two steaming mugs of coffee, there was still no reply.

Lucy placed both mugs on the stand next to Jerry, and leaned in for another kiss.

Jerry did not notice her until she grabbed his chin in her hand and turned his face towards her.

"Is that it then?" she said, sternly. "Now that you've had your fun, you've lost interest?"

"Eh, what?" Jerry looked taken aback. "No, nothing like that, it's just, I received this really strange text from Dan. Well, in fact, it was not from Dan, but Karen, here, read."

He brought back the message and passed her the phone.

Lucy read the screen, and frowned. "Do you think it's for real?" she asked, perplexed.

Jerry shrugged. "Dunno, that's what's so puzzling, I mean, Dan's not the type to play practical jokes. At least, not as long as I've known him."

"I agree, he doesn't seem like the type." Lucy thought for a moment. "You don't think this is maybe Karen's idea of a joke?"

"No idea. I only met her the same day you did."

"That's true, I doubt she knows you well enough to take it

for granted you would think something like this funny." Lucy handed back the phone. "But if it's for real..."

"I know," Jerry completed the sentence. "If it's for real, what should we do? I mean, she's said she's being held captive, so I've sent back a message asking if we should just call the police."

"Do you know where they are?" Lucy asked, lifting her mug of coffee to her lips, and blowing on the steaming liquid.

Jerry nodded. "Dan gave me the details before he left, oddly enough, just in case there was any trouble. But I very much doubt he was concerned something like this would happen."

Just then, the phone pinged in Jerry's hand.

They put their heads together and stared at the tiny screen.

Still in village, held in a cave not far from inn.

They have my baby!

Tried local police when Dan went missing... useless!

Please help me!

JERRY AND LUCY stared at each other.

"Well, she certainly sounds in trouble," Lucy observed.

"What should I do?" Jerry asked, almost imploring Lucy to come up with a strategy he could work with.

Lucy thought for a moment. "OK," she replied, eventually, "just in case this is all a hoax," she held her free hand up, "and I'm not saying it is, but just in case, text back and say you are on your way."

"What!" Jerry looked at her incredulously.

"I know, I know, but if this is a hoax, there's no way Dan is going to let you set off, knowing it's just a wind-up, is he?"

Jerry thought for a moment.

Lucy's idea certainly made sense.

He texted back:

OK, hold tight, I am leaving now.

Will bring police with me.

Send me instructions how to get to you from inn.

Don't worry.

While they waited, they drank their coffee. Both kept their attention firmly focused on the phone, waiting for a response that would either tell them it was all a joke, or that the danger was real.

Finally, it pinged.

Follow path from inn, keeping lake on your left.

Cave entrance on your right, about quarter-mile along path.

Please hurry!

31

JACOBS CRANED HIS NECK TO SEE WHO WAS COMING THROUGH THE door this time. It seemed an absolute age since Polly came down to speak to him, and now he noticed that the daylight that had been shining through the tiny window was completely gone.

He feared it would be Thad, returning to finish him off, as promised.

As the overhead lights came on, he heaved a sigh of relief when he saw the slight figure of Jodie, cautiously taking one step at a time, carrying a glass serving dish in her hands.

She walked over to Jacobs, and stood before him, holding up the dish.

"Dinner," she announced proudly.

Jodie placed the dish on the bench which Thad had been sitting on earlier, and took out a small plastic bottle of water from her apron pocket.

She unscrewed the cap and placed the rim of the bottle on Jacob's lower lip, tilting it forward to allow him to drink.

Jacobs did not realise how thirsty he was, but once the

water began to flow down his throat, he gulped, desperately, swallowing as fast as his oesophagus allowed.

Jodie waited until he was past the halfway mark before she stood the bottle back up and recapped it.

"Not too much, silly," she chastised him, "or you'll end up wetting yourself."

Jacobs managed a raspy: "Thank you."

He was genuinely grateful for the water. His mouth was so parched he was not altogether convinced it was still producing saliva.

Jodie placed the bottle on the bench, and picked up the dish.

As she turned to face him, she whipped off the cloth which had been covering it, and revealed a large slice of meat pie.

"Ta-dah," she announced.

Jacobs looked at the meaty meal and, although his stomach rumbled instinctively, the thought of what Thad had told him went into them made him retch.

He coughed and spluttered, straining against his restraints as he bent forward in preparation for what he knew was coming. However, luckily for him, he had nothing solid left to keep down, so after a few moments he stopped, and sat upright once more.

He could feel tears streaking down his cheeks because of his fit of vomiting.

Jodie too noticed them and, placing the dish back on the bench, she took out a tissue and began to dab his tears away.

"There, there," she said soothingly, "all gone now."

"You'll make a wonderful mother some day," Jacobs gasped, with more than a tinge of sarcasm.

At least his throat was feeling better, thanks to the water.

Jodie spun round and looked about her, as if she were afraid someone else might be down there with them.

Once she was convinced that they were alone, she leaned in

towards Jacob's ear, and whispered. "Don't tell anyone yet, but I've already got me a baby."

When she pulled back, Jacobs stared at her in disbelief.

But in response, Jodie merely nodded excitedly.

"How can you have a child?" Jacobs enquired, astonished by her revelation. "How old are you? You are too young to have given birth!"

Jodie pulled a face. "Well, I didn't give birth to 'er, silly," she replied, her tone mocking him. "But she's mine now, so that's all that matters, innit?"

Jodie could tell immediately from Jacob's expression, that he did not believe her.

She leaned in close once more. "I've got 'er outside in one of Dada's sheds. I'll wait for everyone else to go to bed tonight, then I'll bring 'er out an' take 'er up to my room. She can stay there with me."

The young girl sounded so matter-of-fact, that for a moment Jacobs believed she was being sincere. Or, at least she believed she was.

He could not help but wonder if the poor girl was a trifle touched. If Thad's story was to be believed, Jodie would be a victim of interbreeding, possibly even incest, and history had proven that such a combination often led to the offspring being born with a weak mind, as well as a weak body.

He decided that, in his position, it was probably best to just humour her.

Jodie produced a fork from her apron and used it to break off a chunk of pie. Cupping her hand underneath it, she carried it over to Jacobs like a mother feeding her child.

"Open wide," she commanded.

Jacobs recoiled and turned his head away.

"What's the matter?" asked Jodie, surprised by his reaction. "Mama said you'd be 'ungry, an' I should bring something down for you to eat."

"No thank you," Jacobs said politely, not wishing to antagonise her. "I'm not really feeling very hungry at the moment."

Jodie stared at him, puzzled. "But everyone loves my dada's pies. You've 'ad 'em before – Polly told me."

Jacobs attempted a half smile. "Yes, I know, perhaps a bit later." He coughed once more. "Could I have a little more water, please?"

Jodie shook her head, evidently still unable to fathom anyone turning down one of her father's pies.

She placed the fork with the morsel of pie back in the dish, and brought the bottle back over to him. Jodie let him drink until the bottle was almost empty.

"Oh well," she said, chirpily, "let's hope you don't need to use the bathroom any time soon."

Jacobs swallowed, hard. "Have you any idea what your father intends to do to me?" he asked.

Jodie shook her head. "Not really – they still don't tell me everything around 'ere. I do know that Dada is really mad with my sister, though. I overheard 'im speakin' to Mama while I was in the kitchen."

Now it was Jacob's turn to be furtive.

He gestured with a nod of his head, for Jodie to move closer.

Curious, she complied.

"Do you know that I'm a policeman?" Jacobs asked.

Jodie nodded. "Yeah, I 'eard Mama and Dada talkin' about it."

"Well," he continued, "if I promise that no harm will come to either of your parents, will you do something for me?"

Jodie eyed him, suspiciously. "What?" she asked.

"If you call my colleagues at the station in town and tell them where I am, and what's happened to me, then no one needs to be harmed. Both your parents will be kept safe, I promise you."

As Jodie pulled back, the expression on her face conveyed the fact that she was giving Jacob's request full consideration.

After a moment, she shook her head. "No, sorry, I don't think my dada would be too 'appy with me if I called the police. 'E's always said we can't trust 'em."

"But you can trust me," Jacobs persevered, fighting to keep his tone level and sympathetic. "I won't let them do anything bad to your parents."

The young girl mulled it over again.

Then she asked: "What about me an' Polly?"

"I'll make sure you are both looked after," Jacobs assured her.

"And my baby?"

"Well," Jacobs was still reeling at the idea that Jodie, apparently, had a baby hidden away in a shed in the back yard. "I'll see that your baby is taken care of, too. You have my word."

Jodie planted her hands on her hips. "But I can take care of 'er meself," she said, defiantly. "You just want to take 'er away from me. That's why Dada says we can't trust you."

Before he had a chance to plead his case further, Jodie grabbed up the dish with the pie, and stormed off towards the stairs.

As Jacobs watched her climb, he felt as if his last chance of freedom was leaving with her.

KAREN SAT HUDDLED up against her companion, Dan's mobile tucked firmly inside her bra. She did not want to risk missing a text from Jerry, and with the signal not being particularly strong, she needed to be able to grab the phone the second it went off.

The waiting was agony.

She knew that it would take Jerry at least five to six hours to make it down to Cornwall, even using the motorway. He had said that he was going to inform the police on route, but Karen's biggest fear was that the emergency despatch would connect him to the local station, and if Jerry had as much trouble as she had in trying to persuade them to take action, she could be in for a very long wait.

Even if they did investigate, how would they find her?

She knew that police could sometimes track mobile phones to the nearest control tower, from when it was last used. So that, at least, gave her some hope.

But from there, they would still need to track down her location.

Karen wondered if the cave was a local attraction. A well-known haunt, which one of the officers might remember visiting as a child.

But then, if that were the case, did the locals also know about the cave-dwellers?

Surely not.

Karen was well aware that smaller communities tended to shut their doors to the world, and keep themselves to themselves. But this was not something that they could just pretend was normal.

Furthermore, judging by the state of the woman beside her, it appeared to Karen that these creatures presumably made a habit of abducting women off the streets for their own perverse pleasure.

So how could they keep that between themselves?

These victims must be missed, surely to goodness?

Karen shuddered at the thought. Her main focus was still on finding a way to escape and rescue Charlotte. She dreaded to think what Jodie might be doing to her baby.

Her one consolation was that the young girl had seemed genuinely enamoured by her daughter, and that gave Karen hope that Charlotte would remain unharmed.

Just then, she heard a shuffling noise coming from around the next bend.

Karen tensed, and unconsciously reached out to hold her companion's hand in a show of unity.

As the first of the creatures lurched into view, Karen shuffled as far back as she could against the wall. Unlike her, the woman beside her did not move an inch. There was no doubt in Karen's mind that the poor girl's reason had already deserted her, doubtless as a result of being a prisoner of these wretched things.

As the closest of them shuffled closer, Karen tried to look away, but an unholy fascination kept drawing her back.

Before she knew it, she was surrounded on all sides.

Two rough, hairy hands grabbed at her jeans and began pulling at them.

Karen screamed and tried to fight back, but the effort was useless.

The other creatures soon joined in the onslaught, and before she had a chance to consider how to retaliate, her jeans had been wrenched off her, and discarded to one side.

As she was being held down, Karen knew that surrender might be her only chance of survival. But it was not in her nature to give in so easily, so she continued to struggle and resist as best she could, until the first creature impaled her.

32

"Whoa, easy there, old horse," Lucy called out, slamming her hands on the dashboard in front of her, as if preparing for an imminent impact.

"Sorry," replied Jerry, glancing over to her for a moment, and offering a smile. "I just hate it when idiots dawdle in the middle lane, and only drive at 50 miles an hour."

Jerry had initially asserted that he was driving down to Cornwall alone. But Lucy had other ideas and insisted that she be allowed to accompany him.

Once they reached the motorway, Lucy programmed the address Dan had given Jerry into Google, and they settled themselves in for the long drive.

By half-past eight, they had been on the road for more than five hours and, although she had offered to share the driving, Jerry insisted on taking the wheel. When Lucy cracked a joke about him not trusting women drivers, Jerry explained that he was a terrible back-seat driver, and always grew fidgety.

Lucy ventured a theory that he was just a control freak.

Other than a short stop for petrol, they kept going without a break. The motorway traffic was relatively light, so they had managed to keep to 70 miles per hour, except when Jerry allowed his needle to slip closer to 80.

Lucy had attempted dialling the emergency services when they first set out, but due to the lack of specific details, such as Karen's surname or address, the police operator did not seem to take their concerns too seriously.

Even with Jerry chipping in on speaker phone, they soon realised they had a losing battle on their hands. The only service the operator was willing to provide was to contact the police station closest to where Dan and Karen were staying, and pass on the details. Then, the operator explained, it would be down to them to investigate, or not, as they saw fit.

The operator also suggested that Jerry and Lucy stopped off at the station when they reached the town. But both of them suspected that might be a ruse to pass the buck, so they decided between them that they would make straight for the village to search for Karen, and decide what to do once they had sussed out the lay of the land.

Lucy could tell that Jerry was more concerned about Dan and Karen than he was letting on, so she lightened the mood whenever she could by rifling through his CD collection, and making fun of his taste in music.

They turned off the motorway, and followed the Google directions through the town, and on to the village.

"Do you think we should stop at the police station?" asked Lucy, placing a comforting hand on Jerry's knee.

Jerry shook his head. "It'll just waste time," he said, glancing at the dashboard. "They'll probably keep us there for ages going through our story, and that's time we could spend looking for them."

Lucy could hear the anxious tone in Jerry's voice.

Karen had already mentioned in her texts that Dan was not with her, but Lucy knew that Jerry had not given up hope of finding him, too.

"Should I try texting her yet?" Lucy asked. They had not sent another message since informing Karen that they were on their way. If the situation was as grave as Karen had made out, then they did not want to risk sending umpteen messages, in case it alerted her captors to the fact she was in contact with someone on the outside.

Jerry thought for a moment before replying to Lucy's question.

"Let's wait until we are parked up. She said something about an inn being nearby to where she was being held, so I'll stop there, and we can go in on foot."

Lucy could feel her legs growing restless. She was not sure if it was just the fact that she had been sitting still for so long, or the nerves she was beginning to feel now that they were so close.

She had to admit, it had all sounded a little far-fetched when Jerry first received Karen's plea for help, and she half expected to discover that Jerry had arranged it all with Dan, as a surprise for her.

It sounded quite romantic. A drive to the coast, then a nice dinner somewhere by the sea, and perhaps he had even booked them in to a hotel for the night.

But, although she did not voice her suspicions for fear of ruining the surprise, the more she thought about it, the more ridiculous her idea seemed.

For one thing, they both had work the next day, and neither of them had a change of clothes with them. Furthermore, Jerry's concern seemed genuine, unless he happened to be a brilliant actor.

No, unfortunately, it now seemed clear that this was not some elaborate hoax, but the real deal.

Lucy was all for them diving in and rescuing Karen and her baby, but Lucy now wished she had been a little more insistent that they bring the police along with them.

After all, they had no idea what they were walking into, and it wouldn't help anyone if they ended up being captured as well.

Lucy was just about to pass on her concerns to Jerry, when Google announced that they had reached their destination.

Jerry slowed down as the solid road beneath their tyres gave way to more uneven ground.

The headlights illuminated the hump-backed bridge ahead, and Jerry geared down to second to avoid stalling.

A low mist appeared to have risen out of nowhere, shrouding the way ahead, making it almost impossible to see more than 50 yards in front.

As they crossed the bridge, Lucy studied their surroundings. When she saw the old graveyard outside Jerry's window, with the eerie mist whirling through the headstones, she wished she had kept her eyes in front.

She gave a violent shiver.

"Are you OK?" asked Jerry with concern.

"Not really," Lucy admitted. "This place really gives me the willies."

Jerry nodded. "It does look a little like an old horror-film set," he agreed.

"I wonder if Christopher Lee or Peter Cushing ever owned a place here."

Jerry laughed, in spite of himself. Lucy could certainly brighten up the most depressing of situations. He wondered for a moment why he had ever been reticent about asking her out. As a rule, he refused to allow himself to dwell on mistakes from his past, so he decided to just be grateful that she was here with him, now.

As their car drove slowly down the village main road, Jerry caught sight of the numbers on the cottages to his right.

"Here it is," he announced, pulling up outside one of them. "Look, there's Dan's car parked outside, I'm sure it is."

They sat there for a moment with the engine idling and peered through the window at the darkened building.

"Do you think it's worth trying the door?" Lucy asked. "I mean, I know she said she was being held somewhere else, but on the off-chance Dan has returned, we could do with reinforcements."

"Good idea," Jerry agreed. "You wait here."

With that, he left the engine running while he climbed out of his seat, and approached the front door cautiously.

Lucy watched him through the window as he knocked on the door, loud enough so that she could hear it above the sound of the engine.

He tried twice, without response, then Jerry tried the handle, but the door would not budge.

Peering in through the downstairs window, Jerry could just about make out that there was no one downstairs. He squinted through the darkness for any sign of life, but it was too dim inside to make anything out for sure.

Reluctantly, he returned to the car.

"Anything?" asked Lucy, already guessing the answer.

Jerry shook his head. "Nope, let's carry on down here and see if we can find this inn Karen mentioned."

KAREN SAT HUNCHED up with her arms wrapped around her knees. Her ordeal at the hands of the creatures had lasted for more than an hour as they took it in turns to abuse her.

She gave up trying to fight them off after the second one entered her.

Her struggles were futile against such strong assailants, so she grudgingly decided to give in to protect herself from further harm.

Karen knew that one blow from these creatures would

render her unconscious, or possibly worse. So her main aim was to remain alive in the hope that she could eventually escape, and rescue Charlotte from Jodie.

Once the creatures had finished with her, they slowly made their way back around the corner, and out of sight. Karen could still hear them moving around, communicating with each other in their own unique manner.

After a while, she retrieved her discarded clothes from the floor in front of her, and gingerly slipped them on.

There was a certain comfort in covering herself up, even though she was aware that her apparel would be no obstacle, should her attackers decide to return for more.

To her surprise, the woman beside her moved in closer and placed her arm around her shoulders in what Karen took to be a gesture of solidarity.

But when she turned to offer her companion a smile of appreciation, there was still nothing behind her eyes to show that she was aware of their mutual circumstances. Or, indeed, conscious of the fact that they could be killed at any moment on the whim of one of their captors.

Even so, Karen was grateful for the simple act of kindness, and snuggled in closer like a child seeking the protection of its parent.

She could still feel the comforting shape of Dan's mobile beneath her bra, pressing against her soft flesh. It being her only connection with the outside world, she was grateful that the creatures did not find it and destroy it during their onslaught.

Karen was almost afraid to take it out and check the screen, for fear that either the charge had run out, or the signal was gone. She was not sure how she would cope if such a scenario played out. But by the same token, she knew that she needed to check, otherwise she was waiting for a text that was never coming.

Carefully, Karen slipped the phone out of her bra, and held it in front of her, covering the screen with her hand to ensure her captors would not see the light.

The screen came to life, as a new message arrived from Jerry.

Here at inn.

Going to follow path beside lake.

How many holding you hostage?

KAREN CHECKED that none of the creatures had re-emerged from behind the next bend before she replied. She presumed that they had all come forth to either participate in, or watch her attack, which meant there were six of them, as far as she could remember.

If there were more of them holed up somewhere else in the cave, then she had no way of knowing how many there were in total.

She replied:

At least six.

NOT HUMAN!

BEASTS!

Are police with you?

SHE WAITED, holding her breath. Why had she not mentioned before that those holding her were not human?

Was it because she had been afraid that Jerry might not take her plight seriously?

There was no way Karen could allow Jerry to come and find her, without at least warning him of what he was about to meet. He was walking into the lion's den for her sake, and if anything happened to him, she knew she would not be able to live with herself.

Finally, the response came:

What do you mean, not human?
What kind of beasts?

KAREN WAS ALL TOO aware how ridiculous she must sound to Jerry. If roles were reversed, she wondered if she would be able to grasp the situation. After all, they barely knew each other, and he had already driven all the way down from London to rescue her on the strength of a couple of vague text messages.

Karen thought for a moment before replying.

She could hear the creatures growing restless around the corner.

She prayed they were not preparing from another attack so soon after the first one.

I know I sound crazy, but please believe me.
These things are more animal than human.
Help!

33

LUCY STARED OVER JERRY'S SHOULDER, READING THE LATEST TEXT message from Karen.

"I don't understand," she said. "What do you think she means?"

Jerry shook his head. "Absolutely no idea," he admitted.

From behind them, they could hear the noise from the evening crowd in the bar. After the long drive, they were both ready for a drink and a bite to eat, but they knew that more pressing matters awaited their attention.

"Are we being taken for idiots?" Lucy asked, perplexed.

"If it were anyone else other than Dan, I might have believed that to be so. But he's not that kind of a bloke. You know what he's like."

"So what now?"

Jerry glanced around them. The parking area was relatively full, but they managed to find a spot close to the main entrance. Up ahead, they could see the sign for the lake illuminated by the overhead car park lights.

He wondered if it might be sensible to move his car closer

to the lake for a quick getaway. But then he decided to leave it where it was for now.

Part of him was still unable to fathom the situation fully, and Karen's bizarre messages were not helping his thought processes.

Jerry squeezed Lucy's shoulder and walked around to the boot. He flipped the lid and took out a crowbar, a torch and a hunting knife, which he had packed for the journey.

He opened the belt on his jeans, and slipped it through the sheath, before securing it once more.

He closed the boot, making sure not to slam it as he did not wish to alert anyone in the pub to their presence.

Jerry had no idea whether anyone inside the inn had anything to do with what was going on, but they were in a strange place, in the middle of nowhere, so he thought it best not to announce their presence.

As he walked back around to where Lucy was standing, they both heard a cry echoing through the night.

They waited.

Then the cry came again. It was more prolonged this time, and continued as they glanced about them to try to discover its source.

It was a baby's cry.

The two of them looked at each other, bewildered.

"That what I think it is?" asked Lucy.

Jerry nodded. "Where's it coming from?"

They both scanned the parking area. There was no sign of anyone emerging or entering their vehicles, let alone anyone with a baby in tow.

The crying continued.

"I think it's coming from over there," said Lucy, pointing towards the back of the inn. "Come on, we need to investigate."

"What about Karen?" Jerry reminded her.

"I know," answered Lucy, "but this won't take a minute, we

need to make sure someone hasn't abandoned a baby somewhere out here."

"Do you think that's likely?"

Lucy shrugged. "You never know. You hear about such things on the news all the time."

She pulled Jerry's sleeve as she began to make her way towards the back entrance.

Jerry followed, the torch in one hand and the crowbar in the other.

As they rounded the inn towards the bin area, they came across a large, plastic shed. There were no windows in the structure, and the door was held fast with a stout padlock.

The crying was definitely coming from within.

Lucy grabbed the padlock and pulled at it, frantically.

"It won't budge," she announced. "Someone has actually locked a screaming baby inside here." She turned back to Jerry. "We need to get it open," she urged.

Under normal circumstances, Jerry would have suggested that they go to the inn to report the situation. After all, this was private property.

But then, having a baby locked in a shed, was hardly what anyone would describe as normal circumstances.

Jerry moved Lucy to one side, and placed the fork-end of his crowbar in the shackle of the lock. He pulled back, using all his strength. It took him two attempts to wrench it off, and made more noise than he had wanted to, but at least it worked.

As the broken padlock flew through the air, Jerry made a grab for it, but missed. It hit the ground and rattled along for a few feet before finally coming to a stop.

Jerry flung open the door and shone his torch inside.

In one corner, surrounded by old tools, and discarded bits of machinery, they saw the tiny form of Charlotte in her pram, screaming for her mother.

For a moment, Jerry stood there, stunned.

Although they had both heard the baby's wailing from outside, he still found it inconceivable that anyone in their right mind would trap a baby inside a shed, when the weather was so cold.

Lucy, on the other hand, took the situation at face value, and barged passed him so she could reach baby Charlotte.

Jerry kept the torch beam aimed in the direction of the pram, to afford Lucy maximum assistance in her endeavour. Once she reached the pram, Lucy did not hesitate in lifting the baby out and cradling it against her body.

She cupped her hand gently behind the baby's head, and whispered soothing words to try to comfort her.

Lucy turned back to face Jerry. The light from his torch dazzled her a moment, until he realised what he was doing and lowered the beam, slightly.

"What shall we do with it?" Jerry asked.

"Well, we can't leave the poor thing in here," Lucy replied.

"I know," Jerry assured her. "I mean, should we take it inside the pub and see if anyone in there knows what's going on?"

Lucy thought for a moment.

Finally, she replied. "I don't know, I'd hate to think someone in there did this terrible thing. But who else would have access to this shed, and be able to lock it behind them? The whole thing is barbaric."

Jerry nodded his agreement. "Let's take it back to the car and call the police, they have to come out for this."

"Stay right where you are!"

The voice came from behind Jerry, but with the torch's beam still dazzling her, Lucy had not seen Jodie sneak up behind him.

Jerry turned to see the tiny frame of Jodie, holding a sawn-off shotgun pointed directly at him.

Jerry instinctively raised his arms above his head.

Even though he had never had a firearm pointed at him before, it seemed the only logical course of action, under the circumstances.

"Come out 'ere where I can see you both," Jodie commanded.

As young as she was, there was a menacing edge to her tone that worried Jerry. On top of which, she looked as if this was not her first time handling that gun.

Jerry did as he was told, and moved aside to allow Lucy to step out of the shed, with baby Charlotte in her arms. Her natural fear and trepidation at seeing Jodie pointing a gun at them seemed to transfer on to the baby, who screamed even louder when Jodie came into view.

Jerry tried to manoeuvre himself so he blocked Jodie's line of fire, keeping Lucy and the baby behind him once they emerged from the shed.

"Listen," he began, shakily. "I know what this must look like, but we heard this baby screaming when we arrived just now. Someone had locked it inside this shed and we had to break open the lock to free it."

"An' who asked yer to interfere in matters that 'ave nothin' t'do with yer, eh?" Jodie replied, keeping the barrels levelled at Jerry's chest.

"What were we supposed to do?" demanded Lucy, peering around Jerry's protective form. "We couldn't just leave the poor thing in there crying for its life!"

Jodie ignored her explanation. "You can drop that there bar fer a start-off," she stated, gesturing towards Jerry's raised arm.

In fact, Jerry had forgotten he was holding anything.

Carefully, he bent down, looking at Jodie all the time, and placed the crowbar on the ground. As he stood back up, he turned off the torch and slipped it inside his belt, making sure that he did not pull his jacket back far enough to reveal his knife.

Jodie moved towards them with the gun held high.

Jerry, instinctively held out his arms to protect the girls, and took a step backwards.

When Jodie was close enough, she looked down for a second and placed her foot on the discarded crowbar, before sliding it back behind her along the ground.

Once she was satisfied that Jerry could no longer reach it, she turned her attention towards Lucy.

"Now then," she began, purposefully, "I want you to move over 'ere with me baby," she pointed with the gun towards an area to the side of Jerry. "An' then I want you," she looked at him, "to go inside that shed and bring out 'er pram, understand?"

"Wait," said Lucy, not attempting to hide her astonishment. "This is your baby?"

"Yes!" replied Jodie, angrily. "An' what's it to do with you?"

Lucy stared at the young girl before her. "You're not old enough to have a baby," she said, eyeing her suspiciously.

"Yes I am," screamed Jodie, defiantly, gripping the gun tightly with both hands, and gesturing towards Jerry. "Now get in there an' bring out 'er pram." Jerry nodded, and turned to face Lucy.

He gave her a slight half-smile, as if to assure her everything would be all right. Whereas, in fact, he had no idea what to do to try to defuse their present situation.

He only hoped that Lucy would not say or do anything to antagonise the young girl, especially while she was still holding them at gunpoint.

Lucy did her best to try and calm the crying baby, while Jerry complied with Jodie's command.

Jerry backed the pram out of the shed, and turned it around, moving it forward before locking the brake pedal.

"Now put me baby back in her cot," Jodie ordered.

Lucy glanced at Jerry, then quickly back to Jodie. "She

seems terribly distressed," Lucy pointed out, keeping her voice calm and relaxed. "Don't you think it would be better if we all went inside, out of the cold?"

"What she needs," Jodie insisted through gritted teeth, "is 'er mama. Now stop messin' about an' do as I tell yer."

Reluctantly, Lucy placed the crying baby back in her carry-cot. She placed the blanket over the child to help keep out the night chill.

Once Jodie was satisfied her demands had been complied with, she gestured once more with the gun barrels, and ordered the pair of them to go back inside the shed.

Jerry ushered Lucy back inside. He could tell how reluctant she was at having to leave the baby behind but, at the moment, he could not think past not giving Jodie an excuse to shoot them.

Once they were both inside, Jodie stepped back a few paces and retrieved the crowbar from the floor. She held it in one hand while balancing the shotgun under her opposite arm, and approached the shed.

Without speaking, Jodie closed the door, trapping Jerry and Lucy inside.

They listened from within while Jodie attempted to close the hasp and staple shut, intending to slide the crowbar through the slot to secure it.

However, the force Jerry had applied to the padlock when he was breaking in, had caused the lock shutter to buckle slightly, and Jodie struggled to engage the clasp.

From within the shed, Jerry and Lucy could hear Jodie grunting and groaning as she desperately tried to marry the two ends of the contraption together.

Something metallic hit the ground, outside.

They weren't sure if Jodie had dropped either the shotgun or the crowbar. But either way, it meant that for a split second she might be disorientated enough for them to take advantage.

Without waiting, Jerry charged the inside of the door with his shoulder.

It sprang open, catching Jodie unaware, and sending her sprawling on to the concrete surface outside the shed.

She yelped out in pain as her rump hit the floor hard. Meanwhile, the shotgun flew from her grasp and clattered on the ground, a few feet to one side of her horizontal form.

Before she had a chance to react, Jerry raced forward and grabbed her, turning her over on to her front, before wrenching her arms behind her back, and holding them together at the wrists.

Jodie bucked and cried out beneath him.

Within seconds, Lucy moved in to assist him, grabbing a handful of muslin squares from the changing bag looped around the handle of Charlotte's cot and forcing them into Jodie's mouth to silence her cries.

Unravelling her long scarf from around her neck, Lucy wrapped the material around Jodie's wrists several times over until they were securely bound; then left Jerry to tie a double knot to hold them in place.

The pair of them took several deep breaths of relief, before either of them spoke.

"Now what?" Lucy enquired.

Jerry raised himself off Jodie's bound body. "Help me carry her into the shed," he replied. "You take the half that talks, I'll grab her legs."

They carried their writhing prisoner into the shed and, once inside, Jerry found some twine and bound Jodie's knees and ankles together to stop her from attempting to escape.

The young girl fought strenuously against her bonds, but soon realised her efforts were futile, and relaxed as tears of anger and frustration spilled down her cheeks.

Jerry found a roll of black gaffer tape hanging from a hook by the door, and tore a couple of strips off. He used these to cover Jodie's mouth to ensure she could not spit out the muslin squares and start screaming for help.

As the pair of them gazed down at their helpless victim, the look of pure hatred in the young girl's eyes sent a shiver through both of them.

Once back outside, Jerry managed to jimmy the lock together, and taking a page out of Jodie's book, slid the crowbar through it to secure the door.

While Lucy comforted baby Charlotte, Jerry retrieved the shotgun from where it had landed.

He had handled a shotgun only a couple of times before in his life, when he had accompanied an old uncle who enjoyed clay-pigeon shooting. He was grateful now that he had paid attention to his lessons, as they had at least taught him how to check the safety catch was on, and that the gun was in fact loaded.

They wheeled Charlotte's pram back to the car.

Fortunately, she had tired herself out with her crying, and was now settled and starting to drift off.

"You don't really think this baby belongs to that young girl, do you?" Lucy asked.

"I doubt it," replied Jerry. "I think it's more than likely to be Karen's. Remember how she said they had taken her baby away from her?" he indicated over his shoulder. "I'm more than willing to believe that madam back there had something to do with it."

"What do we do now?"

"Well, I think you should stay here with the baby, and call the police and tell them what's happened. They've got to come out for this."

"Then what are you going to do?" Lucy was suspicious about Jerry's next answer, as she knew he would not want to waste any more time waiting for the police to arrive.

"I'm going to follow the trial by the lake, and see if I can locate this cave Karen says she is being held in."

Lucy was right. "Why can't you just wait with us for the police, it'll make more sense if you try to find the cave with them?"

Jerry placed a comforting hand on her shoulder. "It'll waste too much time. God knows how long she has been stuck in there already – just send the police out after me."

Lucy wanted desperately to argue the point. She hated the fact that Jerry was planning to go out alone, in the middle of nowhere, possibly to come up against six... whatever they were.

But she also knew she could not have an argument with him about it, because his mind was already made up.

Jerry took out his car keys and handed them to Lucy.

"You take the car and drive out of this car park – you're too exposed here," he recommended. "Once you've parked up out of sight, call the police to come and get you."

Lucy took the keys reluctantly, while Jerry unhitched the carry-cot from the frame and placed it on the back seat, buckling it in.

He folded the chassis and put it in the boot.

Once he had managed to usher the hesitant Lucy around to the driver's seat, he leaned in and kissed her.

"Please take care," she begged. "And don't do anything foolish – the police will be here soon."

"Don't worry," he assured her. "Just make sure they follow on as soon as possible."

With that, he waited for Lucy to start the car and drive out of the car park, and then he left.

34

Jacobs felt himself being shaken awake. As he opened his eyes in the murky darkness, he saw the beautiful face of Polly staring down at him. He opened his mouth to speak, but she immediately placed her hand across his mouth, and held her opposing index finger to her lips.

Jacobs understood the gesture.

Polly removed her hand from his face and bent down to kiss him. After a moment, she sat on his lap and began to fondle his hair as she pressed his face against hers, in an act of sheer desperation.

Jacobs could feel himself starting to grow hard, and soon, Polly too could feel his rising member through the flimsy material of her work skirt.

She began to gyrate with her hips and, for a moment, Jacobs was afraid that he might ejaculate into his pants.

Then Polly stopped, and climbed off him.

Without a word, she took a pair of meat shears from the bench in front of them, and slid one of the blades between the rope and Jacob's hands.

Jacobs felt a sudden wave of relief. Before dropping off to

sleep, he had prayed that someone would find and free him, before Thad carried out his threat to make him the following night's special.

He realised how much Polly must be risking by helping him, and her gesture was not lost on him. She was turning against her own family. But why?

Judging by Thad's demeanour, he did not come across as the forgiving type. Jacobs was in no doubt that he ruled his family absolutely, and if any of them stepped out of line, justice would be his to command.

The man was evidently insane. After all, he made a living from killing and eating human beings.

Jacobs checked himself at the thought. He knew that he too was guilty of partaking in human flesh, but at least he had done so unawares. The law could not blame him, any more than it could the rest of the inn's patrons.

Jacobs could feel the knife blade sliding back and forth behind him, but it seemed to be taking for ever, and it was agony for his wrists, which were already sore from his struggles.

He could hear Polly grunting and heaving with the exertion but, from where he was sitting, she did not seem to be making much progress.

"Have you got anything sharper?" he asked, keeping his voice down.

Polly nodded and began to scour the abattoir benches for a more suitable implement. But, in the darkness it was hard for her to see where she was going, or what was available.

She brushed past several dismembered body parts, which Jacobs was pleased to notice made her squirm. There was hope for this girl yet – she clearly did not feel comfortable surrounded by decaying human flesh.

Finally, Polly reached out and cut herself on the upturned blade of a bone-saw.

She yelped in pain, but managed to keep her voice under control to avoid either of her parents hearing her from upstairs.

Polly carried the half-moon-shaped saw back over to Jacobs, and this time he felt more confident that she would be able to get the job done.

Being careful not to catch Jacobs's skin with the teeth of the saw, Polly angled it so she could cut away from his wrists with the cutting stroke.

Jacobs could feel her efforts making progress. The ropes were beginning to slacken. Any minute now.

They both heard the door from the kitchen opening.

Polly stopped her work, and shuffled back into the darkness behind Jacobs, so that she could not be seen.

Just then, the overhead lights came on, illuminating the main cutting tables in the centre of the room.

Jacobs strained against the ropes holding his head in place, to see Mavis Beanie strutting down the stairs, carrying a bucket of water in one hand, and what looked like an empty bucket in the other.

Over her shoulders, she had draped several cloth rags of varying sizes, and dangling from her wrist by a loop of ribbon was a scrubbing brush, like the types people often used in the bath.

Mavis appeared to be relaxed enough as she descended the stairs to where Jacobs sat captive. She placed her accoutrements on the floor in front of him, and smiled.

"Now, you see," she began, "This sort of task I normally give to one of me daughters, but for some reason, I can't seem to find either of 'em, so you'll jus' 'ave to do wiv me, I'm afraid."

Mavis grabbed a wooden stool from under the bench, and plonked herself down on it. Her huge frame looked ridiculous perched on the tiny wooden seat, but it seemed to hold her weight. She then proceeded to undo Jacob's trousers before forcing them down around his knees. Before he could react, she had slipped her fingers inside the waistband of his boxers, and those too were dragged down his legs.

"Now then," she said, grabbing the empty bucket and holding it between his legs. "I dare say you need a pee right about now, so go on – don't be bashful."

In fact, he was desperate to urinate, now that she mentioned it, but whether or not he could do so in this position, under these circumstances, was another matter altogether.

"Come on now," Mavis urged him, "I ain't got all day." Then she laughed out loud. "Speakin' o' which, neither 'ave you."

She seemed to find her own joke hysterical, and Jacobs knew only too well the meaning behind it.

Somehow, he managed to let loose a stream, and looked away as he listened to his jet echoing inside the bucket.

Once he was finished, Mavis moved the bucket to one side and took out one of the flannels she had brought with her. She plunged it into the water, and wrung it out before proceeding to wash Jacobs's genitals.

As she worked, the woman hummed a tune to herself, as if the task were the most natural thing in the world.

Once she was satisfied, Mavis put down the flannel and picked up the brush. Again, she plunged it into the water, and shook off the residue, before scrubbing the area between Jacob's legs, right down to his knees.

The bristles raked against his flesh, making Jacobs stiffen and struggle against his restraints.

Seemingly oblivious to his discomfort, Mavis continued with her task, taking care she did not miss a spot.

The constant strain of fighting his bonds was making his muscles ache, so Jacobs relaxed his posture momentarily.

Quite unexpectantly, he felt the ropes securing his hands start to release. He flexed his fingers to keep the circulation going, and then carefully, not wishing to alert his captor, he tried to slip his wrists free.

It worked.

He was still secured to the pipe, but at least now with his hands loose, he could attempt to untie himself.

Jacobs had no wish to imagine what would happen once Mavis Beanie was satisfied that he was clean. But he suspected this might be his one and only chance to break free.

He struggled against the rope encircling his body, and managed to move his hands around to his waist before Mavis realised what he was up to.

"'Ere now!" she shouted, but it was too late.

Jacobs grabbed hold of the sides of his chair, and managed to lift both legs high enough to aim at the woman's torso.

Without pausing to aim, he shot his feet forward and caught Mavis square in the chest, pushing her backwards. The woman's arms flew out to her sides windmilling as the stool toppled over, sending her crashing back against the bench behind her.

Jacobs paused for a moment, certain that the noise of the falling woman would bring her husband bounding down the stairs to investigate.

But no one came.

Jacobs looked over at Mavis. She appeared to have knocked herself unconscious and, from the position of her head, it looked as if she might have broken her neck in the fall.

From behind him, Polly appeared, she ran over to her mother's motionless form, and placed her hand on the side of her neck.

After a moment, she turned to Jacobs. "She's still alive, I can feel a pulse."

She sounded relieved, and Jacobs could not blame her. After all, Mavis was her mother, regardless of what terrible things she had intended to do to him.

Polly came back over to Jacobs and helped him slip his arms out of his restraints. Rather than waste precious time trying to cut the bonds with her seemingly blunt scissors, Polly held his chair fast while Jacobs stood on it and stepped out of his bonds.

Once he was free, Jacobs dressed himself again before wrapping his arms around his saviour. As they hugged, they heard a low moan escape Mavis's lips.

They both stared at the woman, each expecting her to open her eyes and start screaming to raise the alarm.

But instead, her eyes remained shut, and she stayed in the same position.

"Quick," urged Polly, "we must try an' escape through the kitchen before me dada sees what's 'appened."

Polly grabbed Jacobs by the hand and led him up the narrow staircase.

Jacobs considered going back down for a weapon. There were several tools and saws scattered around the abattoir, which would make fine weapons at a pinch. After all, Jacobs knew he would be no match for Thad if he caught them.

But before he had a chance to mention his idea, Polly had already opened the door a crack, and was looking through it to see if the coast was clear.

She squeezed Jacobs's hand. "Come on," she whispered, "stay close behind me."

They crept through the doorway into an anteroom just off the kitchen.

From their position, they could hear the sound of plates and cutlery being laid out on trays, mingled with calls from the Sunday staff announcing who needed what, and at which table.

It appeared to all intents and purposes like a normal evening in a busy restaurant.

But knowing the truth of what was being served to so many unwitting diners made Jacob's stomach turn.

Just then, they both heard the thunderous voice of Thad

Beanie calling out that there were hungry customers waiting to be fed.

The pair of them automatically crouched down, as if afraid the big man might see them through the walls.

Still clasping Jacobs's hand, Polly led him around the large table that dominated the room, and towards a cubbyhole at the far end of the room.

Once there, she opened the door, and the pair of them just managed to wedge themselves inside enough to hold the door closed.

They waited in silence, both trying desperately to keep the sound of their breathing low. They froze as they heard the unmistakable rumble of Thad's voice as he strode into the anteroom, calling for his wife.

"Mavis, where the bleedin' 'ell are yer, woman?"

They could both sense that he was only a few feet away.

Jacobs tried to prepare himself to pounce, just in case the big man decided to open the cubbyhole door, but his legs were already beginning to cramp from being in such a tight space, so he knew that any effort on his part would be to little or no avail.

"Where the bleedin' 'ell is everyone tonight?"

The big man's words were followed by the sound of the door leading downstairs to the abattoir opening. "Mavis." Thad yelled, "you down there?"

They both held their breath until they heard him start to descend the stairs.

Without speaking, Polly pushed opened the cubbyhole door and crept along to the abattoir door, closing it gently and slipping the bolt into place.

Once it was secured, she leaned down to slot the second bolt into its holder, then finally she closed the hasp and staple and slid the padlock home.

Just as the lock snapped shut, there came a furious banging on the door from the other side.

"What the bleedin' 'ell is goin' on out there? Let me out!"

Ignoring her father's rant, Polly reached out and grabbed hold of Jacobs's hand, and led him out of the anteroom and into the kitchen.

They disregarded the glances they received from the shocked staff members, as Polly led the way past them towards the outside door.

Once they were outside, Polly turned to Jacobs, and looked him deeply in the eyes.

"Run," she commanded, "get away from 'ere and don't ever come back – it won't be safe."

Jacobs looked at her in astonishment. "And what about you?" he demanded. "They knew you let me escape, what will happen to you?"

Polly shrugged. "They won't kill me, I'm still their kin. They'll beat me plenty, but I'll live. The most important thing is you're alive. You need to get away, afore they come after you, or set the clan on to you."

Jacobs looked at her. Running was the only sane thing to do under the circumstances, but something inside him told him that, if he left Polly behind, regardless of her assertions, he would never see her alive again.

At that moment, she seemed more important to him than anything else. He held both her hands in his. "I'm not going anywhere without you; do you hear me?"

35

KAREN CHECKED HER MOBILE AGAIN, THERE WERE NO NEW messages from Jerry. What was taking him so long? She wondered if perhaps he had walked past the entrance to the cave and by now was halfway into town without realising it.

She considered sending him another text, but then stopped herself.

The creatures seemed to be coming closer, judging by the reflection of their shadows on the opposite wall, and that could only mean one thing. They were ready for another assault. Karen closed her knees unconsciously, her instinct for self-preservation automatically kicking in. She knew in truth that neither she nor her companion were in any state to fight off the creatures, and as she had already submitted to some of them, she knew that she would survive another onslaught.

But that did not stop her instinctive inner need to fight. Why should they be allowed to take what they wanted, purely because of their size and strength?

Her position was made even more untenable by the fact that, due to their lack of communication skills, she was unable even to attempt to reason with them.

Whatever they were, they seemed to possess only the most basic fundamental of needs: shelter, food and sex. And while she would never deny any living being the first two, Karen could not help but detest them for the way they seemed oblivious to anyone else's consideration when seeking the third.

Karen wondered how long her fellow captive had been held down here, and for that matter, how many times she had had to allow herself to be subjected to their inhuman treatment.

The poor woman seemed completely unresponsive. Her dark eyes stared straight ahead at all times, regardless of what was happening to her. Karen had made several attempts to speak to her, but none had yielded the slightest result.

In fact, the only sign of life she had witnessed from her since arriving in the cave was when Jodie had fed her.

The thought of Jodie brought Karen's mind back to her baby. Her one saving grace was that, whatever type of person she was, Jodie had not demonstrated anything that might suggest she would hurt her daughter, or let any harm come to her.

Karen only hoped that she might live to see Charlotte's beautiful smile once again.

As the first creature came into view, Karen was shaken from her thought.

She wiped a tear away from her cheek, and steadied herself for what she feared was about to happen.

One by one, the beasts turned the corner, until all six of them stood before the two prostrate women.

As they formed a semi-circle around the women, their yellow eyes seemed to glow in the flickering light cast by the fire.

The largest of the creatures was standing directly in front of Karen. His enormous chest seemed to expand by several inches whenever he took in a breath.

Somehow, Karen knew that it was communicating with the

others, although no grunts or signals seemed to pass between them. There seemed to be an unspoken understanding, as if they were somehow linked by telepathic mind waves.

Either way, Karen braced herself for whatever was about to happen next.

LUCY CHECKED the time on the dashboard clock. It had been nearly 15 minutes since she had spoken to the police. Where the hell were they?

Once she had convinced the officer on the phone to send a patrol car, she texted Jerry to inform him that help was on the way. She hated the idea of him venturing out alone in the middle of nowhere, but she knew there was nothing she could have said or done to stop him. Karen was in trouble, there was no doubt about that, and although her story about being held captive by "beasts" sounded more than a little implausible, she needed help, and Jerry was not the type to sit by and do nothing.

If only they could have convinced the police to meet them there when they first arrived. Then, at least, they would be the ones leading the charge to find the cave, not Jerry.

Lucy turned around to check on Charlotte. The sleeping baby had not moved since Jerry placed her carry cot along the back seat. At least they managed to find her and get her away from that strange young girl before anything bad happened to her.

She had parked Jerry's car a couple of hundred yards along the road, far enough away from the inn so that it could not be seen, but still close enough so that she could direct the police to the path Jerry was following.

Lucy had pulled off the road, which afforded the car the shelter of overhanging trees. She hoped that the police would enter the village from the direction she was facing, so that she could flash her headlights to attract their attention before they reached the inn.

If they arrived from the other side, she would have to turn the car around and drive over to meet them. Much as Lucy loathed the idea of heading back towards the inn, at least with the police there, she should be protected.

As she waited, Lucy continued checking her phone, hoping for a response from Jerry, but when none came, she surmised that he was probably concentrating on the job at hand, which meant at least he was being cautious.

As THEY MADE their way across the car park towards Jacobs's car, they suddenly heard muffled shouts emanating from somewhere in the darkness behind them.

They both looked at each other in shock.

Surely, Thad had not managed to break down the door so quickly?

Perhaps one of the serving staff had heard his shouts and let him out.

Polly gripped Jacob's arm in terror. The look of fear he saw in her eyes was palpable and, under the circumstances, completely reasonable.

Even so, they stopped for a moment and looked back towards the inn.

There was no sign of Thad, charging at them with a bloody axe held aloft.

Jacobs strained to hear where the noise was coming from.

Just then, a movement off to his right, caught his eye. It was one of the out-house sheds which sat just outside the refuge area at the back of the inn.

It appeared to be rocking, but not as a result of the wind, but from the force of something inside moving about.

The muffled shouts were definitely coming from within, as well.

Jacobs took out his car keys and gave them to Polly. "Here, you take these and go and wait for me in the car," he instructed.

Polly shook her head. "No, I'm stayin' with you, you can't leave me."

"I just need to see who's locked in that shed, I'll only be a second," Jacob's assured her. "It might be someone in need of help."

Polly glanced over to the plastic building. She knew only too well that the clan would sometimes drop their latest victims' remains in there for Thad to retrieve later. But, even so, she could not understand how someone alive could be trapped inside.

Gobal and the others would never leave a live offering – it did not make any sense.

Polly looked back at Jacobs. "I'm comin' with you," she said insistently.

Jacobs could tell that her mind was made up, and there was no time for arguments, so he grabbed her by the hand and led the way back towards the inn.

Once they reached the shed, they could both hear the muffled cries much clearer. The movement from within appeared to be caused by someone kicking the inside walls with determined force.

Seeing that the crowbar was the only thing keeping the door shut, Jacobs quickly checked over his shoulder to ensure Thad was not coming at him. Once he was satisfied, Jacobs took hold of the bar and steadied himself to face whatever was about to charge at him once he unlocked the shed.

As he slipped the crowbar out from the lock, the door swung open.

Inside, they were both shocked to see the bound figure of Jodie, lying on the floor.

She had a strip of gaffer tape covering her mouth, and she was screaming from behind it, using her eyes to convey her anger at being left in such a position.

Polly rushed in first and, still clutching the car keys in one hand, bent down and removed the gaffer tape as carefully as she could, trying not to cause her younger sister any undue pain.

Once the tape was off, they could see Jodie's mouth was filled with some kind of cloth, so Polly reached in and carefully removed it while Jacobs placed the crowbar on the floor, and began untying the young girl's binds.

"Quick, we 'ave to catch 'em, before they get away!" were the first words out of Jodie's mouth.

Polly frowned. "What are yer talkin' about girl? 'Oo locked you in 'ere?"

Jodie struggled against her bonds, making it harder for Jacobs to untie them.

"We 'aven't got time fer that," she yelled. "Jus' get me loose, they've taken me baby."

Both Jacobs and Polly stared at each other, perplexed.

"What baby?" Jacobs asked, as he finally managed to undue the knot holding Jodie's feet together.

Without answering, Jodie shuffled over, exposing her bound hands. "Get these off me, I need to get after them, afore it's too late."

Jacobs moved forward and began working the ropes loose.

"What on earth 'as gotten into you, girl?" Polly asked, still taken aback by her sister's previous announcement.

Jodie grunted and strained, again making Jacob's job harder.

When the knot eventually gave way, Jodie jumped to her

feet, knocking Polly sideways. Jacobs only just managed to reach out and grab her before she went over.

Oblivious to her sister's plight, Jodie snatched the crowbar up from the floor, and ran outside into the night.

"Jodie!" Polly yelled, after her, clearly upset by her sister's actions.

Jacobs led Polly back outside. He glanced swiftly towards the back entrance to the kitchens to see if Thad had emerged but, to his relief, the coast was still clear.

Polly stood beside him, her hands planted firmly on her hips, as she watched Jodie disappear down the path that led to the lake.

"What on earth's gotten into 'er, tonight?" she asked.

Jacobs shook his head. "No idea, what was all that about a baby?"

Polly turned back to him and shrugged her shoulders. "No idea what goes on in that girl's mind, sometimes," she admitted. "Shall we go?"

"You mean, go after her?" Jacobs asked.

Polly shook her head. "No," she replied, "I mean get away from 'ere, somewhere safe, jus' you and me."

She reached out and held his hand, placing his car keys in his palm.

Between Jodie's rantings, and Polly's parents trying to murder him, Jacobs had no idea what was going on in that accursed place. All he did know for definite was that Polly was beautiful and caring and had saved his life that evening, so for now at least, everything else could wait.

"Come on," he said, "let's go."

36

Jerry fought his way through the underbrush, using his torch to light the way. The lights from the car park were too far behind him now to offer any assistance, and with the trees closing in overhead, even the minimal brightness afforded by starlight was of little or no help.

He had received Lucy's text, so at least he knew that help was on the way. Whether or not it would arrive in time to be any use was another matter.

Jerry hated losing his crowbar, but under the circumstances it was a sacrifice worth making. That mad girl they had locked in the shed seemed capable of anything, and the last thing he wanted was for her to escape and go after Lucy and the baby.

He hoped Lucy had managed to find a safe spot to park where the girl would not find them, if she managed to somehow break free. Had he have thought about it at the time, he would have left Lucy his hunting knife, just in case. He was all right – he still had that crazy girl's vicious-looking sawn-off but he wished he hadn't left Lucy unprotected.

Still, it was too late to go back now. He still had Karen to think of. If whoever, or whatever, was holding her captive suddenly decided her usefulness was no longer necessary, they might attack and kill her at any time.

He might not make it. She might already be dead.

But he had to know that he tried his best.

As much as he tried to avoid them, the fallen twigs and branches crunched under his boots as he made his way along the trail, announcing his approach to anyone within earshot.

Every so often, Jerry would stop and stand still long enough to try and make out if there was any movement in the dark woods around him.

But the only sound he heard was the wind rustling through the trees.

He suspected that the gang that was holding Karen in the cave would probably have placed a guard on duty somewhere near the entrance. If so, he realised that his chances of sneaking up on them unannounced was virtually impossible.

But it would help if he had some idea how close he was to the cave. That way, he could deploy some form of strategy to perhaps sneak up on the guard and subdue him before he could give a warning to the others inside.

As it was, Jerry suspected that his crashing about through the undergrowth, or at the very least his torchlight, would probably give away his approach long before he even spotted the entrance.

It was a fool's errand he was on, but what other choice did he have?

Suddenly, there was a crackle of dried leaves off to his right. Jerry immediately sank to his haunches, and aimed his torch in the direction the sound had come from.

He stayed there for a moment, holding his breath, his fingers clasped around the handle of his knife. The sound came again, closer this time.

Jerry moved the tunnel of light slowly from side to side, scanning the area before him for any movement.

Finally, something emerged on the path before him, and scuttled off to his left.

Whatever it was, it was no larger than a badger.

Jerry relaxed, and slowly rose to his feet. He felt ridiculous for reacting as he had, especially since, out here, such nocturnal creatures would be plentiful. But, by the same token it also reminded him of how vulnerable he was out in the open.

Taking a deep breath, Jerry crept on. Up ahead, he caught sight of a rough mound of what looked like earth, or an old tree stump, just off the path to his right.

He angled his light towards it, and strained to see if there was any sign of movement around it. There was none. From this distance, it did not look like a cave, but so far it was the nearest thing he had seen that resembled any form of concealed entrance.

Checking the area around him once more, Jerry moved off in the direction of the mound, keeping his torch aimed directly at it for any sign of life.

As he drew closer, his heart skipped a beat. It was an entrance, sure enough.

This had to be it!

WITHOUT WARNING, one of the creatures moved forward and grabbed Karen by her arm. She resisted, instinctively, but she was no match for the thing's awesome power.

She genuinely believed that if she did not succumb, it would wrench her arm out of the socket.

As she was hoisted up on to her feet, Karen felt her phone slip through the flimsy strap which held it in place. Before she had a chance to react, the mobile slid across her belly and landed on the floor on its side, shattering the screen.

For a moment, no one moved. The creature that was

holding Karen swung her around by her arm, and threw her to the floor behind it.

One of the other beasts bent down and retrieved the smashed phone, staring it at closely as if it were some alien object as yet undiscovered.

Once it was satisfied the mobile was of no particular interest, it cast it aside into the darkness, where Karen heard it shatter upon jagged rock.

It suddenly occurred to Karen that for the first time since Jodie had brought her into the cave, there was no one between her and the corridor she entered from. The creatures all appeared to be momentarily engaged by the broken phone, and Karen knew this might be her one and only chance of escape.

She felt a pang of guilt at leaving the other woman behind, but she knew that her fellow captive was in no fit state to try to escape. And, what was more, if Karen did manage to break out, at least she would be able to alert the authorities and send in a search party to help her.

There was no time to think. Karen carefully shifted her weight until her feet were back underneath her, then she sprang forward and started running.

From behind, Karen could hear that her venture had not gone unnoticed.

The creatures began roaring and screeching at each other in a frenzy of, what Karen presumed was anger and frustration, which was closely followed by the sound of them giving chase.

The glow from the firelight afforded Karen the luxury of seeing ahead far enough to spot the next turn in the tunnel, but once she entered the cramped space, she was immediately plunged in utter darkness.

Karen kept her head down as she ran forward. She genuinely could not remember if she had needed to when Jodie brought her in, but that seemed like ages ago, even though she knew it was only a matter of hours, in reality.

She wondered how the creatures, with their enormous size, would cope with the narrower confines of this part of the cave, and prayed that there might be a chance they would have to abandon the chase altogether.

But, the close proximity of the deep breathing behind her soon made Karen realise that, far from giving up, they were gaining on her.

Karen kept one hand out to her side so that she could feel the solid rock of the cave wall, using it as a guide to ensure she had not reached an open space. Her other hand she tried to keep stretched out in front of her, so as to avoid running into a dead end.

It was so dark, no matter how hard she strained her eyes, it was impossible to see the way ahead.

For one horrific moment, she wondered if she was heading in the right direction.

After all, she had not paid attention to the path Jodie led her in on; and who knew how many twists and turns there were in this underground labyrinth?

One thing Karen knew for sure, was that there was no sign of any light ahead.

Just then, the wall to her right she was using as a guide was suddenly not there.

Karen stopped for a moment, and turned to her right, taking a few unsteady steps forward while trying to feel for a solid surface on either side of her.

There was nothing there.

Had she reached an opening?

It certainly felt wide enough, although there was still no sign of any light up ahead.

Karen slid her foot forward along the ground, to test that she had not entered an area with a steep drop. But the ground beneath her shoe felt solid enough.

The commotion from her pursers was growing louder by

the second.

Karen knew her options were limited, and there was nowhere to hide inside the cavernous depths of this structure as, she surmised, those creatures could probably see just as well down here as they could outside, if not better.

Taking a deep breath, Karen held out her hands in front of her and ran forward, hoping that at the next bend she would discover daylight and, hopefully, freedom.

She turned back momentarily when she heard the creatures reach the last turn.

Karen wanted to scream out her frustration, but decided to save her energy for her flight.

Her forehead rammed into a low ceiling with such force, Karen was on the ground before she knew what had happened.

Within seconds, the creatures were upon her, grabbing at her limbs and dragging her to her feet, once more.

This time Karen was not willing to go down without a fight.

Oblivious to the pain in her head from the collision, Karen began kicking and screaming at the top of her lungs. Although she was no match for the beasts' strength, her frantic flailing and scrabbling made their task all the more difficult.

Eventually, one of them managed to grab hold of Karen's wrists, while another secured her ankles.

Karen continued screaming as they carried her back along the tunnels towards their lair.

JERRY WAS NOT MISTAKEN. That was definitely a woman's scream he could hear from somewhere deep within the cave.

It had to be Karen.

She sounded miles away, but he knew that could just be because of the density of the cave's outer walls.

Either way, he had to investigate.

Where the hell were the police?

Jerry moved closer to the entrance of the cave, and shone his torch inside. The beam illuminated the area directly in front of him, but did not stretch far enough in to afford him a proper look.

He would have to go in, there was nothing else for it.

"Aaahhhhrrrrr!"

The scream came from nowhere, echoing through the trees, and before he had a chance to react, Jodie was upon him.

As Jerry tried to turn around, Jodie hit him hard across his shoulders with the crowbar.

The padding from his denim jacket afforded him little protection against the solid iron bar, and Jerry instinctively held up his hands to deflect the next blow.

This time Jodie caught him on the side of his neck, and the force of the strike caused him to lose his balance, and Jerry fell back down the bank towards the path.

His torch and the shotgun went flying from his grasp as he fell, and landed in the undergrowth a few feet away.

Jerry barely had time to recover when he saw Jodie running at him, the crowbar held above her head with both hands, preparing to attack once more.

Jerry fumbled along the ground and managed to locate a stout branch. He grabbed it and held it above him just as Jodie brought the crowbar down for another crack.

The branch held, even though the vibration from the blow sent shudders through Jerry's hands, almost causing him to drop it. But he held on tight, realising it was the only thing standing between him and the iron rod.

Jodie was relentless in her assault.

She swung the bar up and down like a thing possessed, crashing it down on the helpless figure of Jerry as he cowered under his branch.

The scowl on her face was like that of a demented maniac.

"Where's my baby?" she demanded, almost breathless from the continuous onslaught. "What 'ave you done wiv me baby? I'll kill you if you've touched 'er!"

Jerry was in no doubt that she meant every word. But even if she had given him a second to respond, there was no way he was going to tell her the truth, and send her back to find Lucy.

In the distance, they heard a shout.

Jodie paused for a moment, and stood over Jerry, the crowbar still clutched menacingly in both hands.

"You there," the call came. "Stop, this is the police!"

Relieved as he was, Jerry did not dare take his eyes off Jodie to see his cavalry approaching.

Jodie let out a cry of pure frustration.

She glanced down at Jerry, still cowering on the ground at her feet. Her hair was straggling across her face, stuck together with perspiration caused by her relentless onslaught. Her eyes were wide and filled with hatred for the man she believed had hidden Charlotte from her. Jodie raised the crowbar over her head, ready to rain down another severe hammering on to her hapless prey, but just as she was about to let loose, another call rung out, this time from even closer.

"Put that weapon down, now!" The command was accompanied by the beams from a couple of flashlights, which danced across Jodie's face and body.

Jerry could hear the tread of running feet crunching through the vegetation along the path.

Jodie looked back up once more and, seeing how close the uniformed officers were, she turned and scrambled up the incline, disappearing through the entrance to the cave.

Jerry heaved a huge sigh of relief.

Casting his shield to one side, he turned on to one side and shoved at the ground to help regain his feet.

He turned just as the two constables reached him.

"Are you all right, sir?" asked the older-looking of the two, breathing heavily from his exertions.

Jerry nodded. "Been better, but still in one piece."

"I take it you're Mr Grayson?" asked the younger one, also trying to catch his breath.

Jerry looked at him, curiously, then realised Lucy must have given him the details.

He nodded his response.

The older officer pointed towards the entrance to the cave. "And that young lady?"

Jerry shook his head. "Didn't catch her name, she's the one we found keeping a baby locked up in a shed back at the inn, did Lucy tell you about her?"

The older officer nodded. "We thought she was gagged and bound by you."

"She was," agreed Jerry. "She must have managed to get free, somehow." He pointed back to the cave. "But our friend Karen is presumably still in there being held captive by..." Jerry tailed off, not sure what to call Karen's jailers.

The two officers exchanged glances. Then the older one spoke, again. "Yes, the young lady told us what your friend said about being held prisoner, and by what."

"Look," said Jerry, starting to feel irritated by the condescending slant to the man's tone. "Whatever the situation, we need to take this threat seriously."

The younger officer stood forward, holding up his hand. "Not to worry, sir, we're here now, so please leave this to us."

The three of them stood in silence for a moment.

"Well?" demanded Jerry. "Are you going in or are you planning to just wait it out and hope they release her of their own free will?"

"Back-up's on its way, sir," replied the older officer, trying to keep his voice calm and reassuring. "As soon as they arrive, the officer in charge will decide how best to proceed."

Jerry looked back along the track.

There was no sign of any back-up in sight.

He waited, while the two officers spoke to each other.

Jerry could feel his anger rising. He realised, of course, that they had their protocol to follow, and doubtless they were under orders to wait for their senior officer to arrive before they attempted to explore the cave.

Doubtless, they would also have to wait for lighting equipment and dog-handlers, and who knew what else.

Meanwhile, Karen was down there at the mercy of God knows who, or what.

Plus, she now had the deranged Jodie to deal with and, if the baby was Karen's, then Jodie might put two and two together and decide in her own warped mind that Karen had somehow managed to snatch her back.

"Fuck this!" Jerry exclaimed, under his breath.

Before the officers had a chance to react, he ran up the slope and dived in through the entrance.

As far as he was concerned, they could either follow him, or not.

Either way, he was going in to find Karen.

37

Karen struggled for all she was worth, but it was to no avail. The creatures' hold on her was far too strong for her to break.

By the time they had reached the area where she and Matilda were being held, Karen was too exhausted to offer any further resistance.

They carried her over to where Matilda still sat in silence and unceremoniously dumped her on the ground.

The largest of the creatures moved forward and towered over the two women, staring from one to the other and then back again. Its menacingly yellow eyes felt as if they were penetrating straight through to Karen's heart, and she instinctively moved closer to her fellow prisoner for comfort.

After a while, the leader of the creatures turned to the rest of the pack and relayed its orders to them via a series of grunts and gestures.

As before, the others moved in closer on the hapless women, until they were clustered around them, closing off any possible avenue of escape.

Karen had no fight left in her.

She knew that whatever their plan for her and her companion was, she could either comply or die fighting.

Either way, she silently accepted that she would never see her baby again.

One way or the other, she was going to die in this cave, of that she was certain.

The only things she did not know were how and when.

When two of the beasts leaned down towards her, she did not resist. She lifted her weary body off the floor and stood between them as they grabbed hold of her by the wrists.

Two of the others walked around to lift Matilda.

Suddenly, Matilda flew into a rage, and began screaming and shouting and lashing out at the beasts.

It was as if a switch had just been flipped inside her brain.

This was the first time since she had been brought there that Karen had seen Matilda move, let alone fight.

Where was this girl when she tried to make her escape, earlier?

The two beasts holding Karen tightened their grip on her, feeling perhaps that she might be inspired to fight back after watching Matilda.

But Karen was still too exhausted from her attempt earlier.

She watched as Matilda lashed out with hands and feet, swinging wildly and uncontrollably, while the creatures did their best to try and grab one of her limbs.

The largest of them was clearly not impressed by their failure, and began to grunt orders at them, while shaking its enormous fists in the air.

Just then, Karen heard the sound of running feet from around the corner.

Her heart skipped a beat as she immediately thought that Jerry had somehow discovered her location and brought the police with him.

The creatures stopped struggling with Matilda and everyone turned to see who was approaching from around the next bend.

Karen's heart sank when Jodie appeared, brandishing a crowbar, and looking as if she was ready to kill someone.

The young girl made a beeline for Karen, ignoring the beasts.

She lifted the crowbar and shoved the curved hook at one end under Karen's chin, forcing her head back.

"Where's Charlotte?" she snarled, bringing her face within centimetres of Karen's.

For a moment, Karen was stunned by the question. If Jodie did not have her baby, then who did?

Jodie forced the crowbar up a little further, hard enough to make Karen choke.

"I said, what 'ave yer done with baby Charlotte?"

"You took her!" Karen spluttered, trying to twist her face away to relieve the pressure on her throat.

Jodie moved in until their noses were almost touching.

When she next spoke, Karen could feel droplets of spittle hitting her chin as Jodie spoke through gritted teeth.

"Yeah, I know, but then you got those two to take 'er away from me, didn't yer. Now where 'ave they taken 'er?"

Karen stared down at the girl, bewildered. She had no idea what she was talking about, but now she was even more concerned for the safety of her baby daughter.

Her one saving grace throughout this ordeal, had been that Jodie would at least make sure that no harm came to her.

Now, it appeared, someone else had her. But who?

"Tell me," demanded Jodie, "or I'll bash yer 'ead in, right 'ere an' now!"

"I don't know," replied Karen, "I've been stuck in here since you left."

Jodie considered Karen's explanation for a second, but her

eyes told Karen that she was not prepared to see the sense in them.

Jodie removed the crowbar from under Karen's chin, but her relief was short lived.

Karen watched in horror as Jodie lifted the bar back above her head, ready to strike the fatal blow.

"Karen!"

The shout came from somewhere around the next turn. It echoed through the labyrinthine chambers making the caller sound relatively close by.

Karen wondered if Jerry had found her, after all. She did not immediately recognise the voice. But then she had only met him the once, and then only briefly.

Jodie spun around in the direction of the voice; the crowbar still held aloft.

Karen did not wait, she realised that this might be her only chance.

"Help!" she yelled. "I'm here, please help me!"

In a second, Jodie was upon her. She slapped her free hand over Karen's mouth, waving the crowbar in the other in an effort to make her shut up.

"We're in here, please come and help us, they're holding us captive!"

The second shout came from Matilda.

By the expression on her face, Jodie was every bit as surprised as Karen to hear the woman speak.

The creatures all turned to face the direction of the call, then turned back to face their leader as if seeking instruction.

There appeared to be a general sense of panic among them, which gave Karen the strength she needed to start fighting back again.

She opened her mouth as wide as she could and then bit down hard on Jodie's hand.

The young girl screamed and dropped the crowbar as she tried to wrench her hand free. But Karen kept her mouth locked, starting to taste the girl's blood on her lips.

The two creatures holding her had loosened their grip sufficiently for Karen to pull free.

She opened her mouth, releasing Jodie, and in one swift move she shoved the young girl backwards, knocking her down on her back, and in the same moment Karen leant down and grabbed the fallen crowbar.

As she turned back to face the creatures, Karen swung the bar ahead of her, left and right. She did not manage to make contact with the beasts, but she came close enough to make them shuffle back a few steps, to avoid her next onslaught.

"Karen, where are you?" the voice called again. But this time it definitely sounded closer.

"We're here, please hurry!" It was Matilda again, screaming at the top of her lungs.

The stand-off between them all seemed ridiculous to Karen. She was in no doubt that any one of the creatures could disarm her, and probably bend the crowbar into a horseshoe for good measure.

But, for some reason, they just stood there, watching.

It was almost as if now that Jodie had arrived, they had a new leader, and were waiting instruction from her, before acting.

Realising the possible threat, Karen swung round to face Jodie. The fall had obviously taken the wind out of her, and she was still lying on her back, clutching her bleeding hand, and obviously in considerable pain.

The slight twinge of guilt which pervaded Karen's conscience, was soon wiped clear when she reminded herself who it was that had brought her here in the first place.

Karen swung back around and looked over at Matilda.

The two women shared a look that told the other this might be their only chance of escape. The main problem was, the six huge beasts that stood between them.

Matilda took in a deep breath and nodded, almost as if she were giving Karen the OK to make a break for it again, and leave her behind.

But now that Matilda had found her voice, she seemed less of a lost cause to Karen. Prior to that, she was the woman had lost her mind as a result of her situation – and who could blame her?

Now, however, they were in this together.

Karen turned back just in time to witness Jodie trying to make it back up to her feet.

Karen leapt forward and spun Jodie around before she had a chance to regain her balance. Karen grabbed the crowbar at both ends and, standing behind her, held it tight against the girl's throat.

The creatures had all begun to move in, but the second they saw that Jodie was vulnerable, they instinctively stood down.

Jodie flailed wildly, her hands trying to reach up to grab the bar. But each time she did, Karen tightened her hold a little more, until it was Jodie's turn to start choking with the pressure.

Once Jodie stopped fighting, Karen leaned in so her mouth was over Jodie's ear.

"Now, I know that you can communicate with them," Karen hissed, "so tell them to back off, right now, or else I'm going to squeeze the life out of you."

"No, you won't" Jodie replied defiantly. "You ain't got it in yer!"

Karen tightened the bar across her throat. "Oh, no?"

Jodie began to splutter and gag. "All right!" she gasped.

Karen released the bar, just enough to allow Jodie to speak without choking.

"Karen!"

This time the call sounded further away.

How could that be?

"We're here!" Matilda screamed.

"I'm coming. I've got the police with me, don't worry."

"Well?" asked Karen, hoping that Jodie would not have realised that the caller appeared to be farther away this time.

Jodie let out an exaggerated cry of frustration. "Go!" she commanded. "Go on, before the police get 'ere."

The creatures all turned to look at each other.

"GO!" Jodie yelled.

The biggest of the creatures did not appear willing to leave, regardless of the order. While the others jostled amongst themselves, moving closer towards the next turning, the largest one still held its ground, staring at Karen.

Karen could feel her knees starting to buckle under the intimidating gaze of the creature, but she held herself steady, keeping the crowbar in place.

After an agonising moment, Karen asked Jodie. "Why aren't they obeying your instructions?"

"They don't want to leave without me," Jodie replied, seething. "But they don't want to risk you killin' me afore they get to rip you apart."

Karen gulped. She could see that Jodie's explanation made sense.

But at the same time, that did not leave her with an alternative option. Karen decided that this stand-off was not going to end well. Even if her rescuers turned up in the next couple of seconds, unless they were heavily armed, there was not much of a chance that they would survive a confrontation with the beasts.

She had to act fast. It was a gamble, but her choices were limited.

Karen removed the crowbar from across Jodie's neck, and shoved her hard in the back, towards the creatures.

The largest of them lunged forward and caught the girl, before she had a chance to fall.

For a moment, there was silence.

Now that Karen no longer held their leader captive, the creatures all turned their attention towards Karen, as if awaiting instruction to converge on her and tear her apart, as Jodie had threatened.

Karen held up the crowbar in front of her, readying herself for one final assault, should the situation call for it.

"Karen!"

Now the voice sounded close, again. Whoever it was, was making progress.

The look on Jodie's face told Karen that she had realised it too.

Grabbing the beast who had caught her by the hand, she led it away, back around the corner towards the fire; closely followed by the others.

Although there was plenty of room, Karen moved to one side to let them pass, her grip on the crowbar so tight that the whites of her knuckles were showing.

Karen held her breath until the last of the creatures had disappeared from sight.

When they were gone, Matilda walked over to her and threw her arms around her, hugging her, tightly.

"Thank you," she said, sincerely. "You saved my life."

Karen kept hold of the crowbar with one hand, but let it dangle by her side. She placed her other arm around Matilda's shoulders and kissed her on the back of the head.

"Couldn't have done it without you." she told her.

The two women stood there for a while, holding on to each other.

They next shout they heard sounded further away again.

They replied in unison, and kept on replying likewise to every subsequent call, until finally, Jerry's head appeared around the corner.

38

Even after they were found, both women feared that at any moment the creatures would appear out of the darkness, and attack them, or worse still, drag them away with them to another part of the cave, where no one would ever find them.

Even when they finally emerged from the cave to find themselves surrounded by a dozen officers, at the back of both their minds they knew that those present would not be able to protect them should the creatures decide to attack.

With blankets around their shoulders, they were both led to waiting police vehicles.

Lucy was there to meet them, with baby Charlotte asleep in her arms.

The minute she saw her daughter, Karen ran forward and cried as Lucy gently placed her in her arms. Matilda walked up behind them, and hugged mother and baby both together.

Lucy ran into Jerry's arms, and the pair of them did not let go of each other for ages. When they finally moved apart, Lucy punched Jerry several times on the chest and shoulders, before once more wrapping her arms around him.

She knew the risk that he had taken, and she knew why he felt he had to do it. She loved him for both.

Back at the police station, after being given hot coffee and biscuits, Karen and Matilda gave their reports concerning what they had suffered while being held captive.

They both noticed the officers taking their statements glance over at their colleagues with raised eyebrows, every time the creatures were either mentioned, or described.

But neither woman cared.

The following morning, Jacobs returned to work and was brought up to speed on the operation. He made excuses that he had mislaid his mobile when he was informed that the station had tried several times the previous night to contact him.

Taking charge of the investigation, he arranged as a matter of procedure for two officers to go to the inn to question the owners, as it appeared that their daughter Jodie was involved in the kidnapping of a baby, as well as the abduction and imprisonment of Karen and Matilda.

Jacobs had promised Polly that he would not tell anyone of his confinement in the abattoir, nor about what he had seen down there. He explained to her that if, during the course of the investigation, officers discovered her parent's secret, then he would have to act on that information accordingly, and she understood.

As Polly had not had any active part in either the kidnapping of baby Charlotte or the abduction of the two women, Jacobs managed to keep her out of it altogether.

A full excavation of the cave was ordered, and specialists were brought in from three different forces for the undertaking.

But, after six weeks there was still no sign of Jodie, or of the so-called creatures that had kept Karen and Matilda hostage.

No one on the search detail believed that they were looking for monsters.

After expressing their shock and concern when informed of

the exploits of their daughter, Thad and Mavis Beanie disappeared. None of their staff had any idea where they had gone, or for how long and, as there was no official investigation into their activities by that stage, it was decided they had simply left to recover from the loss of their daughter.

Dan's remains were never found, but the case remained open, and Jacobs promised Karen he would let her know if they ever found anything.

She never expected or received such a call.

Karen and Matilda were both offered psychiatric counselling to help them come to terms with their ordeal.

Both refused.

However, they did manage to secure representation from a prominent agent, and sold their stories to the press for a tidy sum.

Karen moved back to her mother's house. With her share of the newspaper money, she had enough for a deposit on a small flat of her own but, with no income, she decided she would prefer to stay at home and watch Charlotte grow up, while her mother fussed over and spoiled them both.

JODIE OPENED HER EYES.

The flickering flames from the fire danced in front of her, and she realised she needed to add some more wood to keep it going.

As she bathed in the warmth, she could hear the others returning from their latest night-time expedition.

Her belly was already rumbling in anticipation.

Sure enough, as Gobal came into sight, he was dragging behind him the dead body of a man. The clothes were already shredded and torn, partly from the initial attack and partly from being dragged over the rough floor of the cave.

The others followed behind, with two more bodies.

Both of these were already naked, and Jodie could tell that some of the others had been too impatient to wait before starting their feast.

Jodie watched eagerly as Gobal sat opposite her and began to eviscerate his kill.

The others joined in with their contributions. The grinding and cracking of the bones as they were wrenched apart mingled with the crackling of the firewood to form a symphony of macabre instruments.

Jodie licked her lips as Gobal tore a massive chunk of flesh from the torso of his victim, and handed the bloody mass over to her.

Jodie tore into the succulent meat, letting the blood ooze down her chin and drip on to her naked swollen belly.

She knew it would not be long now.

The End

Dear reader,

We hope you enjoyed reading *Flesh Eaters*. Please take a moment to leave a review, even if it's a short one. Your opinion is important to us.

Discover more books by Mark L'estrange at https://www.nextchapter.pub/authors/mark-lestrange

Want to know when one of our books is free or discounted? Join the newsletter at http://eepurl.com/bqqB3H

Best regards,

Mark L'estrange and the Next Chapter Team

You could also like:
Ghost Song by Mark L'estrange

To read the first chapter for free, please head to:
https://www.nextchapter.pub/books/ghost-song

Printed in Great Britain
by Amazon

38997623R00216